Godsend

Book 1: A Hero is Called

Godsend

Book 1: A Hero is Called

Written by Mike Apodaca

Story by Jeremy Apodaca

Godsend 1: A Hero is Called
Story by Jeremy Apodaca
Written by Mike Apodaca
Copyright 2011

ISBN: 069232271X

Cover and Title page produced with Gencraft

Put on the whole armor of God that ye may be able to stand up against the wiles of the devil.
Ephesians 6:11

Dedication

This book is dedicated to all those who desire to walk more faithfully with Christ. The Christian life is difficult. It means putting aside all that we are in this realm and embracing the far better things given us in Christ. It is selling all to buy a field for the treasure within. It is bearing our cross daily, seeing our old life as dung, in order to gain Christ. May this series aid you in your journey.

Some of our readers have asked us to provide the pronunciation of the names of a few of the main characters.

Sariel is pronounced Sare-ee-el

Mihr is pronounced Meer

Hecate is pronounced Heck-ate

1

Thursday 6:55 a.m.

A thick, pasty gloom surrounded Alex like a moldy shroud. The stifling, stale air vibrated with a cacophony of wild, discordant noise.

Alex tightened his grip on the hilt of the heavy, glowing sword. Knowing what was about to descend upon him, he warily scanned the horizon and braced himself. He'd been here a dozen times before, and each time was more terrifying than the last.

Fountains of lava broke through the ground's dark crust. Molten rock cast an eerie red glow, revealing the vastness of the cavern. Alex looked down at the short rock pedestal he stood on. The top was just bigger than his tennis shoes.

Then they came. Not hundreds, or even thousands, but an endless sea of creatures poured down the rocky, blood-stained hills on all sides of him. Obscured by a sulfuric yellow fog, the monsters were still too far away to be seen clearly.

Every muscle in his body clenched.

The creature's mind-numbing cries pounded his ears. They screamed not in pain, nor in anger.

They screamed in hunger.

Their earsplitting shrieks grew louder. It was more than he could stand.

Alex's hand went limp, and his sword clanked on the hard, cracked ground. He covered his ears as the rabid creatures came closer.

Now Alex could make them out. Sprinting like wolves, the pale-gray, leathery-skinned demons sprang forward on long, curved, razor-sharp claws. Rows of spiked, needle-like teeth flashed as they screeched triumphantly.

Alex stood on a stone plate—he was the meal.

As they reached him, he closed his eyes.

The demon's screaming morphed into the high-pitched whine of his alarm clock.

Alex's eyes popped open as he gasped.

He threw out his right fist and punched the alarm clock off the nightstand, unplugging it. Shaking his clouded head, he sat up, wiped the cold sweat from his brow, and bounded off the end of the bed.

He threw open his closet, pulled his favorite shirt from the hamper, sniffed it, and decided it passed the smell test. He grabbed his best jeans off their hanger and his phone from the charger on the nightstand before heading to the bathroom down the hall.

He turned on his radio app and heard, *"...news, brought to you by The Center for Bodily Revival. Three more drive-by shootings in Logan County last night. Two people were hospitalized and there was one fatality. Police Chief James Hargis is demanding more cops on the beat while Governor Letcher says that the state doesn't have the funds for new officers."*

Minutes later, he emerged from the bathroom fully dressed, his roughly-combed, blond hair damp. He slipped his left arm into the strap of his backpack and danced down the narrow wooden stairs, his tennis shoes thumping a loud rhythmic beat. With graceful fluidity, he cupped the ball atop the post at the end of the banister with his right hand and used it to sling-shot himself into the next room—the kitchen, where his mom stood near the sink dressed in light-blue scrubs.

Golden-brown raisin toast popped up from the toaster with a hallow thud.

"Late. No time for breakfast," Alex quipped as he breezed toward the door.

As she had done a hundred times before, his mom reached over, pinched a piece of toast from the toaster, and swung her arm out like a barricade in front of a racing train. Alex opened his mouth wide, bared his teeth, and sank them into the toast with a noisy crunch.

He held the toast in his mouth and puffed the words, "Phaaynks Momm." He reached for the door handle, and slipped out. He pushed the door closed with his foot and broke into a fast run as his mom shouted that she loved him.

The warm morning air told Alex that summer was on its way. He sped away on his silver BMX bike, his backpack swaying precariously on his shoulder.

*

About half a mile up the street, young Mrs. Ervin pressed her thumb tightly over the end of her water hose, sending a spray raining down on the suds she'd just lathered over her car. Her daughter, Kari, a toddler of three, bounced her cloudy-pink plastic ball against the concrete driveway.

The mom turned and sprayed a fine mist over her daughter.

As the water hit her florescent-yellow bathing suit, Kari squealed with delight. She jumped up and down, her pink flip-flops slapping the bottoms of her feet.

*

Alex pumped the pedals hard and used the curve of a driveway for a ramp. He got a little air and hit the ground with a loud thump. To get more speed, he stood on the pedals.

Something gray and murky, like a shadow, whizzed past his head and flew into the cab of a delivery truck on the street ahead.

"What the—?" Alex peddled faster.

*

Kari's mother scowled. She moved closer to her car and rubbed her long thumbnail against the windshield, trying to remove a glistening glob of sticky, yellow-orange sap.

Focused on the blemish, she didn't notice the ball rolling down the driveway behind her nor her young daughter bounding after it.

*

Bob Mobly whipped the delivery truck around the corner while he pressed the redial button on his cell phone. His breathing became shallow and sweat beaded on his forehead.

He felt a sudden burst of rage.

He pushed redial on his cell, heard a series of musical beeps, ringing, and then a click.

"Rita, I'm serious—don't you dare hang up. We can work this out. Just listen to me."

There was a flash of bright yellow in the street in front of the truck.

Bob shoved his foot onto the brake pedal. The heavy vehicle groaned and swerved as it skidded forward.

The child in the street froze, her eyes as big as saucers.

The ball continued bouncing across the street.

*

Alex saw the girl's mom twist her head just in time to see five tons of metal hurtling toward her precious little girl. The hose fell from her hand. She lunged forward screaming.

The license plate was inches from the girl's body when Alex yanked her up by the arm. He held her steadily in front of him as the right bumper of the squealing truck grazed the edge of his back tire, knocking it sideways. He kept himself upright, hit his brakes, and came to an abrupt stop.

The child cried for her mommy.

The mom ran over, frantically scooped up her little girl, and held her tight. "My baby, my baby!" She looked at Alex. "You saved her! Thank you!"

The trucker stepped out of the cab and approached. He looked dazed. Alex saw the dark shape of a man, lift from the driver's back and soar into the sky.

Bob put his beefy hand on Alex's bony shoulder, "You all right, kid? I swear . . . I didn't see . . . she came out of nowhere. You're a real hero, kid."

Alex turned his focus away from the sky and whatever it was he saw. He smiled and looked down at his watch. His face dropped. He was late. "I gotta run," he called out, pumping the pedals of his bike. "I'm glad she's okay."

Alex sped away. He glanced at a white-haired man in a white suit watching from the street corner. As he passed him, he thought he saw the man suddenly vanish. He looked back over his shoulder. The corner was empty.

He hit the brakes and fish-tailed to a stop.

"What's going on here?"

2

Thursday, 7:45 a.m.

Kingman High School looked like something right out of Hollywood's heyday. It had been a fancy hotel in the thirties—the haunt of movie stars, oil tycoons, and gin runners. Four stories high, its red bricks were now chipped and worn. In the middle of the wide, main building rose an enormous clock tower, a pointed spire that ascended like a massive obelisk out of the heart of ancient Egypt. On the front of the spire, near the top, was a clock ten feet in diameter. Two wings of the school framed the clock tower like book ends. Once stylish suites now served as dingy, overused classrooms or laboratories. The outside of the buildings were covered with windows stacked in rows and columns as orderly as an egg carton.

Alex made his way up the front steps, gazing at the clock tower, when Conor's bodycheck interrupted him. "Dude! You totally have to ask her today!"

Conor was built like a scarecrow—his joints sharp, his limbs lanky. Alex and Conor had been best friends since the fourth grade and were inseparable. Unfortunately, Conor hadn't grown much since then. But because his hands and feet were huge, he hoped to tower over the others in his class someday.

He pushed his unruly, brown hair away from his eyes, just to have it fall back again. He shifted on his feet. "Hello? Are you listening?"

"I heard you." Alex slung his backpack over his shoulder. "I just—"

"Just nothing. You're chicken." Conor followed this with squeaky clucking as he flapped his elbows and scratched the floor with his fluorescent orange shoes. It was the worst chicken impression ever.

They plodded toward the main building and joined the throng of students chattering loudly with friends or on their cell phones.

"Shut up." Alex body-slammed Conor into a puny freshman, who stumbled forward and dropped his books.

The freshman snarled "Estúpido!" under his breath as he kneeled to pick them up.

Conor kept walking.

"See this?" He held up his hand in front of Alex's face and slowly moved his thumb and forefinger together in a tight pinch, almost catching Alex's narrow nose. "This is your window of opportunity disappearing. The dance is a week from Saturday—ten days away!"

"You think I don't know that? I'm—"

"A loser? Lame? Socially retarded?" They clomped up the steps and into the main building.

Rolling his eyes, Alex stopped and faced Conor. "I'm waiting for the right opportunity."

Conor lifted his head and smiled wryly. "It's right behind you."

Alex turned and he found himself face-to-face with Katie. Her dark-brown hair framed her face. Her bangs, cut long, curled off to the right. She looked like an A-list model in her tank top and skinny jeans,. The moment he saw her, Alex's resolve melted like an ice cream bar on a hot sidewalk.

Katie smiled at Alex. "You didn't answer my text this morning."

Alex took a step backward. He opened his mouth, but nothing came out.

"What's up?" She giggled.

Alex pulled his phone from his jeans and unlocked it with his thumb. A flashing green light told him he had an unanswered text. "Must've been when I was in the shower," he said sheepishly. "Sorry."

Katie looked him over and smiled.

Conor rolled his eyes. "Good morning to you too, Katie," he said as he waved his hand in the air. "I'm fine. Thanks for asking."

"Conor, you're such a dork." She shook her head and turned back to Alex.

Conor mimicked her behind her back. He closed his eyes and puckered his lips repeatedly toward Alex, then laughed. "Catch you losers later," he blurted a little too loudly.

As he passed Alex, he bumped him on the back, which forced Alex to stumble into Katie.

"Later," Katie sang to Conor.

Alex pivoted and walked with Katie to class.

She giggled again and walked close to Alex. "You okay?"

Alex stammered. "Yeah, I guess so. Just having bad dreams."

"Me too! I was a cheerleader, and no one could see me. It was like I was invisible. Isn't that weird? Why do we have to sleep anyway?"

Alex took a deep breath. "So, I was just wondering—"

The clanging bell in the clock tower signaled the start of classes.

"Gotta run." Katie turned on her heels and jogged toward her first class. She turned back and called over her shoulder, "I'll text you after third period."

She disappeared into the crowd of students

Alex sighed. He raised his hand to the end of his nose and pinched his forefinger and thumb together.

*

When he arrived at his last class, Alex was greeted with the usual bunch of morons. A group of boys salivated over pictures on a phone. There was a nerdy kid in the back selling candy out of a gallon-sized Ziploc bag. Many girls—Katie among them—checked their make-up with compacts as if they were getting ready for a photo shoot. One of the boys showed off a new tattoo on his wrist. In the front row, a small group of college-bound kids sat studiously, like they actually wanted to be there.

Their teacher, Mr. Henry Addison, was nowhere to be found.

Alex slid into a desk at the back of the room and dropped his backpack on the scuffed tile floor. Conor held up his hand and pinched his finger and thumb together.

Alex shook his head in disgust. Why couldn't he ask Katie to the dance? What was wrong with him?

Mr. Addison pushed the door open with his wing-tipped shoe and stumbled into the room. He looked awful. His dress shirt was hanging out of his wrinkled pants, and his tie—held in place by a sweater vest—had been loosened and cocked to one side. The greying, curly tuffs of hair that ringed his head like Saturn stuck out in all directions. His eyes squinted hard as he leaned forward. Looking like he was going to puke, he stumbled over his own feet. Students erupted in laughter.

"Burnt biscuits!" he muttered under his breath. He dropped his notebook on the podium in the front of the classroom and addressed the students. "I know I'm late. Just bear with me. I have a splitting headache and it isn't getting any better." He winced.

Alex looked harder at Mr. Addison. Something was wrong. Leaning forward, he rubbed his eyes and stared again.

The teacher's lean frame was outlined with a coarse, jagged shadow. This translucent blanket around him absorbed light like a black hole. It throbbed, pulsing with the teacher's labored breaths.

Mr. Addison grabbed the sides of the podium and swayed like a sailor in a tempest. Heads around the room followed his slow syncopated movements. The room was quiet as the students waited to see if he would collapse.

The darkness rose up behind Mr. Addison. It floated a foot above him, coalescing into a more substantial mass.

Alex's eyes opened wide. He couldn't breathe. Mesmerized, he watched two holes form in the small cloud. They became eyes—flaming, hateful, red, diamond-shaped eyes—that stared down at the teacher with pure, vile hatred.

Alex looked at the other students but could tell by their expressions that none of them saw what he did.

"I can't," the teacher whispered. He looked up and whimpered, "Class dismissed. Everybody head to Study Hall. Read the next chapter in your text."

The stormy mass dropped and enveloped him.

"You okay, Mr. A? You want me to call someone?" a girl asked.

"No. No. I'm fine." The teacher lied. "Go on to Study Hall. Now!"

As the other students shuffled out, Alex scooped up his backpack and approached Mr. Addison.

The teacher stared at the floor like he was trying to remain standing.

Alex leaned in next to his ear and whispered. "Mr. Addison, what…is this?"

"I'm fine, Alex. It's just a headache. I'll be all right," he bellowed.

"But, I saw—"

"I said I'm fine! Now, get out!"

Alex started to leave. He turned back from the doorway and almost dropped his books when he caught a glint of red glow in Mr. Addison's eyes.

Am I losing my mind?

He turned and jogged down the hallway.

*

In Study Hall, everyone sat under the watchful eyes of the grumpy proctors. Number two pencils scraped across college-ruled paper. No one said a word.

Alex noticed Conor in the back of the room. No surprise there.

Alex slid in next to Conor. He pulled a spiral-bound notebook from his backpack and scribbled *that was weird* at the top of the page.

Conor shifted his eyes like an international spy. He slipped the notebook off the edge of Alex's desk onto his own. He wrote in the next line. *Homecoming?* Then he underlined it—twice.

Alex looked at Katie's back and sighed. He reached over and put a line through the word ~~Homecoming~~.

Conor rolled his eyes. He scribbled, *She wants you to meet her at the mall after school.*

Alex wrote, *K.*

After an eternity, the bell rang. The students rose noisily, and Alex looked over at Katie. She turned, smiled at him, and mouthed the words "The mall." She shuffled out the door with her cloud of girlfriends.

*

12

When school was over, Alex ran to his BMX bike and spun the lock's tumbler. It popped open with a loud click. He jumped on his bike and pumped the pedals with all his might. He hopped a curb and powered down the gutter.

As Alex sped away from the school, he saw the man in the white suit watching him from across the street. The strange guy brushed his sleeve then closed his eyes, like he was listening to someone. He stroked his short white gotee with his long fingers.

He nodded, then vanished again.

Alex rode across the street where the man had been.

Nothing. Weird!

*

Alex's legs pumped hard on the pedals as he approached the Willowbrook Memorial Cemetery, which rested between the high school and the mall. It was an ancient burial ground with tombstones in every shape and size. On the near side, beyond the picket fence, rows and rows of simple marble markers stuck in the ground. They reminded Alex of the windows at his school.

Just then, someone built like a bull jumped out of the bushes right in front of the bike.

Adam Murray, notorious captain of the wrestling team and witless bully. Adam had squeezed enough money out of Alex and his friends when they were in junior high to pay his way through college—as if he would ever go there!

The sun glistened off the sweat on Adam's shaved head. His wild eyes bore down on Alex.

Alex was in trouble. He pulled hard on the handlebars and sped past Adam.

Adam buried his vice-like hands deeply into Alex's shoulders and lifted him completely off his bike, which continued forward

13

without him, crashed into the fence, and fell over on its side with the front wheel still spinning.

"Adam, what the..." Alex protested as the boy dragged him toward the opening in the wrought-iron cemetery fence, his legs dangling uselessly.

"Shut up, worm," Adam shouted. His voice sounded like a chorus of many caustic voices blended together. "I was watching you in class. You can . . . see us. You are . . . dangerous."

"Let me go!" Except for the gnarled trees and dead inhabitants, the cemetery was empty. Above, dark spots dotted the sky. Dozens of loathing red eyes stared from the forming billows.

Panicked, Alex kicked Adam hard in the side, like he was punting a football. Unfortunately, the beefy hulk just kept plodding ahead, his bulging eyes set forward. He halted abruptly, changed his grip, moving one hand to Alex's side, then hefted his squirming body high into the air.

Alex looked down. Beneath him, a freshly dug hole, six feet deep, opened like a yawning cave. At the bottom lay a light pink coffin with a shiny metallic top.

"No one will ever find you," Adam hissed.

Alex cried out, "Help! Help!"

Lightning flashed.

Alex was tossed in the air like a rag doll. His eyes wide, he flailed his arms and legs and fell toward the death hole, but something caught him. It held him fast and then gently set him on the ground.

Alex looked up to see the man in the white suit.

"Stay here," the man said in a warm voice.

Adam growled and his mouth opened three times wider than normal, revealing bloody gums. He had crazed eyes and puffed as if he'd run a marathon. His enormous hands went for the white man's throat.

Before he reached him, the man transformed. He became so bright it was hard to look at him. His suit became luminous armor.

Muscles rippled over his body. Two wings grew on his back—foot-long, white feathers overlapped in glistening layers. His noble face grew serious. A large, dazzling sword covered in brilliant flames appeared in his hand. The golden hilt held beautiful designs and ended in a cross.

Alex's knees went weak. He tried not to pass out.

"Stop! I command you by the Name." The angel shouted with a voice like thunder. He pointed his sword at Adam's throat.

Adam shook like he was having a fit.

"Do you challenge me in battle?" the bright being continued.

The wrestler looked like he was going to puke. A chorus of voices choked out of him, "We do not!"

"Then leave him. Now!"

Adam's face screwed up in horror. He whimpered a pathetic whine. Then the frantic voices cried out, "We do not want to go. Do not cast us out."

"You *will* leave him. And you will not return," the holy creature stated with finality.

Adam nodded like a marionette. He leaned his head back and stared into the dark sky above. His face contorted. He opened his mouth wide and screamed. Black wraith-like creatures—shadows with red eyes—poured out of him like a stream of dark vomit and rose into the sky. There must have been dozens of them. The air around Adam hummed and crackled, and a violent deafening wind blew leaves everywhere.

Alex closed his eyes tightly and pulled his body into the fetal position. He shook like he was having a fit.

The din stopped. Everything was calm. Sunlight broke through the clouds. Birds chirped.

Alex slowly opened his eyes. Adam lay on the ground, sound asleep and snoring. The man in the white suit looked normal again as he gently folded Adam's thick arms across his chest.

"He is exhausted, but he will be fine. When he wakes up, he will not remember this." He turned toward Alex and said, "It is time to go."

Alex shuddered. "What do you mean? Go where?" He tried to catch his breath. This must be another bad dream. "Did I fall asleep in Spanish class again?" He blinked his eyes and whispered to himself, "Wake up Alex, wake up. C'mon, wake up!"

The man laughed. "You humans always think this is a dream. Sleeping must be most unpleasant."

Alex remembered the ravenous demons in his dreams and shuddered. "Sometimes."

He slowly stood and brushed himself off. "I gotta go," he said, and headed toward his bike. He found it lying flat on the grass. He scooped it up and sped toward the mall. He wanted to get away and put this weird experience behind him. Looking back over his shoulder, he shuddered.

The man was gone—again.

"Stupid dream!" Alex shook his head and raced to the mall.

*

Alex scanned the mall for Katie. He found her at the food court, in front of the smoothie stand. As usual, her goofy friends surrounded her. Alex wondered how he was going to get her alone.

"We need to talk," a voice next to him said.

Alex looked over and his knees gave out.

Mr. White Suit.

"Why won't you leave me alone?" Alex asked as he watched Katie giggle and sip on a foamy orange drink.

The man stepped in front of Alex, blocking his view. "This is *not* a request. You *will* come with me, *now*."

Alex started to object, but his tongue dissolved in his mouth. It wasn't painful—just so weird. Instinctively, he thrust his fingers into his mouth, which had become an empty cavern. His eyes bulged, and he began to hyperventilate. *Who is this guy? Why is he doing this to me? How do I get out of here?*

"Theatrics," the man complained. "Why must it always come to this? When Moses was called, the Lord had to turn his hand leprous. You should have seen him. I thought he was going to wet himself."

"Mhie tun!" Alex tried to speak.

"Moses was one of my greatest pupils. He started slow, but…"

This was all too much for Alex. He grabbed the man and pushed him against the wall of red and white tile squares.

The man said intently, "Let me go."

Alex look into the man's eyes and his resolve failed. He remembered what this seemingly weak old man had just done to Adam. He loosened his grip and stepped back.

The man straightened his suit and tie, guided Alex to a table, and pushed him into a chair.

Alex looked over at Katie. Everyone in the food court—and there must have been a hundred men, women, and children standing in groups or eating at tables or waiting in line—was frozen. It looked eerily like a 3-D photograph. His eyes lighted on a child whose ball of strawberry ice cream had fallen from its cone and was suspended, midair, halfway to the floor.

What's going on here?

Alex turned to the man. Their eyes met.

"Ah, I see I have your attention. Good." The man surveyed the surroundings and continued. "Something evil has begun in your community. I do not know what it is exactly, but it is serious. In response to this emergency, you have been called. Even as Isaiah, Ezekiel, and Mary were attended by angels at their calling, so are you also attended…by me."

Alex worked to speak, to form words, but without a tongue, his moans came out as a mix of vowels and soft consonants. It was like trying to carry on a conversation with a dentist when he has both hands in your mouth.

"My name is Sariel," the man said and offered his hand. Alex just stared at it. The visitor pulled it back. "Let us start again." Sariel smirked playfully. Mimicking the voice of a game show host, he dramatically announced, "Alexander McKendrick, you have been chosen by the almighty God, the creator and sustainer of all things, to save the world! Congratulations!"

Alex's head began to swim. A dark ring formed on the outskirts of his vision. It closed in until he was nearly blind. He struggled to breathe. His eyes rolled up into his head and his face hit the table with a painful thud.

*

Alex slowly pried his eyes open. He was still in the mall, the people were still frozen, and the man in the white suit still stared at him.

At least his tongue was back in his mouth. He stuck it out and pinched it to be sure.

The man leaned forward. "Sorry I had to take your tongue. But you needed to be focused."

"Who are you? What is all this?"

"Whether you know it or not, you have already begun your training, your discipleship. The first lesson was your confrontation in the cemetery. What did you learn from that?"

Alex leaned back. He would have preferred to be anywhere else—including gym class. "I don't get it. Why . . . why me?"

"Why not you?"

"I'm nobody, that's why. Go back to . . . um . . . God or whoever, and tell him to pick on a priest or minister or someone like that."

The man radiated as he had in the cemetery and was instantly clad in brilliant plated armor. Shimmering wings appeared on his back and extended out in a ten-foot span.

"We do not *tell* the Almighty One *anything*. We listen!"

Alex thought a second before speaking again. "Look, I'm sorry. Um," he looked away, "no disrespect intended. I . . . I just think I'm," he looked back at the angel, "the wrong guy to help . . . God. I mean, look at me!"

The angel turned back into a normal man, white suit and all. "The One who knows every hair on your head has declared that you are the *right* guy. You have been called, Alex. Now, you must be trained."

Alex looked at the statue-like people around him. This angel held all the cards. Since he couldn't see any escape, he tried another tactic. "What do you want from me, exactly?"

"Everything that will happen to you will be for your growth. You will change and become the person you really are in Christ—the person hidden beneath your worldly flesh. Only then will you be ready to fight for God." The man leaned forward and said with intensity, "I will ask you once more. Think back to your confrontation in the cemetery. What did you learn?"

"That Adam sucks."

"Think more deeply," the man demanded.

"What do you want from me?" He turned away. "Look, I don't get any of this. Why can't you just leave me alone? All I want right now is to ask Katie to the Homecoming Dance and to pass my geometry class."

"You have been called to bigger things."

"I don't care."

19

The man shook his head. "You see so little. You are convinced that everything is about you. You think that what you want is what is important. That all this," he motioned around him, "was created for you. In truth, God created all this for Himself and for His glory, not for you."

"I'm just a kid. I'm only sixteen."

The angel responded calmly, "King David was a child when he was called. Samuel had reservations, so the Lord told him not to judge the future king by his size or age. And Paul told Timothy not to allow people to despise his youth. I suggest you do the same."

The angel studied Alex. "I can see you need some time to process all this. Think about it. I will be in touch."

The world moved again.

Alex found himself suddenly engulfed in sound. The little girl's ice cream hit the floor. She wailed.

He looked back. The man…angel…whatever was gone.

"Okay," Alex muttered. "So, now I know what a mental breakdown feels like."

He shook it off and jumped up out of the chair, hoping he hadn't lost the moment.

Katie was looking around for him. He waved at her and she saw him. The crooked smile she made washed away any thoughts of angels or demons or even the call of God.

He moved toward her. In his mind, the world was frozen again. He and Katie were alone, together in a reality of their own. He'd rehearsed the words he wanted to say, but his tongue seemed to have disappeared once again.

His heart pounded.

He swallowed hard.

As he came closer, he blurted out, in a high, cracking voice, "Katie, I have something to ask you."

3

Sunday

All seats in the church sanctuary faced the stage and the pulpit. Padded chairs replaced the pews of old, but were organized in pew-like fashion. The air thrummed with loud rock music. Bright spotlights projected green and yellow beams that brushed across the stage. Special motorized revolving lights with dove-like patterns illuminated the ceiling above the worship leader—a chubby ex-youth director with a scratchy beard, torn jeans, and worn out flip flops. Behind him sat a drummer encased in Plexiglas, a shaggy-haired bass player, and an electric guitarist who ran his fingers up and down the guitar's neck like Jimmy Hendrix.

Smoke poured out on the stage and met the rotating lights, creating eerie, vaporous columns.

Around Alex, people clapped in rhythm and sang along, following the slide show's block-lettered words overlaying a background of streaming video of outer space—stars and massive fields of colorful gas.

Alex had to admit, it was quite a show.

He'd often thought it wouldn't matter what the church was saying or selling—this show would keep people's attention. Sometimes he'd imagine the church selling shoes. Songs would be about the shoes, praising their great qualities, like their heavenly support or their merciful tongues. He even imagined sermons to save the soles of shoes and keep them straight-laced.

When his mind wandered, his mom would lean over and tell him to pay attention, to fill in the empty lines on his outline, and to stop doodling.

There were things Alex enjoyed about church. He liked when the preacher would share his personal stories and Alex perked up when the pastor taught about people being healed. The supernatural piqued his interest. He enjoyed imagining a universe far more interesting than this one.

He thought back on Thursday, when Adam nearly planted him six feet under. He was rescued by that creepy guy dressed like an ice cream man, who knew everything about him.

He shuddered.

Luckily, he hadn't seen the guy since. In fact, he was almost sure that the whole thing was a product of his over-active teenage imagination.

The music's heavy beat reminded him of the Homecoming Dance.

A smile creased his face and he bobbed his head with the beat. He'd done it, and to his surprise, it went well. What had he been so afraid of? He'd asked Katie to the Homecoming Dance, and she'd punched him in the arm for taking so long.

They formed a rough plan for Saturday night.

Everything was set.

*

Mr. Addison released his weight and dropped into an overstuffed chair in his darkened living room. Books covered the walls. Volumes of various sizes and colors stood at attention, like an army of knowledge and wisdom waiting for an order from their commander.

The TV blared, *"In response to a recent report explaining that the War on Drugs is not winnable, and, in fact, has just caused drug use to steadily increase year after year, Congress is considering sweeping new regulations that would legalize many drugs currently considered illegal. They hope this new approach will lessen the ill effects of the drug world. Instead of attempting to eradicate drugs altogether..."*

The exhausted teacher breathed deeply then exhaled through tightly clenched teeth.

The voices inside him came again. *Sinner! Thief! Reprobate! Who are you to teach others? You are a worm, a leech. Your black heart is murderous. You are vile and hateful. Guilty. Obscene. You deceive yourself, telling yourself you make a difference. You are a clown. Your family hates you. Your students hate you. Everyone hates you.*

He shook his head. "Coffee," he whispered to himself. He had to stay awake, had to keep from falling asleep and having the terrible nightmares.

Maybe he'd lost his mind. Was it time to seek help?

As he poured the coffee, the TV continued: *States across the nation are considering releasing thousands of prisoners due to overcrowding in jails. One official recently commented on the spike in the prison population saying, 'Let's face it, people just don't care. They'll cut your throat to get what they want. It's a jungle out there'...*

Mr. Addison picked up his cup and took a deep swallow of the bitter contents. He didn't know how much more of this he could take.

23

*

The day was finally over. Lying in his bed, Alex stared at the ceiling, grinning from ear-to-ear as he thought of Katie.

A shadow crossed the rough popcorn ceiling above him, but there was no one there to cast it. The shadow solidified, hovering directly above him.

His grin fell.

At the top of the churning cloudy mass, two glowing, red spots formed.

Eyes. He was sure of it.

He had to do something. Everything inside him said RUN! But, what about his mom? What if this creepy monster attacked her? What if it possessed her?

He remembered what that weird guy did to get control over Adam.

Alex sat up and stared intently at the eyes. "Um . . . Name yourself!" he firmly commanded.

The pulsating dark mass swirled, rotating quickly, like a hurricane. Jagged black lightning bolts shot out from it and hit the wall. It looked angry.

It dropped right at him.

He gasped and rolled off the bed as the black gyrating mass hit the mattress and disappeared inside.

Great, my mattress is . . . possessed.

He stood and concentrated. "Be gone!" he ordered the thing in his bed.

Nothing happened.

Either a demon had taken residence in his mattress or it had left laughing at him, probably looking for other demons to tell about the stupid kid who thought he could overcome him.

Either way, tonight he was sleeping on the living room couch.

Maybe every night.

As he shut his bedroom door, he wished Mr. White Suit was there.

4

Monday

Alex cautiously entered his bedroom. He rubbed his back, sore from the wooden cross-beam in the middle of their living room couch. He worried over the dismal possibility of having these creepy apparitions invading the different parts of his life.

There was already one in his bed—maybe. He gingerly pushed down on the mattress. Nothing.

What was next, his sock drawer?

His Playstation?

The toilet?

What if they wanted to infest him the way they had Adam? How could he fight … this? And then he remembered the guy in the white suit. What did he say? God had called him for something , , , something important.

What did it all mean?

*

After Alex chained up his bike at school, he saw Conor standing on the front steps waving his hands around, talking to his friends.

Alex had almost forgotten—he was going to the Homecoming Dance!

He came up behind Conor who was boasting to a group of gangly boys about his latest cyber conquest.

Alex spoke in a high girly voice, "Oh Conor, you're my hero! You will save me from all the evil pixels."

Conor sneered. "Shut up, stupid. You'll see. When the zombie apocalypse arrives—and it will—you'll be at my house begging me to save your sorry butt with my laser-guided RPG."

The clock tower rang out for first period to start.

The crowd around Conor agreed with him, giving him a solid round of applause and fist bumps.

Alex rolled his eyes and walked toward his first class. Conor bowed to his admirers, said he had to fly, and sped off after Alex.

"So?" Conor said, pulling his backpack on one shoulder.

"So, who's gonna trust *you* with a bazooka?" Alex countered.

Conor looked exasperated. "Did you buy the tickets?"

"Wouldn't you like to know, Almighty Zombie Killer."

"Quit kidding around. Come on, I gotta get to class."

"If you must know—"

"I must."

"Yes! Pick me up at seven on Saturday. And clean out your car, for God's sake."

"That's great, man. Really, great." Conor noticed the door to his first period class was closing. "Wait up!" he yelled, dashing toward it. "Hold the door!"

As Alex approached his class, he looked to his left and noticed Mr. Addison standing in the hallway, his forehead pressed against the cold metal of one of the lockers. He appeared to be in immeasurable pain.

Alex couldn't take his eyes off of him or the eerie shadow that shrouded him.

He heard a woman loudly clear her throat behind him. "The door is closing, Mr. McKendrick." The first period TA, Megan Bagwell. "Either come in, or head over to Tardy Sweep."

Alex backed into the room, his eyes on Mr. Addison.

*

It was not unusual for Alex to be confused at school. Algebra was like a foreign language, history was an endless string of dates and dead people that made no sense, and chemistry was created just to torture teenagers.

But today, the thing that confused him the most was Mr. Addison. If only he had one personality for the whole day…

In first period English, the guy had come in late and sat in the back of the room. His TA, who was as thrilled as a winner on a game show, had led the class through the period's dry assignments, lecturing like she really was the teacher. It was no surprise that she had a lot of trouble keeping Adam Murray's attention. Alex checked the brute for strange shadows but saw none. He concluded that whatever evil forces made Adam act like such a jerk-wad today were his to begin with.

Even though the banter between Adam and the TA got loud at times, Mr. Addison just sat in the back of the room with his head in his hands.

But now, five hours later, everything was different. Mr. Addison looked like a new man. He was currently engaged in an energetic discussion with his sixth period United States History class, cracking jokes, sharing anecdotes, and having a wonderful time.

"So how would someone get elected to the counsel in the Colony of Virginia? Well, I think you would've enjoyed this, had you been there." The aging teacher grinned with a magic twinkle in his eye. "George Washington started his political campaign with a big party including hundreds of kegs of beer and tons of food. He invited all the wealthy land owners—the voters—to come to his home and drink his beer and listen to him explain why he should be elected."

Alex stared without blinking at Mr. Addison, trying to catch a glimpse of one of the creepy apparitions plaguing him—those flaming red eyes.

Nothing.

Leaning back into his chair, he looked down at his notebook only to realize that he hadn't written anything. He tried to listen to the rest of the lecture but found himself sketching in the margins of his paper the diamond eyes he'd seen the previous day.

Mr. Addison's voice had stopped.

Terrified that he'd been caught not paying attention, Alex sheepishly raised his eyes. Mr. Addison wasn't moving—not just still, but frozen. Alex glanced to Conor, whose mouth was wide open, stopped mid-yawn. He looked out the window and saw a bird floating in midair, its wings outstretched.

"What the...?" Alex slowly turned to his right to find the man in the white suit sitting in the seat next to him.

"Hello," the man said in his mellow voice.

"Bah!" Alex jumped in his chair.

The man grinned. "I have come to hear what you have decided."

Alex gazed at—*what was his name?*—oh yeah, Sariel, with a blank expression. After a few silent seconds, he shook his head and rubbed his eyes, hoping that everything would return to normal. But the strange being was still there, and everything remained frozen.

The man continued. "You know, the topic we discussed the other day? You being called by God to fight for Him?"

"Ugh! Wait, I see what's going on here," Alex said with a frantic tone. "I've . . . I've lost my mind. That's it! The stress of the homecoming and my lousy grades has finally pushed me over the edge. The white clothes—you're from the asylum. You're a doctor sent here to take me to a happier place. Yep, it's the padded room for me!"

Sariel rolled his eyes. "I have revealed myself to you three times now. You have seen one of your classmates under the control of a demonic horde, and a demonic creature appeared to you in your bedroom. What more proof do you need?"

"All of that can simply be the result of a 'mild delusion.'" He picked up this phrase watching crime shows on TV. "Wait a second! How'd you know that one of those things was in my bedroom?" He stared defensively. "Have you been spying on me?"

"Absolutely not. I have merely been keeping an eye on you, making sure that you are all right. I did rather enjoy the bit when you attempted to command the demon to name itself." He laughed heartily at the memory. "That could have been disastrous. However, it did show great courage and the ability to adapt. As always, The Mighty One has chosen perfectly. You will make a great warrior in His army."

Alex remained unblinking. "Wait a second. If you were 'observing' me, why didn't you come in and make that thing go away?"

"I wanted to see how you would handle the situation. Had the demon attached itself to you, I would have stepped in."

Alex scoffed. "Well now, that's reassuring. Come on! You don't wait to save someone after they get shot if you can stop the bullet!"

The angel smirked. "Don't worry. Fortunately, the enemy does not realize how important you are—yet. They only know that you have abilities. They have no idea about your true potential."

"There you go again with all of this 'true potential' stuff. I still don't get what you're talking about!" Alex became irate. "Look, I'm sorry. I'm not your guy. Choose someone else. You know—get a preacher's kid or someone studying to become a pastor. I have my own problems."

"The Lord chose you."

Alex was not about to lose this argument. His sanity depended on it. "If God is all powerful, why does He need me anyway?"

"Silence!" the angel bellowed with such force that Alex fell back into his seat. "I am very patient. However, I will not have you question the Almighty. He has chosen you. That is all. End of story. You are not asked to understand it. All that is expected of you is to believe and obey."

The angel came closer, his eyes narrowed with passion, his voice intense. "Work with me Alex, and become the Champion of Christ you were created to be!"

Alex slowly rose to his feet. He paced like a nervous cat. "Okay, say I accept this. That I go along with you to . . ." he took a deep breath, "save humanity. What am I supposed to do, exactly?"

Sariel approached Alex and put his hand on his shoulder and smirked. "I thought you'd never ask." He dipped his hand into his coat pocket and fished out a 4G Smart Phone, which he deftly turned on with his thumb.

"Wait, wait, wait," Alex protested. "Angels use, um, cell phones?"

Sariel brought up a picture. "What you see as a cell phone, a person at the time of Jesus would have seen as a scroll. An ancient Egyptian would have seen a stone with hieroglyphics. Understand?"

Alex shook his head.

Sariel turned the phone his direction and showed him the picture on the screen. He saw himself dressed from head to toe in plated body armor, far more advanced than anything he'd ever seen.

His hands were clutched in front of him, resting on the ornate hilt of a massive, glowing sword.

"I can do that, with AI."

"God can do it for real. Trust me. I will teach you to use the full armor of God, the tools that will be given to you so that you may be able to combat the evil that is descending upon this town."

Alex's face lit up. "The armor of God. I remember learning about that! That's in . . . uh . . . Ephesians, right?" He recalled the lesson he had heard only a month ago. "It's the sword of the Spirit, the shield of faith, the breastplate of righteousness, the helmet of salvation, the belt of truth, and," he looked at the picture again, "shoes for spreading the gospel of peace."

Sariel nodded.

"But," Alex continued, "the suit we were shown looked like ancient Roman armor. Why's this so different?"

"When the Apostle Paul wrote his letter to the Ephesians, he was chained to a member of the Praetorian Guard in a Roman prison. He explained what he saw. If he had been writing today, the armor would have been described differently."

"I hate to admit it, but this is beginning to make sense." Alex sighed.

The angel stood. "Alex, I have been sent to train you. In time you shall become an athleta Christi. As you grow and develop, you shall become a great threat to the forces of evil. Eventually, the demons shall fear you."

Alex wrinkled his forehead. "Athleta Christi? What's that?"

"It is Greek for 'Champion of Christ.' It is what you were born to be."

Alex cracked a faint smile. "Champion of Christ, huh? I kind of like the sound of that."

Sariel laughed to himself. "Indeed. But there is also a cost."

"A cost?" Alex leaned back in his chair.

The white man sat in a chair next to him. He explained, "Being an athleta is very dangerous. Chances are you will not survive."

"I could . . .," he winced, "die?" His own mortality was something Alex had never really considered.

"Death is inevitable for your fallen race. But, yes, if you agree to the training and become a threat to Satan and his evil forces—"

"Well, that's a deal breaker." Alex shook his head. "You almost had me with the cool armor and all. But, look, I'm not ready to die. You'll just have to find someone else."

"There is no one else." The angel faced Alex. "The Holy One, His Name be praised, chose you."

"And if I don't do it?" Alex raised his hand. "I'm just wondering."

"The light will go out in this place. Satan will win. Many will perish."

"Perish?"

"If you accept your destiny, many will be saved, and the Enemy shall be defeated."

"But I could die."

"Yes."

Alex looked away and his shoulders slumped.

5

Wednesday

Alistair Cain, three-time Forbes Magazine CEO-of–the-Year, barked orders to his inner circle like a sergeant commanding his troops. To his right, his stenographer, a petite young girl with horned-rimmed glasses, pounded away at her tablet, trying to keep up. To her right was Claude Stockwell, top of his class at the Harvard Business School and a technology wiz-kid. His knee bounced uncontrollably, like it was an outlet for extra energy. Next to him sat Cheryl Pierce, a solid-bodied woman with a flair for style. Her flawless makeup and bejeweled accessories were perfect. She was the public side of his company—the best in the business. No one could ever understand how Cain International had overcome scandal after scandal. That is, until they met Cheryl. To her right sat Stanley Weissmuller, the bean counter. He was only seen in one suit—a plain black jacket, white shirt, and thin black tie. His manner was humorless. His only friends were numbers.

Cain ended the meeting as he did after every morning briefing. "Now, get out there and create the greatest company in the world." It was a signal that the meeting was over and that everyone had ten seconds to be out the door. Folders closed, clasps on brief cases clicked loudly, tablets were slipped into covers, and messenger bags zipped shut.

The group exited with machine-like precision, no one saying a word.

When the room was clear, Alistair Cain braced himself, clutching the hand-carved wooden back of his company chair.

His eyes closed as he awaited the transformation.

He released his control over his three trillion cells, allowing his satanic DNA to express itself. In the span of a second, manicured nails became gnarled claws. His Armani double-breasted cream-colored suit turned black as sackcloth. His skin shifted from smooth, bronze-tanned to a pearl translucence, and his short blond hair turned dark and matted like a wild goat's. His limbs doubled in size and rippled with tight, sinewy muscles. His eyes were no longer steel blue but red and serpent-like. Lastly, six inch black horns protruded upward from his chiseled forehead.

It was a great relief to be in his natural state.

Behind him, a smaller creature, with similar features, appeared out of thin air. This being bowed his head nearly to the floor and uttered the word, "Master."

"Report," the Executive Demon commanded.

"The pieces of your wondrous plan are falling into place, just as you expected. Soon, we shall have complete control of the school and of the sacred tower."

The tall one mused. "Has the enemy shown any knowledge of our plans? Have you seen any signs of a counter attack?"

The little demon cleared its rancid throat. "Only the usual: churches and Bible meetings. There's some light coming from these, but not much. We did have an attack that was stopped by what appeared to be a chief angel. It took place at the Willowbrook cemetery. A routine infestation of twelve demons. All were cast out."

"All of them?"

"Yes, sire."

"And who was being attacked?"

Now the demon's face turned to horror. How had he been so stupid? How could he have not seen that the angel protected the human *for a reason*?

He cowered and tried to find words.

As he stuttered and sputtered, the Executive Demon's red eyes became fiery coals. A jagged sword appeared in his powerful right claw. With an effortless, flowing motion he sliced the demon in two.

It vaporized in a small dusty cloud.

A gentle buzzing sounded at the door.

"Come in," Alistair said calmly, bracing himself.

When the door opened, he was the sophisticated executive once again.

*

Alex was in a daze. He leaned back in his padded computer chair, his stainless-steel desk lamp shining down on the steaming bowl of half-eaten Chinese noodle soup. He reached forward, picked up the bowl, grasped the wooden chopsticks between his fingers, and pinched a clump of the steaming noodles.

He imagined himself with Katie at Homecoming. He pictured himself leaning over to steal a kiss, when, in his imagination her image was abruptly replaced by the guy in the white suit. The intruder pointed at Alex and commanded, "Choose."

The angel had been calling him to fight for God. Could he really say no? Could he selfishly condemn all the people he knew?

He shook his head and shoved the noodles into his mouth, slurping up the slippery ends.

He turned his head and was face-to-face with Sariel.

"Bah!" Alex dropped his bowl on the desk and fell backward in his chair.

Climbing back up, he said with disdain, "Don't you ever knock?"

"What have you decided?"

Alex righted the chair and sat back down. "Yeah, about that. I was thinking I might need a little more time." He picked up his chopsticks.

Sariel frowned. "We do not have more time. It is imperative that you begin your training. The demonic forces are on the move."

Alex was stunned by the ferocity of the angel's rant. He was right, of course. But Alex had never done anything important in his life. He'd never had to make any decision harder than choosing which tasteless meal to eat at the school cafeteria.

It was time to man up and take a stand.

He took a deep breath and declared, "Fine, fine. I get it. I guess I can't escape my destiny." He turned away and grabbed his bowl to finish his noodles.

"Finally. I will take that as a definite, yes."

Sariel grasped the back of Alex's shirt collar and forcefully pulled the young man to his feet and close to his white suit.

A portal opened around them. In a brilliant flash, they were gone.

Alex opened his eyes in a completely different environment—one teeming with life. He could smell it in the air. He was surrounded by trees that reached high into the sky. In a narrow ravine between these rough columns, he watched a pack of wild animals eating pampas grass. He couldn't believe what he saw. Alligators ate grass alongside tigers and lions. In the midst of them, relaxed and at peace, were deer, gazelle and monkeys.

The animals were friends.

Alex looked to his right and gasped.

Ten massive pterosaurs had launched themselves from the top of the canopy and were winging their way toward the horizon. In the valley beneath them, three T-Rexes gently walked with a flock of duck-billed dinosaurs and a triceratops.

This was nature as it was meant to be—peaceful, powerful, and harmonious.

This was Eden.

Gathering his senses, forcing himself against his initial shock, he asked, "How? How did you do this? Where are we? What the h— heck?"

Sariel, in his angelic form, smirked. He obviously got real pleasure out of these moments. "So many questions. Where are we? This place doesn't have a name. It is not on any of your maps or any GPS. It is a place of cleansing and training. It is where we will begin."

"But, dinosaurs? Really? Least you could do is warn a guy."

"And miss your expression? Not a chance."

Alex shook his head and turned away from the angel. He just had to have one more look at this place and everything in it. He couldn't get over it. "So, what now?"

Sariel stepped closer. "I must cleanse you of your flesh."

Alex looked confused. "Whaddya mean, flesh?"

"Your earthly self. Think of it as the culmination of all things you have been as a member of the race of Adam. It is your worldly heritage. Although you were made new when you accepted Christ, your earthly self remains. Here, for a time, you will learn what it is like to be freed from this unholy burden."

Alex raised his eyebrow. "So, you're going to cleanse me? How?"

Sariel's angelic body brightened. He slowly lifted his arms and wings over Alex, closed his eyes, and thundered emphatically, "Be free!"

At first, nothing happened. Alex thought the angel must be kidding around again. But then he felt an odd sensation, as if his very skin was crawling. Waves moved from his extremities to his chest. He pulled off his shirt and saw that a pulsating knot had formed over his heart. The tingling sensation turned to excruciating pain. Every nerve in his body screamed out at once. The pinkish mass grew and squirmed as if struggling to break free.

"Ahh! It hurts! Make it stop!"

With one last excruciating tug, the pink ball tore loose from him and shot through the air, splashing in a nearby brook.

Alex stared in terror and disbelief at the bloody, gaping hole over his heart. He couldn't breathe.

He collapsed to the ground, landing on his back, unconscious.

*

It had been months since Henry Addison had known quiet. He couldn't pinpoint the exact day or hour it all started—the murmuring whispers, the cackling, the vulgarities, and the searing headaches. He only rested when he took sleeping pills and drifted into a deep, death-like slumber.

A clicking noise sounded on the slider of his second story apartment. He pulled back the curtains, and the light from nearby streetlamps flooded his living room. He looked down and saw a raven, nearly a foot tall, pecking at the glass. It hopped back and cawed loudly.

"Go away!" he ordered.

The bird didn't budge, but maintained its relentless tapping and screeching.

Addison grasped the cherry wood handle of his balcony's sliding door and yanked it open with as much force as he could, yelling curses at the pest.

In terror, the bird cawed back at him, took wing, and flew away.

Mr. Addison watched until it had flown out of sight.

He took a deep breath and walked to the balcony railing.

The faint sound of thunder rolled in the distance.

A storm approached.

Perfect—a mirror to his inner turmoil.

Henry's eyes drifted toward the street below. His mind whirled.

"I could do it," he said aloud to himself. "Climb on the ledge, jump off, and end all of this."

Coward! One of the voices in his head coarsely whispered.

"Is it cowardly to want to end one's pain?" he plaintively answered as he slowly climbed atop the railing, grabbing a support beam to steady himself.

The thunder became louder and rain fell in buckets, drenching him.

"I'm sick of this! Sick of the pain! It all ends here!"

He leaned his head forward and let go.

A jagged bolt of lightning struck the building not ten meters away, causing an explosion that startled him. As he flailed, the air came alive with a cacophonous squall. Hundreds of ravens descended upon him like a rushing black river, hitting him hard in the chest and thrusting him backward onto the wet balcony floor.

As darkness rimmed Mr. Addison's vision, ravens crowded around him, bobbed their heads, and then took wing as if signaled.

They disappeared into the dark clouds as he lost consciousness.

*

Alex filled his lungs with sweet air and wrested himself out of the weirdest dream he'd ever had. He fully expected to open his eyes and see his familiar bedroom. Instead, the underside of a mile-high forest canopy greeted him.

He jerked up into a sitting position on the spongy, moss-covered ground. Sariel leaned against a tree, watching him. Near him sat a pink pile of wet flesh that reminded him of an organ he'd once seen in an operation video. This pink mass undulated and quickly doubled in size.

He remembered the hole blown over his heart. He put his hands to his chest, but it was intact and he felt no pain.

He pulled his shirt back down, cleared his throat, and asked, "What…what happened?"

The angel watched the pulsating ball of flesh. "In your realm, the flesh permeates your physical body. It is a part of every cell and only at the moment of death are you finally freed from it. However, in this place, it is possible to extract the flesh, temporarily. This way, you can learn and progress unencumbered."

Alex followed the angel's eyes. The ball of flesh had changed again. Five distinct knobs grew from it—two on the bottom, one on each side, and one on top. It reminded him of a baby developing in the womb.

"So, now what?" he asked.

The growth accelerated and the pink ball became the size of a man. Its skin bubbled, and blond hair pushed out of its head. In seconds, colorless eyes formed in sockets on the face. Then its skin became smoother and muscles formed beneath it. Lastly, a Spandex-like covering, which matched Alex's, formed over its body. It started breathing and opened its eyes. It looked just like Alex, but with a crazed expression of raging insanity. It cocked its head to one side, and a maniacal smile creased its face.

Laughing wildly, it reached up and pulled a jagged gray sword from the air.

Sariel leaned against a nearby rock, crossed his arms, and instructed, "You shall refer to this creature as Anti-Alex. It is made

41

of everything that you will leave behind on the earth when you die—everything about you that is not of Christ."

"What do I have to do? Fight him?" Alex asked.

"To walk in Christ, you must fight the flesh every moment of your life. It is a battle that is only won when death releases you. Observe."

A long sword appeared in Sariel's right hand. The hilt was of a white metal and covered his hand. The blade was white with royal blue flames crawling up it. Alex thought it was beautiful.

The angel put his left foot a little in front of his right and balanced his weight. "The flesh wants only your destruction. He will not fight fair. You must not give him an inch."

The thing that looked like Alex leapt into the air, its sword held high above its head. The jagged weapon came down and met Sariel's. The swords clanged loudly and sparks exploded. Sariel didn't seem fazed at all. Anti-Alex thrust again and again, but every time Sariel's lightning fast counterstrikes met his attempted blows. Alex couldn't believe how skilled the angel was with the blade. There were times the weapon moved so fast it appeared only as a blur of light. The fleshly part of Alex reached down and picked up a rock and hurled it at the angel. Sariel swung his sword upward and hit the rock. It soared like a baseball going over the left field fence.

Anti-Alex stopped his attack. His chest heaved. He cursed Sariel and looked over at Alex. "Let me have *him*!" he cried.

"What?" Alex choked out.

"So be it," the angel responded and stepped aside. Anti-Alex's eyes lit up, and he looked at Alex like he was a tasty meal.

The thing circled him slowly.

"What am I supposed to do?" Alex's voice cracked.

"Destroy it. Destroy it quickly, before it destroys you."

Anti-Alex swung his sword. Alex jumped back reflexively, and the sword tore through the front of his shirt. Blood dripped from a thin slice in his chest.

"Ouch! What's your damage!" Alex shouted.

He backed up a few more steps, and still this evil twin charged him. The crazed being swung its razor-sharp weapon with unimaginable ferocity. Alex dodged and ran behind a tree as fast as he could.

"How exactly am I supposed to destroy this thing?" Alex yelled to Sariel. "You know, he *does* have a sword!" Alex continued to dodge the onslaught, trying to stay on the opposite side of the tree.

"So do you!" Sariel yelled back. "The Armor of God exists within you. Trust in the Lord. Extend your hand and believe!"

Alex ducked another mighty swipe. The sword stuck in the bark of the tree right above his head. Alex lunged at his opponent, punched it in the jaw and kicked it in the chest.

Anti-Alex fell to the ground.

Just believe, Alex thought. *Okay, I can do this, I can do this.*

He raised his right hand with his fingers outstretched and tried to focus.

His enemy recovered, jumped up, and approached fast.

Alex proclaimed, "I believe. I call on the power of the Word of God. Help me beat this thing! Please!"

In a bright flash, a shimmering sword appeared in his hand. It was heavy. The green hilt fit his hand perfectly. The blade itself gleamed like it was made of translucent jade. Three diamond-shaped emeralds were imbedded in the weapon—one at the bottom of the hilt, one at the base of the blade, and one near the tip. Alex nodded. It was a beautiful weapon. *Yeah, this will do!*

The feral creature lunged at him with a piercing scream. Alex lifted his sword and met the chiseled blade at the last second. The swords crashed loudly together in a violent flash.

Anti-Alex laughed and kicked Alex hard in the chest. He fell to the ground and rolled on his side. His sword landed three feet away.

The angel shook his head with an expression of sadness.

The creature brought his sword down upon Alex in a final, murderous slash, The boy rolled to the side, scooped up his own sword and jumped to his feet. He swung his blade, which again met the other with an explosive shower of sparks.

Alex noticed his opponent's sword was pocked and damaged by the blow, while his remained unscathed. *Hmm . . . good is more powerful than evil.*

"You must wield the sword. Glide with it. Use it as an extension of yourself," his mentor encouraged.

Anti-Alex backed off and screamed in rage. It lunged forward again, frantically swinging its sword back and forth in front of him.

Alex watched carefully and timed his thrust. He leaned his entire weight into the blow. The sword glided perfectly, meeting his opponent's in mid-swing, stopping it cold. Alex then swung his foot out and swept Anti-Alex's legs out from under him.

With an ear-piercing screech, the creature hit the ground hard. Its sword jarred loose and bounced out of reach. Alex kicked the thing hard in the head.

Its eyes rolled back.

Its body went limp.

It lost consciousness.

Alex straddled his anti-self and put his sword above the creature's neck in a show of decisive victory. His chest heaved as he tried to catch his breath.

"Finish it," the angel commanded. Alex looked back at the angel wide-eyed. "Destroy it while it is still vulnerable."

"What? You saw what happened. I beat him. Can't I just declare myself, you know, the winner?" Alex asked.

"This is not a game. This is the flesh. Destroy it now or it *will* destroy you."

Alex stared at the creature beneath his blade. It was like looking in a mirror. "I . . . I don't think I can."

At that moment, Anti-Alex's eyes popped open. He kicked up hard, catching Alex right between the legs. The boy yelped, grabbed himself, and fell forward.

The creature scurried over to its sword. Weapon in hand, it roused all of its strength for the final blow. It crouched and leapt into the air.

Alex recovered and reflexively jumped up to meet the creature. He focused on the blade bearing down on him as he rose. At the last split-second, Alex twisted his body away from the sword so it missed him entirely. The clone bent forward with the thrust.

Alex spun back and used both hands to plunge his own sword into Anti-Alex's back and through its heart.

Its eyes bulged. It screamed and dropped to the ground. It hit hard, the sword still sticking up out of its back. The being pushed itself up on its knees and turned his head slowly toward Alex. It gave him a snide grin and then froze. Its skin changed from soft pink to a dull gray, stone-like color. It became a man-shaped sculpture of dust. A gentle breeze hit the figure and carried away particles in a dark flowing stream. What was left of Anti-Alex collapsed in a pile of ash.

A euphoric rush of power flowed through Alex. Every purified cell in his body tingled exuberantly. It was like he was hearing the most beautiful music, watching the most gorgeous sunset, and eating the most delicious food all at the same time. "What is this?"

"This, my disciple, is pure joy."

Alex celebrated, leaping, spinning, and laughing with the sword in his raised hand.

The angel mused, "Even as David danced before the Lord."

Sariel walked over to the creature's ashes and brushed aside the top layer. Something glowing red in pulsating rhythms lay underneath the debris. In another moment, it grew cold and dark as obsidian. The angel reached forward and picked up the object. His fingers barely fit around it.

"What's that?" Alex asked, dropping to the floor and trying to catch his breath.

"The core of your flesh—its heart. I shall hold it for safe keeping."

The angel secured the piece beneath his breastplate.

6

Parallel Timescape

The bout with Anti-Alex had drained Alex. He didn't remember falling asleep, so he woke with a start. He stood up, again joyous. He closed his eyes, and a wide smile creased his face.

"You know, Sariel, I never did drugs. I mean, I could've . . . I guess. I was afraid of what my mom would think, and I didn't want to let her down. But drugs can't be better than this."

"The Joy of the Spirit is better than *any* earthly pleasure."

Alex's eyes widened. "You mean better than—"

"Anything."

"Seriously? Wow!"

The angel grinned. "You who bear God's image have been fashioned to possess full joy. Your brains even have pathways specifically designed to ensure that you grow in joy and experience it all the time. Unfortunately, these brain centers can be activated by other things—drugs, sex, overeating, social media, intense gaming, even shopping. It is why these activities become addictive. They are substitutes for the intended source of pure joy."

"So, how do I feel this way all the time?"

"My dear boy, joy is not the goal, it is the by-product. The goal is to fellowship with God and to be filled with His Spirit. Joy comes from living in Him."

"Then count me in."

"Good," Sariel nodded. "We must continue with your training. Some Christians become warriors throughout their lives, gradually learning to win spiritual battles. But the Holy One has called you for a special purpose. It will require a more intensive training, perhaps for months."

Alex's face fell. "What are you talking about? I have to get back. I have school tomorrow. I have to get my suit dry-cleaned and—"

"You must remain here until you have mastered the sword. You beat the flesh, but it was more by luck than skill. Your mind and muscles need training to move faster and with better accuracy. You must become an expert swordsman. You need to learn to walk in the Spirit."

Alex shook his head and waved his hands. "You've got to be kidding me! I don't have time for this."

"Actually, you do." Sariel panned his hand across the horizon. "This realm is not connected to yours. It is part of a completely different timescape."

"Timescape?"

The angel looked up, like he was searching for the right words. "A landscape is a geographical terrain. A timescape is a temporal terrain. Any time spent here does not affect your world. You could spend a thousand years here, and when you return to your own realm, it will be the same moment as when you left."

"What about aging?"

"You never age here."

"What about . . .?" His face tensed. "What if I have to . . . you know . . . go?"

"Go?"

"Oh, my gosh! What if I have to . . . um . . . go to the bathroom?"

Sariel smiled. "This is a spiritual realm. Your body is different here. You don't have to eat here or . . . do other things."

Alex nodded and sat on the ground.

Then the angel announced, "Before you can begin, however, you need to align yourself with the rest of creation."

"How do I do that?" Alex looked up and caught sight of a flock of winged dinosaurs flying high above the canopy. They moved so effortlessly.

"With worship," Sariel continued.

A few moments passed while the angel stared at him.

Then Alex understood. "Me?" he asked.

"You."

"Worship? Now?"

"Now."

After a few moments of thinking, Alex cleared his throat and looked to the ground. He closed his eyes hard and started singing in a cracking voice, "Oh Lord my God, when I in awe-some won-der . . ." He wasn't quite sure how the hymn went after this. *I put my sin asunder? I hear sounds like thunder? I can't get through this blunder?*

"Stop!" the angel said firmly.

"No, just give me a second. I can figure this out. I got it. I humble myself down under. Wait. I'm gonna start again."

The angel put his hand over Alex's mouth and told him, "Stop! That is not worship. To worship is to throw your entire being to the floor before God, surrendering yourself completely to Him. Done correctly, the Spirit within you will resonate with your praise. He will breathe life into your devotion. You will know what it is to completely align yourself with the song of the universe, to harmonize with the angelic hosts, and to move with the stream of all creation."

Sariel knelt, bowed his head reverently, lifted his arms, and gave himself over to God in praise.

The leaves on the trees joined in, vibrating with the beat of his song. The sound of the nearby river splashed and bubbled in harmony. Alex's jaw dropped. He realized that the entire world around him had joined in with the angel's declarations of God's majesty and exalted Lordship. Soon, Alex was dancing again and lifting his arms—caught up in the intensity of the experience. Finally, he collapsed to the spongy floor, exhausted. Gasping for breath, he laughed uncontrollably.

When the glory of God's presence subsided, Alex and the angel simply sat together in silence.

Alex spoke up. "You said something about training?"

Sariel almost appeared giddy, if an angel could be giddy. "With your flesh removed, we can begin. Training in Christ is first and foremost training in walking in the power of the Spirit of God. It is relinquishing more and more of yourself to the control of the Spirit. As you do this, your abilities will improve. This sword," he reached out and picked it up from the ground. He swayed it from side to side, "...will become your greatest ally."

He handed the sword back to Alex. "A warrior must dress the part." He walked behind Alex and opened his arms wide. His massive ivory wings unfurled. He curled them around the boy, enveloping him and drawing him close. An intense brightness flared inside this winged barrier. A rubbery material encased Alex, growing from his core and moving to his extremities. He wiggled and scratched and pulled at this elastic covering.

"What is this—stuff?" Alex called out.

Sariel stepped back and retracted his wings.

Alex marveled at the tight emerald-green second-skin that had replaced his clothes. Jet black pads covered his elbows, knees, feet, and shoulders. He turned his arm repeatedly before his eyes and studied the material.

"Spandex? Really?" He scoffed.

"This is spiritual energy. It will protect you from many dangers."

"Dangers?"

The angel put his hands together. His head bowed, and he appeared to be in deep thought. Alex jumped when a small, grotesque creature appeared snarling about five feet away from him. It kept shifting its weight to jump at Alex, but its feet were somehow anchored securely to the ground.

"This is a minor demon to help with your training."

Alex studied the creature that pulled at its dark purple legs, trying to get them loose. "Is it . . . is it really a demon?"

"Yes. Demons are fallen angels with all of our powers and abilities. With time, they grow more evil, more despicable. I captured this one when I found it nosing around your school. Deal with him."

"What do you want me to do? Kill it?"

"Exactly. But do not underestimate it. All demons are quite powerful and very, very fast."

With those last words, Sariel lifted his hand and the demon's legs were freed.

He sprung right at Alex and sank his wide row of yellow-orange teeth into his right shoulder. It didn't penetrate the material of his Spandex suit, but it was like being caught in a bear trap.

Alex yelped in pain and dropped his sword. He doubled up his fist and repeatedly punched the demon in the head. It didn't budge. He picked up a nearby rock and hit it several times.

Stunned, the demon's jaws loosened, and it dropped to the ground.

Before Alex could take advantage of this, the beast had recovered and bounded toward him again. This time Alex managed to get his hands up and caught the creature in mid-air. It squealed and shook as it flashed its needle-like teeth at him, trying to lock his jaws on him again.

"Only your sword will kill it," the angel reminded him.

"Great!" Alex knew that if he let go of the thing it would catch him and have him for lunch. His arms grew tired and sweat beaded on his forehead.

This had to end.

Alex's mind was flooded with negative voices from his past. He heard himself being called "religious" and "good boy" and "loser." His mind told him that he was lame to go to church or to believe in God. After all, the stories of the Bible were only myths or fables.

The barrage overwhelmed and weakened him.

His arms buckled.

"This one can play with your head—if you let him," Sariel instructed.

And then the voice inside him spoke seductively. *Join us.*

This was too much. The demon had overplayed his advantage. Alex shook his head to clear it. He recalled what Sariel had said earlier, to rely on the Spirit. He remembered Jesus saying that the Spirit, the Comforter, would lead His followers into all truth. He held tight to the creature, at the same time allowing the central part of himself to relinquish control of the situation to the Spirit and His power. Something clean and beautiful welled up inside him.

The negative voices stopped.

Alex lifted the frenzied creature above his head. With all the force he could muster, he threw the snarling beast to the floor. Alex twisted his body and stomped his foot on the edge of his sword. The weapon shot up into the air, and he grabbed the hilt.

The demon came at Alex's face like a rocket. He screeched in utter delight, with his maw wide open and his spiked teeth bared.

Alex thrust the glowing blade vertically up in front of him, holding the sword steady with both hands.

When the creature hit it, the blade sliced it between the eyes, into two hemispheres. The shrieking stopped short, and the slimy blue-green demonic parts disintegrated in a puff of wispy green smoke and shimmering dust.

Alex looked around, dazed.

"Did you see that?" He yelled, jumping up and down. "I mean, really, did you see that?"

"Well done," Sariel said. "That was the easiest one."

Alex's face fell.

"Oh," he groaned, "great."

*

If time were measured chronologically in this place, Alex would have already spent more than five months in training. Sariel led him through exercise after exercise. He fought many demons, each more powerful than one before, each with its' own unique abilities. Under Sariel's guidance he became stronger, more confident, and learned many new combat strategies.

The bouts were broken up by protracted conversations. Sariel made it clear that training the mind was just as important as training the body. His main point of reference was the Hebrew-Christian Scriptures. In his mouth, however, the stories of the Bible were not the ancient religious tales of the past. Instead, they had the crisp reality of an eye-witness.

"I always thought angels were…" Alex looked away. "Well, you're not what I expected."

"How so?" Sariel lay on his back on the soft ground next to Alex. They both watched a spider above them spin new supports onto a huge web.

"I don't know. Like, in the Bible, the angels announced the birth of Jesus and the heavenly hosts sang."

"Yes, I know. I was there."

Alex gasped. "You were at the birth of Jesus?"

"I am an angel, God's servant. I go wherever the Almighty sends me. And on that night, the assignment was glorious."

"Okay, so where else have you been? What else have you seen?"

Sariel reminisced. "There was a winter's morning," he began, "when a certain man named Abram was visited—"

"By three men. You were one of *them*!" Alex's eyebrows rose with realization.

"I was. You see, we were on our way to Sodom, to bring out his nephew, Lot."

Alex searched his mind for the rest of the story, but came up empty.

Sariel continued, "We reached Lot's house without incident. He was such a gracious fellow. Served us food and waited on us like we were kings. He believed our message and was preparing to leave when the men of the city came and called out to him to give us to them."

"They were all . . . um . . . killed, right? With fire and brimstone?"

"Correct. The human soul can only persist in doing evil for so long until it is unable to return to God. The ears stop hearing, the heart becomes hard as stone, and the eyes seek only pleasure and gain. God's gracious message of salvation cannot reach them. When they arrive at this stage, they are—removed."

The spider moved deftly to connect another silky strand.

Alex exhaled. "That's harsh."

The angel closed his eyes. His face tensed with pain. "When one of your doctors pulls the plug on someone who is brain dead, it is sad, but not murder."

"So you're saying they were, like, brain-dead?"

"No. Not their brains—their souls. They had rejected God completely and would never come to Him. At that point, there is no difference between minutes or years. The end is the same."

"So, you're saying they condemned themselves?"

A tear slid between the wrinkles that framed the angel's eyes. "Yes," he whispered.

Alex added this new insight to the dozens Sariel had given him over these months.

Watching the spider weave, he asked, "Did you do anything else I would know about? Anything that's in the Bible?"

The angel smiled, "Well, there was the whole thing with Balaam, son of Beor, while he rode his donkey."

"Let me guess, you were the angel with the flaming sword."

Sariel nodded. "Yes."

"So, did the donkey talk, really?"

"Of course he did. That was God's doing, not mine. Don't look so surprised. Animals speak to humans all the time, mostly in their own ways. You just refuse to listen."

Alex rolled over and faced his mentor. "So, what's it like? I mean, what's it like being in front of God? You must see Him often, right?"

The angel took a deep breath. "Not all angels stand before God in the Holy Place, in heaven. That is the privilege of the Seraphim and Cherubim. Some of us are," he paused, "assigned to this earth. Here we are given physical bodies and live among humanity. I have lived more than two hundred different lives here."

"So, how does *that* work?"

"When given an assignment, I go wherever I am sent—whether Bangkok or Lima or Russia or Africa. My physical appearance matches the environment. I have learned all human languages and customs. I stay and perform whatever tasks I am ordered by God to do. Mostly, I blend in. I make friends and grow older. I go to weddings and funerals. I end up in a rest home and stare at the walls, like many of your elderly. And then, I cause my physical body to appear dead. I am buried. Afterward, I leave the coffin and begin my next assignment."

The spider stopped working on the web and waited.

"And nobody knows?" Alex asked.

"Have you not heard what Paul said, that people have often entertained angels without even knowing it?"

Alex leaned closer. "So, angels like you are all over the place?"

"Not really. There are just a few of us in each geographical area."

"So, you ended up in our town?"

"Actually, I was sent to you specifically. As I said before, you have been called. My job, in this particular lifetime, is to see to it that you fulfill your calling."

"But you still don't know what it is I'm supposed to do."

"True." The angel's eyes sparkled. "But whatever it is, you will be ready, even if it takes an eternity in this place."

"So, what do we do next?"

"It is time for you to learn the laws of the spiritual realm," the angel answered, rising and dusting off his white clothes.

"This place has laws?"

"We can refer to them as natural laws, or rules of operation, if you like. Now, observe." The angel walked to the nearest tree and pulled off a plump pear. He wiped it clean on his jacket sleeve then held it out in his right hand. As Alex watched, in amazement, the fruit slowly dropped through the angel's palm. His hand remained opaque and apparently solid, as did the pear. When it finished its descent, the fruit fell and Sariel caught it with his left hand.

"That's a pretty good trick," Alex said, clapping his hands hard and slow. "What do you do for an encore?"

"That was no trick. What I have demonstrated is one of the rules of this realm. This place is as substantial to you as you want it to be. However, in order to have this much control over the spiritual universe, one must develop focus and be able to bend the rules."

"So, I'll be able to do *that*?" Alex asked.

"More. With focus, in time, and with the growth of your faith, you will be able to pass through solid walls, walk on water, perhaps even fly."

"Fly! Are you kidding me? Okay, I gotta try this. Gimme the pear."

Alex took the fruit and held it in his palm. He stared at it, wiggled the fingers of his other hand at it like a magician, but nothing happened. He wasn't easily daunted. Sariel had said that he *could* do it, when he was ready. He tried to picture his hand transparent, with all the molecules letting go of their physical existence and becoming pure spirit.

Again, nothing happened.

"Now, this is just embarrassing," he said, shaking his head in frustration. "Let me see you do something else. I've got it. Walk through that tree." Alex pointed to a nearby tree with a girth so wide he wouldn't have been able to wrap his arms around it.

Sariel looked at the towering redwood. "That tree?"

Alex thought he'd caught Sariel off guard. He walked over and leaned against the very substantial trunk. Patting the bark, he challenged, "Yeah, Sariel, let's see you pass through this."

"As you wish."

While Alex watched, the angel slowly descended into the ground until his head disappeared.

Alex jumped over to where the angel vanished and stepped on the ground. It was solid. Next thing he knew, the surface of the tree moved. The bark changed shape and Sariel's form could be seen as if he were an ancient relief carved in the tree's surface. His wooden eyes blinked, and he smiled. Slowly, the angel emerged and was free again. He brushed some of the bark residue off his clothes and looked toward Alex.

"You gotta teach me that," Alex said, amazed.

"I can only teach you what you are ready to learn."

*

For three more earth months, Alex continued training.

Sariel exposed him to a whole new set of demons. These were tricky and had unexpected powers. A stout, dragon-like creature cast fire from his eye sockets. Another, a scrawny troll, used putrid projectile vomiting to disgust and distract him. Another hairy type— that reminded Alex of a werewolf—shot gross orange slugs out of its back, which tried to crawl up Alex's legs to make a home in the nearest orifice. Alex learned to innovate, think on his feet, and extended his physical and spiritual powers.

While he rested and recovered, he and Sariel continued their lengthy discussions. This heavenly being had great wisdom and knew how to pierce through Alex's many defenses. He even helped him shift his conflicted feelings about his absent father to begin relying on God as his true Father. As Sariel explained, "You were given an earthly father for a short time, but when you were reborn by the seed of God, this earthly relationship was superseded by that which is eternal. It is vital that you embrace God as your true Father."

The angel showed infinite patience as Alex explained every doubt he ever had. Sariel responded with stories that revealed how ageless truths were woven into reality and could be seen all around him. He would often repeat, "We only need eyes to see."

Over time, Alex developed these new eyes.

And then, after a beautiful time of worship, something was different inside him. He walked over to the tree and pulled off a pear. He held it out in his palm and placed all things, including himself, completely in the hands of God. Taking a deep, cleansing breath, he focused the pear.

The pear shook then dropped through the palm of his hand and bounced on the ground.

"That is a pretty good trick," Sariel quipped, a wry smile on his face.

"Yeah," Alex agreed, "but I'm embarrassed. The pear was supposed to levitate." They both laughed together.

Sariel announced, "This portion of your training is complete."

Alex was stunned. He had become acclimated to this place and was still learning so much. "Do you really think I'm ready?"

The angel nodded. He abruptly stood and placed his hand on Alex's chest. As he stepped backward, he pulled Alex with him through a blazing portal.

In an instant, they were back in the middle of his bedroom.

Sariel vanished.

A bowl hit his foot with a loud clang and noodles splashed over his legs and onto the carpet.

Ugh!

7

Thursday

Alex's arm moved in a smooth arch, perfectly pressing the "off" button and silencing his blaring alarm clock. He hadn't slept much in his months of training. Today he woke feeling like a new man.

He opened his eyes and took in his room. Light refracting off a glass on his window sill created a vibrant rainbow that danced like fairies on his ceiling. The colors in the posters on his walls—mostly of the different cars he'd dreamed of owning—were greatly intensified, richer and more vibrant. For the first time in his life, he noticed the shapes of the furniture and the knick-knacks around him, their internal superstructures. He marveled at the spheres, cones, and prisms that came together to make the ordinary things of life.

"Whoa." He gasped at the beauty and design in everything as he saw the world with new eyes.

His shower invigorated him. He sang songs he'd learned from Sariel and fell into glorious worship. He could have stayed there all morning, singing praises to God under the soothing hot water, but a part of his brain remembered that he had to get ready for school.

When he was dressed, he scooped up his backpack and walked down the stairs into the kitchen. His mom was in her robe, closing the coffee maker and pressing the start button.

How he had missed her!

Overcome with emotion, Alex ran to her and threw his lanky arms around her.

"Alex! What in the world?"

"I missed you so much." Alex tightened his grasp.

His mom pushed down on his arms and wriggled loose. "Okay, okay. What do you want? Whatever it is, we can't afford it."

Alex jumped back with surprise and said with sincerity, "Just glad to see you. That's all."

"You saw me last night. You pushed past me with a bowl of Ramen and scurried up to your cave."

Alex remembered that night and how he had been so self-absorbed. He stepped toward his mom and took her hands in his and looked at her with genuine regret. "I can't believe I did that. It was so...," he choked, "thoughtless and selfish. Will you please forgive me?"

His mom's mouth hung open. She stuttered, "Don't ... don't worry about it. You're a teenager. It comes with the territory. So what're you doing up so early?"

"So, you *will* forgive me?" Alex persisted.

"Of course," she said, looking at him like he was from Mars.

His eyes brightened. "I wanted to see you. I thought we might, you know..." He picked up a cup and poured himself some coffee. "...talk and have breakfast together. Is there anything I can do? Take out the trash? Empty the dishwasher?"

"Okay, now you're really scaring me. What's gotten into you?"

Alex considered how to answer. He carefully said, "Mom, I can't really explain. You might see some," he shifted his feet, "changes in me. Good changes. Needed ones. I've been pretty much living in my own head. Well, I'm done with all that. Here, I'll get the trash." He pulled the plastic bag out of the container, tied off the top, and headed out the door.

That morning, Alex and his mom ate cereal together, drank coffee, and shared their thoughts and feelings. The conversation effortlessly jumped from topic to topic, turned down various alleyways, and camped on things that were funny or particularly meaningful to them both.

When Alex finally left for school, he gave his mom a loving hug, and they both wiped tears of joy from their eyes.

*

Alex's legs were powerful pistons thrusting up and down on his bike pedals. Puffing hard, he reveled with each cool breath. His nose delighted in fragrances he couldn't remember ever smelling before—the robust smell of fresh-cut grass and the sweetness of a honeysuckle hedge.

He looked up past the top of his helmet—a safety device he had never really worn before today—and observed the deep-cobalt sky and the wispy hair-like cirrus clouds. A form like a small airplane or a graceful bird with a massive wing span emerged silhouetted against the cloud. As it moved farther from the glare of the sun, Alex could see it clearly.

Sariel.

The angel soared through the air as gracefully as an Olympic gymnast, his wings slowly beating in curling strokes.

Fondness welled up inside Alex. Sariel was his guardian angel and mentor, and he couldn't have asked for any better.

As he glanced up again, Sariel ascended, entered a dense cumulous cloud, and disappeared from sight.

Alex grinned. He knew he could count on the angel to be there whenever he needed him.

*

Alex walked down the school hallway when Conor jumped on his back, pushing him forward a couple of steps.

"Saturday night," Conor said, a little too loudly.

"That's right," Alex mused. "Homecoming. I'm looking forward to it. Let's make sure we aren't late. We wouldn't want to keep the ladies waiting."

"Funny, jerk-face. Since when have you become all—you know, grown up?" He lowered the tone of his voice for the last two words, trying to mock Alex's newfound maturity.

As they walked together, Alex couldn't help but overhear the dozens of conversations around him, all peppered with F-bombs. He'd barely noticed them before and was known to throw out a few himself for emphasis. Now they assaulted his ears like sharp stones.

He turned his attention back to Conor. "Sorry. I haven't exactly been myself lately. Yeah, I'm looking forward to the dance."

Conor shook his head. "Whatever, loser. I'll catch you later." He dashed down another hall, giggling and tripping a freshman in his way, making him spill his books across the floor.

Alex walked over and picked up the books.

*

Things improved dramatically for Alex when he got to class. He sat in the front row and had deep conversations with his teachers. In English, he understood the emptiness and meaninglessness experienced by John in Vonnegut's, *Cat's Cradle*. In science class, he was fascinated with a discussion over the conflict created in evolutionary circles over those advocating Intelligent Design. In every class he found himself talking with his teachers as if they were co-explorers of the fascinating mysteries of life. He was amazed how interesting high school could be. His teachers all thanked him for his attention and warmly patted him on the shoulder when he got up to leave. The other students jeered at him, calling him the teacher's pet and making sickening kissing noises and tapping their rear ends.

The best part of his day was his last class with Mr. Addison. He participated in an in-depth conversation about Federalism and state's rights.

At the end of the class Mr. Addison announced, "Remember, finish up your essays and prepare for next Monday's test."

The bell rang and the noisy teens poured out the door, cell phones in hand. Several shook their heads at Alex.

Alex approached his teacher. "Hey Mr. Addison, you're looking better today."

"I brought aspirin," the teacher said, curtly.

"I see, well, I'm glad. I guess I better get going. See you on Monday." He headed through the door, delighted with his day.

Mr. Addison called after him, "Actually, I'll be chaperoning the dance tomorrow night."

Alex stepped back into the room.

His teacher continued, "I hear you and Ms. Brinton will be coming together. About time, if you ask me."

Alex blushed and looked down. "Yeah, I finally got the guts to ask her. Well, I guess I'll see you tomorrow."

"See you then."

Alex left the room walking tall. Everything was falling into place. He prayed and the joy of God washed over him.

He arrived home in record time. He hefted his bike over his head and hung it by the front tire on a large hook in the garage ceiling. He left his helmet dangling from one of the pedals.

When he turned, he almost ran into Sariel.

"Ah! I wish you'd stop that. And don't you have any other clothes?"

"So, today went fine?" the white-suited man asked.

"Yeah, but it was weird. I don't know. Everything was different."

"You are different. Your internal architecture is being reconstructed. You have begun to see as God sees."

"I like it, although I didn't exactly fit in." Alex smiled.

"Hmm. And, how was Mr. Addison?"

"Mr. A seemed good. He's going to be at the dance tomorrow."

The angel appeared concerned. "Be careful around him. He is infected with a very powerful demon. His actions may become, well, unpredictable. Watch him."

Alex stopped short. He remembered the dark cloud surrounding his teacher. "Well, can't *you* do something?"

"Actually, I cannot. I am not a free agent, able to do as I wish. I follow orders from the Spirit. Up until now, I have not been given permission to do anything against this creature."

"Permission?"

"Permission. Heaven is the ultimate authority structure—a chain of command. Angels do not do anything without permission."

"So, this demon's allowed to eat away at Mr. A's soul? And you have to let it?"

"This happens more times than you can imagine, and it is always painful to watch. But, everything happens for a reason. There is a grand design and, for all things to come out according to plan, it is necessary for Mr. Addison to be possessed at this time."

"So, you're saying that everything that happens—I mean … everything—happens for a reason? To fulfill God's plan?"

"Yes, absolutely everything," he said with finality.

"So, you're saying Hitler, and . . . and AIDS, and World Hunger, and…and zits, they're all part of *The Plan*?

"Yes."

"And…and what is this great reason? What's the key that makes sense out of all the contradictions? What makes the unfair fair? What makes Hitler okay?"

Sariel took a deep breath. "Alex you *have* grown, and I *am* happy with your progress. But there are many things you are still not ready to hear. But this I can tell you . . ."

"Yeah?"

He touched his lapels. "This is my only suit. I need no other."

And with that, he vanished.

"Of course," Alex said and slammed the garage door behind him.

Any joy he had earlier in the day was gone.

8

Saturday

When the big day of the Homecoming Dance arrived, everything that Alex had been through— the struggles with the demons, the training and relationship with Sariel, and the looming demonic schemes, whatever they were!—were all thrust far into the background.

Today only one thing held his focus—Katie.

He'd received over a dozen texts from her.

Katie: *Alex, what time pick me up?*
Alex: *Conor here at 5.*
Katie: *5:15 my house?*
Alex: *K*
Katie: *R U allergic to Fantasy?*
Alex: *I'm living one.*
Katie: *LOL. Perfume, silly. Allergic?*
Alex: *Don't think so.*
Katie: *Good. My favorite. 5:15 then.*

Alex: ☺

In the bathroom, Alex scowled as he rubbed gritty zit cream on a blemish that was forming on the end of his nose. He hoped that no one—especially Katie—would notice. He put the rosy mass between his index fingers and squeezed.

Several things happened at the same time.

Sariel appeared in the mirror.

Puss spurted from the tip of his nose and splashed against the mirror, right in Sariel's right eye, and his image winced. Alex couldn't help but laugh.

Lastly, his mom knocked on the door and informed him that Conor was downstairs waiting.

He grabbed a washcloth and smeared the greasy stuff across the mirror.

The angel appeared behind him. "This dance is exceedingly important to you." It was a statement of fact left hanging in the air.

Alex kept grooming. He smelled his pits and said, "Are you kidding? This could be *it* for me. I've had a thing for Katie since seventh grade. And I think she might like me, too."

"Relationships are … well … complicated for an athleta Christi."

"What do you mean, complicated?" He buttoned his shirt—a white cotton dress shirt with sleeves rolled up to the elbow. He smiled when he saw in the mirror how great it looked on him. It would go well with his black slacks, red tie, and black jacket.

"Great men and women of God usually remain unattached. It is not easy to divide your allegiance between your relationships with people and your complete service to God. This is why Jesus said that anyone not willing to leave their parents or wives or husbands for Him was not worthy to be his disciple."

Alex tried to remember how to tie his tie. Watching himself in the mirror tying it backward wasn't helping. "But not everyone found this impossible, did they? Wasn't Peter married?"

The angel was visibly shaken. "Yes, he was. That didn't mean it was easy for him. I am impressed that you remembered that."

"Look, I appreciate that you look out for me. I really do. But I'm not worried about it. We'll figure it out. Katie and I will make it work. Besides, I'm not really sure what's going to happen—but I do have my hopes."

"Al-lex!" his mom hollered.

"Coming!" he hollered back and slipped on his jacket. He looked Sariel in the eyes. "You'll be there too, right?"

"Wherever you are, I shall be."

Alex opened the bathroom door. The angel vanished.

He passed his mom on the narrow stairs. She leaned close and asked, "Who were you talking to in the bathroom?"

"My guardian angel," he said, with a wink.

His mom rolled her eyes. "Conor's waiting in the kitchen. You'd better get down there quick, before he eats us out of house and home."

Alex laughed when he saw Conor's outfit. He wore a T-shirt with a superhero on the front and a fitted, light-blue, sleeveless denim jacket. He'd tied his dress shirt around his waist, the sleeves reaching the floor. Superhero boxers showed at the top of his drooping khaki shorts. He wore casual brown laceless Sperrys without socks. To top off his fashion statement, his hair stood straight up, thickly coated in gobs of yellow wood glue.

Sheila, his date, stood next to him. She had chosen to wear modest clothes with muted colors, which made Conor's outfit appear even more extreme.

It was Alex's turn to roll his eyes. Conor certainly knew how to draw attention to himself.

69

*

Classic Heavy Metal music blared as Conor's 1990 faded-red Jeep Cherokee bumped down the road. From the back seat, Alex stared out the back window. Conor talked in a steady loud stream, making a joke out of everything, fully entertaining himself and filling all the empty conversation spaces. To Conor, silence wasn't golden—it was a wasted opportunity.

Sheila sat shotgun, quietly ignoring Conor while texting her friends.

Sariel flew behind them. If only Conor could look into his rearview mirror and see the ten-foot wing span of the angel on his tail.

Maybe it would shut him up.

Maybe.

Alex's mouth went dry.

They turned right—onto Katie's street.

*

Alex stared at the evenly-placed squares in the front door.

"C'mon Moron, we don't have all night!" Conor yelled from the idling jeep in the driveway.

Although he'd fought deadly demons and risked his life for months training with Sariel, this was the first time he was frozen with fear.

He tried to breathe.

He closed his eyes and lifted his knuckles to rap on the door. It abruptly swung opened with a shrill creaking. His eyes popped when he saw Katie smiling in front of him. She looked incredible. Her dress was hotrod red, skin tight, and perfectly complimented her sun-kissed skin and highlighted auburn hair. Alex looked into her dark-chocolate eyes. He bit his lower lip.

"I take it you approve?" Katie quipped, turning from side to side and smiling. She took in Alex's predictable outfit, and her smile faded.

"Wow, you look, amazing." Alex finally got the words out.

"Thanks, you... look great, too," Katie responded mechanically.

Alex noticed the small purse in her hand. "Ready to go?"

"Absolutely!" She turned back toward her dimly-lit living room and called to her dad, "I'll probably be late. You don't have to wait up."

"You know I will," came a deep-voiced response. "Take care of my girl, Alex," he added with a slightly threatening tone.

Katie mouthed the words, "I'm sorry," to Alex.

"I will, sir," Alex assured her father.

Katie smiled and shut the door. "My parents always wait up for me. I don't know what the big deal is. Nothing's ever going to happen to me."

Conor and Sheila were standing outside the car with the back doors opened so that Alex and Katie could climb into the back seat. After Katie was in, Alex shut her door and jogged to the other side of the car.

Katie winced. "Conor, your car is disgusting. I think I just stepped on something that was once a hamburger. You're such a pig."

Alex glanced up through his dirty window. The sun was setting, and the sky transitioning between bright pink and a deep, dark blue. There, still silhouetted against the billowing clouds, was the ever-faithful angel, his wings outstretched.

Alex relaxed on the seat next to Katie as he realized he had his own personal bodyguard.

Conor yelled, "Fasten your seatbelts, everyone. It's going to be a bumpy ride!" He cranked the music way up and pealed rubber.

Alex and Katie's eyes met. They reached for their seatbelts, clicked them shut, and held onto the armrests.

*

The foursome cast ominous shadows across the parking lot as they strode toward the high school's multi-purpose room. Inside, the music was so loud that talking was nearly impossible. As Alex's eyes adjusted to the strobe lights and colored spotlights, he caught sight of couples gyrating on the dance floor. Others were making out while dancing—their hands all over each other, their hips moving together. Chaperones moved quickly toward these couples to tell them to knock it off, but as soon as the chaperones left, the freaking resumed.

Sadness welled up within Alex—the grief of the Holy Spirit over the casual way these kids treated their bodies. The Spirit loved them and wanted better for them.

"You okay?" Katie asked.

Alex couldn't hear her above the din, but he read her lips and got the message.

"Yeah," he responded at the top of his voice, nodding his head to make sure she understood. "Wanna dance?" he asked, dancing two fingers in the air.

"Yeah!" Katie jumped onto the dance floor and bounced and swayed with the beat.

Alex tried to keep up with her. He mirrored her movements and attempted some clever ones of his own.

Before the song ended, Alex had sweat running down his face. He signaled to Katie that he needed something to drink. She smiled and nodded, indicating that she was also parched. Scanning the room, he spotted five-gallon jugs of ice water and paper cups on a table near the far wall.

He left Katie dancing by herself.

Close to the table, a pale-yellow spotlight swept past him on the floor and cast its pallid beam on a ghost-like figure crouching by the water stands.

Mr. Addison, his face contorted and unrecognizable.

The yellow light moved away, leaving the spot in darkness. A red light swept past several seconds later. This time his teacher was bent over. A massive writhing creature clung to his back. The beast's hateful eyes glared at Alex. Momentarily stunned, Alex watched with horror as the demon opened his jaws and sank his dagger-like teeth into Mr. Addison's head. The red light moved on, and the pitiable teacher was again enshrouded in darkness.

"No!" Alex ran to his teacher. But when he got there, he was gone. Alex searched through the crowd, but saw no sign of Mr. Addison.

The scene around him suddenly stopped. All went silent. The dancers held awkward positions, as if a strobe-light flash had frozen them in time. By now, Alex knew what to expect. It was no real surprise when he turned and came face-to-face with Sariel.

He pleaded with the angel. "Can't you do something? Anything? I know you've been ordered not to interfere with Mr. Addison, but we can't just stand by and watch him go through this."

"You are correct. I cannot help the man. But, *you* have been given permission to remove this demon from him," the angel said, solemnly.

Something was wrong here. By now, Alex knew Sariel and could read him pretty well.

"What haven't you told me?"

Sariel responded, "Two things. First, you must enter the spiritual realm alone. I am not permitted to go with you. This is a separate dimension that exists parallel to this one. It is where you will do battle."

"How? What do I do?" His emotions surged with anticipation. He couldn't wait to help his teacher.

The angel reached over and placed his hands on Alex's shoulders. He prayed, "Holy One, please bestow on Alex the mantle of Elisha, who could transverse the spiritual realm according to your sovereign will."

After a moment of intense silence he told the young man, "When it is time for you to battle, simply ask God. If you do not shift between the realms, then you do not have permission to battle. While inside the spiritual realm, you will be invisible to humans but completely visible to the angels and demons who reside there, just as they will be visible to you."

Alex expected to feel a charge of energy or something when he received this new ability, but nothing happened. He guessed he was just going to have to trust that this worked. "You said there were two things," he reminded the angel.

Sariel's tone grew even more somber. "You must understand. This is no minor fallen angel. Normally, it is after years of training that an athleta is allowed to battle a creeper demon of this strength."

"Creeper demon?"

"They are also known as hook demons, because they send out barbs from their arms." The angel looked away with concern.

"Go on," Alex pressed him.

"This is a particularly nasty creeper. His name is Vetis, and he has a knack for destroying men and women. He has driven hundreds to suicide. His more well-known conquests include warriors and kings—Nero, Napoleon, and King George. His attacks have shaped the history of empires. Up until now, we have not overcome him." The angel shook his head. "Alex, he is strong and clever. He has endured for millennia and has learned much about the ways of battle. It was his presence here that first drew our attention to this place. He is only sent on critical errands." Sariel turned to his pupil and added intently, "You must be careful. Use what you have learned."

Alex inhaled deeply and puffed out his chest. "I'll be all right. I just can't sit by and watch this thing chew on Mr. A."

"Never underestimate this vile creature. Try to anticipate his tricks. Have faith in God and wield the Sword of the Spirit. Follow your training and you," he swallowed, "will prevail."

With that, Alex found himself back in the dance with its movement, flashing lights, and deafening noise.

Something grabbed his back. In his mind, he saw the putrid hooks of the creeper demon.

He flew around, taking a defensive stance.

Conor laughed at him. "Dude, lighten up!"

Alex leaned close to Conor's ear. "I'll be right back," he hollered. "Keep a close eye on Katie for me. Okay?"

"Okey Dokey Artichokey," Conor said and headed to the water table.

Now, Alex thought, *where's Mr. A?*

*

"Report," Alistair Cain ordered.

In the corner of his swank New York apartment suite, a demon cowered and cleared his throat. "Nothing unusual to report, sire. We have been observing Vetis day and night, and he seems to have everything well in hand. He is tormenting his subject, Addison, but he has been careful not to let him destroy himself, in spite of his repeated attempts."

"Stop praising Vetis. I know he is talented. How much control does he have over his subject at this point?"

The minor creature thought before speaking. "I believe he could make Addison do anything he wished. When his moment comes, he will be ready."

"He better be."

*

Alex looked down hallways and behind trash cans and lockers trying to find Mr. Addison. He made his way to the school's quad area, where many of the students ate their lunches and hung out between classes.

He heard whimpering.

About thirty feet away, he saw a disheveled, crumpled heap—his teacher.

Alex was filled with compassion. He prayed, "God, Father, please let me enter the spiritual realm. And help me kick this demon's sorry butt." He knew it was irreverent and maybe not the best prayer, but he remembered a sermon where the pastor said that sometimes the best prayers are when people just yell, "Help!"

The world around him shifted. He could still see the tables and benches, the trash cans and blinding yellow-orange beams emitting from tall light poles scattered throughout the quad. But everything now had a muddy, filtered look, like he peered through thin waxed paper.

And his body felt weird. He looked down. His clothing had changed into the green second-skin material he'd trained in.

"Huh, that's convenient," he said to himself. "Now, time to look for this creeper ... demon ... thing."

A warning sounded in his soul. His training kicking in, Alex reached up and pulled down the Sword of the Spirit from mid-air. Its hilt was translucent, as if fashioned from a massive diamond. The long blade shone brightly.

The sword lit up the courtyard and exposed the demon chewing on his teacher. He remembered Sariel's words, *This is the Sword of the Spirit, the Sword of Truth that reveals all.*

The demon looked up at Alex. An expression of surprise came over his hideous face. The beast stood to his full height—nearly seven feet.

Alex studied him. Two curved, sharp horns pointed upward from his bald, gray head. Yellow spittle dripped freely from his gaping mouth. A light armor shielded his torso with thick spike-covered shoulder pads. A roughly-fashioned pentagram was affixed to his chest. Tattered fabric extended from under the armor. The monster had muscular arms and strong hands with sharp talons.

Tape-like black cords ending in hooked, bone-colored barbs curled out from his sinewy forearms. A few dangled freely, the rest were buried deep in Mr. Addison's back and neck.

The demon pulled the cords taut, and the teacher wailed. Vetis squinted and turned his head toward Alex, commanding, "Put out that light!"

"Leave him alone!" Alex squeaked. As soon as the words left him, he wished they had sounded more forceful. He really was new at this.

The creature bellowed, exposing his pointed teeth, "You are not my mission. Depart, while you still have your life."

Alex took a deep breath. He tried not to think about his failure with the shadowy demon in his bedroom. What had he gotten himself into?

"Vetis," he said, loudly. "I command you to leave him."

The demon was shaken at hearing his name, but he quickly recovered. "I know you, also, young one. You are one of the witless children who sit day after day in this pathetic worm's class. Your name is—Alex."

Alex braced himself, taking a fighting stance and putting his confidence in the Spirit of God. His vision had improved slightly. "Fine, now that the introductions are over, I mean it—let him go."

Vetis shifted his hands, and his hooks left Mr. Addison's back and retracted into his arms. Alex's teacher fell to the concrete, unconscious. The demon reached out and pulled a sword from the air. This ominous sword absorbed all light around it like a jagged black hole.

The creeper jumped toward Alex and swung his sword at his head.

Alex ducked, escaping the blow. But as he did, two hooks shot out from the beast's forearms. Alex brought up his sword, slicing the swirling coils just before the barbs reached his neck. Black, oily fluid spurted from the ends and the demon shrieked in pain.

"Who, in the name of everything unholy, are *you*? Confess to me your secrets, young one," the creature screamed.

Alex knew from his training that demons would try to gain advantage through knowledge. He answered, "All you need to know is that I'm a warrior of the Light…and your worst nightmare. Prepare to get your ugly butt kicked."

As his severed tethers absorbed back into his arms, the demon chided, "You are obviously an ignorant child, hardly worthy of bothering over. I would ignore you, but you stand in my way. I will swat you as I would a pesky gnat."

"You talk big, Vetis, but—"

Before Alex could finish his sentence, the towering creature was all over him, thrusting his sword, charging and jabbing. Alex successfully parried all Vetis' vicious attacks, but he was barely keeping up.

Without warning, another barb shot out from the arm of the creature. Alex wasn't fast enough. It pierced through his suit and into his right shoulder.

His resolve failed. The ground collapsed beneath him. Doubt and confusion welled up within. His sword sputtered and dimmed.

What am I doing here?

Who am I to do this?

This is ridiculous.

His fear increased. The demon seemed to grow larger and more terrifying.

This creature's going to destroy me!

I'm gonna die here!

I'm so scared!

And then he heard a scripture play like a recording in his brain. "Greater is He who is in you than he who is in the world."

A voice inside commanded, *Believe. Stand strong.*

It didn't matter how weak he was, only how strong God was.

With his last ounce of resolve, he pulled up on his sword and severed the cord.

Vetis yelped.

Alex pulled the barb out and tossed it.

He shook his head. His mind cleared.

Vetis laughed sardonically.

He turned his arms outward. The skin on his forearms bubbled wildly. "Come to me, young one. Come and meet your fate." Dozens of hooks erupted from the beast. Their shiny barbs shot straight at Alex. They would pierce him from head to toe. There was no way he could cut them all.

Alex crouched and thrust out his left arm defensively. He cleared his mind and entrusted himself completely to the Spirit within him. Whatever happened next would be up to Him.

Suddenly, a shield tall enough to protect his entire body materialized on Alex's left arm. The hellish hooks hit it, sizzled, and dissolved. Disgusting oily liquid splashed everywhere. The stench made Alex wretch.

The demon shrieked with panic. He reached up to bring down his sword for a final crushing blow.

Alex raised his shield.

The sword crashed into it and turned to dust.

Alex stood tall. He hefted his sword with renewed confidence.

Just then, the demon leaped at Alex, his teeth bared, his claws open. New hooks formed in his bubbling arms.

Alex met the attack head on, thrusting his sword upward and through the beast's thin armor and into its belly.

The creature's grotesque face contorted in pain.

79

He shook.

He wailed.

He popped, becoming a dark cloud. The particles wafted away with the evening breeze.

Alex's sword and shield vanished, and he stood in the quad in his homecoming clothes.

After a second, Alex jumped up, yelling, "Oh yeah!"

Sariel appeared.

"Did you see that?" Alex could hardly contain his excitement.

"I am assigned to you until I receive new orders. I see all you do."

Alex noticed Sariel's apprehension. "What's up? I kicked butt back there. I also got the Shield of Faith. And *you* look like I screwed up."

"I am sorry," he said, reflecting. "The barb that caught you," he winced, "I thought you were defeated. This was not my first experience with Vetis." He paused before adding, "One of my former pupils was defeated by him."

"But now that demon is dust. Literally!"

"For the time being, yes. Angels and demons are eternal beings. We cannot be destroyed. If we lose our physical bodies, it is only for a short while. His essence will wander the halls of Hell."

"Really? That's great!"

"But, in time, his form will be restored. You may see him again."

"Hmm. Not so great. But wait, he'll be in Hell, right?"

The angel moved very close to Alex and said in a low voice, "You must be *very* careful. Worship as I taught you. Pray continuously. Walk in the Spirit."

Mr. Addison came to. "Alex, man, my head feels like a nail was just pulled out of my brain." He breathed deeply. "I'm exhausted. Tell Assistant Principal Edwards that I don't feel well and I'm going home." He turned to Sariel and added, "So, who's this with you?"

Alex's tongue went limp. What could he say? He tried to think of something.

Sariel pulled back the lapel of his white jacket, revealing a chaperone badge the parent helpers were given. "I am related to Alex, sort of an uncle. I am a chaperone for the dance."

"Well, thank God you're here. We need all the help we can get at these student orgies."

The teacher stumbled out of the courtyard, whistled down the sidewalk, and disappeared into the shadows.

Alex's eyes followed him. He turned to Sariel. "What will happen to Mr. Addison now? What's to stop another demon from attacking him?"

"It is up to him. He must turn to the light and renounce the darkness and those who dwell within it. If he does not, he may be oppressed again—perhaps even possessed. He needs someone to share with him the good news of Christ."

"I'll begin looking for the right moment. He can see you?"

"I wished it to be so."

"Wow, okay." Alex looked back at the all-purpose building. "This was great and all, but right now I'm heading back to the dance. Hopefully, Katie won't kill me for being gone so long."

*

Alex scanned the room, but he couldn't see Katie anywhere. There seemed to be fewer people at the dance. Several kids were having parties afterward, and some of them apparently started before the dance was over. He caught sight of Conor on the dance floor, whirling with all his might. He walked up to him and shouted in his ear, "Conor, where's Katie?"

"Oh, uh, I have no idea." Conor kept dancing, staring at Sheila, who gyrated in front of him.

"Conor, help me find her!" He hoped she was safe.

"Okay," he yelled to Alex. "I'll be right back," he shouted to Sheila. But her eyes were closed while she swirled her head. Conor shrugged.

The boys walked together, checking every girl they saw. They looked at those dancing, at the young people in groups laughing and goofing off, and at the ones who were leaving for parties. Along the wall, a line of kids stood talking. One of these was the captain of the football team, Brandon Richardson. Katie stood close to him. Her eyes were fixed on his. She reached up, put her arms around Brandon's thick neck, closed her eyes, and kissed him on the lips.

Alex's mouth dropped.

Conor stopped laughing. "Man, I'm sorry, I had no idea she was..."

Alex looked at his friend and knew he had to let him off the hook. He walked him to the front door. "It's okay, Conor. Really. It's my fault. My first date with Katie and I abandon her. What an idiot!" He exhaled hard. "Guess I *am* my father's son. Abandonment's in my DNA."

For once, Conor was speechless.

Alex looked back into the dance. Now he really didn't belong.

He shook his head and said, "Look, I think I'm gonna go on home. Don't beat yourself up. Just make sure Katie gets home safely, okay?"

"What are you going to do?"

"Who knows?"

"You'll go straight home—right?"

Alex rolled his eyes. "Yes, mother."

"What do I tell Katie...um...you know...if she asks about you?"

"I don't know. Just—I don't know."

Alex headed out the door and into the bleakness of the night. He could almost hear Vetis laughing at him from hell.

*

Alex trudged home on autopilot, his steps sullen stomps on the ground.

Sariel was suddenly walking beside him. Alex glanced over with a sneer and then looked ahead, his jaw clenched.

They moved forward in silence.

"You are angry," the angel said.

Alex let loose. "I can't believe it. I'm such an idiot. I should have stayed with her. But, I *had* to go. Mr. A needed me. Why did God pick *me* anyway? Why is this *my* responsibility?"

The angel sighed. "Do not despair, my young friend. You made the right decision."

"Yeah . . . um . . . I think I did. It's just—I don't know. It's hard. I really like her, and I thought she liked me. I guess I misread her too."

"You were not completely wrong. She does care for you—in her own way."

Alex was covered in sweat. He faltered, like he was going to collapse.

"But, for now, we have other matters that require attention. I need to get you home. You have not fully recovered from tonight's battle."

"Yeah. I'm not really feeling so—" Alex's body went limp as he slipped into unconsciousness.

*

Sariel caught Alex, put his arms around him, and shifted them both into the spiritual realm. He transformed, extended his wings, and launched, carrying Alex high into the air.

Minutes later, Sariel gently set down Alex on his front lawn. He kneeled next to the boy, placed his hands on him, and prayed. "Lord, fully heal Alex and help him through his conflicted feelings."

Alex slowly opened his eyes.

"Better?" Sariel asked.

Alex sat up and took a deep breath. "Yeah … much better. Thanks."

*

When Alex reached the kitchen door, his mom was there to greet him.

"Hey, you're home early. What happened? Everything all right?"

"Yeah, I just felt like making it an early night. I was kinda tired," he said, clutching the wood ball at the bottom of the banister and facing the stairs.

"Wait a second." His mom moved closer.

He looked away. He knew that if she looked into his eyes, she'd be able to read the whole situation. There were times he appreciated what she called her "Mom-sense," but this wasn't one of them.

"You know, I wish I could protect you, keep you from getting your feelings hurt."

He couldn't help it. He lifted his head and faced her. As much as he hated it, tears pooled in his eyes.

She continued, her voice cracking, "You're growing up and learning that life is filled with disappointments. And we can get hurt. The secret to being an adult is using these struggles to become a stronger person instead of being destroyed by them."

"Yeah, sometimes things just suck," Alex said.

Then, for a moment, he took his attention off his own problems and considered his mom. He thought about how hard life had been for her. How her first marriage—to an abusive jerk—had collapsed. She left him after a particularly violent beating. How her parents refused to have anything to do with her. They were still angry that she hadn't listened to their warnings about the man. And, how she'd met Alex's father, fell hopelessly in love, and became pregnant, only to be abandoned by him, left to figure out how to raise a child by herself.

She'd risen to the challenge. She went to school at night and started a career in nursing.

The advice his mom gave him now, about strength forged in adversity, had been the theme of her whole life.

He stepped off the staircase and gave her a hug. "I love you, mom," he whispered.

She held him close and patted his back.

Alex pulled away. "Okay, well, good night."

"Goodnight." His mom watched him climb the stairs before she returned to cleaning the kitchen sink.

Alex thought back to when he was little and would sit in his mom's lap and beg her to read superhero stories to him. Afterward, he would wear a towel like it was a cape and pretend to be the hero, battling invisible foes.

Some things never change.

9

Sunday

Alistair Cain's emotions churned. Staring out the window of his high-rise office, peering down on New York City's financial district, he lamented his schizophrenic life. Not that he had failed to play his part well. His rise to power had been an adequate display of his genius.

The towering edifice in which he stood, the American International Building, was constructed in 1932, when America was emerging as a world-wide financial superpower. Located in the center of the famed Financial District of Manhattan, the building's jagged spires made it look like a weapon to be feared.

Produce International, a team of inept visionless brokers helping farmers sell their produce to emerging markets overseas, purchased the building in the 50s and drove it into the ground. In 1997, Alistair Cain, posing as an aggressive young multi-millionaire who'd made a fortune in oil, gold, real estate, and more, stole the company away from them in a hostile takeover.

Under his astute leadership, Cain Enterprises became a worldwide power player. The company had dozens of senators and congressmen at their beck and call. Some wondered if there was anything Alistaire Cain could not do.

And he knew there was one thing.

In spite of all this worldly power, The Executive Demon, knew his master and shuddered at what would happen to him if he failed his important spiritual assignment.

He buried these fears and continued the interrogation, turning back to the puny demon.

"You watched the whole thing and did nothing?" Cain railed. "You were assigned to watch over Addison!"

"It was impossible, I tell you," the creature squealed. His beach ball shape, with its pealing skin, jagged elbows, and gnarly claws, quivered like green Jell-O. "He had a guardian angel. I had seen him before, when on patrol. Sariel is his name. And the young one had a powerful spiritual sword and shield. The mighty Vetis was easily done in, what chance would I have had against him?"

"But you lost Addison! You may have ruined *everything!*"

The demon, generally dim and slow on the uptake, immediately caught the drift of this comment. He stopped quivering and stepped forward. "Wait a minute! You are not going to pin this on me! I acted according to protocol. I was—"

His last phrase was cut off, along with his hideous head.

"I accept your resignation," commented the Executive.

The beach ball vanished in a swirling cloud of black dust.

Cain analyzed the situation. This system needed to be brought back into control.

Sariel was training this boy to be an athleta Christi—the expected course of pathetic resistance. Four hundred years before, a different athleta had been trained in an attempt to stop Cain from fulfilling Satan's plans. Cain eliminated him, bringing things back into stability, and putting the plan back on track with amazing results.

Cain was called a genius.

There was no use in recapturing Henry Addison too early if he was just going to be freed again by this—boy.

What if he *were* set free just before the ceremony? Not only would this affect the balance of heaven and earth, tipping it in the enemy's favor, but Cain himself would be blamed. He was in charge. He imagined himself painfully ground to a pulp, disintegrated, and sent to hell. It would take him a millennium to reconstitute.

He shook his head. No, it was time to live up to his reputation.

He would get rid of Alex now.

The intercom sounded.

He pressed a button on his desk. "Sir," a tense high-pitched voice said. "There's a Mr. Blank here to see you."

"Send him in," Alistair Cain responded, trying to hold his voice steady.

The door to his office opened silently. In the gap stood a nondescript, short man in a double-breasted suit, gripping a sleek leather briefcase. If there were such a thing as a completely average face, height, and build, this would be it.

"Cain," the man said in a monotone voice.

The Executive Demon's defenses fell. His throat went dry.

The visitor broke the silence. "You have been summoned. You are to report to the North American Demon immediately." With that, the unremarkable man turned on his heels and faced the door. It opened on its own, and he exited.

Alistair Cain moved to the center of the room. He knew better than to keep the Smok waiting. He took a deep breath and slid from the physical realm to the parallel spiritual one, transforming to his demonic self.

Launching, he passed right through the tinted window and soared in the crisp night air to Central Park. On a secluded hillside, he found a shimmering circular portal that would take him to the demon's throne room. He retracted his wings and dropped into the spiritual door feet-first. He teleported to a matching portal, dropped ten feet, and landed on solid ground.

He was somewhere in the core of the earth. The seven chief demons who ruled over the largest land masses had all made their headquarters in this place, where they felt secluded and invulnerable.

The outskirts of this voluminous cavern were walls of surging liquid metal. It was like being inside a massive annealing furnace, with temperatures approaching those of the sun.

A dragon-like creature sat before him on a throne made of bloodstained human bones and skulls. His pale tangerine skin mottled with green blotches rippled over his muscle-bound physique. Bright eyes glowed red above his elongated snout. Rows of small, sharp, conic teeth lined his crocodile-like jaws. Spikes of black hair covered his head, back, eyebrows, and chin.

A dozen messenger demons—informants—clung to the bottom of the throne.

The Executive Demon regained his footing. His eyes adjusted to the brilliant light.

The dragon pointed a three-toed claw at him. "Alistair," he spewed in a gravelly voice, "report."

Cain dropped to one knee before the creature. He muttered, "Oh great lord of North America, I have disquieting news."

"Disquieting?" the dragon hissed, his forked tongue darting snake-like between his jaws.

Alistair, still genuflecting, looked to the crusty bloodstained floor. He hoped his information valuable enough to help his master overlook his recent failures. He saw in his imagination a jagged sword quickly drawn and gliding in a wide arc. This time it was his head that leaped from the blade.

He pushed the image away and raised his head.

He started slowly. "I have a theory, based on recent observations, that there is a slight possibility that we may experience interference. It is not completely unexpected."

"What is the worst that could happen?"

"It is highly unlikely."

"Quit stalling!" the dragon's voice boomed.

"System-wide failure, leading to a complete collapse. We have already had one small setback."

The dragon's eyes narrowed. "Setback? What setback?"

Still on one knee, the demon continued, "We have lost Addison—for the time being. Vetis was dispatched by a young man who was with the angel, Sariel."

"You believe Sariel is training another athleta? A champion for the enemy?"

"I do, lord. He has trained others in the past."

"So he has. Your word 'setback' is well chosen. This is serious, but not fatal. I want this mess cleaned up. Reclaim Addison—with a stronger demon this time. No—multiple demons. Gather information on this potential athleta. Find his weaknesses. Exploit them to the fullest—*and crush him!*" The walls shook.

"Yes, my lord." Cain lowered his head.

The dragon leaned forward. Hissing, he said, "There is one more thing. I want you there, now, supervising. This is far too important to be left to underlings. You get on scene, take charge, and see to it that our plan succeeds."

Alistair knew better than to question orders.

He was relieved to be leaving in one piece. Of course, he would have to solve innumerable problems in order to exit his company in New York to take over a high school in a Podunk town in California.

Without raising his head, he simply uttered a reverent, "Yes, my lord."

10

Monday

Alex locked up his bike, shouldered his backpack, and started toward his first class. Sariel walked next to him, in his white suit and shoes, looking like an old plantation owner. Alex was glad he was the only one who could see the angel this morning.

"Today's not going to be good," he muttered.

"Why not?" Sariel countered.

"Because I'm going to have to see *her*, and that's just going to be awkward."

"I must have missed something. I thought you cared for her. Would it not make sense for you to want to see her?"

"It's not that simple. She's probably with Brandon, that guy she was," his expression hardened, "*with* at the dance on Saturday. And I have History with both of them. It'll be hard for me to see them—*together*."

Alex noticed a shadow hovering just behind the hedge framing the walkway. He whispered to Sariel, "Am I wrong, or are we being followed?"

"Make the shift to the spiritual realm and see. You have permission."

Alex didn't want to disappear in front of his classmates. He stepped nonchalantly behind a high spot in the hedge and asked the Spirit to bring him into the parallel universe.

The world around him transformed, and the fuzzy shadow became a small demon. The creature's eyes bugged out when he realized he'd been discovered.

Alex focused his mind and trusted in the Holy Spirit of God. His sword and shield appeared in his hands. He was ready for battle.

But, to his surprise, the demon didn't charge him. Instead, he turned and jumped into the air, flying away on tiny, unstable, bat-like wings.

"A spy," Sariel called over to him, his glorious wings tucked behind him.

Alex yelled, "Don't just stand there. Go! Get 'em!"

"You already know the answer to that."

Alex's shoulders slumped, and his sword and shield vanished. He shook his head. "You don't have permission, right?"

"Correct. But this does tell us something. You are being scrutinized. We must assume that the forces of the enemy know that I am training you and that you are a God-sent threat to their plans."

"What does *that* mean?" Alex's voice cracked.

"Your enemy, the devil, prowls around like a roaring lion looking for someone to devour. It looks like he has turned his sights on you."

"Sariel, don't you think I'm . . . I'm getting in over my head?"

"I agree." With that, the angel reached out to Alex and grabbed him.

All was swallowed in blinding light.

Alex recognized the lush training area and was somewhat relieved.

He needed more strength.

*

Sariel trained Alex for several months, focusing on the boy's fear.

In one of the sessions, Alex held his warrior stance—his left leg forward and his weight balanced on the balls of his feet—with his shield and sword held ready for battle. The angel had been closed-mouthed about what he was about to experience.

Alex stood alone in a vast rocky canyon—waiting, his muscles tensed, at the ready.

A low throbbing hum vibrated the air. He turned around and peered into the horizon.

Slowly, spherical shapes materialized on the skyline. He choked at the stench of rotting meat. The air grew so cold Alex could see his breath. His nose dripped.

As the undulating wave of beings drew nearer, Alex saw they were vicious animal skeletons, with bony hands and feet scraping the ground, trailed by flowing red streams of smoke. What took Alex's breath away was the sheer number of them.

It was his nightmare—all over again.

The circle closed on him.

There was nowhere to hide.

He raised his sword and began slashing in wide arcs, spinning his body in circles and ducking behind his shield. At first he held his own, chopping through bones that instantly turned into clouds of white dust. But ultimately, the onslaught was too much for him. He was pounded from all sides. One skeleton grabbed his shins and yanked his legs out from under him. He crashed to the ground, which knocked the air out of him. Two more grabbed his arm, careful to avoid his sword. They shook the weapon loose, and it fell with a thud on the soft ground.

Alex cowered under his shield, holding it over him with all of his might. But it wasn't enough. A group of skeletons tore it out of his arms.

Exposed and vulnerable, Alex stared into the skeletal faces of death and yelled, "Sariel!"

The angel didn't come.

Skeletons ripped at Alex's clothes, hair, and skin. Some pounded on him while others pulled at his limbs, dislocating them. A series of heavy blows pummeled his body and head. One punched him square in the nose. Blood ran down his face and the back of his throat. Another blow split his lip. His jaw was broken with a horrible crunching noise. Repeatedly kicked in the side, his ribs cracked.

He never imagined there could be pain like this.

As he lost consciousness, he glimpsed the euphoric expressions of dozens of animalistic skulls howling in victory around him.

*

Alex opened his eyes in the bright, timeless realm. He hurt all over. Wincing with every movement, he rose on his elbow.

Sariel stood nearby.

The angel spoke. "God was merciful and healed you immediately. But I was told that you needed to experience the pain. I am afraid you will be sore for a while."

"So, Sariel, what *was* that?"

"What did you learn?"

"That I can still get my butt kicked."

"True. What else?"

"That my head feels like it's going to fall off. Look, I can't do this. I need...I need more help."

"I was commanded not to interfere with your battle. When you collapsed, I only had seconds to revive you. I prayed for your healing. God repaired the damage. If He had not, you would be dead now."

There was an uncomfortable pause.

Alex finally broke the silence. "So, why do I get the feeling I'm not going to like what you're going to say next?"

"You failed. You will have to do this again and again and again until you are victorious."

Alex looked down and shook his head. "No. I can't," he moaned. "You saw what they did to me. I can't go through that again. I can't."

"You are correct. You can't beat them that way. No one could. You need more protection and more power. Tell me, what is it that allows you to be a warrior?"

Alex knew the angel was trying to lead him and, in reality, he was never more willing to follow. "The answer is God, but that's far too obvious. There's something else. It's not my training or my physical strength."

"So, what gives you a place in this celestial battle?"

This question told Alex he was on the right track. But he couldn't think of where to go from here. He took a shot. "Uh … I'm going to heaven?"

"This is also true but not relevant to our discussion. Hopefully, it will be some time before you will go to heaven. What else?"

Alex wished he'd paid more attention in church. He had to admit, most of the time while the preacher taught the word of God from the pulpit, he was checking out the girls around him and wishing the service was over. He returned to the question.

What did I gain?

He thought out loud. "I've gained a new life, my life in Christ. I've gained an inheritance in Him. But, most of all, I guess...I've gained...salvation." This sounded right to him.

"Yes. Trust in your salvation and you can prevail."

"I can?" Alex was excited. He sat up and shocks of pain ran through his back, side, and head.

"You can. It remains to be seen if you will. You need some time to overcome your soreness and for more training. Then, you will face these demons again."

"Great. I can hardly wait." Alex lay back down and closed his eyes.

*

Sariel prayed more fervently.

As a warrior angel and a trainer of athletas, he knew the importance of the mind in winning battles. He had engaged Alex in discussions meant to provide him with a wider understanding of reality. Now the angel felt the Spirit wanted the young man to see his part in the amazing flow of history and to provide the real purpose behind his battles.

Sariel thanked the Spirit for his direction. He approached Alex and put his hands on the young man's shoulders.

Alex tilted his head. "What's up?"

The two of them vanished and re-entered the timeline of history, emerging by some trees in a lush and humid jungle near a wide, forest-green river. A battle raged nearby with a clanging of swords and men yelling orders. Horses pounded the ground with their hooves, and elephants clamored like living tanks, trumpeting loudly with each thundering step. Blood painted shields and swords. Arrows and spears whizzed through the air and found their marks. Soldiers on the march trampled the fallen.

"Alexander the Great's attack against King Porus of India," the angel explained.

"Alexander the Great was an athleta Christi?" Alex asked, stunned.

Sariel shook his head. "Not at all. He was debased and evil to the end. He cared for nothing but surpassing the urban legend of Achilles and being recognized as the greatest conqueror ever."

A spear flew into the chest of an Indian soldier and he collapsed. Sariel turned toward Alex.

The boy's eyes showed his disgust. "So, why'd you bring me here?"

Sariel could tell the bloodshed was getting to the boy. This wasn't one of his video games. These were real people bleeding and dying. "This is the side of reality that you are used to seeing—the side your human senses are attuned to. But there is another side that your mortal eyes do not see. It is the most important part—the part that is most real."

The angel moved his hand in front of him, like he was pulling back a curtain. Alex now saw angels and demons engaged in a fierce battle on the ground and in the air. A bare-chested youth dressed in puffy white balloon pants, a turban, and earrings wielded a shaft with balls on both ends. The young man faced down a brutal knight demon.

"This is Banudu, an athleta from ancient India," Sariel explained.

"Wait…um…the people of ancient India knew about Jesus?"

"No. But then neither did Abraham, and yet he was declared righteous because of his faith in what he did know. From his youngest days, Banudu accepted the revelation he saw—God's signature in the beauty of creation and the wonder of his own humanness. He sought out the Person behind all things. He reached up, and the Spirit reached back. I trained him at a young age and he became a powerful warrior—one who changed the course of history."

The knight demon slashed his black sword at the young Indian. The boy easily dodged the blade. Before the creature could react, the athleta pushed off the ground with his powerful bare feet. He clubbed the monster hard with his weapon and landed gracefully behind him.

"Observe," Sariel whispered.

Alex's eyes were fixed.

This young man was always one step ahead of the beast. The demon's sword slashed time after time where the boy had been a split-second before. This athleta used his whole environment to aid in his attacks. He sprung off passing elephants and soared through the air like an acrobat. It was more like a dance than a fight.

As soon as he had an opening, the warrior reached for the bright dagger strapped on his leg and dealt a fatal blow. With one fluid motion, he slashed the creature's sinuous throat.

The beast's eyes went wide and its sword fell to the ground. It grabbed at its throat, attempting to stay the flow of dark blue blood. It roared in fury and pain and disappeared in a cloud of dust.

The athleta moved on to the next massive demon.

Alex turned to Sariel. "I don't get it. Why would God send an athleta here?"

"The Almighty One dispatches his forces, including athleta Christis, to fulfill his will. Alexander's role was to establish the Greek language as the universal medium of communication across the Mediterranean world. Once it was in place, the New Testament could be written in a language understood by all."

"Hmm, I see. So what am I being trained for?"

The angel left the question unanswered.

He took Alex to several other spots along the timeline. They observed athletas battling demons in Africa, China, and ancient America. In each place, people turned toward the living God.

"So," Alex said, "there is a plan. I mean, history and all. God's doing something all the time."

"Doing what, exactly?" the angel queried.

"Saving people, I guess."

Sariel smiled.

When Alex and Sariel returned to the training ground, they fell into their regular pattern of worship and praise to God.

"You are ready," Sariel declared.

*

Alex took his stance once more, his sword and shield in hand. He waited, trying to calm himself and to commune with the Spirit.

And then it began, the buzzing and rumbling.

The frantic horde approached.

They appeared to be the exact same skeletal army that had defeated him before. Seeing Alex again, they yelled with excitement, likely anticipating another brutal throttling.

As they approached, Alex reviewed what Sariel had told him. He had salvation as a result of Christ's death and resurrection. Because of this, he was a part of the grand exchange—Jesus had taken his sin and he had received the righteousness of Christ. Lastly, he was now a part of God's plan to bring this message to others.

He thanked God for his salvation and trusted himself fully to the Spirit.

The demons closed in.

A helmet enveloped Alex's head. It was close-fitting with a black visor over his eyes. It was so light that soon he forgot he was wearing it.

The demons shrieked in pain as they touched the helmet and exploded in puffs of dust. Alex's sword strokes killed dozens more. He caught sight of Sariel perched far off in the sky above. The skeletons poured in from all directions, like a bony avalanche, only to be ground to dust. After a few moments of intense battle, Alex stood on a pile of the pulverized remains of his assailants.

When the last skeleton collapsed with a shriek and a confused look on its bony face, Alex bowed his head and thanked the Spirit, the Father, and the Son for this great victory.

His skin-tight suit, helmet, shield, and sword all vanished. He was back in his regular clothes.

When Alex raised his head, his faithful guardian landed nearby and retracted his wings.

Sariel announced, "You have acquired the Helmet of Salvation. This is a powerful tool that the enemy cannot comprehend. With this part of the armor, and with those you will soon receive, you can overcome any onslaught."

Alex nodded his head. "Hmm, so, as long as I wear this armor, I'm pretty much invincible?"

"Nearly invincible. But do not be mistaken. It will not be easy to keep the armor and helmet in place. There are many distractions in your realm, many things that can take you off task. You must never give your fleshly self an opportunity to reassert itself. You cannot wear the armor while wearing the flesh. We have lost many strong warriors who have slowly, systematically walked away from their faith and become enamored with the things of this world. Ultimately, they put their own selfish desires above their calling. In time, this becomes their habit and they are no longer able to battle."

Alex hoped this would never happen to him.

Sariel came near. "It is time to return." The angel put his hands on Alex's shoulders.

They materialized back at his school, right where he had been when they left.

"You must hurry to your first class," the angel said.

Alex took in his surroundings. "You're right. Mr. Addison will kill me if I'm late again. You coming?"

"No. I need to meet with the other angels monitoring this town." The angel ascended.

"Well, good luck with that," Alex said and ran into the student herd entering the school.

*

Four creeper demons slinked furtively through the administration hallway. People walked past them, through them, without the slightest notice of their presence. The evil creatures were like lions walking through a compound of gazelles. Even though their mission was clear, it took extraordinary self-control to refrain from sinking their hooks and teeth into the foolish and vulnerable humans around them.

When they reached the middle of the building, all four stood outside the office of Principal Holmes. They pressed their hideous bodies against the door and passed through it.

*

The whole first period class moaned when Mr. Addison announced there would be a pop quiz. Pencil in hand, Alex closed his notebook and slid it under his desk. He grabbed the stack of papers that had reached him, took the top one, and passed the others.

Unease swept over him, and panic clawed at the pit of his stomach. He brushed sweat off his forehead and tried to calm his breathing. He hit the side of his head and dug at his ears with his little fingers, attempting to stop the excruciating ringing.

At first he thought this was all because he was unprepared for the surprise test. But, a voice inside told him it was something else. There was an emergency in the spiritual realm. The Spirit of God in him sounded an alarm so intense he found it hard to stay in his seat.

He whispered to himself under his breath, "Now what?"

*

The creepers found Principal Holmes at his desk, examining the file of one of his students—Chad Johnston. His eyes scanned the timeline in the file made up of Chad's "incidents": The incident when he lit fireworks in the bathroom, when he tagged the school, when he wrote his name on the wall in orange spray paint, when he punched a kid who walked too close to him in line and stepped on his new shoes, when he downloaded pornography on a school computer and made it the desktop wallpaper. In every case, Chad promised the principal it would be the last time he would see him in his office.

Now he'd been caught cheating.

The dark forms crossed the room and stood right in front of Mr. Holmes.

The fattest of the foul demons spoke up, "I will sink my hooks into his soft-pink pig flesh. You three stand guard."

"This one is mine!" snarled a second creature. "I claimed him on the way here." He bumped his shoulder into the fat one's chest, knocking him out of the way.

"Oomph," the portly demon winced and flailed his arms to scratch his attacker.

"You're both wrong, he's mine," the third demon announced. Hooks bubbled up from his arms and shot toward the principal's head.

Before they made contact, the fat demon reached out and grabbed them in mid-air. He tugged them to his crooked mouth and bit down hard. "Yum, lunch," he laughed. Black fluid sprayed from his mouth and ran down his chin.

While the other three brawled, the last demon—a seasoned monster—pulled a wavy blade from its charcoal-gray sheath with a metallic whine. The sound brought all to a standstill.

The powerful one lunged forward, pushing the blade deep into the body of the fat one. The corpulent creature bellowed in pain before disappearing in a shimmering puff. The other two froze, staring at him in horror.

"Now that I have your attention," he began, "we can get to business. The Executive, Cain, put me in charge of this operation. He authorized me to kill all of you, if need be. Nothing is to interfere with our mission. Do we understand each other?" He waved the blade in front of their faces.

"Yes, completely. But, I don't know your name," the third demon said, retracting his limp hooks.

"Hunger is my name. It is my specialty to make humans covet what they cannot get and to make them ungrateful for the riches they already possess." He moved behind Mr. Holmes and looked past him to the other two demons.

"This is what we shall do," he stated with finality and pointed to the second demon. "You will hold the principal. He is the bait for our trap. You will take control of him. He needs to be our puppet for the next few days."

This was the first time that the other two had been made aware of the timeline.

"So, how many days from now?"

The commanding demon grabbed this creeper by the throat and put the blade to his eye. The demon's giant red pupils dilated.

"Focus!" Hunger commanded, tightening his grip.

"Yes....yes, I will," the creature choked out.

Still holding him above the floor, Hunger said, "We must protect this possession. There is one who will attempt to set him free. We must be ready."

He dropped the gasping creature, then nodded to the other demon.

The terrified creeper moved behind the seated principal. He stretched out his arms, as if to hug the back of the chair. The flesh on the forearms bubbled and hooks broke through the skin and shot out on black cords like writhing snakes, toward the man. They passed through his clothing.

Principal Holmes didn't flinch. His countenance fell, and he put his head in his hands.

The foul demon relished in the man's growing emptiness. He raised his head and howled in ecstasy.

The other two joined him.

*

Alex kept checking the kids around him for dark shadows. He bombed the quiz. At lunch, he found a secluded place and worshipped God as Sariel had taught him. He asked God for direction and understanding, but the Spirit within him remained silent.

Sariel never returned.

While riding his bike home, Alex realized he had to wait. When the time for battle arrived, he would be summoned. Until then, he needed to trust God and live his life.

He wondered if Mr. Addison would give him another crack at that test.

11

Thursday

Days passed. Alex fell back into his normal routine.

In his last period class, Alex tried to keep his focus on Mr. Addison's presentation on the Boston Tea Party and its importance as an example of orderly dissent. He also tried to forget that Katie and Brandon were sitting together behind him.

It wasn't easy.

Conor had invited him to sit in the back of the class with him, but Alex had declined. Better to sit in the front where he couldn't see the happy couple.

He looked out the window to his left and peered down into the quad. Lovers walked hand-in-hand. At various tables, students embraced and kissed.

He shook his head, exhaled, and turned back to the lecture.

Concentrate!

Mr. A's views were so different from Sariel's. Alex guessed there was more than one way to look at historic events. What seemed to matter most was the person telling the story.

Mr. Addison ran an ancient projection machine, showing old filmstrips of various examples of civil disobedience, including Henry David Thoreau—who went to jail for withholding his taxes in protest—and a brave young man standing in front of the row of tanks at Tiananmen Square in China.

The teacher brought his presentation to a climax. "All of history is a struggle between those in power, who exploit the masses, and the lower and middle classes who must fight for their fair slice of the pie. It's truly the haves against the have-nots."

Alex smiled. *That's your view.*

Alex looked down into the courtyard again. What he saw sent shivers down his spine. Shadows were everywhere, following the students and, in some cases, hovering above them. All at once they fell on their prey and latched on. It was a predatory massacre.

Alex popped out of his chair and rushed for the door.

Mr. Addison stopped his lecture and asked him, "Do you have a pressing appointment, Mr. McKendrick?"

Alex turned and walked backward toward the door. "May I be excused…um…to the restroom? It's…uh…sort of an emergency." Kids snickered.

The teacher rolled his eyes. "We wouldn't want an accident, would we? Take the hall pass."

But Alex was already out the door.

The students jeered him.

*

Alex moved swiftly down the hallway to the restroom. He ducked into one of the stalls, where Sariel appeared in front of him.

"You have permission to battle these creatures. Something serious is happening."

"Great." The young man assumed a posture of prayer and asked to be put into the spiritual realm, but nothing happened. "I don't get it," he finally said. "You said I had permission."

"Are you sufficiently focused? Not distracted?"

It came to Alex like a slap in the face. All he could think about was Katie and her stupid new boyfriend. Was it that easy to be taken off track? He kicked himself mentally and turned back to Sariel. "I'm sorry. I've taken my eye off the ball. Please forgive me. It won't happen again." With that, he bowed his head, asked God to forgive him, and gave himself completely over to the Spirit. He instantly shifted into the spiritual realm and his protective green suit.

He bolted for the courtyard.

Alex had been in this other-worldly place before, but it had never been like this. Demons were everywhere. Most were little with hairless bodies, bony arms, and flailing legs. Three menacing creepers landed on the courtyard looking like they were about to consume an all-you-can-eat buffet. They attacked the humans—biting them, shooting them with hooks, and burying their faces into the backs of their heads. Alex thought of them as hellish leeches.

He concentrated. His helmet formed over his head, his shield appeared on his arm, and his sword took shape in his right hand.

A couple of the demons spotted him. "He's here! He's here!" They chanted in unison.

The demons let go of their victims. They turned as a unit toward Alex, and swords appeared in their hands.

"Really?"

He'd been set up. These demons had been sent to draw him out, to test his strength, to see what kind of threat he posed to them.

He intended to show them.

He took his warrior stance and leaned on the Spirit within.

The little, scrawny demons scuttled at him first. Alex swung his sword like a baseball bat, knocking these little monsters away as fast as they approached. It was fun.

Next, three Creepers attacked him from all sides. As the one in front shot forth its hooks, Alex charged, holding his shield in front of him. The hooks and their cords dissolved as they touched the holy metal. Before the creature could react, Alex was on him, slicing him through and turning him to dust.

His momentum carried him face-to-face with the brick wall of the building. Two other demons came up behind him. Alex jumped and pushed off the wall, catapulting himself into a back flip up over the demons and the hooks they had just launched at him. Landing behind the ugly brutes, Alex brought them both down with one clean slash.

When he looked up, the courtyard was surrounded by bright angels nodding their approval. The demons were gone. Sariel appeared in front of him as Alex's weapons disappeared.

"That was intense," Alex said.

"Yes," Sariel replied pensively. "Do not let down your guard. The battles will soon grow far more difficult."

"Well, it shouldn't be that much of a problem. I seem to be getting stronger with every fight. I should be able to handle it, right?"

Sariel patted his shoulder with affection. "That you should, my young friend. That you should."

Alex saw worry in Sariel's eyes.

*

Alex walked back into class. The other students were working on a quiz. Mr. Addison must have passed it out while he was away.

He slid into his seat and picked up the paper sitting on top of his desk. Scanning it, he realized that the quiz was on the material that had been covered in class that day. He'd be okay on the first part, but he wasn't even in the room for the rest.

With frustration, he started the test.

He hoped athletas were lucky guessers.

*

Alex moved out the door with his classmates. Conor came alongside. "Man, what was with that test? It was so hard!"

"Did you listen to the lecture? Did you take any notes?" Alex shot back, avoiding the crowd coming toward him.

"Of course not. I was going to, but I found a better use of my time."

"Which was …?"

"Well, playing the new game app on my phone. What else?"

They stepped outside and took their usual position on the stairs in front of the school's main building.

"You're hopeless." Alex shook his head and laughed.

"Yeah, but don't worry, there's still plenty of hope for you."

"I don't know about that. I messed up pretty bad with Katie. Can you believe she's going out with *that* guy?" Just as he said it, Katie and Brandon walked past, holding hands.

Both boys looked away and whistled.

When the couple had passed, Conor said, "I know. I did *not* see that coming. What gets me is that, even though she was on the date with you, she went after him. I mean, who does that?"

"Katie does. I don't know. Maybe she got scared and needed an easy way out of being with me. I just can't stand to see her with that—jock. He doesn't deserve her."

Conor waved his arms. "Yeah, you're right. Man, just think, if you didn't have to pee at that very moment, you guys would be together. The body is always our enemy."

This was one of the times Alex wished Conor didn't turn everything into a joke. "Thanks man. You always know just what to say. I'll see you tomorrow."

Conor smiled. "Okay, well, see ya later, Loser!"

"Later."

Alex headed to the bike rack, hopped on his BMX, and headed home.

*

Later that night, Alex had a fitful sleep. He dreamt he was at school, running through dark twisting halls lined with endless classroom doors. He frantically searched for something, but didn't know what.

He turned a corner and came to a shadowy circular stairwell. Grasping the icy handrail, he was drawn upward into the void. He climbed several stories. The stairwell abruptly ended at a large metal door. Alex reached for the doorknob.

The door came to life. It glowed red and the heavy metal bulged, creaking and groaning. The lump receded and the eerie light dimmed. It swelled again and again in a rhythmic breathing pattern. He heard a hoarse, eerie voice. "Alex, enter."

And then everything was still.

The door creaked open on its own, and Alex peered into the night-black room toward the only source of illumination—a humming, ten-foot-wide pentagram that shone red and orange on the floor. Alex stared, transfixed.

He carefully approached the circle and star and the oppressive evil that emanated from it. He reached toward the harsh glow. His hand blistered in the intense heat.

Crying out in pain, he wrenched back his hand. The pentagram flashed. A deafening hum assaulted his eardrums. He choked on the suffocating scent of sulfur. His eyes stung and watered.

Without warning, the pulsating circle became a hole in the floor. The ground rumbled. Black sludge gushed from the hole, knocking Alex off his feet. It spewed like a fountain and the tar-like substance rose, enveloped him, and weighed him down. He couldn't stand. He couldn't swim. He couldn't move. It flowed up his nose and down his mouth, closing off his airways.

The darkness consumed him.

Alex's eyes popped open, and he gasped. He was in his bed. His room was dark and quiet.

Sariel sat nearby, his countenance painted with concern.

Alex looked out his window and saw two other angels atop his neighbor's roof.

"More angels?" he asked. "Reinforcements?"

"Yes," his guardian replied. "These are stationed here to protect your home. Others will join me in guarding your person. You shall never be alone."

"That's comforting. Who needs privacy, right?"

"Your safety is far more important. The demonic activity in this area has increased dramatically. It is a full invasion. We will meet it with the overwhelming force of light." He affectionately put his hand on Alex's shoulder. "You still have a vital part to play in whatever is going on here, my disciple. Remember what I have taught you. Stay faithful."

"I'll do what I can, Sariel." He yawned.

The angel stood. "I know you will, Alex. Now sleep. I must confer with my supervisor. He may know more about what is going on here and how we can counter it. Do not worry. Today you have demonstrated your power, and there are plenty of angels to protect you. Be on your guard. I will return as soon as possible."

"Okay." Alex breathed deeply, letting his sore, tired body relax.

Sariel stood in the windowsill, transformed to his glorious form, and launched himself into the night sky.

*

Alex's guardian angel ascended past the earth's atmosphere, his wings flapping slowly and silently. He turned and looked back down to the earth and sighed. This planet had been his home since the earliest ages, but he relished the times when he could enter the courts of heaven to confer with his superiors.

He turned away from the earth and pulled his body tight, like a missile, and launched.

Artists throughout the centuries have portrayed heaven as a place in the clouds. It is, actually, a place amidst the stars.

Faster than the speed of light, Sariel raced through the vast vacuum of space. He soared through multi-colored nebulas and passed near a gas giant. The glories of the universe filled him with awe. He slowed as he approached his supervisor's dwelling.

Mihr lived on a crystalline platter a mile in diameter hung in space. The outer rim was covered with elongated prisms that split the bright light of nearby stars and nebulae into spectacular rainbows.

Sariel's wings were bathed in color as he landed. "Mihr?"

No response.

Sariel stared up at the wispy blue and purple streaks of a vibrant nebula, illuminated from behind by a vast curtain of shimmering white stars. A comet raced across the face of the nebula. It slowed, stopped, and changed direction, barreling backward in a tight curling spiral.

Sariel decided to investigate. He unfurled his wings and rocketed off the crystal platform.

Reaching the nebula, he saw that the celestial event he witnessed was not a comet after all. A team of sixty angles flew in such a tight formation they were a ball of blazing light. Their wings overlapped each other and flapped in perfect harmony. The ball looked like it was breathing.

112

Mihr flew in the center of this blazing sphere, encouraging his team, bellowing like an opera star singing about the wondrous glories of God. Sariel noticed that the beat of the song perfectly corresponded to the flaps of the angelic wings.

Oh glorious One enthroned on high,
All creation lifts its eyes to You
We storm forward on Your wings of power
To conquer in Your holy Name.

As the team passed close to Sariel, the angels drew their swords and spun their blades, their arms moving above their heads like a bunch of cowboys roping steers.

And then it all went bad.

A couple of angels fell out of step with the others. Swords hit against each other and sparks flew. Wings clashed. The beautiful song became a pitiful shout of, "No! No! No!" The ball fell apart. The angels spun out of control and hurtled in all directions until they came to a stop and righted themselves.

"Is everyone all right?" Mihr called out, surveying the team.

The angels nodded and said they were fine.

Mihr broke out in a hearty laugh. "Praise be to God. Well done, everyone. Almost had it that time."

Mihr noticed Sariel hovering nearby. "You're all dismissed. We will meet again at the appointed time. Bless you all."

The angels dispersed, many nodding in acknowledgement to Sariel as they passed. Sariel nodded in kind. He had great admiration for these warriors.

Although angels do not age, Mihr gave the impression of ancient wisdom.

"Sariel, my dear friend, it is good to see you," Mihr said, cheerfully greeting him with a hug. "Come, let's talk."

The two angels flew to Mihr's crystal platform. They sat on elegant glass-like chairs the size of thrones. Mihr leaned forward. "How is your young disciple holding up?"

"He is doing well—so far—but the war rages on. I fear the battles will soon grow fierce."

Mihr looked into Sariel's eyes. "I can see through you, my friend. You are afraid he is going to fail—like the others."

Sariel winced.

Mihr reached over and put his hand on his friend's shoulder. "Now, none of that. We all know that this young man could not have been placed under a better wing than yours."

"But he is not ready. And the enemy is on the move. They know of him."

"Yes, that has been reported to me. The Lord has a special plan for Alex. He always does." Mihr leaned in closer and recited a common adage among angels. "The best always happens."

"I know. I know."

"Yet, you are worried."

"He is so easily distracted."

"Yes, he is a product of his age. Sariel, you must have faith in him. Guide him the best you can and *trust*. He may surprise you."

This was exactly what Sariel needed to hear. "Thank you Mihr, I will." He walked a few steps away and looked out toward a cluster of stars. "Is there any more intelligence? What is the enemy planning? Is it what we have feared these many years?"

"Unfortunately, you know everything I know at this time. Something malevolent is developing—something that will have a sizable impact on the spiritual battle. Unfortunately, it is still veiled in shadow," his friend explained. "We must—"

"Trust the One who knows all," Sariel responded with another common angelic adage. "It would just be nice to know more."

Mihr grinned and nodded. "We know what we need to know." He leaned closer. "Now, I have summoned you here for a reason. I have something important to tell you."

*

Just say the words "school lunch" in a group of students, and you'll hear stories that will turn your stomach. The Kingman High cafeteria was on a "healthy" food kick and had stopped serving chocolate milk, had begun using tasteless whole-wheat flour, and had replaced red meat with gelatinous tofu.

Alex reluctantly took a bite of his tasteless flatbread veggie sandwich.

Conor stood and yelled, "Here's to cholesterol, a man's best friend." He pulled a giant piece of pepperoni pizza out of a plastic bag in his backpack. He held it high like a victory pennant. The students cheered as he stuffed the entire thing into his mouth. When the last of the crust passed his lips and filled his cheeks, he thrust up his hands in victory, reveling in the applause of his many admirers.

Euphoric, he took a bow and ceremoniously sat back down.

Adoring friends patted him on the back and mussed his hair.

He looked across to Alex and his eyes filled with panic.

Conor mumbled, grunted, and sputtered through the pizza fragments. He started communicating through hand gestures and facial expressions, ending with him pretending to put a gun to his head and pull the trigger.

"They're right behind me aren't they? Gah!" Alex couldn't stop himself. He looked back.

Conor chugged some soda and swallowed hard. "I told you not to look. Man, you're taking this hard."

"Wouldn't you?"

"Yeah, I guess so. But hey, look at the bright side. This can't last. Brandon's a royal loser. She'll figure it out—sooner or later."

"I know, but right now, this sucks." Alex got up, shouldering his backpack. "You coming?"

"I wouldn't miss fourth period for the world." He wiped pizza sauce off his cheeks with the back of his sleeve and walked next to Alex, keeping his stride.

Alex took one glance back and saw Katie kissing Brandon. He turned away fast, another indelible picture in his head.

As the boys entered the main building, they almost bumped into Principal Holmes, who marched down the hallway like a man with a purpose. Alex's mouth dropped. A dense shroud of darkness surrounded the man.

Alex leaned over to Conor and mumbled, "I gotta talk with Principal Holmes. I'll see you later, in sixth period."

"You talk to the principal? What about?"

Alex didn't answer.

"Okay, man. I'll save you a seat in the back."

"I sit in the front, remember?" Alex shouted back.

When Conor was out of sight, Alex turned toward the stairwell. He had to get away from all these people so he could disappear into the spiritual realm.

He opened the door. A freshman girl charged down the stairs and out the exit. Alex pulled the door closed, quickly took his warrior stance, and forced himself into the spiritual realm.

He looked back at the door. He didn't want to open it and possible freak out the students in the hall. He concentrated and gave himself to the Spirit. Alex stepped forward and passed through the door.

Cool!

He stood in the hallway wearing his armor, hunting a demon.

He found the Principal further down the hall, but instead of one demon torturing him, there were three.

He took a deep breath and called out, "Hey, slimeballs. Get off him, in the Name of the Lord."

The demons stopped chewing on Mr. Holmes and looked up with bloodshot eyes.

The largest one called out in a deep, hoarse voice, "Ah, here he is, the tiny gnat that has been buzzing in our business." He laughed, reeling in his hooks and leaping off the principal's back. He pulled a sword from the air. "Come on, warriors, our master will be thrilled to hear we killed off this brat."

The other creepers also brandished swords. All three licked their lips with anticipation.

Alex took his fighting stance. Sweat beaded on his forehead. Where was Sariel? What was keeping him? Maybe he should have waited before jumping into this fight. But didn't his guardian say that being able to shift was proof of permission? He couldn't remember.

The first demon charged. Alex raised his shield and sword. But the demon stopped and with another vile laugh snarled. "Alex, isn't it? How's Katie? She is so happy with … um …. Brandon, isn't it? She likes kissing him." He made a sickening, sloppy kissing sound.

"Shut up!" Alex became enraged. These taunts were red hot pokers. He wanted to annihilate these hideous creatures.

His sword grew transparent and faded, along with his armor and shield.

The creeper lifted his sword, muttering, "Too easy," and brought the putrid blade down hard. Alex lifted his arm, but his shield was gone.

He thrust his sword up.

There was just enough of his blade left to deflect the direct force of the stroke. The weapon hit his chest. It didn't pierce his green suit, but the blow knocked him off his feet. He fell hard to the floor.

His head ached. He had to do better than this.

Instantly, the three demons surrounded him. They turned their arms over simultaneously, and dozens of sharp hooks spurted from

117

their bumpy skin. Pain cried out as the hooks implanted themselves into Alex's flesh.

A wave of loss crashed over him. Why was Katie with Brandon? Why had she rejected him? Was he just patently undateable? Maybe it wasn't him, maybe it was her! How could she not see through Brandon's shallowness? His mind was bombarded with images of Katie and Brandon making out.

She was all he hungered for.

Nothing else mattered.

Nothing.

Alex looked up through his pain and saw the three demons leaning over him. Globs of yellowish drool fell from the bottom lip of the biggest one. Alex closed his eyes tight as the rancid stuff hit his face and slid down his cheek. Before he could breathe the monsters were on him, shredding him with their teeth and claws.

The vile creatures stood back, howled in triumph, and lifted their swords for the kill.

Alex lost consciousness as the entire world around him blazed in white light.

*

Sariel smiled as he left the outer courts of heaven. Mihr, his trusted friend, had shared with him news that would affect both his life and that of his charge.

He hoped Alex hadn't gotten himself into trouble while he was gone.

*

"What now?" Alex heard a muffled voice above him.

An authoritative voice said, "Check him for hooks. Be thorough. A single barb left behind can prove lethal. You saw the effect they had on him."

"He's clean," a third one said. "And now, the healing."

Alex heard angelic voices singing praises to God. Hands touched him and warmth moved over his body. His choppy breathing deepened and became more regular.

He drifted out of consciousness again.

*

In his office, Alistair Cain braced himself for the news.

The minor demon, a runt called Malice, trembled before him. This was not a good sign.

Alistair lifted a piece of ice from the metal bucket before him, held it to his aching head, and said, "Spill it."

"Please! Master, I beg of you! Do not kill me!" the demon pleaded.

"If our lord could afford to lose another demon, you would already be gone. Report!"

The demon could barely get out the words. "The creepers have…um…they have failed…uh…temporarily. They had the boy…and uh…they were just about to kill him…um…but…"

The Executive grabbed the demon by his scrawny throat. "Let us understand each other. I may not be able to kill you, but I *can* hurt you. Now, tell me what happened!"

The Executive demon released him.

Malice rubbed his throat, took a deep breath, and said, as steadily as he could, "The room filled with angels. They poured in and disarmed the demons. They severed their hooks.

I hid.

I watched.

The demons rallied. They shot through the ceiling. They were chased, but got away. When the angels left, the demons re-established their hold on the principal."

"But the boy escaped. They had him, and he got away."

The gargoyle-like creature giggled nervously. "Yes, my lord."

Cain drew back his arm and caught Malice with the back of his hand. He bounced off the wall like a soccer ball. When he landed, he held his head in pain.

"See, you are not dead," Cain muttered. "At least, not yet."

*

Angels floated Alex through the window and into his bedroom. They gently placed him on his bed, then brought him back into the physical realm.

Trembling, he winced, pulled his legs and arms close, and turned to the wall.

Broken bones had been mended, arteries reconnected, and tissues made like new. Yet pain screamed from each nerve ending, and the horror of the memory of those creatures biting him and tearing him apart made it hard to breathe.

An angel gently pulled the covers over him.

The heavenly beings, clad in white armor, all put their hands out toward the shaking boy and prayed.

12

Friday

Sariel arrived in Alex's bedroom just after midnight and found the boy unconscious.

Angels guarding Alex filled him in.

Sariel transformed to his human form, sat on the chair near the window, and waited.

After several hours, the young man opened his eyes. When he saw Sariel, he turned away in disgust.

"Ah, good, you are awake," the angel said.

"Where were you?" the boy hissed, wiping away tears.

"I am sorry you were hurt, Alex. But you must know that I am not the one to blame for your ... condition."

The boy didn't turn. "Of course, *you* never make mistakes. *You're* perfect. It must have been part of God's perfect will for me to nearly get killed."

There was a painful silence.

"Were you directed to battle?"

Alex didn't respond.

Sariel pressed him, saying, "No angel told you that you had permission? Did you feel the Spirit inside you leading you to fight?"

"No. Okay? I figured that since I could shift to the spiritual realm, I was supposed to attack. I guess that's what I get showing initiative."

Sariel studied Alex's clenched teeth and balled fists. He tried a different approach. "You must understand, I did not leave you without protection."

The boy sat up in bed and stared down the angel. "So, why didn't they stop me?"

"They wanted to. They were not given permission to interfere—until the last."

"All part of *God's* plan," Alex spit out. "The *perfect* plan."

Sariel scowled. "The Almighty can handle your impudence. In fact, He has infinite patience for it. I, however, find it most distasteful. Even though you were not told to go in, you were allowed to and could have prevailed. The truth is, you were distracted. Rather than being focused and guided by the will of God, you allowed your attachment to this world—to that girl, Katie—to overwhelm you. Those creatures knew just what buttons to push. Admit it. You failed because you lost focus."

Alex climbed unsteadily out of the bed saying, "I want out. I told you, you've got the wrong guy. I'm not a hero. You can't make me one. I just want to live my life, and I can't do that if I'm always, you know, chasing spooks."

Sariel leaned forward and spoke with great care. "You have come to an important crossroad. Jesus explained that nothing else must come close to your devotion for Him. You must be willing to sacrifice everything, *including your life,* to His will."

Alex sighed and shook his head. "He asks for too much."

Sariel spoke with passion. "Yes, Jesus asks that you give up all for Him. But remember, He also willingly gave up all for you." He took a deep breath to control his emotions. "Imagine how difficult it was for all of us, the entire heavenly host, to have to stand back and watch God's Son dying on the cross. He could have spoken one word, and ten thousand of us would have come to His rescue. We all wanted to. We were dying to. But we were not given permission. His death was also the Father's will—part of His plan. And we sadly accepted it."

Alex turned away. He shut tight his eyes, his mind, and his heart.

*

Alex trudged toward his school. His aching body moved along slowly, so he knew he'd be late for his first period class. He didn't care. Thankfully, he saw his bike still safely locked in the bike cage.

He spent first period in tardy sweep, staring mindlessly into space and twirling a pencil between his fingers.

He was dead inside, partly from the poisoned hooks that had pierced him the day before. But there was also something else. The whole situation was just too big for him. He was an ant in the path of a steam roller.

He went through the motions in his classes and didn't say two words the entire day.

Riding home on his bike, he knew Sariel flew fifty feet above him.

He never looked up.

They moved together in silence.

*

The ecstatic Kingman fans stood, cheered, and shook pom poms when Brandon Richardson scored a third touchdown—single-handedly securing another win for the record books. This would move the team to second place in their division and give them a clear shot at the championship.

Alex knew Conor could care less about the game. He was there to have fun and to mess around with his friends. He threw a jelly bean toward the band that caromed off a tuba and hit the drum major in the cheek. To avoid suspicion, he turned and pretended he was talking to Alex.

Alex tried not to stare at Katie and her new friends. She'd traded up and now hung out with Brandon's circle of "beautiful people." These were the students at the top of the food chain—the Most-Likely-to-Succeed crowd. The yearbook would be all about them while Alex would be lucky if he was in anything more than his student mug shot.

Conor threw a handful of jelly beans down on the band geeks. The multi-colored projectiles bounced off their instruments and cylindrical hats. The musical nerds all looked in his direction.

"Crap!" Conor exclaimed, sitting still. "Just act normal."

"I need some air." Alex got up and worked his way to the aisle.

Conor stood. "We're outside! What do you call *this*?" He waved his arms.

"I'll be right back." Alex stomped down the stairs.

Alex didn't see the hideous creeper demon move in behind Conor. Hooks sprang from the creature's arms and buried themselves deep inside the boy's back. Conor laughed uproariously.

Alex stood under the bleachers, staring out into the parking lot. Suddenly, above the frosty light of the street lamps, he saw a squadron of shadows flying through the air.

Sariel appeared beside him. "I have seen numerous evil gatherings in my day—times when the enemy's forces have descended on a geographical location, attempting to take mastery over it. This is what is happening here and now."

"Don't you get sick of it? It's like you're in a war that never ends."

"Ah, but it shall end someday. The Lord will be victorious and will rule over all." The angel had a far-away look in his ancient eyes. "The amazing thing is that the Lord allows us to participate in the battle. Now understand—he does not really need us at all. He could vanquish the forces of evil with a thought. It is for our benefit that we are allowed to fight. In the process, we learn and grow."

"So, God could change all this, if He wanted to?"

"If it would better fit His will, His ultimate purpose, He would."

Just then, Alex saw Principal Holmes duck out through the gate and head for the school. Dark forms crawled all over him. Alex imagined the three grotesque demons he'd battled chewing on the man, like he was a delicious feast.

It was more than he could stomach.

He looked away.

"Turning your back will not make this all go away."

"Not my problem."

Sariel leaned closer and whispered, "The only thing keeping those things from crawling all over you and those you love is your faithfulness and our protection. If you give up, you will also be theirs." He put his hand on Alex's shoulder. "We do not always choose the situation. We do choose our response to it."

Alex considered. There was no place to hide. He was either God's or Satan's. There was no neutral ground.

Alex breathed deeply and turned back toward the principal and his tormenters. He shook his head and trudged forward.

Sariel said, "I thought you were done with all this."

"Try to keep up," Alex said to the angel, heading after the principal.

"I shall try," Sariel said, tongue in cheek.

*

As Alex approached the school building, a dazzling light blinded him.

"Hold it right there! Campus security," the man said, forcefully.

"I need to talk to Principal Holmes," Alex rebutted.

"Whatever it is, you can take it up with him on Monday, son. Go on back to the game. If I see you back here, I'll have to take you in."

Alex nodded and turned back toward the stadium.

"Is he looking?" Alex asked.

"He just turned away," Sariel responded.

"Good." Alex shifted into the spiritual plane. It took a second for his vision to adjust to the muddled colors and streaking lights.

The campus policeman looked back again and muttered, "What the—? Where'd he go?" He flashed his light all around.

Alex, in his armor, and Sariel, in full angelic form, turned the corner where they'd seen the principal go. They found themselves confronted by a dozen Creeper Demons.

The biggest one, a drooling slimy beast who'd tormented Alex before, musically shouted, "Surprise!"

Alex slashed with his sword. He cut Mr. Holmes loose from the gnarled cords, then spun and faced his enemies. They surrounded him.

To Alex's surprise, Sariel stepped in. He held a flaming sword that lit up the entire portico. The demons turned away and stepped back. But the angel didn't engage them directly. Instead, his wings beat hard. He rose above the fight to a position where he could keep any creatures from escaping. "Alex, they are all yours."

The lead demon approached the athleta. "It's time to finish what we started. Have you not heard? Have they not told you? Sariel keeps so many secrets from you, poor boy. I have been given

126

permission to kill you." He guffawed and then proclaimed to the others, "Hunger will conquer this puny pretender to the glory of his master."

The band of demons cheered their leader on.

Emboldened, the creature continued. "You know, you are not my first."

"And you're not mine," Alex retorted, leaping at the beast.

Hunger lifted his sword to block the assault. Meanwhile, the other demons shot dozens of hooks at Alex. They hit his helmet and shield and disintegrated.

"I saw Katie kissing Brandon," Hunger started in again. "It must hurt so deeply to be rejected in this way. Poor Alex, you are so mistreated."

Alex remained quiet. His armor and sword never faltered. He shook his head and hissed, "Why don't you shut up and fight!"

The athleta lunged forward threateningly. The smaller demons recoiled in fear. He thrust his sword at Hunger. Again, the demon blocked it. Alex could feel real strength in this creature.

"Alex, behind you!" Sariel called down as two creepers quickly ran up behind the young warrior.

Alex swung around. The sword of the smaller demon was so badly aimed that when Alex dodged it, the blade passed through the neck of his grotesque partner. The pierced creature dropped his own sword and clutched his throat, trying to stay the gushing blue-black ooze. In a moment, he was gone.

The horrified demon realized what he'd done and wailed.

Alex sliced him in two.

Alex turned just in time to clash swords with Hunger. The beast battered his head with its leathery wings to distract him.

The other creeper demons scurried into the courtyard, anxious to get into the fight.

"Aim for his legs and feet," the lead demon commanded his reinforcements.

Stinging barbs hit Alex below the waist. He slashed at them but the lingering effects of their poison nibbled at his resolve. *I need more armor*, he thought.

In a flash, segmented black and gray plates formed over his feet, shins, and thighs.

The hooks that hit his new leg armor sizzled and evaporated.

The young warrior, greatly encouraged, turned his body and kicked Hunger square in his barreled chest. The demon lost his balance and fell, rolling to the side of the courtyard.

Alex jumped to the other demons, his sword swaying before him. Three of the creatures leaped upward, trying to fly away, but Sariel cut them down.

Their trap had backfired!

In desperation, the foul creatures pulled out their jagged swords and charged.

Alex turned and slashed the creatures one after another. Their faces flashed pain and horror before they exploded in demon-shaped clouds of ash.

Hunger recovered, pushing himself up on his muscular legs. Alex raised his sword and went after him. His attacks were met by the demon's blow for blow.

"You are beginning to tire," laughed the creature.

"I'm sure getting tired of you." He drove his sword high and the demon countered, but before Hunger could react, Alex shoved his sword into his belly.

The creature's eyes went wide. His voice gurgled, "We … we will get you yet, athleta."

He became a wispy cloud.

Sariel landed next to Alex and retracted his wings. "Adequate," he commented.

Just then the campus policeman's flashlight lit up the corner of the portico where they stood.

"Oh my God," he choked out. He pulled a radio to his lips and said in a shaky voice, "This is Chansler. I need backup in the corner of the East Quad. I've got a real problem here."

*

Conor was having a terrific evening. He'd eaten far too much junk food. He'd yelled with the cheerleaders and mimicked their inane routines. Best of all, a group of guys who acted like even bigger idiots than he did had called him over to join them.

Katie plopped herself down beside Conor, trying to ignore his goofiness. She wore Brandon's letterman's jacket, which was twice her size. She pulled up the long sleeves until they looked like accordions. She cleared her throat, leaned closer to him, and spoke into his ear. "Conor. A bunch of us are going to the beach tomorrow. Wanna come?"

Conor ran his fingers through his straight, brown hair. "Sure, I mean, if I don't have anything else going on. Wait, tomorrow? That's Saturday, right? I have … um … nothing. Okay, I'll be there!"

"You're *so* weird."

"Takes one to know one." He laughed. "I miss you, Katie girl. I mean, now that you're hanging with the letterman class, us lowlifes never get to see you."

"You can see me tomorrow. And," she breathed deeply, "can you bring Alex?" She looked away uncomfortably. "There's been a lot of tension between us lately. I just want us all to be friends again."

Conor's brow furrowed and he wrung his hands. "Yeah, I'll ask him."

"Great. Thanks. Oh, and don't tell him I told you to invite him, or he might not come."

Conor rolled his eyes. "Uh, gotcha. No problem."

"Okay, thanks again. See you tomorrow!" she said brightly as she stood, turned her back on the bottom-feeders, and headed back to her new friends.

Once she was gone, Conor's face dropped. "Ugh, why am I always in the middle?"

The beach.

Sand.

Bathing suits.

Food.

Friends.

He pictured Alex's shocked face when he saw Katie there—with Brandon. He imagined Brandon and Katie arguing over Alex.

It would be chaos.

A crooked smile crossed his face.

The creeper demon loosed its hooks and flew away.

*

Alex sat in the empty spot next to Conor and his goony friends, like nothing had ever happened.

The security guard had found Principal Holmes crumpled in a ball in the quad and had called for backup. Alex and the angel, still in the spiritual realm, had walked right past him unnoticed. Alex had shifted back to this realm when he neared the stadium.

Alex cleared his throat. "You moved. I had to find you. Did I miss anything?"

"The game? You're kidding, right? Old Brandon boy started kicking their butts in the first quarter and hasn't let up. Look at the score—forty-eight to seven. This isn't a game, it's a massacre."

"I can relate."

"So, um … what are you doing tomorrow?" Conor asked, like he was trying to appear nonchalant.

Alex looked over at Sariel, who stood in the aisle close by. The angel nodded toward Conor.

"I don't know," Alex said. "Why?"

"Uh…um…a bunch of us are going…to the beach…uh…you should come along. Who knows, it might get you out of this pissy mood you're in."

"The beach?" he asked, looking at the angel for permission.

Sariel grinned and nodded his head. Alex's shoulders relaxed. "Sure," he said, a little surprised. "I could really use a break."

Conor howled. "A break from what? Dude, your whole life is a break, interrupted occasionally by school."

Alex shook his head.

If only that were true.

*

Malice entered the endless hallway toward the Executive Demon's suite at the top of a New York high-rise.

He cursed this stupid assignment. Why should he have to constantly report bad news to the Executive? In spite of all this, he took comfort in the fact that the Executive couldn't afford to destroy him. He himself had noticed how thin the demonic horde had grown upon this ridiculous planet. It was coming to the point where every demon, no matter how incompetent, was vital to the cause.

Good.

Malice looked forward to a time when the earth would be covered with demons, when the Dark Lord would rule majestically from an exalted throne of skulls. Maybe then he would get a decent assignment and be allowed to feast on humans. It had been centuries since he'd gnawed on anyone.

The door was ajar. He entered the suite and gasped. The Executive Demon and Smok, the North American Demon, were kneeling, their foreheads on the floor. Before them stood a being whose darkness absorbed all light. He eyes belayed incredible intelligence and cunning. Behind him, dragon-like wings spanned the space from his head to the ground.

Malice immediately lunged forward and did a face-plant on the floor. He'd been in the presence of the mighty one giving orders to his legions many times, but he'd only seen him from afar. He mentally cursed himself for walking into what was obviously an extremely important meeting. He wondered if he could sneak away and come back later.

"Malice, report," Lucifer spoke in a voice that echoed off the walls like thunder.

The demon kept his head down for fear of losing it. He cleared his throat and spoke. "Your worship, I fear I have nothing but . . . nothing but bad news to report. Our traps have backfired. We have lost the creepers who had control of the principal."

"How many?" Satan asked.

"A dozen creepers in all, my lord, including Hunger."

"That will be all, Malice," the dark lord hissed. "Continue to monitor. Report all to Alistair."

Malice glanced over at Cain, then lowered his head. "Yes, your worship." He crawled backward, his eyes riveted to the floor, until he was out of the room. Then he shot down the hall like a bullet, thrilled beyond belief. He had survived delivering bad news to Satan himself. And, what's more, his supreme master knew him by name.

*

Satan spoke in a raspy whisper, "You may stand, both of you. We must talk. This is as I had foreseen. Our enemy knows our plans, and he is training a champion to thwart them. Time is now of the essence. I understand you are moving on site earlier than you planned, Alistair."

The Executive responded. "Yes, my lord. I had to make arrangements. Everything is in place. I leave tomorrow morning."

"Satisfactory," the Demon Lord hissed.

*

Sariel sat in Alex's room and patiently stared out the window. He worshipped and praised the Lord with all his heart.

Alex came in and closed the door. He sat on the edge of his bed and unlaced his shoes. "It's all settled. Mom said I can go to the beach tomorrow."

"That is good to hear. You have permission from heaven as well. It is what you need."

"So, you going to tell me about the fancy footwear?" Alex stretched out on the bed, putting his arms behind his head. "I gotta say, I thought I was a goner before those shoes appeared."

"You are speaking of the latest part of your armor. You have now been given the shoes of the Gospel of Peace. Peace means completeness—wholeness. Tell me what happened to you out there. What were you thinking while fighting those demons?"

Alex reflected. "Well, I was going after the big ugly one, but the little ugly ones kept shooting me with their hooks. It ticked me off. I felt that the Spirit within me said I could walk away at any time. He said my salvation was secure, that I wasn't saved by fighting, but that I could fight because I was saved. He said that if I were to continue, it would be completely by my choice."

The angel turned to face Alex, listening.

Alex continued, "In that moment I knew what my life was really about. I mean, this stuff with Katie still hurts, but I think I've wasted a lot of emotional energy on a relationship that only really existed in my mind. I guess that was when I let it go. All I wanted, in that moment, was to stop the evil from spreading. But, I couldn't do it with my legs and feet exposed. The demons were getting the best of me. When the armor appeared, I knew they were licked."

"You are beginning to sound like an athleta Christi," the angel mused.

"Uh, is there something wrong? I thought this is what you wanted?" Alex pulled off his socks, tossed them toward his hamper and missed.

"I have trained many athletas in my lifetime. But never have I seen one advance as quickly as you have. You lack only two pieces of the armor— the Breastplate of Righteousness and the Belt of Truth. I am sure you will acquire these when the time is right."

There was a flash of dark lightning on the horizon.

Alex sat up.

"The enemy is bringing in reinforcements. While you are at the beach, I will confer with my angelic brothers."

The young man gasped. "You won't be there with me?" "You have permission. I do not."

"Maybe I should stay here and help you."

"We do not always understand what we are called to do. You should have seen Joshua's face when he was told to march around the city of Jericho for seven days. It didn't make sense to him, either. But he obeyed and took the city. You have been called to go to the beach with your friends tomorrow. It is where you belong. I belong here."

"So God says you belong here, in a boring meeting, and I belong with my friends at the beach." Alex yawned and threw the other sock. He missed the basket again.

His head hit his pillow, he pulled his covers over him, and his eyes closed.

"Sucks to be you."

13

Saturday

The digital alarm clock on Alex's nightstand read 2:45 a.m. Alex tossed in fitful jerks on his bed.
Sariel stood over the boy.
The angel worshipped and prayed.

*

Alex dreamed he was at school. Everything seemed so real, so normal.

Katie approached, looking incredible—not the girl dolled up for the Homecoming Dance, but the Katie he'd fallen for. Her straight auburn hair fell in feathered layers down her back, and her startling blue eyes shone with vibrant life and innocent curiosity.

And now those amazing eyes were completely focused on him, as if he were the most important thing in her world.

She reached him and placed her hands on his shoulders. She pursed her luscious lips, her eyes slowly closed, and she pulled Alex close. Alex enjoyed the warmth and softness of her lips against his. He kissed her hard and wrapped his arms around her. It was incredible. That is, except...well, something was not quite right. He struggled to ignore the distracting thoughts nagging at his consciousness and to simply enjoy this moment.

It wasn't too hard.

When the passionate kiss ended, Katie nestled her head on his shoulder.

He held onto her like he would never let her go.

That's when he noticed they weren't alone. Someone stood nearby, facing away from him.

The person slowly turned. As his face came into the light, Alex realized who this guy was.

It was him—the fleshly version of him—that Anti-Alex he had defeated in his first training session.

Suddenly, thunder shook the world and Alex watched a jagged bolt of black lightning streak the sky. It hit the ground next to Anti-Alex. When the smoke cleared, a demon with the face, wings, and claws of a dragon and the body and legs of a man appeared.

The fierce creature howled and bounded toward Alex.

Alex tried desperately to move, but was paralyzed. He tried to call out to Katie to get behind him, but couldn't open his mouth. Impotently, he watched in horror as the dragon grabbed Katie in its talons. Cowering in his claws, her eyes wide in terror, she screamed to Alex to save her. Horrified, all he could do was watch.

The demon laughed and sank his razor-sharp claws deep into the girl's shoulder. Blood spurted from the fresh, open wound. In her agony, she called, "Alex, please! Please do something!"

The scene changed. They were no longer at the school but in a dark dingy room. In the center a red pentagram had been painted on the floor. It shone with red and orange light.

Alex's body was freed from the gripping paralysis. As his sword appeared in his hand, he lunged at the dragon demon.

Anti-Alex yanked Alex's arm back and laughed sardonically, saying, "Not so fast, brother."

The evil twin reached out and knocked the sword from Alex's hand. It hit the floor and vanished. Anti-Alex wrapped his arms around him and held him fast.

*

Sariel, dressed in his white suit, stood over Alex's bed, closely monitoring the sleeping boy.

Alex's breathing had become more labored, his pulse rate elevated. He was in some kind of distress.

The angel's jacket pocket vibrated slowly. He reached in and pulled out the stone heart he'd acquired from Anti-Alex. It pulsed as red as it had when he first retrieved it.

Sariel quickly put the stone back in his pocket, placed his hand on Alex's shoulder, and prayed over him.

*

Alex tried to pull away from the laughing Anti-Alex. A bright bolt of white lightening pierced the ceiling and hit the floor. When the smoke cleared, Sariel stood nearby.

"Alex, you must resist him," his mentor called out to him. "Remember all you have learned and worked so hard to attain."

Anti-Alex yelled at Sariel in Alex's own voice. "Shut up, you idiot! You're nothing but a fake!" To Alex the clone whispered, "Brother, you and I are meant to be together. We are two halves of one! You know this is true. You agonize over your incompleteness. I am the piece you are missing. You need me. I can make you strong." His replica reached out an enticing hand to him.

Alex shook his head resolutely. "You're wrong! You may have been a part of me before, but now, I don't want anything to do with you." Alex swatted his twin's hand away, and his sword materialized. He held it out threateningly. "Now, back off!"

With that, Anti-Alex, Sariel, and the dragon demon all faded and were gone.

The pentagram grew dull and vanished.

All that remained was Katie. "Alex," she cried, running to him, her arms open wide. They were about to embrace…

He woke up.

"Ah! What was that?" he moaned in a groggy voice.

Sariel leaned over him. "You were having a nightmare. I was able to calm you by laying my hands over you and praying."

Alex rubbed his eyes. "That was too weird. It felt so real. I thought I was actually there, and that *she* was actually there."

"Who did you see?"

"I saw Katie and that anti-me thing. He was trying to bond with me or something. Then you came and told me to fight him off."

"As I warned you during your training, Anti-Alex will reassert himself. For some, this happens after days or weeks. For others, just hours. Hmm…Did you see anything else?"

"There was this huge Dragon Demon I've never seen before. Oh yeah, and there was this pentagram. The dragon captured Katie in his claws and," Alex took a deep breath, "he bit her. It was awful."

"Did the dragon have spikes running from his head to the end of his tail?"

Alex nodded. "Yeah. How'd you know?"

"The demon you described sounds like the Demon Lord of this continent."

"Demon Lord? There's a Demon Lord?"

"There are seven to be precise, one for each continent." The angel sat on Alex's desk chair. "What else do you remember?"

"Not much, really. He appeared in a black flash and bit Katie." Sariel looked concerned. "So, why was he in my dream?"

"God often speaks in dreams. The meaning will be revealed in due time. Try to sleep. I will keep watch over you and pray."

Alex yawned. "Thanks, Sariel. I want to be awake at the beach tomorrow."

Sariel sighed and nodded in agreement.

*

We'll return to our investigation of child molesters living in your neighborhood, but first, here's Kelsie Holmes with your weekend weather. A chipper female voice sang out of the radio app. *This is a perfect day for all you beachgoers. The sun is already burning off the morning marine layer, and the surf is high.*

Alex lay on his bed, sprawled out like a dead man.

The cell phone on his nightstand played a booming string of electric guitar licks and drum beats that roused Alex into a sitting position. He pushed the hair out of his eyes, grabbed the phone, swiped the lock with his thumb, and punched the send key before he brought the receiver to his ear.

"Hey, Rip Van Winkle—you awake?" Conor shouted.

"Am now. What's up?" Alex answered with a groggy voice.

"Look at a clock, moron. I'll be there in about fifteen minutes. Be ready!"

"Okay, okay. See you when you get here." He hung up.

Alex gave his room a once over. "Sariel, you there?" He stood.

Where could he be?

Then he remembered Sariel had a meeting.

He grabbed his swim suit, T-shirt, and flip-flops and raced to the bathroom for a quick shower.

*

Mihr's eyes lit up with a blazing internal fire. "Praise be to the Creator of all, who has brought you to my home."

Sariel agreed, though not as exuberantly. "Yes, praise be His name."

Mihr turned away, avoiding Sariel's stare. "You have come to request more angelic warriors."

"I had planned on building my case for this first, but yes, we need more help. I fear things are," his head bowed, "far more difficult than we ever imagined."

Mihr turned back and met Sariel's eyes. "What has brought you to this conclusion?"

Sariel put out his hands plaintively. "The demonic warriors—there are so many."

"Go on."

"Overall we outnumber the creatures two to one. And they have been significantly diminished through displacement. Yet their forces in Willowbrook continue to increase at an alarming rate. And, last night, Alex had a disturbing dream." Sariel paced. "It involved his anti-form attempting to gain control over him. He also saw someone. I believe it was the North American Demon Lord."

Mihr pondered this. "Hmm, Prophetic? You believe your athleta may be seeing into the future?" The angelic commander's voice was strained.

"It is possible. Once he came into contact with Anti-Alex in the dream," Sariel took a heavy artifact out of a compartment in his white armor, "its stone heart glowed, as if reacting to Alex's thoughts. I am afraid his anti-self still has much control over the boy."

"You must take great care to keep the heart out of the hands of the enemy. With the potential power this boy possesses, there is no telling what they could do with his anti-self."

"Do you have a safe place in mind?"

"Storing it in heaven is impossible. It is tainted. At this time, the safest place is in your care."

"I understand." Sariel tucked the heart back beneath his armor.

Mihr came close and looked deeply into his friend's eyes. "Tell me, Sariel, what would you wish?"

"I request the opportunity to plead our case before the Angelic Council. I must help them understand our plight. I am hopeful they will reconsider and authorize reinforcements."

"They will not change their minds. The Holy One will have to change His orders first."

"Moses got Him to change His mind about Sodom," Sariel reminded him.

Mihr laughed out loud. "You and I both know that's because it was what the Lord had planned all along."

"So true," Sariel agreed. "I just hope He has also planned all along to send reinforcements."

*

Alex thought the whole town was at the beach. Parking lots were full. Conor finally came across a spot about a mile away from the beach, curbside. He was thrilled he didn't have to pay for parking.

Conor jumped out of the car and look around. When he caught his image in his car's side mirror, he smiled at his reflection. "Sick!"

Alex toted his beach bag with all their beach stuff. His mom had packed them a healthy lunch so they wouldn't starve. How would he break it to Conor?

With his flip-flops dragging, Alex plodded along. He'd been out of it all morning. Stupid dream!

Conor claimed a spot on the hot sand among all the blankets, towels, and lounge chairs. The boys spread out their big towels and plopped down.

Alex stared down, looking as if Christmas had been cancelled that year.

Conor snapped his fingers in front of his friend's face. "Hey, Mr. Gloomy. What's with the long face? We're here to have a good time."

Alex felt bad for spoiling the morning. "Sorry, man. I had a really weird dream last night and I can't shake it."

"Probably ate a bad hot dog at the game last night. Where do they get those things anyway—the pound? Hey, speaking of food, let's get some. This bad boy's starving!" Conor jumped up and looked at the vendors. "Let's see, they've got pizza, burgers, hotdogs, pretzels, Asian food, gyros, Mexican. Oh yeah! I'll take one of each!"

"My mom packed us a lunch," Alex said, sheepishly. He opened his bag and showed Conor the food sealed carefully in individual plastic tubs.

"Yeah, that was nice and all, but I'm not really in the mood for anything...healthy. No cardboard sandwiches for me. This is the beach, and I declare this a junk food day. Say, I got it, you eat...um...that and I'll have the good stuff."

When Alex didn't respond, Conor looked back at him. "What now?"

Conor joined his gaze.

Katie emerged from the surf. She looked perfect in her black two-piece with white trim.

"Uh-oh," Conor gulped.

Alex's whole body tensed. "What's *she* doing here?"

Conor tried to recover, saying, "Yeah, what a crazy coincidence. I...um...can't believe she's here."

"You were never a good liar. You planned this, didn't you?"

"No, really, I didn't. She did." He pointed at Katie, who approached.

"Hey guys! I'm so glad you could make it!" Katie said, waving with genuine excitement. She hugged Conor and looked at Alex but kept her distance. "Uh, I'm sure you guys know Brandon."

Brandon came up soaking wet in his baggy swimsuit and put his arm around her waist.

Alex's whole body clenched.

"Of course we know him," Conor spoke up. "Who wouldn't know Kingman High's own Brandon Richardson? That was some game last night!"

"Who invited these dorks?" Brandon mocked and pulled Katie away.

"Brandon, be nice," Katie scolded.

"Sorry babe, I guess I'm still pumped from the game last night. It *was* awesome! Well, *I* was awesome!" Brandon laughed heartily.

Alex looked at Brandon to see if he was oppressed by a particularly monstrous demon, but nothing was there. He decided the football player was just a jerk by nature.

Brandon and Katie turned and walked away.

"Well, we'll catch up with you guys later," Conor called after them. "We're going in for some empty calories. See ya."

They didn't turn around.

Alex and Conor trudged through the sand toward the food. There was no way Alex was going to eat a sack lunch now.

They got to the end of the line in front of the burger place. After a few seconds, Alex sighed and said, "I can't believe she's with that . . . that idiot! I've seen fungus smarter than that guy! She's way too good for him."

"I agree completely. But ask yourself, are you angry because she's going out with him, or because she isn't going out with you?"

Alex turned toward him. "What's that supposed to mean?"

"You know. Dude, this whole thing boils down to you being jealous. Why can't you just be happy for her?"

"Because I know *she* isn't happy."

"Are you kidding? She's a walking advertisement for happy."

"Ah, just forget it." Alex turned away.

"How could she not be happy? She's going out with Brandon Richardson, star of the football team! She's at the top of the food chain! Katie girl's fine, my friend. No need to worry about her. No, you're the one I'm worried about."

"I guess…" Alex rubbed his aching head. He sighed. "Maybe I'm just crazy."

"Now, there's a novel idea—you being crazy. Wait, I have the perfect therapy. What you really need is a chimichanga grande."

Alex sighed and threw up his hands. "Yeah, okay."

Maybe a chimichanga would be just the thing right now.

*

The Learjet buzzed faintly as it cut through the atmosphere at 35,000 feet above the Arizona desert. Alistair Cain set his wine glass down and stretched his legs. His lunch—tiny, square, crustless sandwiches—melted in his mouth. Although he hated and despised the vermin humans that infested this planet, he had to admit he did enjoy the lavish perks of his present assignment.

And now he supervised the most important demonic event in four hundred years.

He reveled at his own brilliance and his ability to shape events. No one else had the finessed required to take over Kingman High School.

Cain had long sought to create classrooms that would make children more susceptible to demonic influence. Best to indoctrinate young minds.

By working his contacts in the California legislature and the California Department of Education and greasing the palm of a governor desperately looking for sizable re-election contributions, Cain had pulled off the impossible—taking over Kingman High, a low performing public high school, promising to make it an example for high schools throughout the state. He assured the California State

Superintendent of Public Instruction that, once successful, he would send teams throughout the state to train principals in his proven techniques. To show how serious he was about this enterprise, he promised to personally supervise the transition to excellence in their model school by serving as its principal.

The only catch—he had to begin immediately.

He sipped the last of his wine and took a deeply satisfying breath. Soon he would control millions of young people, making them fit for Hell.

*

Alex watched Katie jump up to reach the volley ball far above her head. The tips of her manicured fingernails scraped the ball, but it went on behind her. Brandon saved the play and set up the front line for an easy spike and point. His teammates clapped and cheered.

The food the boys ended up with—a pepperoni pizza, French fries, and stale corndogs—was tasteless. Alex took his last bite, but couldn't recall having eaten anything at all.

He stared at the thunderous crashing waves.

Conor sat next to him on the recycled-plastic table, his eyes darting here and there, taking in all the activity.

"Come on man, really. Lighten up," Conor pleaded. "I know it's tough to see her with that guy, but at least she's having a good time."

Alex didn't change his gaze. "Conor, if you want to play, go ahead. I really don't mind. I could use the time to think."

Conor jumped up. "Thank You! If you need me, just yell and I'll be right over...um...or at least I'll wave at you, sucker!" Conor bounded from the table and ran out onto the beach, kicking up sprays of sand in his wake.

Alex picked up a soggy fry from Conor's plate. He stirred it around in the pool of catsup and deftly drew a bright red circle on a napkin. He scooped up more catsup. Inside the circle, he scribed five bold lines, creating a catsup star. He stared at the gloppy red pentagram and grew cold inside.

He smeared out the design with the fry and pushed the plate away.

He looked out on the crowd. Where others may have seen families or cute kids digging in the sand with bright plastic tools, Alex only saw couples holding hands or embracing. A young pair ran into the surf, kicked up the foamy brine, and fell into each other's arms.

And, of course, they were all exceedingly out-of-their-mind happy.

Ugh!

Then something else entered his field of vision—a hulky bald-headed guy with a wiry goatee and a thick, tattooed neck. His chest could have been chiseled from stone and his abs looked like they could be climbed like a rock wall.

But this was not what caught Alex's attention. It was the deep darkness that surrounded the guy. Alex, who felt invisible anyway, did a quick shift to the spiritual realm.

In this parallel universe, he saw things that made his shoulders clench.

The bruiser had two creepers attached to him by their sinewy cords. They took turns biting into his head.

Behind them stood a creature Alex had never seen before. This thing was more than twice the size of the brute he shadowed. A thick, second skin of cream-colored armor rippled over his massive muscular physique. Silver shackles hung on his forearms. Large textured pads covered his shoulders. He wore a tight-fitting helmet on his skull-like head. It framed his ghostly eyes with a sharp jagged edge. Bony spikes stuck out of holes in the armor at his shoulders, head, and cheeks.

The massive monster opened his mouth, obviously barking orders at the other two. Alex's blood curdled at the needle-sharp teeth jutting from the creature's enormous maw.

Alex whispered, "Sariel, where are you?"

The young athlete shifted back to the physical realm. Thankfully, no one saw him reappear on the bench.

Alex watched the hulky baboon step on an elaborate sand castle some kids had been working hard on for hours.

"Hey, jerk!" they yelled through their tears. The goon just laughed. He kicked sand onto blankets nearby and shoved anyone aside who happened to be in his way. He was headed toward Katie.

Alex stood and backed himself into a row of mulberry bushes behind his table. He bowed his head and pleaded with the Spirit to shift him to the spiritual realm and to equip him for battle.

Nothing happened.

He tried again.

Still nothing.

He tried a third time and was shocked when he heard the Spirit distinctly say, "No."

"Really?"

The bully closed in on Katie and Brandon. Alex imagined the damage this guy could inflict, especially under demonic influence. He had to do something.

The muscle-bound jerk pulled a huge beach umbrella out of the sand, yanked hard on the top, and threw the entire canvas covering to the ground. He hefted the six-foot pole above his right shoulder like a spear. Testing the weight and balance of the weapon, he zeroed in on his target—Katie.

As the brute leaned into his throw, Brandon inadvertently stepped in front of Katie, right in the line of fire. His eyes widened when he saw the spear aimed at his head.

Alex ran through the sand with all his might, lunged forward, buried his head and folded arms into the brute's mammoth chest.

The bully was knocked off balance. The spear plunged into the sand while the muscular creep slammed into a corpulent woman wearing a fluorescent-yellow, island-print Mumu. The two of them fell down together, the possessed man flailing on top.

The woman screamed and swatted the clumsy oaf. The goon rolled off the woman and laughed out loud. He looked at Alex and snarled, "This is not our day, athleta, but it will come soon." He turned and trudged down the beach, laughing and kicking buckets of sand on everyone.

*

"No way," Brandon muttered.

"What?" Katie watched Alex brush the sand off his board shorts.

"That jerk over there was going to throw a spear at my face."

"What?"

"I saw the whole thing. That jerkwad had a spear. He was getting ready to throw it when that guy rammed into him and knocked him down."

"Alex saved your life?" Katie's eyes went wide.

Brandon scowled and blurted out, "Not likely. I would have caught the spear in mid-air and beat the jerk's butt with it."

Katie leaned into Brandon and hugged him. She teased, "Could my hero please get me a soda with ice?"

Brandon puffed out his chest. "Sure, babe." He strutted toward the refreshment stands.

When Brandon was out of range, Katie ran to catch up with Alex, who walked back toward his table.

*

Katie approached Alex. "Thank you. That was really something," she said above the noise of children playing in the sand and the pounding surf.

Alex stopped and looked into her eyes. "I couldn't just sit there and let that guy…um…anyway, I…" His tongue was tied in knots. He hated this.

She smiled at him. "So, what have you been up to lately? Are you still saving for a car? Is Conor still driving you crazy? I miss hanging out with you guys."

"Nothing really new," he lied. What could he say? *Yeah, I've been enlisted by an angel who's training me to do battle against demons that want to take over the world—or something like that. We're not really sure what they're up to. Anyway, I've been called by God to stop it. That is, on most days we can stop them, just not today. I don't have permission. Oh, and you should see my helmet, shield, and sword—and my fancy footwear. They're way cool. Oh, and I had stop that buffoon because he was controlled by three demons who were trying to kill you.*

No, he decided silence was best.

This was okay. Katie filled all the empty spaces in the conversation. "Look, there's Alice and Doug! Aren't they cute together? I was hoping they'd show up. You know, he's had a crush on her, like, forever." She continued with a story Alex pretended to be interested in.

Brandon caught up with them, standing with a thirty-two ounce soda in each hand, his biceps bulging. "Hey, what's going on here?"

Katie responded in a sickeningly sweet tone, "I was just thanking Alex for helping my hero boyfriend."

Brandon's muscles relaxed. He turned toward Alex. "Yeah, um . . . that was a good tackle, man. Maybe you should . . . um . . . go out for the team." He laughed so hard he choked.

Alex looked away. "Yeah, that's not really my thing, but thanks anyway. Well, I'd better get back to…uh…sitting over there." He pointed back to the tables.

Katie smiled. "Yeah, okay, thanks again." She took her soda and curled her arm in Brandon's.

Alex sighed and strode slowly back to his table.

He had a killer of a headache.

*

Farther down the beach, the giant demon grabbed the backs of the creepers and dug his talons deep into their flesh. The two demons shrieked and writhed in pain.

"Release your hooks," the knight demon commanded.

One-by-one the black coils retracted into the bumpy arms of the two creepers. The demons both fell off the back of their charge. The goon continued down the beach without them, still acting like a jerk.

"Sire, why did we let the human go?" one of the creeper demons huffed.

"I want a closer look at that athleta," the massive creature murmured as he walked back up the beach toward Alex.

"But, what is he to us?" the other creature whimpered, trying to keep up with the giant demon's steps.

"Know you nothing?" the massive knight spat out. "This is the young one who has been sending you weaklings into hell. The master is shifting his forces. He has placed knights, like myself, in this area to take care of this pesky insect."

*

The two angels glided silently through space, their great wings unfurled. In the spiritual realm, they moved at lightning speed.

150

Arriving at Mihr's quarters, they landed, retracted their wings, and moved toward the center of the crystal platform. They were filled with the ecstasy of the Spirit and bowed in worship and thankful prayer. Their voices dropped off, and they simply rested in the sublime quiet of God's presence.

Mihr's calm voice broke the silence. "You must not become discouraged over the Council's rejection."

"It was a fool's errand. You warned me of the likely outcome. I…I just had to try."

"Of course," the supervising angel agreed. "Hopefully your current troop allotment will be satisfactory and you shall prevail. If not, your failure shall serve the greater good. Do you foresee another possibility?"

Sariel stood and faced Mihr. "No, my friend. As usual, you have
summed up the situation perfectly. I just…"

"Your feelings for the boy are as obvious as the wings on your back."

"It is the danger of my calling."

Mihr stared intently into Sariel's eyes. "Be ever on your guard, my friend. Your deep affection for Alex clouds your judgment."

Sariel chuckled. "You and I both know that objectivity is an illusion. We walk in love. Praise God, it is the lens through which all our choices are made."

There was no need for more discussion. Sariel knew that having his request for reinforcements rejected was the best decision possible, he just didn't know why.

He reached out and affectionately squeezed Mihr's forearms. "Thank you for accompanying me and for pleading my case. I am most grateful for your help. No one could have been more convincing. Now, I must leave you and return to Alex."

151

"Of course. Farewell, my friend. I shall always be here for you."

With that, Sariel turned away, unfurled his wings, and lifted off the crystalline surface. Once he was far enough away, he retracted his wings, became a light beam, and hurtled toward earth.

*

The three creatures headed toward the boy.

A deafening sonic boom stopped them in their tracks. For a moment, they stared up at a blinding streak of spiritual energy that hit the upper atmosphere. They quickly ducked behind a lifeguard stand and watched in horror as the beam reached the earth and materialized into a white angel with uplifted wings. Long white feathers laid over each other as the wings retracted and the angel left the spiritual realm. He morphed into a man in the white suit and approached the boy.

*

"Sariel. There you are. What took you?" Alex asked.

"Satan is increasing his forces in this region. I petitioned the angelic courts for reinforcements, to meet the challenge with equal or greater force."

"Speaking of force, check out these guys." Alex leaned his head toward the three distinct dark shapes looming behind the lifeguard stand. Sariel saw them for what they were, two vicious creepers and a far more deadly beast.

"The ominous one behind them is a knight demon," explained Sariel. "He is a highly-trained killing machine, not to be underestimated. It is imperative that you do not let him pierce you with his blade."

"Why? What'll happen?"

"You shall die. Rely on your shield for protection." The words hung in the air.

Alex now understood why he hadn't been allowed to shift into the spiritual realm earlier.

He jerked his head toward Sariel. "Wait. So, you're saying I have to fight *that thing*? Do you at least get to go in with me...to...um...help me?" Alex's throat closed. He had no illusions. The victories he'd had up to this point were more a result of luck than skill.

This could be the day his luck ran out.

Sariel didn't answer. Instead he asked, "What happened while I was away?"

"Those creepers had control of some big jerk. He was terrorizing everyone on the beach. All of a sudden, he grabs the pole off an umbrella and gets ready to hurl it at . . ." And then he understood. "Katie! He wasn't aiming at Brandon." Alex shook his head. "How could I have been so stupid? He was aiming at Katie!"

Sariel's brow furrowed. "Alex, you must focus. Worship. Give yourself over to the Spirit. Submit to the will of God. Trust Him. Lean not on your own understanding. Above all, do not let the forces of evil exploit your weaknesses."

"Easy for you to say." Alex clenched his teeth.

"Not at all. If I could take your place, I would."

"I would let you," Alex replied. "So, what do you think's really going on here?"

Sariel scowled. "I wish I knew. You must not fear the size of this beast. Remember, David faced Goliath. Gideon conquered the Midianites."

"Yeah, with God all things are possible, right?"

Sariel nodded and put his hand on Alex's arm. "It is time. Go with God and you shall prevail, young warrior."

Alex shifted to the spiritual realm, acquired his armor, and walked toward the monsters.

*

The Knight demon stood with the creepers, watching Alex and Sariel. What were they were talking about?

He studied them. He'd never gone into a battle unprepared and thus had never failed.

If Sariel were to enter the fray, he would have to retreat—and fast. There was no contest between the two of them. But if the boy came at him alone, his victory was assured.

He hefted his massive sword before him, leaned forward, and charged the boy.

*

Alex tensed and gripped his shield as he ran past people on the sand. The knight bore down on him, his weapon raised high.

Alex dove to the side and the demon's massive sword slashed past him. He side-rolled and jumped back onto his feet.

He tried to focus on Sariel's training. He remembered discussing the importance of reach—that the warrior with the greatest reach has a distinct advantage. The knight demon's muscle-bound arms were over five feet long! His massive sword was twice the size of Alex's. In fact, if given the chance, Alex was sure he wouldn't even have been able to lift it.

Advantage: ugly demon.

The knight recovered and laughed, "More! More! This is fun!" He twisted his torso and brought his sword in a smooth flowing motion to the left, where Alex stood. Anticipating this move, Alex spring-boarded off a nearby ice chest as the blade passed beneath him. He landed on the left side of the demon, away from his enormous blade. He pulled his shield to the left, raised his sword, and pointed it at a seam in the demon's heavy armor.

Before he could thrust, his adversary shifted his weight and the evil blade swung back at Alex. Their swords clashed, sending sparks in all directions. The force of the contact knocked Alex off his feet and onto his back.

The demon bellowed. "If I had an ounce of sympathy, I would feel sorry for you, my sacrificial lamb. You are probably hoping for a quick end. Unfortunately for you, I take great pleasure in making puny ones suffer. You shall drown in pain and despair and only then shall I let you die."

The bulky demon nodded toward the creepers who fanned out. Alex spring-boarded up to his feet and tried to take a stance that would allow him to defend himself from all sides.

But the creatures moved away from him—one heading straight for Katie, the other for Conor.

The knight howled with laughter. "They have permission to bring pain and suffering on your friends, and I have permission to take your life." With that, he swung the sword back and forth in front of him.

"You lie! I know the stakes. You've been given permission to *try* to kill me." He glanced at the other two demons. "Now, let's keep this between you and me. Leave my friends out of it."

The demon railed, "You are appealing to my honor? Or perhaps my sense of fair play? Look at me, human. I have none of these sensibilities. I want nothing more than to inflict insurmountable pain. You and your friends are today's entertainment."

He swung again.

Alex ducked and slammed his shield forward, hitting the back of the beast's arm. No effect. Alex quickly stepped back.

"Where are you going?" the demon jeered through sharp teeth. "Come and play, little one!"

Alex looked at the giant, trying to find a weakness. Heavy armor encased his body from head to toe. Alex had speed and agility, but this advantage would be useless if his sword did little or no damage. Eventually, the demon would overcome him, and he would be toast.

He swung his sword as quickly as he could, like a propeller, hoping that speed might win out after all. Alex leaped forward. The demonic hulk swung a perfectly timed thrust that crashed into Alex's shield. He was thrown off balance and nearly lost his sword.

The beast raised his blade upward, extending his body for a killing blow.

Alex dove through the demon's muscle-bound legs. He rolled forward on the ground and pushed himself up quickly.

The demon completed his power swing. He laughed again when his blade passed through empty air and hit the sand.

"More!" he thundered.

Alex bit his lip in frustration.

His reach was too short.

His abilities too inconsequential.

He was out of ideas.

He was beaten.

"More!" The beast stepped forward. "You are pathetic! You are no athleta."

Alex glanced quickly behind him to see that the creepers had reached their prey.

Hooks lunged from their arms to Katie and Conor. Then, the frothing one above Katie drew close and bit her in the neck. She winced and pressed her hand against the spot.

People around Katie and Conor walked by and played around as if nothing unusual was happening.

It was all too much.

The Knight laughed and poised to strike.

Alex took his warrior stance, prayed, and did the last thing any practiced swordsman would ever do—he pulled his right arm behind his head, shifted his weight, put all his energy into his arm, and threw his sword with all his might.

The gleaming blade flew straight as an arrow. The beast tried to shift his mass but couldn't get out of the way fast enough. The sword pierced the armor protecting his right arm, just below the shoulder. The blade didn't sever the arm, but it pierced the bone, shattering it.

The creature howled and quickly dropped his own sword to the sand. He yanked at the glowing weapon sticking from his massive bicep. He tugged hard at the hilt and finally yanked out the blade. The tip was coated with thick blue gunk.

The blade disappeared from his hand and appeared in Alex's, clean once again.

The knight snarled at his opponent, "You got lucky today, amateur. Next time we meet, I will be the one cutting you to pieces. This pain is nothing compared to what I'm going to inflict upon you when I return." He ran across the sand, jumped into the air, unfurled his wings, and flew out of sight.

Alex faced the creepers and shouted, "Looks like it's just us, boys. Come and get it."

The creepers immediately retracted their hooks and jumped grasshopper-like on their spindly legs. They followed behind the knight, whimpering pathetically.

"Yeah, and don't come back!" Alex yelled after them.

His armor and weapons disappeared.

He walked closer to Katie, knowing he was invisible to her. She and Brandon were seeing who could eat their shaved ice faster, in spite of the accompanying brain freezes.

She was laughing, her eyes bright.

She *was* having a great time.

He looked at the happy couple and sighed.

His deep feelings for Katie were putting her in danger.

He had to get over her, for her sake.

He would try to let her go.

He would try.

*

Alex appeared next to Sariel.

The young man poked him. "Nice beachwear, by the way."

Sariel glared at Alex. "My first inclination is to knock some sense into you. What were you thinking?"

Alex's face fell. What had he done? "I'm sorry, Sariel. I let him get to me. I attacked in anger. Truth is, he pushed me into a blind rage. I lost control."

"No, that is not what I mean. Not all anger is evil. Fury aimed in the right direction can be useful. God has said, 'Be angry, but do not sin.'"

"Let me get this straight. It's okay that I attacked in anger? I mean, it doesn't sound very Christian."

"The Almighty often acts out of anger." The angel furrowed his brow. "I am talking about throwing your sword. *Never* do that again. It could leave you utterly defenseless."

"I'm sorry. I was desperate. It'll never happen again."

"It had better not."

Alex bowed his head and wished *he* could disappear.

*

In just two days, Alistair Cain's minions had secured him a beautiful two-story house in the Willowbrook suburbs. The mansion was stocked, its cupboards full. His personal effects had all been put in place. The utilities were turned on, and he had full television and WIFI. Dynamic hand-motion-activated computer pads hung everywhere.

When the limousine dropped him off, his personal assistant met him at the front door and handed him the keys. The assistant gave him a tour of the house and showed him all the nuances that gave the place "personality."

Later, in his demonic form, Cain let his muscles relax in the Jacuzzi-sized bathtub. It had already been drawn according to his liking—with scalding hot water and the faint smell of sulfur. He closed his eyes and tried to become one with the scorching fluid. And yet, his anger seethed. His talons scratched deep lines in the marble tub. Why hadn't this athleta been destroyed?

He had to keep this boy from ruining everything.

Three creatures materialized in his bathroom. The biggest—a towering knight demon whose head almost touched the vaulted ceiling—was wounded and bleeding. Oily blue gunk dripped onto the white tile floor.

A fourth demon, a messenger, appeared next to Cain. He was small with extremely large wings.

Alistair Cain leaned over to the messenger. "Summon a repair demon. Be quick about it!" The last part had an implied, "or else..."

The little creature flew toward the ceiling and vanished.

The hulking monster swayed, and his eyes rolled up in his head. Alistair braced himself as the Knight lost his legs and fell backward. He crashed into the wall, busting out tiles and knocking a chunk out of the marble sink. He hit the floor with a thunderous thud. The creature's eyelids drooped, and he lost consciousness.

"What is this? Explain yourselves." Alistair yelled at the two cowering creepers.

"He...he lost. The athleta..." The creeper's tongue froze when he saw Cain's reaction to the word.

"Curse that athleta! What will it take to destroy this gadfly?" Alistair snarled.

Bowing their heads and closing their eyes, the creepers awaited destruction—but it never came. Slowly, one ventured to open an eye and look at Cain.

"There were some developments, my lord." The creeper kept his head bowed. "Heroes are destroyed by their friends," he recited the Satanic adage. "This athleta has two close friends, along with Sariel, his supervising angel. He is quite dependent on the angel and must still be in the early stages of his training."

"Anything else?" The Executive Demon's anger was assuaged somewhat. This intelligence might prove valuable. While the creeper searched his memory for more details, the messenger demon returned, a repair demon in tow.

The repair demon moved close to the knight and sunk his pointy teeth into his muscular neck. Cain knew this was to tranquilize the massive brute and keep him unconscious. More than a few repair demons had lost their physical existence working on knights before putting them to sleep.

When the repair demon was sure it was safe, he started removing the layers of heavy armor.

"Anything else?" Cain continued the interrogation.

The creeper pulled his attention away from the repair. "There was something I noticed during the fight. Something about his armor. Oh yes, I got it. I have only seen an athleta once before. I can remember the key pieces of the armor—pieces this boy wasn't wearing."

"Which pieces exactly?" the Executive Demon pressed.

"It was—I believe, but I could be wrong—the breastplate and the belt. Yes, these were missing."

"Vulnerability." Alistair grinned.

*

Alex rode shotgun in Conor's old filthy Jeep. Conor had explained more than a dozen times how he got the car. His Uncle Tony'd bought it new and put almost a hundred thousand miles on it. The red "tank" was passed down to his Uncle Richard, who drove it

160

for only a year. Richard sold it to his brother David, Conor's dad, who turned around and gave it to Conor.

Because it was a gift and not the result of any planning, saving, or hard work on Conor's part, he'd trashed it. A heavy layer of dirt and grime coated everything. Alex wondered how Conor could see out his windshield.

Nor could Conor see that Sariel sat amid the backseat trash.

"Man that was cool! What a great day!" Conor announced for the hundredth time.

Alex was silent.

Conor glared at him. "What is it with you? Why can't you just let her go?"

"Actually, I did, at the beach. I realized it's ridiculous to hang onto something that never was. She's too good for him, but, well," he shrugged, "it's her life. She'll have to live with her choices."

Conor snickered. "Listen to you, so mature and grown up."

"You're such an idiot."

"Thanks, Dad." Connor laughed. "So, you hungry? I'm hungry. There's a burger place up ahead. You got any money?"

"Sure. I brought gas money, remember?" He handed Conor a ten dollar bill.

"Well, now it's burger money."

They pulled into the drive-thru. While Conor studied the confusing menu, Alex looked across the street. His skin crawled.

There was a simple box-like building with flashing Christmas lights strung around the top of the roof. They lit up a poorly painted sign that read "Center for Bodily Revival." The front door was painted dark purple. The shadows crawling over the place grabbed his attention.

He reached for the door handle. "Order me a plain burger with nothing on it and a soda. I...I gotta stretch my legs." He popped the door open and closed it before Conor could react. He took a few steps away from the car and peered across the street, toward the building.

Sariel appeared next to him.

"Whaddaya see over there?" Alex asked under his breath.

"I see a horde. There are a dozen smaller demons, about twice as many creepers, and three massive knight demons on the roof."

"Why, I wonder? You know, I've heard about this place in church. It's a cult. No wonder it's crawling with demons."

The angel shook his head. "Few false roads need much help from the evil ones. They are maintained by two things: man's insatiable need to be reunited with the true God and his stubborn unwillingness to walk on the only road that will get him there."

Alex digested this. "So what is *this*?"

Conor called over, "Hey, earth to Alex. I'm done ordering and I'm moving up to pay. If you're not in this car on time, I'm leaving you here and eating your burger."

Alex waved him off.

The angel answered. "This is important. Over the last four centuries, the number of demons on earth has been reduced significantly. For them to station so many in one place, this must be a vital stronghold for the enemy."

Alex searched the Spirit inside him for permission to do something. The answer was a resounding, "No!"

Conor honked his horn. Alex turned and ran. He jumped back in the jeep while it pulled away.

Sariel appeared again in the back seat. "This could be the reason you were called—to stop whatever is going on at that place."

Alex turned back to the angel.

"Turn around and face forward," Sariel commanded.

Alex scooped up his hamburger and put it to his mouth.

Conor chattered about the day like he was the host of an entertainment show reporting on the Oscars. He critiqued everything from the food to the swim suits.

Alex nodded and grunted at appropriate moments and kept his hamburger to his mouth.

"Meanwhile," Sariel continued, "we have to be careful. They may also be guarding someone here. I will dispatch an angel to watch over this place. In time, we will know the truth."

With his mouth full, Alex blurted out, "I just feel like we're running out of time."

Conor replied, "I know, man. Look at us, we're juniors! One more year and we're out of this place! My mom keeps pushing college. Guess I have a year to sell her on my whole bumming through Europe plan." His soda gurgled as he sucked out the last of the fluid. "Everything comes to an end," he proclaimed, tossing the cup into the back seat and onto Sariel's lap. The angel gave it a shove, and it joined the other trash that littered the floor.

"Ha! Now, you're a philosopher?" Alex quipped and took another bite of his burger.

Conor stopped at a red light. The front of the Jeep protruded over the line and into the intersection.

"Philosophy…" he mused. "If my mom wins and I end up in college, I'm so making philosophy my major!"

The light turned green, the Jeep's wheels spun loudly, and the car raced off into the night. Conor yelled out the window, "I think, therefore I am—I think!"

14

Sunday

Alex sat next to his mom in church. She hung onto every word and dutifully filled in the lines of her notes. He balled his fists. It was all he could do to keep still.

For the last half hour, the minister had been teaching a message called "Christianity Anybody Can Do." It was delivered in a friendly, sitting-in-your-living-room style that made the audience comfortable. The presentation—a heavily bulleted slide show—featured slick graphics and short video clips of people walking in the park, giving each other hugs, or kissing cuddly puppies.

For the first time in his life, Alex really scrutinized what the preacher said—and, more importantly, what he wasn't saying.

The preacher walked to the front of the stage. "The world is good and, when we think positive thoughts, we drive evil from our lives."

Alex scanned the theater seats. A woman sat in the back, withered and hunched over, her face the picture of pain. Alex winced when he saw the deep shadows hovering over her.

The preacher continued, "The power is within all of us. Just claim it!"

Shaking his head, Alex looked down the aisle he sat in. A young man nearby looked like he was going to hurl. More shadows undulated above him. Alex imagined creepers with their vile hooks.

Demons in the church?

Alex wanted to shift—to attack—to free these poor people. The Spirit within him said, "No!"

With tears in his eyes, the athleta decided he would do more than nod affably at the pastor when he greeted him at the back door on the way out.

*

Alex saw Pastor Spangler, stuffed inside his tight-fitting out-of-style chestnut-colored tweed sports coat, forcing a plastic smile at the church's back door. The last few parishioners shook his hand and told him, "That was inspiring, Pastor," and "What an excellent message."

Alex had stalled so he and his mom could be at the end of the line. He clenched his fists in anger.

The pastor shoved his meaty hand toward Alex but spoke to his mother. "Virginia, who is this strapping young man with you?"

Alex took a deep breath. "Pastor Spangler, can I ask you something . . . about your . . . um . . . message?"

"Sure." He turned toward Alex, giving him his undivided attention.

Alex's mom stepped back, her eyebrows raised.

Alex bit his lip and tried to hide his distaste for the man. "What is the purpose of your preaching?"

165

The pastor's smile remained pasted on. "There are many things that can happen in a sermon. I try to meet the people where they live. You know, help them sort out their problems, learn new ways to live their lives productively, and to let seekers know—"

"What about the demons? Man, open your eyes! Couldn't you see that people brought powerful demons with them into your service this morning? They were here for help, and you didn't help them."

The pastor forced a chuckle and patted Alex's shoulder. "Now, son, you might want to cut back on those video games."

Alex's mom frowned and apologetically nodded agreement.

Agitated, Alex paced as he ranted. "Wow, so now *I'm* the one with a problem? Look, there's something going on here in Willowbrook. Demons, huge ones, important ones, are being sent here. We have to fight them!"

His mom grabbed his arm. "Alex, come on. It's time to go."

Alex shook his head and pulled his arm from his mother's grasp. "Mom, please, this is important."

"Alex, we're leaving now."

"I gotta go, son," the pastor added. "It's been great talking to you."

Alex's mom pulled his arm again. He stumbled forward. As they passed the minister, she hurriedly nodded and thanked him.

When they got to the door, Alex turned back and shouted, "The forces of Satan aren't afraid of you! That's . . . that's the whole problem! You do *this* week after week while evil grows steadily all around you. In their eyes, you're a joke!"

He shook his head and stomped off, slamming the church door behind him.

*

"That was patently unpleasant," Alex's mom groaned. She hit the gas, and the car squealed out of the parking lot. "What *was* that? What's gotten into you?"

Alex stared out his window.

"Don't even think about giving me the silent treatment, Alexander. I don't deserve it." Her steel-blue eyes narrowed.

She was right. He cleared his throat and glanced back at her. "I just…um…I mean, it's complicated."

There was a pause. His mom finally said, "Alex, normally I wouldn't even ask you, especially after all the talks we've had. But this stuff about demons…" She took a deep breath. "Ok, here it is. Are you on drugs?"

"What?" Alex's eyes popped and his hands flew forward plaintively. "What?"

"You sound like you've had a bad trip or something."

"No Mom, I don't do drugs. Never have."

"Honest?"

"Honest."

"Then, what *is* it?"

"Demons, Mom. Okay? This place is crawling with them." He sighed deeply and slumped.

His mom glanced at him with concern. Awkward minutes passed.

She cleared her throat. "So, don't you think it's time we, you know, talked?"

Alex knew where this was going. It was the taboo subject, the one thing they'd never discussed. There were times he wanted to talk about it, but she wasn't ready. When she wanted to talk about it, he could never get past his anger. But now he was up to anything as long as it changed the subject. And who knows? Maybe finding out what happened would strengthen him.

He took a deep breath. "Yeah, I think I'm up for it."

His mom cleared her throat. "Okay, let me start at the beginning. When I was getting ready to graduate nursing college, having recovered from a messy divorce, I went with a handful of friends to Florida for spring break. While I was there, I met someone. He was very handsome and knew far more about life than I did. We had an instant connection—a love-at-first-sight sort of thing. I was deeply attracted to him."

"Okay, okay. TMI. Please, spare me the details!"

She smiled and shook her head. "*Anyway*, I ditched my friends and had dinner with this amazing man. He was so tall and rugged. His voice…his voice was strong and made me feel like there was good in the world."

Her smile faded. She looked down. "We ended up in his hotel room. I wanted to be with him more than anything. I didn't care if it was wrong or stupid. I was so lonely. And it felt good to be wanted."

The car continued for a few blocks, neither of them saying anything.

"When I got up the next morning, he was gone. I remembered that he'd said he'd only be in town that one night. I looked for a note or something, but there wasn't one. For days I went back to the restaurant where we met."

"Let me guess. No luck."

"No. Later I found out I was pregnant."

Alex's eyes hardened.

"My dad blew a cork. He never stopped yelling. Couldn't accept the idea that I wanted to raise you by myself."

"Must have been awful for you."

"It was tough. Your grandma helped. She told my dad that he would be kicked out before I would. I left you with her a lot while I finished school."

"Is that what wrecked your relationship with her?"

"Your granddad called her bluff. He left us, and she found she couldn't live without him. She couldn't find work. I decided it was time for us to go."

"That's how we got to California?"

"It's the farthest I could go. So, anyway, I started a new life for us. I wasn't interested in getting married or anything like that. You were the only man I needed in my life. Actually, men were scared off as soon as they found out that this was a package deal."

"So, you...*him*...one time?"

"Yeah. I sound like the perfect spokesperson for safe sex, huh?"

"Again, TMI."

"The weird thing is I never stopped loving him. Never had anything but positive feelings and, Alex, I wish you would feel the same."

They drove along for a while.

Did she realize what she was asking? Did she know how he felt? Did she understand that he'd harbored feelings of hate and resentment toward this man his whole life?

"Mom...um...I don't know." His mom had leveled with him. Now it was his turn. "There's more to it than that. You're a great mom—the best. But, I...I needed a father. This guy may be something great in your eyes, but to me, he's just a jerk that got what he wanted and then," Alex turned away, "he left."

"Alex, I can see how you could look at it that way, but you're not being fair. He doesn't even know you exist. If anyone did wrong, it was me. After I found out I was pregnant, I stopped looking for him. You see, truth is, I kept you from him. I'm sure he would have been proud to have you for a son."

Alex swallowed hard. "I guess in these situations, there really isn't a roadmap. I guess you do what you think is best. You try to pick up the pieces and make your life work. You did that, and...I do...I mean...I love you for it." He quickly looked away.

169

"My, my. You really have grown up." She smiled. "You okay?"

Alex took a deep breath. "Yeah. Thanks for ... you know."

They drove for few minutes in heavy silence. When they pulled up to the house, Alex's mom pushed a button and raised the garage door. She turned to Alex. "So, think you're ready for driving lessons this summer?"

"Absolutely." He grinned.

"And, do me a favor, okay?"

"Anything."

"Let up on the pastor. He's just doing his job."

Alex could not have disagreed with her more.

As if reading his mind, she added, "For me?"

"Okay," he agreed. "For you."

*

Hovering high above the empty high school, the angel, Melioth, batted his majestic wings. This heavenly warrior had challenged and chased off a dozen demons since sunrise.

He waited somberly for the pudgy cherub to reach him. There was news, and lately the news was not good.

This cherub had the shape of a child and small wings that flapped like a hummingbird's. His words, however, displayed his age-earned wisdom. "Glory be to the One who reigns in the heavens! Melioth, you have been called back to the heavenly courts. Once there, you will receive a new assignment."

With that, the butterball turned and sped off, his little feet kicking the air behind him.

Without question or debate, Melioth turned upward and propelled himself toward heaven. Other angels joined him, streaking from the area in mass, leaving Willowbrook to the demons.

This made no sense to Melioth, but he continued on his course undeterred.

*

The sound of a faint buzzer echoed off the walls.

"Brandon, customer!" a hoarse voice shouted.

Brandon rolled from underneath a lifted Chevy 4x4 on his heavy plastic mechanic's creeper board. He sat up, pushed himself to his feet, and grabbed a dirty rag to wipe the grease off his powerful hands.

"Got it," he called back to his uncle, who was pulling the head off an old Ford truck engine, exposing the oily pistons inside.

Brandon backed into the dirty windowed door that separated the shop from the small reception area. Turning around, he found himself eye-to-eye with Cindi Langster.

Cindi was a cheerleader, new to the squad this year. Brandon had been watching her at games. Short and petite, she had the face of a supermodel and a body to match. Strawberry blonde hair flowed over her shoulders. What had gotten Cindi on the elite squad was her tremendous energy. In fact, in every possible way, she was known to be intense—a real handful.

She folded her arms across her chest and smiled at Brandon. "So, if it isn't Kingman High's own Brandon Richardson. I didn't know you worked here."

Brandon smiled his winning smile. "I come down here on weekends. You know, to help my uncle. He's getting on and can't keep up with everything. And it gives me some extra spending money."

"Hmmm, I see. Do you guys fix brakes? Mine are squeaking something terrible."

"Sure." Brandon leaned his elbows on the counter, flipped the pages on a thick invoice book, and started writing Cindi's name.

"So, what's this between you and Katie Brinton? Not serious, I hope."

Brandon looked up at Cindi. Her blue eyes bored through him. She wanted him. She brought her dainty hand to her cheek and tilted her head.

Brandon leaned closer and smirked. "We're not engaged or anything. She doesn't own me."

"I have to admit, I was a little surprised to see you two together. I mean, not to be mean or anything, but isn't she kinda…I don't know…boring? I would have thought you would want someone more…oh…exciting in your life."

Brandon laughed. He loved where this was going. He turned to the side and tightened his bicep. "You know how it is. Katie's someone to hang out with. Kinda like a pair of comfortable shoes, that's all." He leaned closer to her. "But I got lots of shoes."

15

Monday

Antsy all day, Alex didn't even remember riding his bike to school. He couldn't listen in his classes and forgot there was a quiz in Algebra 2. He'd apparently left his quadratic abilities at home. He didn't even flinch when he walked past Katie and Brandon making out in the hall.

He sat in his last period class—history—doodling the picture Sariel had painted in his mind Saturday night when he described what he saw at the Center. He sketched a rectangular prism, added doors, Christmas lights around the perimeter, the sign, and a parking lot.

Alex could hear Mr. Addison's droning voice but paid no attention to his words.

He drew creeper demons in front of the building, starting with their powerful legs and feet ending in two toes with razor-sharp claws. Their torsos he sketched short and hunched over. He added arms, and, lastly, he drew their impish heads with two gnarly horns on top. He scribbled in their eyes—black as death. He made their spiky teeth run the length of the lower part of their jaws.

Around these creatures, he drew assorted smaller demons—miniature versions of the creepers, but without the hooks.

Then he drew three large knights on the rooftop. They were bulkier than body-builders and encased in strong armor. His pencil moved fast, creating the skull-like heads and bony horns. He slowed down when he got to the swords in their claws. The shiny hilts had curved spikes like a bat's wings. The blades were wide and jagged—far too big and heavy to have been wielded by a human.

While Alex drew, oblivious to the world, Kevin Kiser, a nerdy boy who sat in the desk next to his, watched in amazement.

"Man, Alex, you're really good," Kevin whispered. He brushed his greasy hair out of his eyes with both hands, like a hamster grooming himself.

"Thanks," Alex whispered under his breath.

"I know that place." Kevin leaned in closer.

"What?" Alex kept sketching.

"The building in your drawing. It's the Center for Bodily Revival. I see that place on television every week. It must be amazing."

Alex stared at the knight demons on the paper and shook his head.

*

That evening, Alex chained up his bike at the supermarket, half a block from the Center.

He noticed that his bike looked a little small for him. Maybe he would start the new school year driving.

That is, if he lived that long.

Sariel materialized next to him, wearing his usual suit. He looked like he wanted to hit someone.

"There you are. What's wrong?" Alex asked. He followed the angel's eyes and spied the shadows crawling all over the Center. "Don't tell me, we don't have permission to go in there."

"Not exactly. I am not to enter the Center with you. You are to go in—alone."

"Against three of those big ugly guys? You kidding me?"

"You are right, of course. You must not go in there. It would be suicide." The angel placed his hand on Alex's shoulder.

An upwelling of joy and confidence infused Alex. In the midst of it, he heard a distinct message. *Be strong and courageous. I am with you!*

At first he thought it was his imagination. Then he closed his eyes and listened with his heart. The voice grew stronger. He turned to the angel. "No. I have to go in. I . . . um . . . don't know why. I don't know what's gonna happen in there, but this is what God wants me to do."

With that, he shifted to the spiritual realm. Instantly his helmet, shoes, shin plates, shield, and sword were in place. He leaned forward and moved with purpose toward the building. Demons jumped up and down and shouted curses at him. Taunting creepers shot out their hooks, retracted them again, and howled in raging laughter. The knights glared at him from the roof. They looked as tall as trees waving their giant swords in the air.

Alex gulped, took his warrior stance, tightened his muscles, and waited for the attack. None came. They just continued their taunting.

After a tense minute, the double front doors opened. The Center's administrator—a small, crumpled figure in a bright-red kimono—emerged. He spoke to Alex with a thick Asian accent. "Welcome, young warrior. You have been summoned. Follow me."

Alex moved closer, his sword at the ready. When the Director turned, Alex saw a creeper latched onto his back with his claws buried deep in his shoulders. He almost barfed when he realized the demon had his head pushed into the Director's, using the man like a ventriloquist's dummy. It was the creeper who spoke.

"This is the Center of Bodily Revival." The small man announced. "We take your damaged life and help you learn how to make it whole once more."

Alex walked past him and through the doors, keeping a wary eye on the demon.

The front doors slammed shut.

The demons jumped into the building through the walls and roof.

Sariel bit his tongue in frustration.

Alex's sword lit up the atrium. A dozen minor demons raced toward him. He lifted his green kite-shaped shield just in time for two of the horrid things to hit it. They disintegrated with high-pitched squeals. Alex lowered the shield and swung his sword, catching two creepers and another small demon by surprise. They puffed out of existence.

Alex ran down a hall to his right, mowing down creatures stupid enough to get in his way.

Then, without warning, something grabbed his arm and roughly pulled him into a side room. He choked on incense and smoke. High-pitched twangs of Indian music assaulted his ears. Murals depicting an assortment of various Hindu gods and demons covered the walls. Colored lights swirled around the room.

Alex hung in mid-air, his arms pinned above his head, his sword useless.

The knight demon that held him spoke to another nearby. "Now, cut him."

The other knight pulled back his sword like a ball player getting ready to hit a home run.

As the sword came forward, Alex swung his lower body above the knight's arm and out of the way. The shimmering blade— colored by the swirling psychedelic lights and bubbling lava lamps—

swung straight and true. With a sickening crunch, it plunged deep into the other knight demon's armored torso. His face screwed up, and he screamed in pain. Dark fluid spilled from his waist.

Alex was released. He scrambled to his feet and sprang toward the other knight, his sword before him. The blade found a chink in the armor near the waist. It slid through and into the beast's leathery flesh.

The creature shrieked and backed away in horror and pain. Like two massive demon-shaped balloons, the knights popped and disappeared. Alex's blade hung in the air, fell to the floor, disappeared, and reappeared in his hand.

"Excellent." Alex approached the doorway. He peered both ways down the hall. No one in sight. He moved from wall to wall, looking all around him. When he was almost to the atrium, he heard someone clear his throat behind him. He spun around to find the Asian man staring up at him. The demon that had possessed him was gone.

"You *must* come this way," the man pleaded.

The man shuffled down the hall. Alex followed. It was probably a trap, but he was ready.

The man stopped in front of another set of doors and smiled. He put his hands together, bowed respectfully toward Alex, and then slowly opened the doors.

Alex walked into a huge amphitheater with rows and rows of red plastic fold-out chairs all facing a huge carpeted podium. The entire room was lit with rows of ceiling lights and strategically placed spot lights. Two box-like TV cameras hung mounted on massive robot arms connected to the ceiling.

The doors slammed shut and locked behind him.

"Of course."

He heard repeated thunderous clacks across the room. Dark sparks flew as the remaining knight demon savagely pounded his sword against a chain bolted to the floor. He wasn't making a dent in the four-inch-thick links.

The demon looked up at Alex. His face screwed up in panic. He hit the chain again and again and again. Sparks showered like a fireworks show.

Alex wondered what the beast was doing.

A jagged streak of demonic lightning cut through the air at the far end of the cavernous room and struck the ground right next to the knight demon. More bolts flashed in the air, dark streaks that absorbed all surrounding light and left the room in utter darkness. The only light that remained was the cold, blue light of Alex's sword. When the barrage of crackling streaks ceased and the lights came on again, a striking girl about Alex's age stood where the dark lightning had hit the floor.

She was clearly annoyed by the pounding sword. "Stop that, you moron!" she yelled in a high-pitched screech.

Close to Alex's height, the girl's shoulder-length dark hair was streaked with purple highlights. She wore a black floor-length dress with silver trim at the top that matched the belt around her slender waist. Her neck was ringed by a purple choke collar with a diamond-shaped crimson-colored gem in the front. In her right hand, she held a seven-foot black staff topped with three jagged blades.

The girl strode up to the demon. "He's mine, fool." She swung her blade at his skeletal head. The knight shrieked. Alex could see that this brute was terrified to raise his sword against the girl.

The demon jumped back and fled hastily through the wall.

The girl slowly turned to Alex. She sauntered across the room to him. "Hmm. You're the athleta I've heard so much about." She studied him. Her black lips curled into a smirk. "You don't look like much."

Alex was speechless.

The temptress walked slowly toward him, then circled him like he was her next meal. He kept his sword at the ready and followed her with his eyes. She lifted his chin with a finger. Alex noticed a pentagram tattooed to her palm. "You're kinda cute though … yep … in a Hardy Boys sort of way."

"Who?"

"Hmmm. Not a reader, eh?"

"If you're going to attack me, just do it."

"Calm down, warrior." She studied her black fingernails. Satisfied with their perfection, she continued. "I'm not the one who's going to annihilate you. I will leave that to my baby. My pet. I call him Cuddles."

The girl reached for the pendent around her neck and pushed her thin fingers into the kite-shaped gem. The thick chain the knight had been hitting cracked and crumbled and turned to dust. Alex saw that its trail continued onto the stage, to the back wall, and behind two massive doors extending up to the top of the thirty-foot vaulted ceiling. This back room had probably been designed to hold props and scenery. What was back there now?

As the chain disintegrated, he heard the sound of hydraulic pistons. The giant doors creaked open. Alex couldn't see anything in the darkness inside, but he heard loud, labored breathing.

"Prepare to meet your doom!" the girl yelled dramatically. She chuckled. "I've always wanted to say that. All right, gotta fly. Things around here are about to get…well…messy."

She lifted her staff, pushed her pendant, and vanished in another crackling black lightning bolt that pierced the ceiling and shook the room with a thunderous clap.

Alex tensed. He looked over at the thirty-foot doorway. Near the top, a giant pea-green head with pointy ears pushed through the opening. Snake-like yellow eyes scanned the room. The creature let out a blood-curdling roar, baring foot-long fangs in its maw.

Alex stepped back and froze. Now what?

A muscular behemoth barreled through the parted doors. It rose up onto its powerful hind legs and hit the ceiling with its head, knocking loose the panels. The monster howled, fell back on all fours, and huffed steam from its nostrils.

"Not good." Alex shuddered as the creature's eyes fell on him. The beast roared again and pounced in a blur of claws, muscles, and teeth.

"*So* not good!"

*

Sariel knew better than to disobey orders. He was expressly told not to enter the building. He knew that whatever happened in there, whether Alex was winning or dying, the angel was not to interfere, under threat of the supreme punishment—becoming a demon himself.

He would obey, but he would do so closer to the building.

He silently crossed the parking lot.

*

Alex snapped into action. He ran close to the wall on his right and ducked as the giant's razor-sharp talons pierced through the wallboard just above his head, showering him with white dust and debris.

Quickly changing directions, Alex jumped under the creature and rolled between its back legs. He then sprung to his feet and hacked at the muscular legs with his sword. The blows did little except make the monster angrier. The beast scratched back with his leg and kicked Alex in the chest. He soared through the air and hit the far wall with his back, knocking the wind out of him. He slid to the floor with a thud.

Shaking his head to clear it, Alex stood just in time. The bloodthirsty creature raced toward him. If Alex didn't move quickly, he'd be sliced into ribbons by its massive claws.

He ran again. The mindless killing machine behind him swung his arms, slashing the walls and splintering the furniture. Alex raced through the middle aisle. Behind him, chairs flew through the air like waves behind a speedboat. Alex circled the room, returning to the place where the claw had ripped the wall open above him. He tucked his head and rammed his shoulder full-force into the weakened wall. The wall gave, and he found himself tumbling into the main hallway.

The demon's arm crashed through the wall. It felt around, searching for him.

Alex rolled to his feet.

His shoulder screamed in pain. It had to be dislocated.

The claw, nearly as big as Alex, came toward him. He jumped back, lifted his sword with both hands, and stuck it deep into the top of it. The massive hand shot up reflexively, catching Alex. It lifted him up and sent him crashing through the ceiling, up onto the roof. He flew off the creature's hand and rolled to the roof's edge.

Aching from head to toe, Alex pushed himself up on shaky legs.

The creature's ugly head burst through the roof not fifteen feet from him. The beast roared and ripped apart sections of the plywood and asphalt, pushing hungrily toward Alex. He swam through the building like a bloodthirsty shark.

Alex backed to the roof's edge and tried to gauge the drop. It must be thirty feet. The fall would break his legs or maybe even kill him.

But he had no other options.

He took a deep breath and lunged forward as the creature's snapping jaws reached him.

He shouted, and his arms flailed as he fell.

Sariel caught him.

The angel's powerful wings flapped hard, propelling them high into the cold night sky.

The enormous creature burst through the front of the building, sending debris flying in all directions. It leapt into the air and grabbed for the rising pair, just missing them. As Sariel carried Alex safely away, it howled.

*

The creature looked around. Dust clouded the air. Cars stopped. People gathered in groups on the sidewalk and pointed at the devastation.

He was invisible to them.

They looked delicious.

As the massive demon took a thundering step toward the crowd across the street, a bolt of dark lightning flashed and enveloped him.

He howled, frantically waved his muscular arms, and disappeared.

*

Sariel held Alex's limp body in his arms. The boy's armor and weapons were gone. Now, he was just a kid in trouble.

The angel gently set him down on a grassy spot in his own back yard and went to work.

He laid his hands on the young man, bowed his head, and prayed. At once the healing power of God passed through his hands and into Alex. The athlete relaxed, and his breathing stabilized.

Sariel lifted his wings and hands and held his face upward, praising God for His mercy toward Alex. In the midst of this intense worship, the icy fear that had gripped his heart was released. A rush of emotions overwhelmed him, like a dam bursting. He collapsed next to the boy, sobbing uncontrollably.

16

Tuesday

Alex woke the next morning in a great mood.
Getting ready for school, he kidded Sariel, assuring him that he would never again use the "jumping off the roof" strategy.

The angel scowled.

*

Alex chained up his bike at school, hefted his backpack, and strode toward the main building.

Sariel grimaced beside him.

"So, what's wrong now?" Alex said under his breath, nodding to people he knew.

"You seem to be under a false sense of security," Sariel said in all seriousness.

"Yeah? Why do you say that?"

A lanky kid came close to Alex. He patted him on the shoulder. "I saw you save Brandon from that A-hole at the beach. Way to go, Alex!" He gave him a thumbs up and continued on to class.

Alex's smile grew.

The angel kept pace. "Although you have done incredibly well so far, you must understand that permission to do battle is not a guarantee of success."

"I appreciate your help, Sariel. You've been amazing. But, you don't get it. When that thing was chasing me around last night, I knew I was done for. I never expected to get out alive. The way it turned out, I'm only here because of your fast thinking and a lot of luck."

"Luck does not exist. You are alive because the Almighty wills it so. Your survival was part of His preordained plan."

"I stand corrected." Alex chuckled.

The angel pressed him. "I fail to understand how you can possibly be so elated this morning."

"Because, I think I finally get it—what you've been trying to teach me—and I'm okay with it. Really." He faced the angel. "Last night I came closer to death than ever before, and you know," he patted the angel's arm, "it was fine. I was ready for anything. I know things could have gone either way, and now I can accept that."

Sariel's chest puffed with pride. He put his arm around Alex's shoulder. "This is very good. What about your feelings for Katie?"

"I would have loved it...you know...if something had worked out. But it didn't. Obsessing over her was tearing me apart. I let her go."

"And?"

"And it was like a bunch of knots inside me suddenly untied. Now, I'm ready for whatever comes."

As they stepped into the building and headed down the hall, Sariel added, "Clarity is important, especially since that massive behemoth is still out there seeking to destroy you."

Alex shuddered. "I've been trying *not* to think about that."

"But you must." Sariel met his eyes. "Ignoring evil shall only make it more powerful. You must think through what happened last night and learn from it. Otherwise . . ."

Alex shook his head and muttered under his breath, "I know." He ran a finger across his throat. "You really know how to dampen a good mood, Sariel."

The angel nodded and disappeared.

*

Alex strode toward his first period class. He rolled his eyes when he saw Conor walking backward down the hall toward the front door, telling a wild story to a circle of admirers. Conor told the crowd, "Later," and ran to catch up with his friend.

"Hey, dude, where you going?" Conor asked.

A tide of students passed them and poured out of the building.

The field trip to the Mission! Alex had forgotten all about it. He turned and joined the throng with Conor.

At the buses, Alex saw that the students were being divided up by Social Studies classes. Alex and Conor found an empty seat in the middle of the bus.

A girl behind them had a face covered with piercings like she'd been hit by shrapnel. Her fluorescent hair looked like it was on fire. Apparently, she knew only one modifier—the F-word. She used it to color every noun and verb. The girls in front of him flaunted their sexual exploits, who they were doing it with and where. Two freshmen—he couldn't tell if they were girls or boys—across the aisle were dressed in black Goth clothes with stringy raven hair hanging in front of their faces. They reminded Alex of lifeless zombies, staring ahead with expressionless eyes.

When had high school become such a freak show?

The bus engine turned over with a loud thrum. They lurched forward and got in line with the other buses, which lumbered out of the parking lot like a train of elephants.

"Hey, d'ya hear about the changes?" Conor nodded his head to a girl at the front of the bus who smiled at him.

185

"Changes?"

"If you'd check the Facebook account I made for you, you'd know that our lame school was taken over by some huge company and that they're getting rid of all the top brass. Seems this company has a better way to educate us stupid youngins." His face contorted and his eyes crossed. He guffawed.

Alex sighed. He could care less about school politics.

Conor bolted up and caught a piece of candy thrown from the front of the bus in his wide-opened mouth. He threw up his hands in victory while those around him cheered. He sat back down, not missing a beat.

He continued through his smacking. "But the sweet part isn't the new principal—it's what the principal's bringing with him."

Alex braced himself as the bus took a sharp turn and crept onto the freeway onramp. "And what's that?"

Conor shook with excitement. He pulled out his cell phone, thumbed the screen, and shoved it into Alex's hand. "That's *my* definition of perfection."

Alex almost dropped the phone when he saw the image. It was the lightning girl, dressed in regular street clothes and smiling with black lips.

"Seriously?" He choked.

"I know, right?" Conor took back the phone and kissed the screen. "The principal's daughter! Ha! I'm gonna have to fly right from now on."

"The principal's daughter? Great. How did you get that picture, anyway?"

Conor laced his fingers behind his neck in pride and said, "Dude, never underestimate the investigative powers of Conor Turosi."

"Or Google." Alex jabbed him with his elbow, making him spit out his candy.

*

The busses groaned to a stop and the kids spilled out, pushing and shoving. Alex clomped off the bus and looked around for the tour guide for his class. He followed Conor. After introducing herself, Alex's guide—a short Hispanic woman with a thick accent—turned and led the way, telling her group to "Keeep up…keeep up."

They examined the priest's quarters, walked through the lush gardens, and checked out the graveyard with its crumbing tombstones. The docent never stopped chattering, explaining everything from the sanctuary's four-foot-thick walls to the winepress in the vineyard.

While on the way to the gift shop, Alex lagged at the end of the group. Grabbed from behind, he was pulled into a small dark space inside a monk's austere cubicle.

A hand covered his mouth. "Shhhhhhhhh," a girl's voice cautioned. "They'll hear us."

Alex gasped.

It was the girl from the Center of Bodily Revival.

The girl with the pet knight giant.

The girl Conor wanted to marry.

"Now," she said in a sultry voice, her lips pressed close to his ear. "Let's understand each other." She leaned her curvy body into him.

His eyes widened in panic, and he tried not to tremble.

"Well," she smirked. "I believe I have your attention, athleta."

Sariel, where are you?

Alex tried to phase into the spiritual dimension, but nothing happened.

He froze.

187

The girl let out a deep, throaty laugh. "Trying to shift on me, weren't you? You're *such* a newbie." She chuckled and backed off a little. He sighed with relief.

"I...I don't know what you're talking about," Alex countered.

"If the athleta were organized enough to have a code, it would go something like this: *athleta may only enter into spiritual battle when they—or someone else—is being threatened.* Seeing as I pose no real threat to you, at least not a violent one, you can't do battle with me."

"So, what do you want?" Alex tensed his jaw.

"Only to see you up close. That was no mean feat you pulled off the other night. You're the only one who has survived playtime with Cuddles."

"What crazy pet store do you shop in, anyway?" Alex tried to shift again.

No luck.

"He's a gift from my father. Sadly, he's really a brute and has only one thought left in his puny brain—to kill you. And he won't stop till he gets what he wants."

Alex's heart raced. He took a deep breath. "Father? But I thought demons were fallen angels. You're saying they ... reproduce?"

"Well, they do—just not with each other. You see, I'm something of a, well, half-breed. I have the best of both worlds—part demon *and* part human."

Alex considered. He focused on the fact that she was half human. That may be important.

"But," she continued, "I've chosen to focus on my demon side—way more perks." She smiled, pulled back her black lips, and bared her sharp teeth.

Alex looked away from her and toward the wall.

In less than an instant, the girl reached into her left sleeve and drew a dagger. She reared back to plunge it into his jugular. As she thrust, he disappeared into the spiritual realm. Her blade stuck in the wall behind where he had stood.

The girl laughed out loud. "This *is* going to be fun." She chuckled, pulled the knife from the wall, and put it back into her sleeve. "Shame I have to destroy him. He's kinda cute."

*

The Executive, currently in his demon form, worked at home at his massive computer station, which took up an entire wall in his study. The polished pewter desk was tailor-made to his needs. A motion-sensing pad read his intricate hand gestures. Flat-screen monitors surrounded him on three sides with multiple open windows.

The screen directly in front of him streamed information about his company—its productivity, internal office memos and e-mails, financial transactions, market volatility, shipping efficiency. You name it. Below this, another thirty-inch screen was split into dozens of video windows, each showing the real-time activities of politicians and power players from around the globe. Nothing happened that he did not know about. In any meeting, Cain was the smartest person in the room. It was as close as he could get to omniscience.

On the monitor to his left, he received feeds from every major, and a few minor, news organizations across the globe. He watched these in many different languages to track events brought about by his Satanic brothers. Politicians were caught with their pants around their ankles, while legislators shifted the nation's wealth away from the needy and into the coffers of the rich.

The last monitor, the one to his right, was used to analyze the cultures of the world. He studied the works of contemporary artists, filmmakers, and game designers. He monitored religious organizations. He kept his eye on the world of fashion and the common media. Lastly, he tracked the work of key scientists and engineers around the globe.

He would work behind these screens for the next eight hours. After all, demons never sleep.

There was a powerful "shave and a haircut" rap on his door.

"Come in," he commanded, turning his chair toward the door and standing.

The door slowly opened, revealing his daughter. She dropped to one knee and lowered her head.

"Hecate, you have news, I trust."

The girl avoided eye contact. "I have met this so-called athleta. I can tell you, he's no champion. My guess is that he has just been lucky. Well, his luck is about to run out."

"You have a plan."

"Wouldn't call it a plan, really—nothing so elaborate. He's no match for my pet. I just have to, well, arrange another playdate."

"And I assume you have this matter under control?"

"Affirmative."

The demon took a step closer to the girl, and his red brow furrowed deeper. "You must understand, this boy could ruin everything I have worked so hard for these last four hundred years." Alistair placed a gnarled hand under the girl's chin, raising her head. She looked into his grotesque face with admiration and fear. "If you can accomplish this," he continued, "I will see to it that your name will be included among those responsible for replenishing the demon race. It will help to remove some of your—shame."

"It is a great honor simply to be of service," she said, her black eyes hypnotically locked on his.

The demon pulled his hand away and turned back to his computers. "You are dismissed," he muttered.

The girl stood to her full height, turned on her heels, and left.

When she was gone, a messenger demon appeared at his master's elbow.

"My lord, do you think she will be able to complete her assignment?"

The Executive Demon continued scanning the screens and waved his hands. "She has as good a chance as any. Of course, I would never leave such an important assignment to chance. All does not depend on her. I have a plan of my own."

A maniacal grin crept across the messenger's face.

"So, why are you interrupting me?" the executive snapped.

"To tell you—th-th-the Ruler of North America is on his way." The creature ducked. It didn't help. Without looking up, the furious executive let out a loud groan and caught the measly creature with his knuckles, sending him rolling across the room.

He had to get rid of this boy!

*

Hecate entered her cave-like bedroom and sat on the edge of her queen-sized bed. She reclined against her satin pillows, picked up her electronic pad, and surfed the social networking sites, looking for anything about Alexander McKendrick from Willowbrook. All she found was a flimsy Facebook page that hadn't had any action for months.

She muttered, "What a loser."

She searched the school records, scouring all databases related to Alex. She had no trouble getting past the firewalls—her father had given her all the passwords. In no time, she knew about Alex's absent father, his single mother, and that he was an only child. She winced when she saw his mediocre grades. "Serious underachiever."

Lastly, she tapped into the yearbook committee files. Alex wasn't in any of the pictures—not the band, drama, campus clubs, ROTC, ASB, or any sports teams. Did this loser even go to this school? She found the thumbnail of his class picture, double-clicked, and waited while it filled her screen.

Alex's kind eyes met hers and she froze. Her pupils dilated, sweat glistened on her forehead, and she trembled. Short of breath, she stared at the screen for a full twenty seconds before throwing the cursed tablet across the room, knocking a silver lamp off her desk.

She breathed deeply and tried to calm her heart.

When her infernal human emotions bubbled to the surface, her father always ranted in disgust that she had, "the fever."

Demonic emotions were simple. They knew the entire range of fear—from mere concern to wretched panic. As one of the highest demons had said, "Fear is the beginning of wisdom." And, of course, there was hate—again, from mild disgust to utter detestation.

Hecate had no problem with hate. She hated everything—especially herself.

The other emotions—the human ones—troubled her, and she fought with all she was to control them. One aberrant emotion was an innate feeling of right and wrong. Like a festering splinter under her skin, her subconscious mind often told her that her thoughts and actions were "bad."

Duh! Of course she was bad. She was half-demon. The infuriating thing was that this stupid internal moral compass also told her that she *should* be "good." She would have given anything to silence this perpetual sense of personal condemnation.

The worst human emotion of all, however, was love. It was a feeling so intense, so much bigger than she was, it took constant concentration and force of will to keep it in check.

She would never love.

Never.

As a little girl, she often cried out for love, only to be punished. How many times had demons performed horrendous tortures on her to rid her of this constant need for attention, approval, and affection?

The demons believed that after years of work, they had completely hardened the girl and eradicated any remaining desire for vile love.

As she became a teen, they trained her for special operations like this one. She proved exceedingly efficient. Over time, she was given more important assignments.

Best of all, she was allowed to live.

She wiped tears from her eyes, took a deep breath, and filled her mind with images of Alex being torn to bits by her amazing pet.

Her countenance changed. Her brow furrowed, and her pupils shrank to tiny black beads.

She breathed deeply. "Better."

The corners of her mouth raised until she bared her pointy teeth like a vampire.

*

Mr. Addison had thrown up more than once at the Mission—fortunately, in trash cans. When he got back to the school, he had a million papers to grade.

At nine o'clock, he finally made it home.

All he wanted now was a bowl of canned soup and his bed. Maybe tomorrow he'd call the doctor.

*

A creeper had his hooks in the teacher while two Knights stood guard, counting themselves fortunate for such an easy assignment. All they had to do was keep Addison out of commission until the big day. So they gave the man excruciating shingles, something this creeper was particularly adept at.

They howled in laughter as the man writhed in agony.

The demon leaned forward and sank his pin-like teeth into Addison's back. Within seconds, the man had the irresistible urge to hurl. He ran into the bathroom and heaved again.

The creeper on his back laughed and bit him again while the knight Demons howled.

17

Wednesday

Conor met Alex at the bike cage, waving his arms like a madman. People nearby turned to look. When they saw it was Conor, they rolled their eyes.

"So, get this, my new game, if the aliens catch you, they hold you still." Conor put his hands out before him to demonstrate. "Then they bring their giant slimy mouths close." He grabbed Alex by the head. "And they chew you to death with rows and rows of shark-like teeth. Ahhhh!" He pretended to gnaw on Alex's scalp, making horrible chomping noises and laughing hysterically.

Alex pushed Conor off, cursing him under his breath. A group of punkers with eight-inch mohawks stepped aside, laughing.

Conor's snorting laughter abruptly ceased. His jaw dropped and he stopped dead in his tracks. His glassy eyes widened as he stared toward the parking lot.

"What?" Alex stepped back.

A wide smile slowly crossed Conor's face. "An angel," he whispered, transfixed.

Angel? Alex turned, fully expecting to see Sariel in his angelic form. Following Conor's gaze, he almost lost his breakfast. Coming toward him, looking like she owned the place, was that girl—the one who tried to stab him. The half-demon/half-human. Today she donned dark sunglasses, a short black skirt, and a black short-sleeved top with a purple lightning pattern down the right side.

"Dreams do come true." Conor ran his fingers through his messy brown hair. "Do I look okay?"

Before Alex could answer, the girl was there. She lifted her shades and looked at Conor. "So Alex, who's your handsome friend?" She put her glasses back on and extended her dainty right hand. "Hecate."

Conor grinned stupidly.

Alex grabbed the girl by the arm and rushed her away behind a hedge, leaving Conor behind. "Just what the hell do you think you're doing here?"

"Interesting choice of words, athleta. What the hell are we all doing here?" She opened her arms, motioning toward the school. "Wasting our time for a piece of fancy paper? We do this so we can go to college to get another fancy paper and work like mindless drones for the rest of our lives. Yeah, you gotta love the system!"

Alex couldn't argue. He felt that way every day. But he needed to keep his edge. "So, where's your—pet?"

She tipped her head. "My baby? My precious? You miss him already, don't you? He's also very fond of you. You're all he thinks about—literally." She giggled. "Don't worry. You'll be reunited soon enough."

"Why don't the two of us just end this now? I'm up for it if you are." He took his warrior stance.

Hecate waved her index finger at Alex and taunted, "Ah, ah, ah. Remember the rule. I'm not attacking anyone. I'm just a schoolgirl on the way to her first period class."

196

She went back to Conor. "It's great to meet you, Conor. Let's get together soon, okay?" She pulled up her shades and winked at him.

"Yeah. Sure." Conor panted like a lap dog.

The girl took one last look toward Alex and waved. "Tootles!" she mocked and headed for the school's main building.

Conor turned to Alex and whooped loudly. "I can't believe this! My life just took an unbelievable turn for the better." He looked at Alex like he had just woken from a dream and said, "What the hell am I doing here with you?" He turned, waved, and yelled, "Hecate, wait up!" and raced to catch up with her.

Sariel appeared next to Alex in his human form.

"Now what?"

"This creature has one great limitation—being half-human, she will not be able to possess your friend."

Alex shook his head. "Too late, I think she already has."

*

When Alex entered his first period class, his knees buckled. Hecate sat in the middle of the front row with Conor. His friend clowned around, making strange sounds and telling stupid jokes. It was an act Alex had seen a thousand times. The whole class—including Hecate—focused on him.

The only desk left empty was next to Conor. Alex sighed and slid into the chair.

"Don't you need to get to your class?" Alex grunted at Conor.

"I told them I had to talk to my counselor," Conor responded, his eyes locked on Hecate.

Hecate leaned over and whispered something in Conor's ear. She could have asked him to set himself on fire and he would have complied with glee. Hecate and Conor switched places. Alex turned his back to Hecate.

"Now, this is cozy." She smirked.

A lanky young woman clamored through the door, precariously hefting a cloth grocery bag, a designer purse, and a fancy coffee-house beverage. Her outfit—a white blouse, dark vest and knee-length skirt—was simple, close fitting, and professional.

She plopped her stuff on the table next to the podium and proceeded to write her name on the whiteboard in flowing script with bright-pink ink—Nikki Bales. Next to her name, she wrote the words, *No talking, or else.* She switched markers and wrote in black ink. *Pages 134-147, questions 1-10 due by the end of the period. No excuses.*

Students around the room pulled tablets out of their backpacks and thumbed to the pages.

One of Alex's classmates asked, "What's up with Mr. Addison?"

The sub merely put her finger to her lips and referred him to the message on the board as she sipped her steaming coffee drink.

Alex sat back and glanced over at Hecate and Conor. The girl sped read the chapter, brushing her hand flat over the paragraphs as if she absorbed the information through her skin. Conor pretended to read with his tablet upside down.

Hecate reached the end of the chapter, leaned over, and whispered something to Conor. He dug into his backpack and handed her his spiral notebook and a pen. She carefully tore out three pages and handed the rest back to him.

Alex watched her write in heavy, deliberate strokes. She curled the paper toward him. Across the top of the page it read, "OMG, I'm in all of your classes!"

Alex's stomach clenched.

He turned back to his own work and tried to remember what he'd already read, but nothing came to him. His eyes had brushed over the words, but his mind had been elsewhere. He'd have to start over.

He glanced up at the sub who poured over Mr. Addison's lesson planner, scowling and shaking her head.

They were both lost and confused.

Hecate dropped the paper on Alex's desk. Below her words, she added a picture that showed her in her long black dress with lightning surrounding her. Next to her, she'd drawn the face of her pet chomping on a guy who looked a lot like Alex. The caption read, *Cuddles loves Alex.*

He crumpled the paper in a tight fist, shoved it into his jacket pocket, and peered over at her desk again. She'd already finished the first six questions. Her flowing script—that looked like calligraphy—covered an entire page.

His paper was still blank.

*

Alex sat alone at a table in the quad, stared blankly forward, and chewed his tasteless bologna sandwich. From time to time he glanced over at Conor and the she-demon, who sat at a nearby table. It was like watching a puppet master and her empty-headed marionette.

"You must be very careful," Sariel's voice sounded before his body appeared on the bench next to Alex. "Her strategy is transparent. She wants to rattle you, to get to you through your friend."

"Duh! You don't think I know this?" Alex swallowed hard.

"We have bigger problems."

"What else's new?"

Although no one could hear him, the angel leaned in closer. "Our situation grows worse by the hour. Many of our forces have been," he breathed deeply, "reassigned. My pleading for reinforcements has been refused. Meanwhile, the forces of evil have multiplied ten-fold. This town is crawling with demons—creepers, knights, and knight giants. I fear worse creatures may be on the way."

"But it's all according to the plan, right?" Alex muttered, sarcastically.

"Yes. But sometimes the plan is to fail miserably. In the history of Israel, they were victorious against the massive stronghold of Jericho—"

"Only to be defeated afterward by the nearly defenseless village of Ai. I get it. So what do we do?"

"The only thing we *can* do. Stay the course—and pray."

*

Sariel put his arm on Alex's back as the two walked down the hallway toward Alex's next class.

"Well, don't you two make a cute couple?"

Alex spun around and grabbed Hecate by the arm. He pulled her out of the flowing student herd and closer to the wall.

"Wow, someone likes it rough." She gave Alex a sultry stare. "I'm game if you are, athleta."

Sariel's voice resonated, "Alex, let her go!"

Alex's chest heaved with seething anger. He was sick and tired of this...she-creature. He stood taller and gave her a warning look before he opened his grip.

Hecate acted as if nothing had happened. "Alex. Sariel. I'll see you two in class." She rejoined the student flow and was gone.

"What a witch." Alex groaned.

Sariel turned toward him. "Alex, listen to me. You are losing control. You cannot let this girl get under your skin. It weakens you and strengthens her. Perhaps another training session is warranted." The angel reached over to Alex and held him by the shoulders.

Alex braced himself for another transition to the lush training center.

It never came.

The angel dropped his hands, his face awash in panic. He looked like he was going to have a heart attack.

"What? What is it?"

The angel looked agast. "I do not know. This has never...I mean...I just do not know."

The crowds in the hallway had thinned. A hall monitor—an aging portly woman packed tightly into her faded jeans, school T-shirt, and oversized fluorescent yellow vest—approached Alex. "Gonna stand there all day, son? Go on, get to class."

Alex nodded and turned to go. After two steps, he spun around to face the angel. "You coming?"

Sariel simply stared into space.

*

Hecate glided through her front door and called out, "I'm home."

She strolled into the immaculate kitchen and swung open the refrigerator door. After she lifted out a Cobb salad, prepared according to her unique specifications, she opened the freezer and grabbed a chilled fork.

She crunched forkfuls of the greens as she headed for her father's study. He'd be working, but had demanded they talk when she got home.

Hecate opened the door to the study a crack and asked, "This a good time?"

"Enter," the Executive Demon commanded.

She went down on one knee and then slipped another bite of greens into her mouth.

Her father knew she had to eat to survive. It was a weakness inherited from her mother's side, a reality he'd come to accept.

"Report. Of course, I have received intel from others, but I want your perspective."

"May I sit, master?"

The demon nodded toward a padded chair nearby. Hecate sat, crossed her legs, and took another bite.

"Always salad, like your mother," Cain said.

"Am I really like her?"

"Your mother was a convenience, nothing more. Her ambition was to be a trophy wife on the arm of a successful businessman. I used her to gain credibility for my assignment as a human."

"So, how did I fit in?"

"You, Hecate, were an accident. I would have killed your mother, and saved you the burden of a half-breed existence, but the empty-headed twit announced her pregnancy to the press. There was a media explosion. The public, the press, and my board of directors were elated."

"And your demonic superiors?"

"They decided to use the swell of good will to our advantage. You would be born."

"I've seen the archives on the web." Hecate chose her words carefully. "Did you kill her, after all?"

"No, I'm afraid I did not. It was you. You killed her. Her heart failed giving birth to you."

Right, Hecate thought, but dared not show her disbelief.

"The media was abuzz. You became America's baby. Everyone wanted to claim you as their own. Doors suddenly opened for me. Senators who wouldn't return my calls were calling me expressing their unfailing support. I even secured a meeting with the President."

"So, I became an asset?"

Cain did not answer.

Hecate took another bite of crisp greens. "Today was interesting." Hecate spoke with her mouth full. "Conor's wrapped around my little finger. We have a date tomorrow night."

"Good. And the athleta?"

The girl mused. "Alex? I tormented him all day. At one point, I thought he was going to choke the life out of me right there in the school hallway. He was so pissed."

The demon nodded. "And Sariel?"

Hecate rolled her eyes. "You know, I thought this place was crawling with angels? Isn't that what we were told? I didn't see any today, except that old fossil."

"It would be a grave mistake to underestimate that old fossil." Her father's last words carried a tinge of pain. There was more to what he said, but Hecate knew better than to ask. He would tell her what he wanted her to know. It wasn't hard for her to fill in the blanks, though. She imagined he and Sariel had met before, and whatever happened, it wasn't pleasant for her father. She made a mental note, took her last bite of salad, and set down the bowl.

The demon stood to his full height. "You shall join me in the training area. The more prepared you are for any eventuality, the better."

The demonic girl couldn't help but wonder if this training session was for her benefit—or his.

He put his claw on her shoulders and they disappeared.

18

Thursday

*W*orship is connecting with a person—your Creator.

Sariel had repeated this during training. Alex had to chant it like a mantra. It was one thing to say the words and another to experience their reality.

It had taken concentration and effort for Alex to block out the cares of this world and to enter into worship. But now, here he was, his arms lifted up, wrapped in God's presence. Joy overcame him. This is what he was created for. In the afterlife, he would worship like this in a radiant new body, free of the flesh and every stain of sin.

He thanked God for this taste of eternity.

When he opened his eyes, Sariel stood beside him, worshipping, enraptured, face toward the ceiling, his eyes closed.

Mike Apodaca and Jeremy Apodaca

Alex needed to get ready for school, but he didn't want to disturb the angel's worship. He got up silently, tiptoed across his room, gathered his clothes, and headed for the shower.

His guardian spoke. "You have made the right choice, you know."

Alex glanced back at him and then continued to the restroom, where he pulled off his socks and T-shirt. "What choice was that?"

"Some would have prepared for the coming battle by doing push-ups or something silly like that. Others might have studied books like *The Art of War* or watched cheesy Kung Fu movies. But the battles you are about to fight will not be won with brawn nor brains. Our battle is not against flesh or blood, but with principalities and powers. These you will defeat by your connection to the Spirit."

Alex leaned around the corner. "Thanks, Sariel. I don't know what I'd do without you." He smiled and then jumped into the shower.

After a few moments, the angel said, "I have to leave."

Alex poked his sudsy head from behind the shower curtain. "What? Did you say, leave?"

"I have been summoned by my superior, Mihr. I shall try to return as soon as possible."

*

Hecate raced along in her fully-restored black and purple '64 Mustang convertible. A few blocks from the school, she pulled hard over to the curb, screeched to a stop, and killed the engine. Her eyes glowed red as she scanned the region for demons.

Convinced the area was clear, she reached beneath her leather choker. She retracted a micro-chip, pushed it into the slot on the side of her phone, and slid her thumbs over its surface.

She found the document that had been given to her a month ago by the nurse who'd helped deliver her. Words appeared on the

205

screen. They were her mother's words, spoken with her last breaths. Her mom'd made the nurse swear she would deliver the message when Hecate was old enough to hear it—when she turned sixteen.

Through a blur of tears, she read the following:

My beautiful daughter, Hope,

Please forgive me, honey, for not being there while you were growing up. I bet you're incredible. I know I would be proud. There are so many things I wish we could have shared. I will always love you. I will wait for you in heaven.

Mom

Below this, the nurse added:

Your mother had me write this down for her just before you were born. She held you in her arms as her heart failed, never taking her eyes off of you. I believe she still watches over you now—from heaven.

Sincerely,
Deborah Mobly, RN

Hecate wiped tears from her high cheekbones, pulled out the memory chip, and tossed her phone into her purse. She carefully slipped the chip underneath her choker, pushed her large sunglasses onto her face, fired up the car's engine—which roared a powerful lament—and sped off.

*

What was with everyone? Katie felt like she'd shown up to school naked. Everywhere she looked people stared at her, pointed, and whispered. Friends turned their backs and pretended they hadn't been looking at her.

Then she opened the message on Instagram. Through horrified tears she saw picture after picture of Brandon with Cindi Langster—drinking, kissing, and embracing. She rubbed her thumb across her phone and opened Facebook. More pictures.

She could barely breathe. Part of her wanted to run, to disappear. But a bigger part of her wanted Brandon's head on a pike.

She scowled and strutted to the parking lot. Others who saw where she was going followed.

There he was—the stupid jock, leaning against his car, looking at his phone, laughing with his friends. They were probably making fun of her.

"Hey, babe," Brandon called out in his suave voice.

"How could you!" she screamed. Heads around the parking lot turned. A crowd gathered.

"What're you talking about?"

"This, you slime." She held up her phone. Brandon's friends laughingly chimed in with, *You're in for it now*, and *The ball-and-chain is mad.*

Brandon tilted his head. "Look, Katie. I'm an athlete. Watch the news sometime. This is what athlete's do."

Katie sobbed in anger and pain. "You said, I was special."

Brandon raised his voice. "Oh yeah, and you said you loved me. But do I ever get any action from you? No way. You're the most frigid girl I know. Maybe I just got tired of waiting."

"But..."

Brandon puffed out his chest. "You know, now that I look at you, I'm not sure why I even bothered. You were a charity case from the start. Why don't you just go crawl back under that rock where I found you."

Katie lunged, claws out. But she was held back by her friends, her nails inches from Brandon's eyes.

His buddies all laughed and cheered.

*

In last period, Katie sat with a full-sized Kleenex box, continuously pulling out tissues and wiping her nose and puffy eyes.

Brandon stared out the window—his jaw set like concrete.

Hecate pushed a note onto Alex's desk. It had the usual picture of him dying by a bloody dismemberment at the hands of her demon pet. This one was particularly gruesome, and the sight of it made him seethe.

Underneath it, she'd written:

Katie's available now, you moron. Make your move!

Alex crumpled the note and stuck it in his pocket. He acted like it didn't faze him at all.

While Mrs. Bales wrote on the whiteboard, Hecate leaned over to Alex and whispered, "You're pathetic, athleta."

"Not listening." Alex copied the notes from the board.

"I would give you a whirl myself, but I'm . . . you know . . . involved." She winked.

Alex gritted his teeth as he turned to her and said, "Stay away from Conor."

"No can do, best buddy. You see, Conor and I have a hot date tonight. And with any luck, my demonic friends'll get him so deeply possessed, he'll completely lose his mind. When we're done with him, he won't be able to form a coherent sentence—not that he can now, you understand."

Alex snapped his pencil in two.

The classroom door opened and Vice Principal Edwards entered with a man in tow. "Sorry for the interruption, everyone, but I wanted to take this opportunity to introduce you to our new principal. He's a champion in the business world and someone I've always admired. Join me in a warm welcome for Alistair Cain."

The class gave a tepid response, but Mr. Cain didn't miss a beat. He moved in front of the teacher's desk and faced the class. For a moment, he studied their faces with his piercing black eyes.

"Good afternoon. Is there any one of you that would buy a gaming system from a company that had a failure rate of twenty-five to fifty percent? Not likely. And yet, that is the failure rate of America's high schools. This is unacceptable. The education system in America is broken. Up to this point, there has been a lot of finger pointing but no real solutions. This ends today. From this point on, Kingman High School's motto is 'Success at all costs.'"

Mr. Cain turned his attention toward one particular student, Stephen Stanley. Big and brawny, he looked like someone had tried to squeeze a rhinoceros into a school desk. His blond buzz cut was streaked with bright red dye. Ear spools the size of silver dollars made thick hoops on the sides of his head. His skull-covered gray clothes were baggy and saggy. On his forehead was a bright red tattoo of a QR code, which took people's cell-phones and devices to his disgusting Facebook page.

The principal glared at Stephen with intense distaste. "Mr. Stanley, it is no secret that you are one of the reasons why Kingman High fails. Stand up."

Stephen leaned back and smiled. He rolled his eyes and gave the new principal the finger.

His friends laughed.

Mr. Cain stared at Stephen as if taking him apart one molecule at a time.

Alex and Hecate were the only students who saw what was really going on.

The principal had entered the room surrounded by dark shapes. When he singled out Stephen, these demons sprung at the boy and crawled all over him like maggots on a dead rat.

Alex began to respond, but the Holy Spirit said, "No!"

While the rest of the students watched, Stephen's expression changed. Glistening sweat beaded on his forehead, and his smirk drooped. He winced. He stopped giving the finger and started thrumming his hands on his desk. Blinking, he tried to look away from the new principal, but demons held his head fast.

"Just what is your plan, Mr. Stanley? Where do you think this current path will lead you?"

"You sound like my grandpa," the boy choked out.

The principal's eyes narrowed. "Let us get one thing straight, Mr. Stanley. I am not your grandfather. Your grandfather tells you to get your pathetic act together and quit being a total loser because he loves you and wants you to have a good life. I do not love you, Mr. Stanley, and I could care less if you succeed in life or if you end up pushing a shopping cart filled with aluminum cans and chasing cockroaches for your next meal. Now, stand up."

There was a moment of absolute silence.

Stephen shifted his weight and slowly stood.

"Let me tell you what I do care about, Mr. Stanley. My company. And my company needs a continuous supply of new talent. It needs customers who have good jobs and money to spend. It doesn't need bottom feeders whose life plan is to leech off the system, either through welfare, food assistance, or prison. In other words, Mr. Stanley, we don't need you."

Alex watched as rhinoceros boy started choking, struggling to breathe. His body shook uncontrollably. He leaned over and tried to stabilize himself, but his knees buckled. He fell to the ground, jerking and frothing at the mouth.

The students around him jumped up from their desks.

"Oh, my God," Mrs. Bales shouted. "Call 911!"

Nearly every student in the class whipped out cell phones, punched buttons, and reported what had happened. Some snapped pictures and posted them online.

"I don't think he's breathing," Katie yelled. Students around the room gasped. Girls started crying.

Stephen lay sprawled on the ground with his arms wide, his eyes staring into space.

The substitute teacher kneeled down beside him and wretched. She tugged off her scarf, wiped the froth off Stephen's mouth, then put her mouth over his and blew in. She sat upright, laced her hands one on top of the other, leaned the heel of her right hand on his sternum, pressed with her whole body weight, and rhythmically shoved down hard. His chest heaved up and down, up and down, up and down.

The entire room panicked.

After minutes of this, Stephen remained unresponsive.

He was dead.

Mrs. Bales stopped and wept.

"Good to meet you all. Now, let's create the greatest school in the world. Success at all costs." Mr. Cain smiled, turned on his heels, and left.

Hecate leaned over to Alex and whispered musically, "That's my dad."

*

Cain climbed the circular stairs to the office he'd had installed in the clock tower. He liked having the students feel he hovered above them. It gave him a distinct psychological advantage.

He flattened his hand on an ID plate on the wall next to a heavy metal door. The lock made a loud metallic scraping sound. He pushed open the door and stepped in.

A series of 70-inch surveillance screens lined one wall. Cain could see every inch of the school, some areas from multiple angles. Two security experts carefully scanned the monitors. Whenever a student stepped out of line, they were immediately taken to a reprocessing center to be fixed, like broken parts. The video footage of their behavior was catalogued in their personal files. Cain imagined these videos being used for blackmail or shown at parent conferences. Stupid kids would be horrified. Parents would yell and trust would be broken. The school would become a place of fear and mindless compliance.

The thought satisfied Cain to the core.

Whereas public schools could never get away with this kind of invasive surveillance, this school had now become a division of Cain International.

Teams around the room all snapped to attention when Cain entered.

"Back to work, everyone. We have a lot to do and very little time. Hustle!"

"Yes, sir," they declared with a military snap.

"As you were." He nodded and stepped back out the door. In the atrium outside his office, he glanced at another locked door—the one to the stairwell—and smiled.

*

This was stupid and Alex knew it, but he didn't care. Sariel would have tried to talk him out of it, but then, Sariel wasn't here. In fact, he was barely ever here. Alex had begun to grow weary of his guardian angel's perpetual absence.

And he had permission to go—from his mom.

Dressed in dark clothes, Alex kept his distance from Conor's clunky Jeep. He stood on his bike pedals, pumping with all his might. Conor made a right turn about a half-mile ahead of him.

They headed for the only theater in town.

*

Principal Cain hefted a padded cot from his office, folded the legs, and carried it out to the door in the atrium. He slowly pressed his hand flat against the ID plate. As a loud clicking of tumblers greeted his ears, the door opened and revealed a steep, dusty, spiral staircase. Cain picked up the cot and began the ascent. The stairs ended at a metal door that opened to a storage room behind the massive clock. Cain looked disapprovingly at the mess. The former administration had kept everything—dust-covered sets and props from old plays, massive costume snake heads used by several generations of Kingman mascots, and racks covered in obsolete sports uniforms. Were they saving these relics for a future Kingman High museum, or what?

A six-foot wide pentagram with heavy, crimson candles on every vertex was painted in dark, dried blood on the floor. On the wall beyond it stood the back side of the tower clock—a four-inch thick, circular, rusty metal frame. Ten feet in diameter, it reached from the floor to the ceiling.

Cain set up the cot beside the pentagram—positioning it in just the right spot. He closed his eyes and played out Saturday's events in his mind. He saw a montage of slit throats, rushing blood, hordes of demons, and screams of horror.

Everything was going according to plan.

He kneeled, placed his forehead to the floor at the top of the pentagram, and chanted an ancient incantation in a language not of this world.

The candles sputtered to life. Flames danced on the wicks around the circle. The blood between them bubbled. Cain continued chanting. The enormous metal frame behind the clock shone red.

Cain reverently raised his head and stood to his full height. He slowly stepped around the pentagram and stood before the metal frame. He raised his arms, chanted more incantations, furrowed his brow, and peered into the circle. Its surface changed. The clock's mechanism—a dense overlapping of gears—melted into formless blobs of color swirling in surreal patterns. Dark lightning flashed across the surface. The colors coalesced into a dark, inky void.

With careful steps, he drew closer. Colors slowly appeared in the blackness of the circle's surface. These color smudges formed shapes. The shapes became distinct figures that connected across the circle's surface, creating a moving picture of a hellish cavern. A swirling lava ceiling spanned a large rocky expanse. Demons milled about.

Cain inhaled deeply. He put his hand into his pocket and took out a rectangular piece of metal two-inches wide by four-inches long with an engraved inscription. It said only one word.

Assemble.

He tossed the message into the middle of the circle. It hit the surface, setting off black sparks. He watched it continue in the world on the other side. It hit the rocky ground with a metallic clank.

A tall hideous demon approached it. He snatched it up, gazed at its surface, turned his ugly head upward, and stared at Cain through the glowing frame. He lifted the metal piece high in his right hand and nodded.

The image disappeared, becoming gears and springs once more.

*

After chaining up his bike and buying a ticket, Alex headed toward the theater doors. There was only one movie Conor would be even remotely interested in—a slasher flick full of gratuitous nudity and violence.

The ticket seller didn't ask for proof of Alex's age. But then, they never did.

He moved cautiously down the dark hallway leading to the theater, hoping he could find a spot near the top where he could watch over Conor and that she-devil undetected. He scanned the area for the dark shapes of demons, ready to shift if necessary, but he saw no demons here.

At least, not yet.

He entered the darkened theater. His eyes slowly adjusted.

Something was wrong.

No movie played. The seats were all empty. He didn't see Hecate or Conor.

His first thought was that he had the wrong theater. Then he saw movement near the screen.

"What's it like to be so completely predictable?" Hecate's voice rang out from the front of the theater.

He glimpsed something laying on the short wooden stage in front of the screen.

Conor. He wasn't moving.

The she-demon stepped out from behind the side curtains, dressed like she had been that first night, in her black and purple get up.

"Hecate, what the heck?" Alex called, as he made his way to the stage.

"Your friend is tougher than I thought. I assumed he'd be easy to possess. I was even going to let him have a hand in your destruction. I guess I misread his loyalty."

Alex stepped closer to the stage. He held his hands out to his sides. "Hecate, think. You don't have to do this. You're half human. You *can* be saved—you *can* choose to walk away from the darkness."

The girl laughed sardonically and snarled. "You don't know anything about me, athleta. Don't you dare lecture me about what's possible."

"Think about it. Whaddo you have now? What keeps you on Satan's side?"

"Forget it, Alex. Not going to happen. My life is with the demonic. I was raised demon. I am a demon. It's all I know."

"Hecate, think," he pleaded. "You're only looking at one side. You're half human. Think of your mother. Is this what your mother wanted for you?" Hecate looked away. "As to your spiritual side, I've learned a little about this. The demons were originally created as angels, loyal to God. When Satan rebelled, he took a third of the heavenly host with him. They became demons. They … well … they're stuck now, forever. They'll always be demons destined to spend eternity in Hell."

"A myth we completely reject."

"That's because you're still convinced this is a fair fight. It isn't. Satan *is* strong, but he isn't another god. He's only a fallen angel, just like your father. When this is all over, he'll be banished to Hell along with the rest of them." Alex read her eyes. He could see her resolve falter. "The difference between you and them is that you're human. You *can* still choose. Hecate, give your life to God. Accept the forgiveness paid for you by Christ on the cross and walk in His light."

Hecate laughed. "Where's the hokey organ music playing *Just as I Am*? You are such a loser, Alex! Did you really think I was going to give up my amazing life? You *are* crazy."

"Hecate."

"No, Alex. Not today. Not ever. I've made my choice."

With that, she reached to the pendent on her throat and concentrated. Dark lightening swirled and flashed in jagged branches, filling the theater. Puffs of smoke billowed from where the black bolts hit the walls.

Alex shifted to the spiritual realm.

The lightning coalesced in the middle of the room. When it dissipated, it left her enormous pet monster. This time he stood upright and held a ten-foot sword.

"You remember Cuddles?" She laughed. "Playtime."

Alex gulped. He positioned himself for battle. Instantly clothed and equipped, he held tightly to his sword and shield.

"Goodbye, Christian. Enjoy your afterlife. It begins now," Hecate mocked and once more seized the pendent on her neck.

*

"Oh glorious One enthroned on high,
All creation lifts its eyes to You
We storm forward on Your wings of power
To conquer in Your holy Name."

Mihr sang out the battle cry. The ball of angels again hurled through space, their swords spinning in circles.

Sariel noticed that the circles were tighter, probably to eliminate the risk of the swords clanging together.

"Now!" Mihr yelled. The sphere spun faster and faster until it became a brilliant blur.

Then it came apart. An opening formed in the blazing ball and spread throughout until the whole thing collapsed into sixty bright points of light moving quickly apart.

In the middle, Mihr.

He laughed heartily. "When we get that, it will be spectacular and quite deadly. I cannot imagine any horde of demons that could stand against it." Mihr saw Sariel and proclaimed to his team, "We are done. We will meet again to train at the appointed time."

He whizzed past Sariel. "Sariel, join me at my home."

The angel dutifully followed.

When they landed at the crystal platform, Sariel blurted out, "Mihr, what is it? Please tell me quickly. I am afraid to leave Alex alone. Our numbers are so few now."

Mihr patted his shoulder soothingly, pain in his eyes. "You are not going back."

Sariel was stunned. "I've been," the angel could barely speak the word, "reassigned?"

Unthinkable.

"I'm sorry, my friend. I know what Alex means to you."

"He … he will not last a day, Mihr. Not with the horde that is assembling in his town. Something is going on—something of enormous importance to our enemy. We need to stop it."

"And we both know it is all part of the plan."

"What if it is Salem all over again?"

"Now, now."

"Alex will surely be destroyed!"

"What athleta has not been destroyed? If this is to be the end of his earthly story, then Alex is leaving honorably and will be rewarded eternally. You must be happy for him."

"Yes, of course in the long run this would be best."

"But still you are not at peace."

Sariel took a deep breath and confessed, "Alex dying now would not be best for me. Mihr, my friend, you do know what Alex means to me, how much I love him. If he were to cross over now, we would be separated—he in heaven and me fighting demons on earth until the Lord returns. I am not ready to let him go."

*

The bellowing cry of the beast filled the movie theater. Hecate held her pendant high. Before she could summon her black lightning and transport herself away, her pet leaped for the nearest prey.

Unfortunately, it was her.

In less than a second, she was tightly in its grasp, her arms pinned. She couldn't reach her jewel. She screamed as the massive demon smashed her into the wall, nearly breaking her neck.

Alex ran to the beast. "Let her go!" he yelled and stabbed into the armor on its right leg. The giant howled and swung at him with its massive sword. Alex ducked and pulled out his blade, coated with slimy blue blood.

The huge demon was no longer interested in the girl. After all, she wasn't moving and could no longer fight. He dropped her. Hecate hit the stage with a clunk, right next to Conor's motionless body.

"That's right, Ugly. It's just you and me." Alex ran up the left side aisle as the beast swung its sword back and forth in front of him.

As Alex reached the back of the room, debris from the seats showered over him. He watched the demon's arm pull back for a fatal blow. In the portion of a second he had left, Alex turned his shield upside down and used it as a sled. He skidded down the steep steps, right past the creature. The giant's blade crashed through the back wall of the theater.

Alex lost control and fell off the shield just before it reached the last of the stairs. He tumbled across the sticky carpet in front of the stage.

The monster recovered quickly and stamped down the stairs after him.

Alex rolled onto his back, threw up his legs, and back-sprung back onto his feet. He willed his sword and shield into his hands and faced the demon coming at him. He jumped to the left, and the creature turned in that direction with him.

The beast raised his sword, and his massive body became airborne in a deadly pounce.

Alex quickly dodged to the right.

The demon crashed into the end of the stage, busting it to splinters. Alex ran with all his might to the steps that led up the right side of the theater. Near the back of the room, he ran into a row of seats, jumped up, and stood on the arm rests.

The giant creature picked up his sword and pulled itself up to his full height, his head coming close to the ceiling. He puffed out his armor-covered chest. His nostrils flared and his eyes narrowed. He roared at Alex, baring his razor-sharp teeth.

Alex roared back, then yelled, "Come on! Come on you… you…thing! Can't you even catch me?"

The demon was the size of a small mountain. He plodded forward, his gnarled feet crushing the first several rows of seats. He stopped in front of Alex and tightened his grip on his sword.

Alex braced himself. "Do it! Come on, you wimp. Do it!"

The monster pulled back his arm for a final deadly thrust. His sword shot forward as if fired from a cannon—right at Alex's stomach.

As the blade came close, Alex jumped in the air and pulled his legs up under him.

The long weapon slid below him, plunged into the concrete under the seats, and, for a split second, held fast.

Alex landed on the flat side of the wide blade, got his balance, and used it as a narrow ramp. He ran up it and across the arm to the demon's horrid head. Alex extended his arm and shoved his sword full-force into the beast's throat. The blade plunged through the leathery gray skin, between the vertebrae, and severed the creature's spinal cord.

For Alex, the rest was a tangle of falling, rolling, sparkling dust, and pain.

*

"Alex, hey Alex. C'mon now, you're scaring me. I mean it, Alex, quit fooling around."

At first it sounded like Conor spoke from far away. Then Alex felt his cheek being repeatedly slapped. Reflexively, Alex grabbed Conor's hand.

"Stop that," he said, groggily.

"There you are, moron. I thought for a minute there…"

Alex slowly sat up and looked over the room. There was no sign of the monster. "What the—"

Conor said, "Dude, I don't know what happened. Someone knocked me out cold. You and Hecate too. She's bad, man. You gotta help her."

Alex pushed himself up and ran to the stage. He leaned close to the girl's nose and mouth. She wasn't breathing.

"Call 911." He ordered Conor.

He put his mouth over Hecate's and pushed air into her lungs. He put his hands into position and set the heel of his hand onto her sternum and thrust down hard. As he pushed, he prayed, "C'mon, Father, please help her! In Jesus name and power, please."

The girl's eyes fluttered.

"It's working!" Conor shouted. "Keep it up!"

Alex went down again, placing his lips over Hecate's, only this time her hand reached behind his head and she kissed him hard.

"Oh now, that's just not right," Conor said, shocked.

When Alex lifted his head, he stared into the girl's beautiful eyes. "Hecate?"

"Hope," she corrected him with a weak voice. "My name is Hope."

*

Cain pored over an ancient book of spells he'd used at the time of the Salem Witch Trials. The handwritten book was twice the size of a family Bible and bound in rough leather. Ornate designs and satanic symbols were pressed deep into the cover. Brass clasps and hinges held it together.

Turning the fragile, browning velum pages with a light touch, Cain found the incantations he needed and placed a cloth bookmark inside.

He was almost ready for tomorrow night.

"Sir," the young data specialist interrupted him.

"What is it?" Cain growled.

"It's your daughter. She's been in an accident. She's being transported to Willowbrook General Hospital. She's a little banged up, but they don't seem to think her injuries are life-threatening. They do want to examine her."

Without a word, the Executive Demon headed out the door. In the hall, he disappeared into the spiritual realm.

His gray double-breasted suit became black as night. Ten-foot wings sprang from his back. Horns pushed out of his forehead. His eyes deepened and their sockets widened.

Hecate had done nothing but leech off him her whole life. When he thought she showed some potential for fighting, he began training her. He gave her the giant Behemoth—a vicious killing machine—to observe in battle and to learn from. And what did she do? She botched her most important assignment and got hurt.

Infuriated, he sprang through the wall, his massive wings lifting him high above the school and the streets below.

Stupid girl.

He knew what was wrong with her—the pathetic human weaknesses inherited from her mother. He had hoped he could scrape this blight off her soul, but, as of late, he'd seen more and more of its unnatural and disgusting presence.

But he would soon be free of her.

As he imagined tomorrow's two sacrifices, two throats slit in honor of the momentous event, his destination approached. He landed just off the hospital grounds and retracted his wings. After passing behind a tall hedge, he emerged as Alistair Cain, concerned father.

He entered the emergency room door and approached the information desk.

*

A half-hour later, Cain's stretch-limo waited outside the hospital. The driver opened the door for Hecate. She climbed out of her wheelchair and slid in, careful not to bump her sore wrist. As soon as possible, she would trade out this grotesque light-blue sling for a black and purple one. If her arm felt any better in the morning, she would just trash it. After all, weakness was not part of her image.

Her father slid into the seat next to her. The driver shut his door.

As they pulled away from the curb, Alistair spoke. "Report. Leave nothing out. And, be careful. I will know if you are lying or omitting anything."

She sighed. "I know this is not what you want to hear, but the truth is, I was unconscious for most of it."

Alistair studied her face with cold dead eyes. "So, what *did* you see?"

She knew she had better give him real information. "It's all my fault," she started. "I'm such a screw up. I materialized my pet closer to me than to Alex. It was really a stupid creature, a monstrous killing machine with the mental capacity of a slug. It had no sense of loyalty or authority. Before I could dematerialize, the beast grabbed me and smashed me into the wall, knocking me out and hurting my arm and neck. The next thing I knew, the paramedics were carrying me out."

"Recite the elements of failure."

These rolled off her tongue. "Failure to plan. Failure to acquire adequate resources. Failure to acquire adequate knowledge or skills. Failure to understand your enemy. Failure to ready one's self for any eventuality."

"And?" he prodded.

The car made a sharp turn.

"And general screw-ups," she finished. *Would he kill her now, or later?*

223

"And your pet paid the ultimate price for yours. Do you realize how important behemoths are, especially now?"

Tears welled up in her eyes. "It won't happen again," she said, trying to keep her voice from cracking.

"There is a way for you to repair what you have done." He said, his voice calm and soothing. "I have a plan. It involves your new friend, Katie Brinton. This time, you will not fail me. If you do, it *will* be your last."

"Yes, my lord," she gasped.

*

Scraped and bruised from head to foot, Alex was sure he'd knocked a tooth loose—at least that's what his tongue kept telling him.

Conor's car pulled up to the curb in front of Alex's house. Conor killed the engine, cleared his throat, obviously trying to breach the awkwardness of the silent car ride. "So . . . you and Hec—, I mean, Hope. Dude, how long has *this* been going on?"

"Don't know what you're talking about," Alex said, slumped in the seat.

"Dude, you got to first base on *my* first date with Hope. You did it right in front of me. How do you expect me to feel?"

Alex sat up, stunned. "Look, firstly, I'm really sorry if your feelings got hurt. You know I would never do anything—I mean *anything*—to hurt you. You're my best friend, and I would never put a girl above our friendship."

"*Hello!* You kissed her!" Conor's jaw hardened.

"She kissed me, remember? She was probably just trying to upset you. She gets her kicks by stirring everything up."

Conor stared off into space. "Yeah, that's one of the things I like about her."

"Look, Conor. I have no interest in Hope, other than to be her friend."

Conor stared at Alex, thinking. His expression softened. "Okay, I get it. Thanks."

Alex reached over, and the boys bumped knuckles.

He got out of the car and grabbed his bike out of the hatchback. "Thanks again for the ride."

"I'll add it to your tab. I think you owe me, like, a trillion dollars by now. You're my retirement fund."

"I better start saving." Alex chuckled as he slammed the back shut.

"I know what'll make us even." Conor started his Jeep. The engine roared.

"What's that?"

"You can be my best man when Hope and I tie the knot."

Alex fought the urge to dump cold water on his friend's dreams. He knew that anything could happen between now and when Conor would be ready to get married—if he was ever ready. But this wasn't about the real possibility of Hope and Conor becoming man and wife. It was about something else, something between him and Conor.

"I would be honored." Alex patted the top of the car twice and headed toward his garage to put his bike away.

"You'll be honored, all right," Conor called back. "It'll be the best party ever!"

*

She should have been dead to the world, but Hope was having trouble sleeping. The pain medication they gave her had worn off and now her arm and neck hurt, but she didn't want to dull her senses with another dose.

If her father knew what she was about to do, he'd kill her.

225

She'd never access the Bible on any of her electronic media. Her phone, electronic pad, and laptop were all monitored. Her father would know the minute she digitally opened anything to do with—*the enemy*.

Jesus.

Demonic lore portrayed him as a real dope for following his father's orders and allowing himself to be crucified for mankind. He was so weak that Satan easily defeated and humiliated him through public execution.

Her life had been defined by the demonic cause—to thwart every effort of the enemy to extend his influence, to retain the satanic ground they had already secured, and to extend their kingdom over mankind. After all, Satan was the god of this world. Jesus was merely a usurper trying to overturn the proper order.

And yet, as she grew older and began to think for herself, the story made less and less sense.

Deep inside she knew her relationship with her father should have been characterized by love and admiration. But all she ever knew was fear.

One day she would step over the line or screw up one too many times and would end up dead.

She thought he would take her life tonight, but instead, he'd offered her a way back into his favor.

Weird.

How much longer could she live like this—without real love in her life?

She was so confused.

She'd been awful to Alex. She had tried to kill him. And what does he do in return? He saves her life, risking his own. He prays for her. And then there was the feeling she had—a presence ... something she thought of as a brush with pure goodness and love. The experience warmed her entire being.

Unsettling.

Hope sat up and her eyes glowed red. She scanned her room for demons. Surprisingly, her bedroom was clear.

She turned on her side and punched buttons on her cell phone, accessing the flashlight app. Then she slipped the contraband Alex had given her from inside the sling on her arm.

She opened the New Testament, the size of a small deck of cards, and read about Jesus.

19

Friday Morning

lex's eyes popped open. He sat up in bed and anxiously looked around his room. His clock read 3:15 a.m. A gentle breeze brushed thin forest-green curtains, shifting them eerily back and forth. The room was awash with moon light, contrasted by deep dark menacing shadows. In them, he thought he could make out the shape of a creeper demon here and a knight demon there. But when the curtains shifted, the shadows did as well. His stomach turned.

Was he losing his mind? Seeing things that just weren't there?

And yet, something inside him stirred. He was learning to depend on this inner voice, and now it blared like an internal alarm.

He spotted a winged creature, larger than any living bird, beautiful against the full moon, gliding toward him. Sariel—his mentor, his protector, his friend—was back!

Alex jumped up. "Yes! Yes! Yes!" He gyrated in a crude victory dance.

He knocked the dirty clothes off the metal fold-out chair next to his window and sat.

The angel entered the room, more radiant than ever.

The brightness slowly dimmed.

Alex's face dropped.

Not Sariel.

Alex looked away in disgust.

"Hello, Alex. I am Mihr, Sariel's trusted friend and superior. I have been sent to watch over you during these difficult times." The angel carefully folded his massive wings and transformed into a man in a bright white suit, just like Sariel's.

Alex sighed with disappointment. "But, where's Sariel?"

"Alas, Sariel—my, this is difficult—he requested to be transferred." The angel sat in the chair next to the window and looked down at the floor.

Alex's eyes went wide. "He . . . what? Why?"

"He cited irreconcilable differences. Seems you are very difficult to manage, my boy. He said you always choose your own way instead of following your training. He referred to you as something of a—how do you say it? Ah yes, a rogue agent. Well," he laughed heartily, "that ends now."

Alex shook his head in disbelief. Sariel was fast to point out when he had been stupid or reckless—and there had been a couple of times he had, well, innovated—but Sariel had never shown anything but love and approval for him personally. How could he have so completely misread the relationship between them? He felt like he'd been punched in the gut.

The angel surveyed the cluttered room around him. Alex had always used his floor as a shelf for dirty clothes and anything else he didn't want to put away. "Now, this is not the most favorable place for your...um...retraining. We shall have to shift to the training area." The angel's jowls jiggled when he spoke.

"Yeah, okay, I guess," Alex said.

Mihr came closer and put his hand on Alex's shoulder, and they transported through a portal to a different place.

But it wasn't the lush paradise Alex had trained in twice before. Instead, they sat at a small wooden table in an upscale coffee bar. The angel had a steaming cup of black coffee in front of him, while Alex held an iced mocha latte topped with a tower of whipped cream and a crisscross caramel design. The far wall was lined with Alex's favorite video games.

Alex looked down. He was still in his boxers. He closed his knees, put his hand over his lap, and hoped no one else would come in. It was like being in a bad dream.

The angel took a sip of his coffee and waited for Alex to do the same.

Alex put the straw to his lips but realized he was in no mood for something this sweet. In fact, his mood was terrible. He didn't want to be here. He was tired and his head was fuzzy. But he thought he had to be flexible and willing to accept what he was given without complaining.

After all, he had a bad reputation to live down.

What he really wanted was Sariel.

"This drink is not to your liking? You can have anything you desire. I will get you anything you ask for." The angel's eyes sparkled. "Anything at all."

"I'm...not thirsty," Alex said, his voice flat. He slumped in his seat.

There was a long pause.

"So, let us begin." The angel cleared his throat. "What did Sariel say was the purpose of your training?"

Alex thought. "Well, the purpose was to strengthen my faith so that I could battle the forces of evil."

The angel smirked condescendingly. "Evil . . . evil . . . evil. Angels like Sariel are always getting caught up in the idea that reality is black and white. Well, it is only like that at the extremes—where the whackos live. You are not a wacko, are you, my boy?"

Alex responded with a firm "No."

"The truth is far more balanced, more moderate, as you will soon discover."

This made some sense to Alex. He'd seen crazy people, like those who carried signs declaring the end of the world and stuff like that. Talk about extremes!

He added, "Sariel also trained me in the use of the Armor of God."

Mihr visibly flinched at this last reference and then said smoothly, "Armor and battles. Are we barbarians? Seriously, I am shocked at Sariel's old-fashioned notions. The poor angel still lives in the ancient past." He leaned forward. "You and I do not function this way. No, my boy, this is a modern age, a time of instant information—of smart phones and data pads. The key is to be on top of things, aware of the changes. We have to be smarter than everyone else."

Alex became more confused by the second. He asked, "Then, who's the enemy? What about all the demons?"

As the angel smiled, the wrinkles around his eyes deepened. "That is just the point, my boy. The only enemy is ignorance and bone-headed absolutist thinking."

"I…I don't understand." Alex sighed.

"Try your best to keep up, Alex. Ignorant people believe there is only one answer for everything—one universal truth. This is simple and easy for their small minds to grasp. They hide all ambiguities and unanswered questions behind their absolutist religion. They deny and devalue the beautiful ancient religions of others declaring that their way is the only *true* way. A far more modern, more enlightened view, is the understanding that we all create the truth that makes sense to us—the truth that makes our lives

231

whole and livable. You see, each of us really creates our own way to happiness."

What the heck was this angel talking about?

Alex was in over his head. True, everyone saw the world differently. Everyone looked at things through their own lens and saw things their own way. And who was to say which perspective was better than the others? Who was to say which way was the *right* way? Maybe they were all equally correct and all equally incorrect. Maybe things just are what they are.

"But...but..."

"Yes?" The angel slowly sipped his coffee.

"But what about murderers and rapists? What about people who kill children and stuff like that? To follow your logic, they were just living out *their* ideas of what worked for them. If nothing is absolutely right, then nothing is ever really absolutely wrong either."

"Of course, you immediately go to the extreme." The being of light shook his head. "Maybe you are a wacko and you just don't realize it."

"No, this is right." Alex engaged. "Nobody's so crazy as to say that killing babies is okay. What *you're* saying is crazy. If people followed your logic, there'd be no law, no civility, and no compassion. There'd be chaos." He stood and announced, "So, long story short, you're just wrong."

Alex picked up the cold drink and dumped it over the angel's head.

The angel transformed into a shrieking demon with a hideous, impish face, jagged teeth, and razor-sharp claws.

Alex shifted into his armor.

The beast lunged over the table at him, and Alex jumped back. A belt formed tightly around his waist. The belt blazed with blinding light and the beast sizzled out of existence with a crispy sound.

In that moment, Alex remembered what he had been taught at church. This was the Belt of Truth. He now knew for certain there was only one reality that mattered—God's.

Alex stood with the Spirit sword, salvation helmet, faith shield, peace shoes, and the belt of truth. Only one piece was missing.

In an instant, his armor disappeared and he stood in his bedroom again. He looked at the clock.

Still 3:15 a.m.

He crawled back into bed, breathed deeply, and fell asleep as if nothing had ever happened.

*

Alex greeted the morning with renewed confidence. He headed for the bathroom with a spring in his step.

It sucked that Sariel was still gone—he would have loved to have him there for back-up. He missed him. Still, he had taken care of two pretty nasty demons on his own. He'd stood up to the overwhelming power of Hope's monstrous pet, and he saw through the subtle lies of the tricky demon in angel's clothing.

Maybe he was an athleta Christi after all.

But who could he tell?

Who'd ever believe him?

"Alex, you almost ready?" his mom called from downstairs.

He spit toothpaste into the sink and yelled, "Coming."

It was Friday. His mom had asked him if he wanted to drive the car to school—with her in the passenger seat, of course. He hoped Conor was there when he drove up. Maybe he'd get off his back about driving.

He grabbed his backpack and bounced down the stairs. His mom set the house alarm, and they both headed out. She locked the door behind them.

In their dark-blue Toyota coupe, Alex's mom recited her safety checklist. "Adjust the seat. Fasten your seatbelt. Check the mirrors. Start the car. Check all the warning lights on the dashboard, and look three-hundred-and-sixty degrees around the car for anything in the way."

Alex did his best not to roll his eyes. He took a deep breath, put the car into drive, and pulled away from the curb.

Everything went fine—until they got close to the school.

A Chevy pick-up came out of nowhere and barreled toward them. Alex swerved the car out of the way, avoiding a head-on collision, and squealed the tires as he hit the brakes.

The truck hopped the curb behind them and continued on.

Alex and his mom shuddered.

The truck drove across a lawn and thunderously crashed through the front of a house.

They stared in disbelief at the massive hole.

Alex's mom jumped out of the car. Her eyes hardened and she became a first responder nurse.

Alex looked above the house. "Oh my God!" He gasped.

Dark shapes dotted the blue sky as far as the eye could see. They were various sizes—some smaller than him and others as big as a house. All had the shadows of wings at their sides. He turned his head and followed their trajectory.

They headed for his school.

Why were they going there?

Alex's mom called 911. She got the recorded message that said because of the sudden increase in calls they would have to wait for an operator. She cursed, left the phone on speaker, and headed for the house.

Alex had a sudden realization that horrified him. "Mom, wait!" he yelled. He caught up with her and grabbed her arm. "You're not safe here. You have to go away. Grandma Ruby, in Oklahoma— you could stay with her."

"Alex, knock it off. I've gotta see if anyone's hurt. You go on to school. I'll be fine."

Alex shook his head. "No, I'll stay." They rushed through the jagged truck-sized hole.

The ground was littered with glass, wood, plaster, and the remains of the living room. The debris-covered truck had lodged into the kitchen wall.

Alex reached into the open driver's seat door and killed the engine. The cab was empty.

"Hello?" Alex's mom called out, looking around. "Where are you? I'm a nurse. I'm here to help."

They heard a low moan and followed it into the kitchen. Two bodies laid face-down on the floor. Alex saw dark shapes crawling all over them.

He shifted into the spiritual realm, and everything around him shimmered. Six small demons chewed on the fallen bodies.

Alex's sword lit up the room.

The demons stopped feasting and looked up in unison.

"Now that I've got your attention . . ."

Alex lunged at the creatures, but they were fast. In a flash they scattered like cockroaches, two in front, two behind, and two on the ceiling. He stopped, took his warrior stance, and held his glowing sword with two hands.

The two demons behind him pounced, but he swung around and sliced them both with one swing. As he turned, the two in front bared their razor teeth and shot forward. Alex spun and dispatched them. Then the two demons on the ceiling dropped. Alex jumped aside and swung his sword like a baseball bat, sending them both to hell in a cloud of shimmering dust.

Easy peasy!

He phased back into the physical realm and found himself face-to-face with his mom.

"Alex. What in the world?"

235

Eyes wide, Alex stammered, "Mom, I can't explain right now."

"You…" She choked on the words. "You disappeared … and reappeared. How?"

What could he say? Confused and afraid, he shouted, "It's why you have to leave. It's not safe here."

"Why? Alex, you're not making any sense."

"It's because . . . because . . ." He tried to catch his breath. "Please, Mom. Just trust me. You have to go to Grandma Ruby's. Now."

"Alex, that's not how life works. We can't just drop everything and go to Oklahoma whenever we feel like it. I have a job. I have responsibilities." She brushed his hair out of his eyes. "I have you, honey. I can't just leave you."

A siren sounded as an emergency vehicle approached.

"Go to school. There's nothing more you can do here."

He hated to admit she was right. He knew where he was needed. Still, he didn't want to leave her.

"I've got this. Go."

The Spirit within confirmed her words. "Just be careful, Mom, please."

"I promise." She smiled warmly. "My, you really have grown up." She hugged him, and he hugged her back tightly.

He stepped outside, hid behind a bush, and shifted again. He ran full speed in his skin-tight armor. Hundreds of demons passed overhead. At the school, hundreds more landed on the grounds, retracted their wings, and ran into the campus.

For the thousandth time, he wished Sariel was there with him.

*

"He's here, Mr. Cain," a female security officer announced.
"Good. Let him in."

Alistair's countenance brightened. One by one the variables were coming under control.

Alistair loathed uncontrolled variables. They added an element of unpredictability and unwanted surprise. Random variables—even minor ones—could take a plan off course and even cause complete system failure. In every project, he brought all variables into submission and, when possible, turned them into assets.

The door to his office opened to reveal a disheveled Mr. Addison supported by two of Cain's brawny assistants. The man had lost ten pounds in the last two weeks and looked like he was about to hurl. His hair was greasy and tousled, and he reeked of body odor and booze. His eyes wandered aimlessly.

Cain found encouragement knowing the essential elements were finally in place. Only two parts were still needed, and they were, for the most part, window dressing.

"Stabilize him," Cain barked. "If he dies, I will personally kill every one of you!"

The assistants nodded vigorously and ushered Addison away.

Cain turned to face his computer screens.

One random variable left to deal with—Alexander McKendrick, the athleta Christi, and any of the enemy's forces that came with him. Alistair was not afraid of the few angels that remained. He had plenty of demons on hand to battle them and to protect the plan.

As for Mr. McKendrick ... within hours, he would no longer be a variable.

Cain watched with malicious glee as his minions escorted Addison to the heavy metal door to the left of his office—the door to the spiral staircase. Within minutes the teacher would be strapped securely to the cot next to the pentagram.

Now, for the last variable. Cain focused on his wall of monitors, studying the flashing amber boxes of the facial recognition software that bounced around and framed student's faces.

No match for Alex.

Where was that infernal boy?

*

Alex ran at full speed. He imagined students all over the campus being tormented by small biting demons, creepers with their poison hooks, and knights with their powerful swords. Knight giants could be pulling kids apart with their bare hands. And who knew what other hellish creatures he would find?

Was this what he'd been training for?

He mustered his faith.

His will was set.

He would rise to the challenge.

Even if it killed him.

Instead of the anticipated pandemonium, he found an even more disturbing situation.

Creatures landed and took positions throughout the campus— but they weren't attacking anyone. Students walked right past them— and sometimes through them—talking, laughing, and texting as if nothing unusual was happening.

Alex's armor and sword disappeared and his body phased back into the physical realm—right in the middle of everyone. Kids passed him on both sides. Some bumped into his arms. No one paid him any attention.

Typical.

He walked toward the main building.

"This place is starting to look more like home every day."

Hope's voice.

She strode up next to him.

He was glad to see she was okay.

"Ho—", he started to say, but the fierce look in her eyes told him he'd better not. "Hecate, what *is* all this?"

"Get out of my way, Alex," she ordered and barreled past him in a rush.

He jogged up beside her and said, "Don't you think we should...you know...talk?" Without looking, she shoved her arm out and pushed him into a concrete bench. He lost his balance and fell unceremoniously to the ground.

Students laughed and heaped insults and abuse on him.

Alex got up, wiped the dirt off his jeans, and stared at Hope.

What in the world was going on?

*

Conor plopped into his Jeep's bucket seat and tossed his ragged three-ringed notebook onto the passenger's seat. He slammed the heavy door and clicked his seatbelt before he slipped the key into the ignition and the engine rumbled to life.

An excruciating pain started behind his eyes and traveled through the center of his brain.

He winced, shook his head, cursed, and slowly backed the old red Jeep out of the driveway. The car bounced into the street and sped off. Conor drove on autopilot, trying hard to see past the row of shimmering stars obstructing his vision.

At a stop sign, he hit the brakes. He took a deep breath and rubbed his eyes.

The air split with a deafening screech, a thundering crash, and the tortured sound of metal crunching. Conor was thrown forward and the seatbelt hit him like a fist, knocking the wind out of him.

His neck ached and his head hurt more than ever.

He glanced in the rearview mirror and saw a silver SUV on his butt. Shaken, Conor looked around, cursed again, and lumbered out of his car. He rubbed his throbbing neck.

When he looked up, a huge guy with wild wiry red hair, bulging eyes, and dirty frayed clothes barreled toward him. His tattooed right fist clanged a rusty metal baseball bat hard against the asphalt.

The man cursed and yelled, "What's the matter with you, punk?" He swung the bat right at Conor's head.

Conor ducked. "What's your problem, man? *You* hit *me*."

"I'll hit you." The man's backswing caught Conor's side.

Conor shoved the man with all his might, pushing him to the ground. He kicked the bat out of his hand.

As his assailant quickly rolled onto his knees, Conor kicked him square in the face, jumped into his car, and sped off.

*

Katie walked down the school hallway, deep in thought. She slowed when she felt the tug on her sleeve.

"Hecate, you startled me," she smiled at her new friend.

"Sorry, I just wanted to chat before first period."

"What's up?" She continued down the hall.

The she-demon forced a smile. "We're still on for tonight, right?"

"Yeah, sure."

"Great." The girls approached Katie's classroom door. "Dad's going to be away. I've stocked the kitchen with snacks, and we can order any movie we want."

"Sounds terrific," Katie said, smiling.

Hecate looked away and spoke with a cracking voice. "You don't know what this means to me. It sucks being the new kid and not fitting in. I'm just happy I met you. You're a real friend."

Katie hugged her. "I'm so glad you came to Kingman. I . . . well, you know."

Hecate stared wide-eyed as Katie entered the classroom.

*

Conor tried not to hurl. That idiot busted at least two of his ribs. At first he considered calling the police, but, since he didn't exactly have insurance, he decided against it. Should he go to the hospital? Did they do anything for cracked ribs? He wanted to see Hecate. If his ribs continued to bother him, he could just check in with the school nurse. If nothing else, he'd score some pills from friends. Then he'd feel no pain.

He came to a stop sign in front of the highway. The road was nearly empty. A van approaching from his left slowed to make a right-hand turn. Conor checked for cars then pulled out to make a left into the empty traffic lane. A beat-up gray Nissan Sentra swerved around the van and crashed full speed into Conor's car on the driver's side.

Pain engulfed him. It started in his side where the Jeep's door caved into him. He was jolted hard. His brain screamed in agony and his insides felt like they exploded. His stomach turned as the Jeep was hurled into the air and flipped upside down. And the sound—a deafening blast of metal and glass smashing, busting, and exploding—assaulted his ears.

He fought to breathe and not pass out.

The Jeep hit the ground hard and rolled onto its side.

Everything stopped.

Conor hung limp from his seatbelt. He hurt all over.

Blackness overtook him.

20

Friday, 1:07 p.m.

Alex spent the morning with frayed nerves. Shadows covered his school, but none of the demons attacked. He went from class to class looking over his shoulder, ready for anything.

He walked up to the edge of the Olympic-sized swimming pool. Baggy turquois swim trunks hung loosely to his knees. He gripped the porous cement tiles under his long toes, bent his knees, took a deep breath, and lunged forward.

With a big splash he entered the underwater world. Light played on the bottom of the pool, forming slowly moving, shimmering spider webs. Alex enjoyed being enveloped by the cool water. He loved the peace and quiet. It reminded him of his training time with Sariel, where he was taken out of the troubles of this world and given a different orientation and focus.

His head broke through the surface of the water. He wiped the water off his face and kicked his feet hard to stay afloat.

Was that a girl yelling?

He turned and saw Katie pull her arm away from Brandon as she told him to go away and leave her alone.

The stupid jock didn't seem to be getting the message.

Brandon told her, in a loud threatening tone, that he just wanted to talk.

Alex climbed the stairs out of the pool, dripping water on the concrete.

Hecate approached Brandon yelling, "Are you deaf *and* stupid? Just lay off, loser. She doesn't want to talk to you."

Brandon fired back. "Who asked you, you scary witch? Get back on your broomstick."

Three football players behind Brandon laughed. "Good one, dude."

Alex pushed Brandon away from Katie and shouted. "Leave her alone!"

Brandon quickly gained his footing and stood eye-to–eye with Alex.

Alex didn't back down. He set his jaw. His eyes smoldered, his hammer-like fists clenched, and his muscles tightened, ready to strike.

For an intense moment, time stood still.

Then one of the football players remarked, "Hey man, one more fight and they're gonna kick you off the team. This punk isn't worth it."

Brandon stepped back and released his fists. "Okay, okay. Look, I just wanted to talk to Katie. I think I hurt her feelings. Anyway, I wanted to see if we still had a chance." He turned to Katie. "So babe, let me know when you're ready to talk."

Katie shook her head. Her hard eyes declared it was over.

Brandon stepped away and told his goons, "C'mon guys, let's beat it."

Alex came closer to Katie, who was on the edge of tears. "You okay?" Alex lifted her chin and their eyes met.

"Alex, watch out!" Hecate yelled.

Before he could respond, there was a hard jerk on his wet trunks. He felt them slide to his ankles.

"Now that's what I call microscopic!" Brandon yelled, pointing and laughing.

Alex quickly pulled up his trunks, pivoted, and pounded Brandon's nose with a hard right cross. The jock stumbled back. His nose gushed blood. He wavered like he was drunk. His eyes rolled back in his head and his knees buckled. He collapsed on the wet concrete with a thud.

The three jocks glared at Alex. Pouncing in unison, they punched him, knocked him down, and kicked and stomped on him.

Alex's world went black. Yelling voices faded.

He faintly heard the harsh metallic sound of a whistle blowing and the coach yelling, "Hey! Knock that off, right now!"

He lost consciousness.

*

Alistair Cain had told his personal staff they would regret interrupting him for anything that wasn't life or death. The assistant who dared to stand before him now must have something vital to report.

"It's the boy you told us to watch, sir. He's been in a fight."

The assistant plucked on the keyboard at Alistair's command center. A video box popped up on one of the monitors and Cain watched the replay of the encounter with intense interest.

"There are times when events, for no apparent reason, simply go your way. We couldn't have planned anything better," Cain mused.

"Yes, sir."

"Let the others go with a severe warning. Bring Alex McKendrick to me."

"Yes, sir."

*

Alex had been taken by stretcher to the nurse's office. Smelling salts jolted him awake with a sting. His physical injuries amounted to a few cuts and bruises. The greatest wound he suffered was to his pride. Two large security guards fetched him and ushered him to the top of the stairs and into the foyer outside the new principal's office.

He was told to stand there and wait. The air was chilly. Still dressed in wet trunks, he held his arms across his bare chest for warmth. "How 'bout a towel? Or my clothes?"

The guards chuckled and headed back down the stairs.

"Thanks a lot," Alex called after them.

Another guard, a broad-chested hulk, loomed menacingly and tapped the gun in his holster. "Now, we're not going to have any problems, right kid?"

"No, sir," Alex muttered. He shivered and looked at the floor.

*

For over an hour Alex froze in the hallway near an armed guard. Each time he asked what was taking so long, he was told, "The principal's busy." When he asked if he could put his clothes back on, the guard told him nothing at all.

Finally, the guard ushered him into Principal Cain's office. He had to sit in a cold metal fold-out chair near the principal's enormous desk. Armed guards stood at attention behind him.

Alex looked up with amazement at the dozens of large monitors on the wall above the principal's head. Opened windows showed locations around the school in real time.

Alestair Cain had watched his every move.

Cain pushed his posh rolling chair back from his desk and stood to his full height. He paced in front of Alex. When he finally spoke, it was methodically, as if orating in a court of law. "Firstly, I want it fully noted that I am not attacking you or anyone else. The demons stationed around the campus are under strict orders to leave the humans alone. You, therefore, have no reason to attack us. Frankly, I am not even sure that you can."

"W-what's…what's this all about, M-M-Mr. Cain?" Alex wished he could get his teeth to stop chattering.

Principal Cain glared at him. "Alex, you are a royal pest, a random variable I simply cannot afford."

"So, do something about it. Destroy me now. Get it over with."

Cain smirked. "You cannot bait me, kid. That is my game."

The powerful man leaned on his desk. "I know you well. Every demon that pulls a weapon on you ends up back in Hell as a slimy pile of goo. However, I cannot allow you to ruin our plans." Cain steepled his fingers. "I have arranged a safer solution, something we in business call a win-win."

"The only s-s-scenario I s-s-see is we win, y-y-you lose," Alex snarled between stutters.

"Well, perhaps this will change your mind." Cain scooped up a remote from his desk and pressed a button.

The wall of screens flickered and showed live video feed of his mom, taken from more than a dozen different camera angles. She was at her nursing station, talking to someone on the phone. She looked concerned.

"Your mom is receiving very bad news. Firstly, one of our school counselors will tell her that her son is being suspended from school and may have charges pressed against him for assaulting another student. We have plenty of eye-witnesses and a video that will corroborate this."

Cain referred to the screen. A frozen image appeared with Alex's fist on Brandon's nose.

The demon said, "Look at her confusion and the pain in her eyes. Read her lips. *I don't understand*, she's saying. This is just great."

"Brandon attacked me first," Alex yelled. "There were p-plenty of witnesses."

"That is not what my security cameras will show. The entire section where your shortcomings were publically revealed? Well, let's just say that never happened. From what I understand, you and Brandon were vying for the same girl, am I right? So we have motive."

Cain paced again and continued, "I have signed affidavits from ten witnesses that will corroborate this story. Secondly, your mom is about to discover that the hospital she works for has been purchased by Cain Industries and that her department is being restructured. In layman's terms, my boy, she is being canned."

Cain walked behind Alex and clicked another button. The images changed. He viewed his house on some screens and a bank on others. "The bank, another Cain holding, has decided to foreclose on your mother's mortgage. You see, times being what they are, she's been late with her payment on more than one occasion, thereby voiding her contract. It would not be fiscally responsible to allow you and your mother to stay in your home. We are forced to, forgive the pun, repossess it."

The Executive Demon relished the pain in Alex's eyes. He had outmaneuvered this puny boy like a battlefield general, outflanking his opponent, neutralizing any possible assault and cutting off the avenue of retreat.

Cain now mustered his forces for a final crushing blow. "You do not watch the news, do you? Ignorant of current events? Well, allow me to enlighten you. Seems this town has some very unseemly characters in it—mass murderers, rapists, and the like. Your mother is rather attractive. My forces have brought her to the attention of these vile reprobates. As we speak, they are—shall we say—making plans."

"M-m-monster."

"Of course I am." Cain faced Alex and his eyes flashed red.

Cain straightened his tie, ready to close the deal. This was an old game—show the opposition they were out of options and then get them to give away the farm—and no one played it better than Alistair. "You have only one alternative, Alex. One that, I might add, is not all-together disagreeable. You told your mother to go to Oklahoma today, to visit your grandmother."

"How do you know that?"

"Knowledge is my business. You will convince your mother that it is time for the two of you to relocate to Oklahoma permanently, before something most unpleasant, most violent happens to her."

"No! You can't!"

"Of course I can. And what is more, you stupid fool, you cannot stop me."

Alex stared into the man's black eyes. Cain told the truth. He shivered violently and his breathing grew labored. He was beginning to go into shock.

Cain continued, "You will go to Oklahoma and leave all these difficulties behind you. Life might not be ideal in the Sooner State, but I shall see to it that your mother gets a good job and that you live comfortably for many years."

Alex shook his head. "N-n-no. I do kn-n-now who I'm d-dealing with. M-m-monsters don't make deals like this."

Cain smiled. Like all great businessmen, he had saved his trump card for the last. He leaned close to Alex's left ear, making sure he didn't block the view of his mother. "Have you noticed how thin the angelic protection has become in this town? Where is your guardian, Sariel? The forces of the enemy are in retreat. Nothing can stop my plans. Be assured, athleta, if you and your mother are not in that car by six o'clock tonight, I shall send a legion of demons to those vile criminals. They will torment her. They will violate her. They will make sure her end is as slow and painful and as brutal as possible. And you will watch."

"You bast—!" Alex tried to lunge at him but Cain's strong assistants held him back.

Cain howled in laughter. "Who is the real fatherless one here, Alex?" He lifted the remote again. "Oh, one more thing . . ." The image on the screens flickered and suddenly they all worked in unison, each monitor one piece of a wall-sized puzzle. There— unconscious on a hospital bed, tubes running all over his body—lay Conor.

Alex slumped in his chair, his eyes filled with pain. "What have you done?"

"What I had to do. You are a pest. I have tried to exterminate you. I have sent demon after demon to wipe you off the face of the earth, but, like a cockroach, you survive.

"My only recourse is to get you to choose to walk away of your own volition. Now, you would never do this just because I want you to. So, I have made it worth your while. I did this to your friend to remind you of my power. Your choice is clear—your misguided sense of mission, or your dear mother's life?" He smirked. "What is life, after all, but a series of choices? You cannot have everything, Alex. I think we both know what is really more important to you."

The screens switched back to Alex's mother, showing her from a dozen angles. Her brow was furrowed, her eyes full of fear.

Alex stared, his eyes full of tears.

*

Alex was gone for good. Cain had won.

Now that the last variable was secured, all would go according to plan.

Three knight demons accompanied him to the clock room. The years of accumulated clutter—band uniforms, mascot heads, etc.—had all been removed and the room cleaned.

Two experienced physicians tended to Addison, who lay on the raised cot.

On the far end of the room, affixed to the wall, a metal circle ten feet in diameter showed a massive assembling of the hordes of hell. There were bat-sized demons that zipped back and forth in front of the circle. There were demons in armor, demons ten feet tall, and half-formed demons in the process of restoration. Each faced the circle, waiting expectantly for the chance to return to the earth to settle old scores with their ancient enemy and His forces.

Cain transformed into his demonic self. His forehead puffed out and rippled. Two short black horns pushed out from between the ridges. A black wiry beard covered his cheeks and ended in a sharp point on his chin. His eyes became snake-like.

He faced the creatures behind him. "You do understand the importance of your assignment? The honor that has been bestowed upon you?"

"Yes, my lord," they said in unison.

"You know what to do?"

"Yes, my lord."

"You shall not fail me. Do you understand? You will shadow the athleta and make sure he is out of the way. If he deviates from our plan, even in the slightest, you will kill both him and his mother. Is that understood?"

"Yes, my lord."

Satisfied, the Executive Demon positioned himself before the knights. He took a wooden box from his pocket and lifted the lid.

"Open your mouths!" he ordered.

The creatures let their jaws fall. Cain pinched a dead fly from the box and dropped it into the gaping mouth of the demon nearest him. He did this again for the second and third demons, then closed the box and put it back into his pocket. He raised his arms slowly and closed his eyes, envisioning the transformation. Recalling the spell from the witch's book, he chanted the Latin words, *"Convertere in insectorum ad gloria malum."*

The Knights eyes widened. They looked at each other in horror. Their leathery skin bubbled. They shrieked in agony as they struggled to breathe. Confused, they complained of being hot and tore at their armor. All at once, they fell forward, landing on their hands and knees. Bones snapped loudly inside them. Their eyes rolled back in their heads, and they screeched even louder.

Three sets of limbs—long, black, hairy sticks—pushed out through the putrid, undulating flesh on their sides. Meanwhile, their own legs and arms dissolved into a puddle of green goo. Yellow structures pushed through the thick skin on their backs, extended, then fanned out into two pairs of jagged transparent wings.

The three demons wailed.

Their jaws popped and dislocated. They almost lost consciousness when their mouths extended and bent down, forming giant mandibles. The horns on their heads dissolved and segmented antenna broke through their skulls right above their eyes. Their eyes split like dividing cells, becoming two—four—eight. These new eyes flooded their brains with multiple images as if they peered through a kaleidoscope.

The three demons began to shrink—growing smaller and smaller and smaller. In no time they were the size of raisins.

As the blinding pain subsided, they gazed around the room. At first, it was hard to get their bearings. Their senses were all off. And then, slowly, as their brains' wiring became complete, they could hear, smell, see, and touch with heightened acuity.

Alistair Cain changed back to his executive self.

The three creatures rubbed their front feet together.

Cain flatten his hand in front of him at waist level. He said, "Come."

The flies flapped their wings so fast they became a frost-colored blur, lifted off the floor, and hung buoyantly in mid-air.

They ascended and landed on Cain's hand.

The Executive Demon leaned his lips near the tiny flies and whispered, "Go. Complete your mission. Do not fail me."

Three flies buzzed loudly and left his hand, following Alex's scent.

21

Friday, 6:03 p.m.

The sun sank low in the sky. Wraith-like shadows stretched across the Cain mansion.

The girls had been laughing and chattering for over an hour. Hecate had carefully planned the entire evening. They started with a personal spa, getting a complete massage, facial, manicure, and pedicure. Afterward, they wore comfortable loose-fitting black silk pajamas with their names embroidered in purple on their right pant leg.

Katie appeared to revel in the special treatment.

The girls ate chicken cordon bleu, crisp spinach salad, and crunchy sweet potato fries expertly prepared by Mr. Cain's personal chef.

"So, what's up with you and Conor?" Katie dipped her spoon into her luscious mint and chip ice cream. "Come on, all the juicy details."

Hecate smiled shyly. She relished this time with Katie. They had a real connection—something she had never known before.

Hecate put her spoon into her mouth and let the cold burst of sweetness coat her tongue. "Conor is Conor. With Conor, what you see is what you get. I think he's one of the most honest guys I've ever met."

Katie looked surprised. "Yikes, that's amazing. I've known Conor forever, but I don't think I could have described him any better. You're really something, Hecate."

Hecate, raised on hatred and abuse, found it impossible to accept compliments—especially tonight. Soon this girl, the only friend she ever had, would be dead. Her throat slit in honor of tonight's glorious events.

She had to stop thinking about it.

Hecate forced a smile. "What about you? Brandon is your past, who's your future?"

Katie looked coy and stared at her ice cream. "I do have my eye on," she raised her eyes, "someone."

Hecate pretended to look surprised. "Really? Spill it."

Katie took another lick of ice cream. She rolled her eyes toward the ceiling and slowly grinned. "It's Alex. I like Alex. And I think he liked me too…uh…for a while, but now I'm not sure."

Hecate scraped her spoon against the bottom of her metal ice cream dish, gathering every last drip of sugary goodness. "What about today at the pool? He seemed to care about you then, didn't he?"

"Yeah, maybe. It's just so soon after Brandon. My feelings are all screwed up. I…I just don't know."

"Men!" Hecate rolled her eyes and giggled.

"Yeah, men!" Katie nodded and rolled her eyes as well.

Three heavy white doors opened around them. Katie eyes went wide when tall muscle-bound hulks who looked like secret service men, stepped through and approached.

"Miss Cain, it is time to go," one of the men said.

"Where you goin', Hecate?" Katie asked, her spoon halfway to her mouth.

*

Alex stared at the California High Desert outside the car window. Rolling hills and deep water-cut washes raced by. In spite of the harshness of this arid landscape, he saw lush vegetation, even colorful flowers here and there. Life and beauty surviving against impossible odds.

His mom drove, both hands clenching the steering wheel. She stared forward, lost in her own thoughts.

Alex considered how he got here.

When he'd arrived home three hours ago, a large moving truck was parked in his driveway with a full crew loitering outside. His mom met him at the door and sat him down at the kitchen table. She explained that her hospital was letting her go. Fortunately, she was offered her dream job in Oklahoma, just fifteen minutes from her mom's house. The package included a salary nearly double what she made now—a small fortune in Oklahoma. Cain Enterprises offered her a beautiful rental to live in, which she could later buy from the company at a greatly reduced price. Even better, they offered to move her family free of charge.

The only catch?

They had to leave now.

Before making the decision that would uproot them and change their lives forever, his mom wanted to ask Alex what he wanted to do. In fact, she left the entire decision up to him.

Alex, his eyes pooling with tears, had agreed that they should go.

Cain really had thought of everything.

And so Alex stared out the window and tried not to cry.

His mom cleared her throat and took a deep breath. "So, it sounds like you had a big day. Wanna tell me about the fight?"

"There's not really much to tell."

"The counselor told me you went off on the boy and fractured his nose."

Alex was silent.

His mom sighed. "Yeah, it's probably time for a fresh start. I wasn't really getting anywhere in Willowbrook. Maybe being closer will...well, who knows? Maybe I can build some bridges with my parents." She was quiet for a moment. "Maybe they'll actually become grandparents. Anything can happen." She sighed. "I guess the clincher for me was what happened today. I've noticed the drop in your grades this year. I was hoping it was just a phase or something. But after today's meltdown—well, I can see there was a bigger problem."

Alex didn't respond. He considered the things he'd lost. There was Katie—although, to be honest, he never really *had* her. And Sariel. They'd only begun his training when the angel just disappeared. And now, he was losing everything else. Conor—the image of him in the hospital still haunted Alex—his friends, his school, his home.

Alex felt like he was fading away, like a water color painting held under a running faucet. Soon there'd be nothing left.

Worst of all was his shame over betraying his God and losing any standing he had before Him. He had been an athleta, a chosen warrior for God.

Now he was nothing.

The enemy was mobilized.

Something horrific was about to happen at his school.

And he was AWOL.

With pain-filled eyes, he glanced over at his mom. She was all he had left.

*

The guards approached Katie. She dropped her bowl and lunged for her phone, which sat on the dining room table in front of her. One of the guards deftly plucked it from her hand and smashed it on the floor under his heavy shoe.

"Who the hell do you think you are?" She swung her fists at the guard. Another man pushed her back into her chair. "When my dad finds out you broke my phone, he's going to kick your—"

One of the men produced a syringe while two of them held her down.

"Wait! Wait! What's that? Stop! You can't!" She turned to Hecate. "Hecate! Make them stop! Call your dad! Do something!"

The girl, who she thought was her friend, simply turned away and said, "Don't fight it, Katie. There's nothing I can do."

Katie gasped. Hecate was in on this?

Katie screamed, kicked, and flailed against the strong hands that held her. She tried to pull her arm away as the guard plunged the needle into it.

She yelled obscenities and sobbed. In seconds, her body became unresponsive. She couldn't speak or keep her eyes open. She desperately tried to hold onto consciousness.

Then all went black.

*

One of her father's security officers carried Katie out over his shoulder, fireman style.

Hecate followed, holding back tears.

Twenty minutes later, Katie's eyes were closed and her limp head bobbed as she was carried up the circular stairs to the top of the clock tower and to her destiny.

*

"So," Alex's mom asked. "What was that at the truck accident today?"

"Huh?" Alex turned from the window and faced her.

"Hello? You disappeared. I saw it. And then you reappeared. As weird as it was, it didn't seem to faze you at all. You just went on as if nothing had happened."

Alex's mouth went dry. After giving up everything to save his mom, he couldn't bring himself to lie to her. "Okay," he sighed, "I'll tell you, but you won't believe me."

"Try me." She glanced at him and gave her *I'm waiting* expression.

Okay, Alex said to himself, *here goes*. "I've been . . . um . . . in training."

"Training? For what?"

"To become a soldier for God, something called an athleta Christi. It all started a few weeks ago. I was trained by . . . by an angel, named Sariel." As the words crossed his lips, their reality seemed far off, like a distant night's dream.

His mother glanced at him again. "Go on."

"Well, I was given powers and spiritual equipment—the armor of God. I fought demons and destroyed them, and . . . well, I was getting pretty good at it." He grew suddenly quiet and looked over at his mom. He shook his head. "I can only guess what you're thinking." He impersonated her, in a high-pitched raspy voice, "*My poor son. We'll have to see if the Oklahoma hospital has a good psychiatrist he can see. Maybe two.*"

"Never pretend to know what anyone else is thinking. And, as your mother, I forbid you to ever use that voice for me again. Understood?"

"*Absolutely*," he responded in the voice.

They both laughed.

"Alex, listen to me. I've never been more proud of you than I am right now. Of course your grades fell! You were focused on fighting for the Lord. You disappeared to fight a demon this morning?"

"Six. They were easy."

"And that fight today, with the boy, you were fighting for the Lord, right?"

Alex looked down. "No. Not really. That was all me."

His mom chuckled. After a pause, she said, "I wish you would have trusted me and told me this sooner."

"So, you...you believe me?"

"Alex, I'm a Christian, remember? How could I say I believe the Bible and not believe there are angels and demons all around us all the time?"

He considered this. "Yeah, I see your point."

"So, what comes next for you, athleta?"

Alex turned away stone-faced and stared again out the window.

His mom probed. "What's wrong?"

After a moment, he whispered. "I've retired."

"Hmmm. God told you to retire?"

He shook his head. "Not exactly."

And then the entire situation—the new job, new house, and fresh start—made perfect sense. Her voice became sharp. "You're protecting *me*, aren't you?"

Alex didn't answer.

"Aren't you! Alex, be completely honest with me. You were told to back off or something terrible would happen to me, right?"

He looked down and admitted, "Yeah."

Alex's mother pulled the car over to the emergency lane and turned off the engine. Other cars swished by, their headlights momentarily lighting up the area around their car.

She spoke in her stern, *Now, you listen here young man* tone, saying, "How dare you decide this for me, Alex?"

"But Mom—"

"Don't you *but Mom* me! What were you thinking? I can't order you to obey God. If I did, you wouldn't really be obeying Him as much as obeying me. This is something you have to do because *you* want to. But, don't you *ever*, I mean *ever*, choose to disobey God because you're protecting me."

Alex's phone signaled in short beeps that he had a text.

"Go ahead, read it," his mom said. "It may be important."

Alex retrieved the text from Hope, which read:

help!
katie in danger
school clock tower
gonna kill her!
hurry Alex!

He shoved the phone back in his jacket pocket.

"So?" His mom asked.

Alex shook his head. "I can't. If I do anything, he'll kill you."

"Listen to yourself. You keep mixing things up. You think that if you obey God, you'll be responsible for my death. But if I die, it won't be your fault, Alex. I know that."

He started to object.

"No, you listen to me. Being a Christian means surrendering our lives to God. He owns us. He chooses what's best for us and for His kingdom. Whether we live or die, our lives are His to use as He wills."

Alex couldn't help himself. He sobbed. "But I can stop them. I can keep you safe."

His mother took a deep breath, pulled his head over to her shoulder, and ran her fingers through his hair. "Alex, recently I said you were growing up. I meant it. It's time you became an adult in this area. You can't hold onto me forever. I've been placed in your life for a short time, and, don't get me wrong, I've loved every second I've been your mom, and I've tried to do my best to raise you as a Christian man. But I'm asking you, please, take me out of your equation. I'll gladly accept whatever God has for me—life or death. But you need to either walk in obedience, or not, because that's what you've chosen for yourself. Either way, I will always love you."

Alex remembered Sariel's words, *Eeverything that happens is God's will. This is the best of all possible universes because it reveals the most about God. If a better universe could have been made, the all-powerful God would have made it. No matter what happens to us, it will be according to God's plan and for His glory.*

Alex breathed deeply. "I've made my decision."

*

Hecate stepped into the clock room and her jaw dropped. Two physicians attended to a disheveled, unconscious man. On the floor next to him was a pentagram eight feet in diameter with unlit candles at every vertex. She looked across the room. On the far wall, by the window, hung the thick iron back of the clock—a massive circular opening to hell. Her stomach turned at the sight of the sea of demons clambering in front of this portal. She had heard of the place of eternal imprisonment and suffering but had never really seen it.

Glancing above her, she saw demons the size of wolves positioned across the vaulted ceiling, hanging like vampires. Their maniacal eyes followed her as she entered the room.

To the left of her, three big chairs, like thrones, were set in a place of honor like box seats at a stadium. The first and largest was constructed of blood-covered skulls fused together in expressions of torment and horror. The second, smaller and less ornate, was made of wrought iron, and the third, built of plain oak, was normal human size.

Although the thrones were empty, she suspected they wouldn't be for long.

The guards laid Katie's limp body on the floor. They stretched out her arms and legs and secured them in metal shackles with chains connected to thick eyelets in the planked floor.

Hecate noticed a second empty set of restraints next to Katie's.

Her father, in his demonic shape, came close. "Ah, there you are, Hecate. As you see, we are finishing our preparations. The ceremony shall begin at ten o'clock. The procedure shall be a lengthy one, I'm afraid. One you will probably find rather boring. That is, everything except the beginning—the sacrifice."

By the hungry look in her father's eyes, she assumed those empty shackles were meant for her.

"What *is* all this?" Hecate asked in a small, controlled voice.

"It is time for you to continue your education." Her father grabbed her arm and pulled her over to the unconscious man. "You have not met Henry Addison. He is a teacher on staff here at Kingman High. Mr. Addison is important. He carries a promise in his bloodline. You see, just over four hundred years ago, our glorious lord, Lucifer, brilliantly outmaneuvered the enemy. He tricked Him into forging a deal and, of course, the enemy cannot go back on a deal."

Her father steered Hecate to the large circular hole in the wall. "It was simple. Our lord accused the heavenly enemy of being a sadistic bully. He cunningly showed Him that this fight between our kingdoms was patently unfair. What sense does it make for His forces to outnumber ours two-to-one? Why should our armies be systematically reduced in battle while His vast minions remain stable? Our vanquished demons are imprisoned in hell, whereas, when the enemy's warriors are defeated, they are taken to heaven, healed, and returned to service. In the end a deal was made, and the enemy foolishly agreed to allow our forces to be replenished—under certain conditions."

"Conditions? What conditions?" Hecate stepped away from her father and closer to the hole in the wall. She stared at the swarming throng and shuddered at the thought of all those angry demons coming back to earth.

"A human blood line was chosen to be the key to reversing the polarity of this portal to hell. Currently, the doorway only goes in one direction. We can send things into hell, but nothing can come back this way. But at midnight on the 50th birthday of any male in the Addison bloodline, the portal reverses—for one minute only."

"Why so small a portal? Why not make it huge?"

"The size of the portal was part of the bargain—ten feet in diameter, or less. In a little over two hours, we will have one short minute to get as many demons as possible across this threshold."

Her father leaned over the man strapped on the gurney.

He whispered in his ear, "Happy birthday, Mr. Addison."

*

Alex sighed as his mom got off the freeway. She turned the car around and headed back to Willowbrook.

"I'm proud of your decision." She smiled at her son. "I support you one hundred percent."

Alex heard the loud frantic buzzing in the back of the car. He turned and saw two dark shapes the size of softballs flying at him. He swatted at them, but they stopped in mid-air and dodged his swipes. He saw a third bug fly to his mom and latch itself onto the back of her neck. She screamed, and the car swerved out of control.

Alex leaned his entire being on the Spirit of God within him and prayed, *Father, please give my mom eyes to see into the spiritual realm.*

He shifted to this parallel dimension and was instantly in his full armor.

Alex grabbed the bug off his mom and threw it into the back seat.

His mom tried to regain control of the car, swerved to avoid an oncoming truck, and rammed into the guard rail on her right, creating a shower of sparks. She hit the brakes hard, bringing the car to a sudden stop.

"Alex, get out of the car!" she screamed.

Alex and his mom both jumped out and slammed the doors shut, trapping the creatures, but they busted through the windows.

His mom ran down the road, chased by one of the enormous flies. It had gotten so much bigger.

The other two creatures, barely visible in the darkness, were transforming—growing and changing color and shape—becoming demons.

Before the nearest one could fully form, Alex halved it with his sword. Its dark blood spurted and it disappeared.

Alex watched his mom fall down on the rough pavement, badly scraping her leg and hurting her arm. She turned over and sat up, the headlights shining on her like spotlights.

In front of her, the mega-fly bubbled and transformed. In seconds, hairy black legs dissolved, the compound eyes melted, and the mandible fell away. The creature's natural DNA reasserted itself, reconstructing the knight demon—a terrifying silhouette in the bright headlights.

She screamed in terror.

A sword appeared in the creature's right hand. It looked down on Alex's shuddering mother and smiled as it raised its sword high for a killing blow.

Before the creature could bring down his jagged blade, a glowing sword tip popped out of his chest, and gunky blood bubbled from around it and down its armor. The creature's expression turned from victory to horror. It dropped its sword, wailed, and vanished in a dense cloud.

Behind the cloud stood Alex, his sword in hand.

"Thank you." His mom smiled with pride.

Alex looked over his shoulder. "Be right back."

*

The athleta spun and lifted his cross-covered shield to block a blow from the third knight demon.

The demon stepped back. "You are nothing, boy! When I'm through with you…"

Alex smashed the beast in the head with his shield. The demon stumbled. Alex took advantage of this split-second opportunity and brought his sword down on the creature's exposed neck. The head rolled away and the body convulsed before both became shiny dust.

Alex shifted back to his regular clothes and returned to his mom, who sat on the pavement.

She shook her head. "So this is normal for you?"

He laughed. "Pretty much. You okay?"

She nodded.

"We need to go." He offered her his hand. He pulled her up, but her knees buckled and she threw her arms around his neck to keep from falling.

She looked at her right hand and gritted her teeth. "Ow! I think it's sprained, maybe broken."

Alex supported her as she hobbled back to the car, not putting any weight on her right leg. "Better put me in the passenger side. I can't drive. You'll have to do it."

"You're kidding, right?" Alex's voice cracked, an expression of horror on his face.

*

Alistair Cain smiled with satisfaction. Everything was progressing according to plan.

He looked out the window on the face of the tower, next to the portal. The demons in the courtyard below stood guard against any angelic attack, elated at the prospect of seeing their partners in evil once again. Together they would be a strong army—one that could really challenge the angels and win.

Then something caught Cain's eye. It ascended the horizon, just above the rising moon. Dark energy in the form of a chariot streaked through the sky leaving black flames and smoke in its wake. Drawn by eight majestic dragons beating enormous wings, it looked like hell's version of Santa Claus's sleigh.

Cain's heart raced. The massive demon crowd below stopped dead and stared upward at the satanic vessel streaking through the sky.

"Okay, places, everyone! He's here," Cain announced, holding his hands tightly together.

The room filled with smoke and dark flames as the phantom sledge passed, soaring through the front wall and leaving through the back.

It left a commanding being in its wake. Nearly ten feet tall, he wore a robe of black fire. His coal-black skeletal head had foot-long, upward-pointing horns on each side.

At the sight of him, everyone dropped to their knees and cowered.

"Rise," the chief demon hissed. He slowly glided to the throne of bones and reclined.

The dragon-faced North American Demon, Smok, then flew into the room. He bowed before Satan and took his place on the metal throne. Lastly, Alistair Cain sat on the plain, wooden chair.

Cain spoke to Satan. "In honor of your superior genius and ultimate victory, my lord, I have arranged a special entertainment. I hope it pleases you."

He nodded toward two assistants who grabbed Hecate and dragged her screaming to the floor. While she fought and kicked, they closed the shackles on her wrists.

"Let me go!" She snarled and pulled against the restraints. Then she looked at Cain. "Father, you can't do this. I did everything you asked. I fulfilled my mission. Please, father!"

Cain faced her. "You are just one less variable in the equation." He spoke to the physicians. "You may begin."

Hecate screamed. Satan and the North American Demon leaned forward.

The physicians gave Katie smelling salts. She reacted violently—coughing, choking, and forcing open her eyes. Hecate lay quietly next to her, looking away.

Katie tried to get up, but metal dug into her wrists. She glanced at her restraints. She shook them hard, but they only clanged as if laughing at her weakness. She looked around at Hecate, the witches, the moving picture on the back of the clock, and the empty thrones.

A witch stood above her. She waved gnarled hands over the girl's head and chanted an ancient incantation.

Cain watched as Katie's vision changed and she acquired the ability to see the spiritual realm. She looked up and gasped at the creatures hanging from the ceiling. Her eyes darted around the room, from demon to demon. And then she looked toward the thrones.

Her eyes fell on the largest throne. When she saw the horned skull and its glowing eyes, she shook with terror.

Smok chuckled and tapped his fingertips together with deep satisfaction.

Katie screamed at the top of her lungs.

Hecate sobbed.

Cain looked over to Satan. His master leaned forward and hissed with delight.

Horror, shock, betrayal, murder.

Most entertaining.

22

Friday, 9:46 p.m.

The time it took for Alex and his mom to return to Willowbrook turned into one long driving lesson. Alex had never driven on the freeway, nor had he ever driven at night. His mom talked him through every move and proceeded to bite her lip when he wandered into the next lane, scold him when he tailgated, and praise him when he occasionally kept the car steady.

Alex parked under a streetlamp in a quiet neighborhood three blocks away from the school. He shifted to the spiritual realm and looked around. There were no demons nearby, so he reappeared in the driver's seat.

His mom shook her head. "I don't think I'll ever get used to that."

Alex looked at his mom. She cradled her arm. "I still think you belong at the hospital."

"I'm a nurse, remember? Don't worry. I'm fine, just sore. This is where God wants you. I can go later, if I have to."

He thought for a second. "Okay." He nodded. He got out of the car and closed the door. Before he moved, he took one more look around and checked for shadows. Then he walked around to the passenger side and spoke through the open window. "You should be okay here. I'll...I'll be right back."

"I still think we should call the police."

"And tell them what? That the high school's been taken over by demons? They won't see them. They'll think it's a prank. It's not a fight they're prepared for."

She considered. "Well, you be careful, understand?"

He shook his head. "I hate leaving you here alone."

"You have no choice. If you need anything, call me on my cell. Somehow, I'll get help to you." She touched his face. "God has called you to be an athleta Christi. Go, obey God. Save the girl. Be the hero. I can wait. But *be careful*—I mean it. I'm just gonna have a little nap." She rolled up the window, moved her seat back, winced as she found a comfortable position, and narrowed her eyes.

"I'll be back soon." Alex placed his palm on the window and smiled the little boy smile that only moms and their sons share, then he turned and, for the second time that day, he left her and ran toward the school.

He shifted into the spiritual realm and his spiritual gear. Carrying his sword and shield before him, he stepped onto the school grounds.

His jaw dropped. Hundreds, maybe thousands of demons of all sizes rallied in the courtyard.

Alex looked up to the ancient clock in the clock tower. Hecate, no—Hope, had texted him that Katie was in danger there. A storm cloud hung above the spire with dark lightning shooting through it.

He held his shield tight and thought of what Mr. Addison had taught him about Constantine. Going to battle against Rome, he saw a vision in the sky—a shield with a cross on it. A celestial voice proclaimed, *"In this sign you will conquer."* Constantine had all his soldiers paint crosses on their shields. They defeated the superior army in Rome. Alex glanced at the green cross on his shield. He prayed for the same victory now under the same emblem.

Once one demon saw the athleta, they all saw him. The entire satanic multitude turned toward him. They jeered and stomped the ground. The closest ones, a group of short, vicious monsters, instinctively raced forward to attack.

They were vaporized under his sword.

Alex glared at the rest and took his fighting stance. His blade shone brightly.

For a moment the hellish horde wasn't sure what to do. Then they screamed in unison.

Alex winced and covered his ears. Windows shattered on the surrounding buildings.

Satanic warriors screwed up their courage and prepared to attack. Jagged swords appeared in gnarled fists.

The commanding voice of the Executive Demon called out from the open Clock Tower window. "Stop, you idiots! He shall destroy you all! Step back, now, and bring forth our mighty champion."

At these words, the multitude stepped back, forming a circle and revealing a vile monster Alex had never seen before.

Cain called out to Alex, "Behold athleta, your worst nightmare—a midnight demon."

The beast stood over ten feet tall. Thickly matted, dark-brown fur ran from his waist to ankles. His muscular legs were bird-like, bending backward and ending in two powerful toes pointing forward and one pointing back, each one tipped with razor-sharp talons. His brawny humanoid upper body was protected by well-fitted armor. His floor-length cape ended in sharp narrow spikes on both sides.

Alex cringed at the face. Five black horns ringed his head. Tall ears pointed skyward. His eyes were black with narrow, yellow vertical lines streaking through them. Piercing fangs in the giant mouth curved out of his face like spikes on a bear trap.

Sparks ignited in his right claw. A swirling cloud of dark energy with sputtering lightning bolts inside.

Alex shouted at the creature, "I am a Champion of Christ, and I serve the Lord of all. Leave this area, or I *will* destroy you." This sounded far more convincing in his head.

He took a deep breath, planted both feet firmly, and leaned his entire being on the power of the Holy Spirit within him.

The terrifying creature shouted like a banshee. He turned toward the clock tower and acknowledged Cain, his master, bowing his ugly head. He then quickly turned to face Alex, ready to pounce.

They circled, facing each other. The scene reminded Alex of the Roman Coliseum—he was the Christian and this thing was the lion.

Before the threatening monster attacked, he projected words and images into Alex's mind, scratching thoughts directly into his consciousness. The words "disloyalty," "lying," "laziness," and "failure" echoed through his head. Images of missing the mark in nearly every area of his life flooded his soul, filled him with guilt, and crushed his resolve. Who was he to stand for the holy God? He was just as evil as the creatures he fought. He was full of sin and had lived a selfish life. In reality, he was nothing but a complete Christian screw-up. This charade had to stop.

Alex's armaments began to fade.

And then a different voice spoke within him. Alex remembered what he'd heard in church from his earliest days, the words that were spoken over him at his baptism—that it was not his sinfulness that mattered, but the sacrifice of Jesus which covered his sin. That now, because he had chosen to be in Christ, he was clothed in His righteousness.

He remembered grace.

Alex listened to the Spirit and took his warrior stance. When he did, his armor grew solid and strong once more.

A new piece, a segmented gray breastplate covered his upper body. It clung to him like a Kevlar vest. The front was covered by a blazing green cross that ran from his neck to his belt. This was the Breastplate of Righteousness. It completed his armor and made him stronger than ever.

His confidence soared.

Alex stood his ground. The midnight demon leaned forward and shot straight up into the air like Superman. The creature flew swiftly from one side of the courtyard to the other in front of the clock tower. He came down right on top of Alex—talons first.

The athleta held up his shield, and the creature hit it hard. Sparks flew. Alex was knocked on his back. The flying demon wailed and backed off, hanging in mid-air, just above the athleta. It pounded the shield with its wings. Alex tried to hang on.

The midnight demon rose into the air triumphantly.

The demonic horde laughed and cheered wildly.

*

From inside the clock tower, the Executive Demon announced, "This is the beginning of the evening's entertainment. You will all be treated to the messy demise of the athleta, Alexander McKindrick. I will kill this pathetic agent of the enemy and then replenish the forces of Hell on earth. Let the painful slaughter begin."

Even Satan sat a little higher and watched expectantly.

*

The midnight demon beat his wings, keeping his position above the courtyard. He held up his right claw. The ball of dark energy buzzing around it coalesced and shimmered with dark lightning.

The creature called out to Alex, "I promise you a painful death, puny one. Agony, fear, and shame will be your fate. In the end, you will beg me to kill you."

Alex yelled back, "Bring it on, you ugly . . . um . . . rooster. When I'm done with you, you'll be crowing in hell."

The demon threw back his head in fury. He reared his arm and hurled a sparkling ball of dark energy at Alex.

Alex jumped to his feet, braced himself, and held up his powerful shield. The sparkling energy sphere hit the shield like a missile, and dark lightning sprayed in all directions. The shield held, but Alex was knocked back five feet and landed on his butt.

The athleta shook it off and quickly regained his footing. He called up to the creature, "Looks like I hit a nerve. What else you got, chicken legs?"

Before Alex could react, the Midnight Demon fired another swirling ball at him. The missile hit his right arm, sizzled and sparked, and penetrated his armor. Immediately, his arm screamed in agony, went numb, and his hand opened. His eyes widened in shock when his spirit sword dropped to the ground and disappeared.

The hovering creature lifted higher above the courtyard and held up his right claw once again. The way he kept glancing up at its claw, Alex figured he was waiting for the energy to build so he could throw another powerful bolt. He appeared to have all the time in the world.

Alex watched helplessly as the black fuzzy ball around the beast's hand grew and grew and grew.

"Oh, my God, help!" Alex said under his breath. He knew it wasn't much of a prayer, but he meant it.

The flying creature pulled back his right arm and launched a black sparkling mass the size of a small car right at Alex. The demonic horde followed the energy ball down, twisting their heads to track its path.

Just before it hit him, Alex jumped away. But, to his surprise, he didn't land—he soared. The energy sphere hit the ground and harmlessly dissipated into the concrete. Alex looked below him and grinned.

He yelled with pure excitement. "Yahoo!"

He was flying!

Alex willed himself to dart forward and backward. He spun in place and did a flip. Then he braced himself and soared high above the school, passing the midnight demon on the way up.

The beast grabbed for him, but he was too slow.

"Whoa!" Alex yelled as he came to a stop, hovering high above the school. "Now, this is what I'm talkin' about!"

The demon turned toward Alex and fired dark energy with each hand—a steady volley of spheres the size of softballs. The round missiles pounded Alex's shield with no effect.

Alex leaned to his right and took off, holding his shield in front of him. He found flying easier than riding a bike. He made a full circle around the quad while the midnight demon threw small energy balls that continuously fell far short of their mark.

Alex soared past the main school building and neared the clock tower. Dark bolts shot past him on both sides. The midnight demon was in hot pursuit.

Alex returned to the courtyard and descended. He dropped down to ground level and aimed his shield to plow down a group of demons standing near the walkway. Their eyes and mouths opened wide in horror as the shield knocked them off their feet.

Alex tried to move his right hand. He could bend his fingers, and they no longer felt numb.

Good.

He flew like a rocket, streaking through the air with the midnight demon close behind.

The creature hurled black energy spheres that whizzed past his head—so close their crackling rang in his ears. This beast learned fast and now anticipated Alex's movements. It was only a matter of time before a lucky shot immobilized him and took him down.

Alex flew back toward the school building and braced himself behind his shield. He aimed for the front door. He skidded on the ground and hit the door so hard he crashed through, sending a million splinters into the air. He rode the shield forward like a toboggan. It hit the ground and skidded down the hall, rammed a couple of trashcans, slowed, and finally came to a stop.

Alex jumped up, took his warrior stance, and held up the shield.

The midnight demon raced through the open doorway with his ear-splitting banshee cry.

Alex realized his mistake. He was stuck inside a narrow corridor with a powerful monster, and his ability to maneuver—his only real defense—was lost.

The demon also realized his advantage and came at Alex in a dead run, firing energy bursts left and right.

Alex reached over to his right and turned the door handle. He fell through the door just as the barrage hit. Standing in his first period classroom felt weird. Keeping his attention on the door, he backed into the room, bumping into desks.

He listened for any movement.

If only Sariel were here.

Alex braced himself for the worst.

But nothing happened. An eerie quiet filled the room. Alex crept toward the door one deliberate step at a time.

Holding his shield to the side, he opened the door a crack, leaned over, and peered back into the hall.

It was clear.

Weird.

That's when the demon raged through the back wall of the classroom.

Alex was knocked clear into the hallway and onto his back with the wind knocked out of him. His shield skidded about ten feet away. He heard desks knocked aside. The demon appeared in the doorway, glaring at him.

Alex rolled up and started to stand, but a giant talon flew forward and hit him square in the chest, knocking him to the floor.

The demon smiled. His right claw lifted and black energy swirled and sparked around it.

Alex scrambled up and reached for his shield, but the creature darted forward and kicked him in the back, forcing him down again. Alex rolled. Before he could get up, the creature pinned him down, his clawed foot resting hard on his chest.

He couldn't breathe.

The horrid creature yelled a cry of victory and reared his crackling arm back for one last powerful missile.

Alex prayed to the Spirit and willed his sword into his hand. It appeared. He shoved the fiery blade deep into the creature's feathered leg.

The midnight demon shrieked and jumped backward in pain.

Alex followed with another thrust, burying the weapon deep into the demon's chest.

The creature writhed wildly as he tried to pull out the blade. With a forlorn banshee cry, it disintegrated in a thick, dark cloud.

Alex, still carrying his sword and shield, stumbled wearily out of the building to the deafening jeers of an angry crowd of vengeful demons.

"You guys just don't know how to treat a champion," he quipped.

*

Cain's jubilant smile fell. He stared in shock and disbelief. Rage exploded within him, and he commanded the demon horde to "Kill him! Kill him now!"

With one deafening cry, all the creatures lunged toward Alex.

*

"Oh, man!" Alex yelled.

As the demons reached him, he sprang from the concrete and lifted into the air, heading straight for the clock tower. Demons took flight behind him, like bats from a cave, their wings pounding the air.

Cain jumped back as Alex burst through the window and landed just inside the room.

He turned back to the window and shoved his shield into it, covering the opening.

The cross on the holy shield radiated. Demons in front hit the shield and sizzled into oblivion. The rest stopped short and backed away to a safer distance.

Alex's eyes darted around the room. Satan and the North American Demon glared at him from their thrones. On the wall near the window was a giant hole to Hell where a field of demons, as far as the eye could see, stood like they were waiting for something.

Hecate—or was it Hope?—stood in the back wearing a black cloak with a group of women who looked like witches. A pentagram glowed red on the floor at his feet. Katie . . . poor Katie ... lay shackled to the floor next to it.

And then his knees buckled in shock.

Alex's mom was chained to the floor beside Katie. Upon seeing her, his shield, sword, and armor faded and disappeared.

Two of Cain's assistants grabbed his arms and held him fast.

Cain stepped forward. "Mr. McKendrick. I thought you and I had a deal—a pretty sweet deal for your family, I might add. You double-crossed me. We had no trouble finding your mother in the car

278

and bringing her here. Now, she will pay for your deception." He pulled out a dagger and moved toward Alex's mom. He smiled. "After all, a deal is a deal."

"Don't touch her!" Alex yelled as he pulled hard against his captors.

They held him fast in their iron grip.

Satan hissed with pleasure.

The North American Demon ran his forked tongue over his conical teeth in anticipation.

Cain kneeled down and held his blade to Alex's mother's exposed throat.

Alex's mom closed her eyes and prayed intently, "Our Father, who art in heaven…"

The demons shrieked and covered their ears.

Alex seized his opportunity and jerked his arms out of the guards' grip.

Cain yanked a piece of bloodstained linen from the floor and stuffed it into the praying woman's mouth. "That is quite enough of that," he snarled.

Alex stepped forward and tried to take his warrior stance, but the goons on either side of him recovered, grabbed his arms, and pulled him back.

The Executive Demon brought his blade to his mom's throat again, bowed to Satan, and exclaimed, "For your pleasure, my lord."

Alex watched as his mom closed her eyes and gave herself completely to God's will. No matter what happened, she would accept it as His loving servant.

Cain tightened his grip on the knife.

Hope threw off her black cloak. The room filled with a blinding light that exuded from every pore of her being. The demons, including Satan himself, turned away from her brilliance.

Hope lunged at her father, hitting him hard and knocking him to the floor. She stood tall and lifted her arms. Her hands, with white crosses in the palms, filled with swirling white light and crackling sparks.

"Alex!" she yelled as she hurled two balls of shimmering lightning at his guards. The swirling current encased them and their bodies shook convulsively. Their eyes rolled up into their heads and they fell to the floor unconscious.

Alex took his warrior stance. His sword and armor returned. His shield solidified and glowed bright green once more.

Alex pointed his blade at Cain's head. "It's over. Release my mom and Katie! Now!"

Hope raised her right hand, which blazed with swirling white light, and said, "Do it, father."

Cain glared at her with utter contempt.

"Now!" Hope ordered.

The Executive Demon reached out and waved his hand toward the shackles. They popped open with a loud clang. Katie and Alex's mom sat up, rubbing their wrists.

Alex's mom yanked the stale rag from her mouth and spit.

A midnight demon, the size of a linebacker, emerged from the shadows behind Satan's throne. He pulled back his arm and fired a ball of black energy. It hit Alex in the chest and swirled over him. His muscles screamed in pain and his body stiffened. His sword, armor, and shield faded and disappeared again.

Two witches grabbed Hope from behind, jerking her arms high behind her back.

Cain rose up behind Alex's mother and buried his blade deep into her back.

Her eyes went wide and she gasped.

"No!" Alex screamed.

Alex's mom turned toward Alex. Her eyes met his. "I love you, son," she stammered. "You are God's warrior and . . . and I'm so proud of you." Her eyes closed and her body collapsed.

Cain ran the blade across her throat, then held up the bloody weapon victoriously.

Alex shook in horror. "I'll kill you!"

He tried to move, to tear Cain apart with his bare hands, but his muscles were frozen. All he could do was curse and wail.

Cain seized Katie's arm and twisted it high behind her back. She yelped and winced in pain. He brought the bloody blade to her throat. His eyes blazed. "This is just not your day, athleta. We have nearly two hours. This one will die slowly, painfully."

"Keep your hands off her," Alex yelled.

Cain smiled with slanted eyes. "Oh no, athleta. We are going to put our hands all over her."

Hope pulled her arm back, smashing her elbow into the nose of the witch on her right. Her right hand freed, she fired a crackling bolt of white energy at her father's head. It encased him like a helmet. He dropped his knife and fell to the floor, blinded.

Hope turned toward the witch on her other side and punched her square in the nose. Blood gushed down her chin.

Hope then turned to Alex and threw a flashing lightning bolt right at him. The charge hit him and surrounded his body, neutralizing the effects of the demonic energy. Instantly, his body was released and he could move again.

Alex looked down at his fallen mother. Her eyes stared forward in death.

He fought back tears and willed his sword and shield into his hands. A blast of dark energy hit his shield as it materialized.

The demons all around them pulled swords from the air and crouched, ready to attack. The demons on the ceiling released their grip and shot toward them.

"We gotta get out of here!" Hope yelled to Alex and Katie.

"This way!" Alex led them toward the open door leading to the stairs.

The dragon-faced North American Demon lunged from the middle throne. He raced between the girls and snatched their arms.

He hurled himself and the two girls through the portal and into hell.

"No!" Alex yelled. He dropped his weapons and scrambled toward the radiating circle.

In the distance, he heard a booming voice ring through the demonic din.

"Oh glorious One enthroned on high,
All creation lifts its eyes to You
We storm forward on Your wings of power
To conquer in Your holy Name."

Alex looked outside to find a blazing ball of light the size of a hot air balloon rolling over the demon horde, scraping a wide line like a lawn mower cutting tall grass. The demons shrieked and scattered.

Alex turned and jumped toward the portal.

The room filled with light as Sariel snatched Alex from behind and pulled him out through the open window and upward into the moonlit sky.

*

Cain pushed himself up and stood on shaky legs. He crossed the room, winced, and looked out the window. Brilliant angels filled the sky, their swords drawn. His demon horde in the courtyard below cowered and averted their eyes.

All at once, the angels looked upward and shot into the night sky.

Cain turned back to the room and yelled to one of his assistants, "Triple the guard on the clock tower. Be quick about it! The time of the reversal approaches!"

He wasn't finished yet.

And then, in the quiet that follows a raging storm, he heard one discordant sound—the repeated soft striking of the pads of ancient hands brought together again and again.

Cain looked back to the thrones, and his jaw dropped.

Satan was slowly clapping.

23

Friday, 10:26 p.m.

Alex tried to push himself loose from Sariel's strong arms by twisting his body and kicking his legs. If the boy's arms hadn't been pinned, he would have knocked the angel's block off.

"Where've you been, Sariel! I trusted you—now . . . now my mom's dead!"

"Hold still, Alex!" he commanded.

"What about Katie? And Hope? They're in hell! You couldn't come ten minutes earlier?" Alex kicked out again and tried to shake free.

"Alex, stop!" Sariel ordered.

"Let me down!" Alex squirmed more violently. "I don't want anything to do with you! I hate you!"

Sariel placed his right hand over Alex's forehead "I'm doing this for your own good," he said quietly.

The boy stopped fighting, his eyelids fell, and his body went limp.

The angel held him tightly, enclosed him in his protective feathers, and rocketed through the atmosphere and into outer space faster than the speed of light.

*

When Smok had come through the portal, into the acrid air of hell, he found himself standing in front of a sea of demons stretching into the horizon. They stared at him curiously.

"I know him. He is the Lord of North America," one of the smaller demons called out. He prostrated himself. "Welcome, your highness."

"He is, he is," others in the horde agreed. All at once, the massive throng lowered themselves to one knee and bowed their ugly heads in respect.

"Look," another yelled out, rubbing his hands in delight. "This lord—he has brought meat!"

Demons cheered and stepped closer.

The dragon-faced monster dangled the girls by their arms like piñatas.

The vile creatures shouted and raced forward as one.

The girls screamed in terror.

*

Sariel landed with a crunch on a pure white, iridescent floor of the outer rim of heaven, the level where the celestial courts were held. He prayed softly and gently as he laid Alex down in the shallow layer of glistening diamond crystals that covered the ground. His massive wings folded neatly onto his back, nearly disappearing.

Now he would wait and pray.

He peered into the expanse before him. The glistening floor looked like a snow-covered plain extending endlessly in all

285

directions. Vibrant red, blue, and purple hues from nearby nebulae and stars reflected off the surface, creating a vast sparkling prism. Dots of color danced on his white angelic armor. The never-ending melodic music of the heavens softly sang out in harmonic perfection all around him.

Sariel continued praying.

On the horizon, he saw the spires of the heavenly city shining brightly against the night sky. It was in these lofty spires that angels were prayed over and healed after brutal demonic battles. After their recovery, they would be reassigned and join in combat once again.

Two dazzling dots appeared over the heavenly minarets and streaked toward him. Moments later, a pair of muscular warrior angels, both nearly ten feet tall, landed in front of him with a gentle crunching sound. The glorious angels wore brilliant armor over their torsos and helmets that covered their heads but left their rugged faces showing.

They slowly tucked their massive wings behind their backs.

Sariel greeted his brothers with a reverent bow. "Gabriel, Michael, praise be to the Name of the Glorious One."

They responded in unison, "All praise and glory to Him." These were not idle phrases, but an angelic idiom that summed up their entire reason for existence.

"My brothers, there has been an egregious breach of the holy order." Sariel shook while he spoke. "One of the seven Archdemons, the North American Demon, has carried two humans—alive, and against their will—into hell."

The two angels towering over Sariel stepped back in shock.

"This cannot be!" Michael's wings flew open as he shouted in disgust.

Sariel continued, "Be that as it may, it has happened." He looked down at Alex. "I have brought this human—my athleta Christi. I believe he is able to help. Time is of the essence."

Michael stared at Alex's motionless body then nodded. His voice boomed, "All right then, Sariel, Wake him up."

*

As the horrid creatures approached the demon lord, he yelled "Eat!" and threw the two screaming girls fifty feet into the air toward the swirling magma ceiling. They tumbled and shrieked, their arms and legs flailing wildly.

Demons lifted their hands to catch them, while others extended their wings and launched in an attempt to get the first bites midair.

Suddenly, all were blinded by a comet-like streak of light.

The demons shrieked and recoiled from the resplendence.

In a flash, the blinding light reached the girls, caught them both by the waist, and swept them away, vanishing with them through an opening in the rock-face to the left of the circular portal.

The demons howled viciously and fell into hot pursuit. Their thunderous footsteps shook the coarse, dried-lava walls of hell.

*

Alex stood on wobbly legs and squinted against the intense illumination. Still dressed in his spiritual armor, he found himself face-to-face with two giant angels.

Sariel spoke, "Alex, let me introduce Michael and Gabriel, angelic warriors in service of our God and King."

Remembering his Scriptures, Alex resisted the urge to fall down before them and their dazzling glory. Had this been any other time, he would have flooded them with questions.

Alex remembered the clock tower and buried his head in his hands.

Sariel spoke quietly to the angels. "Alex has had a terrible shock. Just a few minutes ago, the Executive Demon, Alistair Cain, slayed his mother in front of him."

Michael's voice pounded the air like thunder. "I am most sorry, Alex, for your terrible loss and for the pain it has brought you. You obviously loved your mother a great deal. You need not worry about her welfare. She resides here now, in the heavenly courts, reveling in perfection, no longer subject to the sin and degradation of her earthly flesh. Someday, if you continue in faithfulness, as she did, you will join her and the two of you shall spend eternity together in the glorious presence of our God."

Alex found help and healing in the angel's words. He wiped away his tears.

Sariel spoke again. "Alex, time is of the essence. Angels are not allowed to enter the vile region of hell under any circumstances. It is one of our most serious restrictions. But, *you* have divine permission. You can go in and possibly save these girls."

"But Sariel…" Gabriel objected.

Alex cut him off. "I'll go. I'll do it."

Puzzled, Gabriel and Michael looked at each other.

A voice emanated from all around them, shaking the very heavens. "He is *my* athleta. It *is* his destiny."

All three angels brightened at the confirmation.

Alex fell to his knees and faced the floor.

"The decision is made. Boy, stand and put out your hand," Michael commanded.

Alex rose, looked up at the angel, and held out his shaky hand. The massive angel dropped something heavy into Alex's palm.

A beautifully carved crystal key.

*

The girls' blood-curdling screams echoed throughout the narrow halls of hell. They soared through caverns lit by fiery lava pits spewing glowing molten rock into the air and creating eerie shadows along the distant walls. The streak of light that carried them banked and weaved, averting the lava.

The cracked dark stone floor beneath them shook, crumbled, and fell piece-by-piece into the fiery lava below. Falling boulders sent up new splashes of molten lava.

Just as Katie thought she would burst into flames, frosty air hit her exposed skin. They'd entered a blue cavern of luminescent ice. Crystalline stalagmites and stalactites made the cave look like a giant's mouth filled with sharp teeth ready to chomp, chew, and swallow them.

This icy chamber led to another where the rancid air was filled with loud moaning. Katie trembled as she heard sad voices pleading for one more chance, promising to live a better life, or cursing God. Looking closer at the remote walls that lined the cave, she noticed movement. The walls themselves were alive—thick, tangled knots of snow-covered, shivering human bodies frozen into a sparkling glacier.

Katie, her teeth chattering uncontrollably, almost fainted.

Hope gasped.

Terrifying, ravenous creatures—some running, some flying—remained hot on their trail as the girls continued to be carried through the halls of hell. At every turn the screaming demons tried to cut them off, but the light carrying them somehow anticipated every trap.

The girls held tight, not about to fall into the jaws of the pursuing horde.

At the end of the corridor, a patch of vibrant light illuminated the darkness. Katie squinted when they reached it.

The light beam gently set the girls down.

The vicious demons stopped short at the edge of the luminous rocks and thunderously roared obscenities and threats. In disgust, they slowly turned and disappeared into the shadows.

Hope reached over to Katie and took her arm. "I'm … I'm so sorry Katie. Please forgive me. I had no choice."

"I could see that. And, after all, you did try to save me."

Breathless, Katie turned and watched as the blinding light that had carried her dimmed, revealing a man dressed in full medieval armor. He belonged in a feudal castle in Europe. His helmet was two heavy, hinged metal halves—a thick piece that wrapped around the back of his head and a thinner visor. From head to foot, he was encased in plates of segmented metal.

His armor slowly transformed. A tall hat made of dark brown fur now sat where his helmet had been. His glistening breastplate turned into a heavy, fur-lined coat, which covered a ruffled cream-colored shirt. His leggings became loose-fitting pants ending at the knee, and his iron boots were now high-topped black leather shoes with shiny silver buckles.

A man right out of their history book looked them over, laughed heartily, and said, "Unc béon fæger sigewif."

The girls stared at him, their mouths open.

"Excuse me?" Katie asked.

The man blushed and laughed again, louder this time. He closed his eyes and seemed to be concentrating. He scratched his head, raised it, opened his eyes, and said, "Ah, thee art lassies fair indeed. Alas, if I were but thirty years my younger . . ." He hooted jovially, as if he didn't have a care in the world. With a wave of his hand, he announced, "I bid thee, fair lassies, welcome to my most humble abode. May God bless ye both."

"Thanks," the confused girls said in unison. They looked about them. This area of bright light extended hundreds of feet with fresh, clean air. It was so quiet and serene.

Katie and Hope noticed small groups of strangely luminescent people and angels surrounding them. As Katie's eyes adjusted, she saw these were not real beings, but statues carved out of the shining rock. She took Hope's hand in hers and approached them, only to discover they were carefully arranged into scenes, events from the Bible—the fall of Adam and Eve, David and Goliath, Jesus on the cross—with verses carved into the floor near them.

"Look!" Katie exclaimed, pointing to a nearby clearing. The girls stared at a vast carving in the floor labeled "hades" in two-foot letters. It was an enormous map, over sixty feet in diameter. This place of light in which they stood was in the center. Surrounding this was a labyrinth of narrow hallways leading to wide spaces, twisting and turning tunnels, and voluminous caverns. A large hammer and chisel lay nearby.

The edges of the glowing map appeared unfinished.

Katie asked breathlessly, "You did all this?"

"Aye," the man answered. "A smith I am, with a fair eye for carving."

Hope stared at the artistry. "It must have taken forever."

"Aye. My residence hath been interminable."

Hope turned back to the odd man. "Who are you and what are you doing *here*…in hell?"

The man drew himself up. With a twinkle in his eye, he explained, "Ye shall have to excuse me, lasses—ye being the first of my human kind to venture into these putrid halls of perdition during my…well, my lengthy residence. I have nary conversed with a soul in more years than I can imagine. I thought I might have…well, forgotten the habit." He chuckled. "My name is Addison, Cornelius Addison."

"Addison? Really?"

He looked surprised. "Ye possesseth familiarity with the name?"

"Addison was one of my teachers," Katie said, straightening her robe. She took a seat on a rock structure and put her arms around her knees. "The last time I saw him, he was all tied up and, I don't know, drugged or something."

The man looked pensive, and then said, "Some hath restrained him, then? To what purpose? Would he be a common criminal? Or a reprobate?"

Katie responded, "No, nothing like that. It was a nightmare. I was kidnapped and taken to the clock tower at our school. We were surrounded by weird . . . creatures. And there was this huge red circle on the floor with a star inside—"

"Aye, and a sizable circle affixed to the wall proceedeth unto this dreadful place? It is too true an evil."

"How . . . how'd you know?" Hope asked.

"Tis the fiftieth birthday of thine teacher, Mr. Addison, on this cruel day—even as it was mine those many years yon. At the witching hour tonight, the portal which has been opened to this putrid place will, in itself, become reversed."

"What are you saying?" Katie asked.

"I beseech ye to understand. This happened in my township, in Salem. In that time, it was I who was beguiled into forging that infernal band. I knew naught what I accomplished. The forces of the Evil One used that band on the fiftieth anniversary of my birth to infest our township with legions of hellish demons." His eyes stared off into the distance and his voice grew faint. "For one minute alone the portal is reversed. And for one minute only, Hell regurgitates its vile membership."

"And it sounds like they're getting ready to do it again," Hope said.

"Aye, that it does," Addison agreed, nodding his head. "That it does."

*

292

Led by the three angels, Alex took a short hike to another section of heaven. They came upon a crystal door, just taller than Alex, standing in the middle of nowhere. The facets cut in the door reminded Alex of a diamond. Below its bulbous handle was a crystal keyhole.

Alex walked around the door and shrugged his shoulders.

"I don't get it."

"This is the doorway to perdition. It has never been used . . . until now," Michael informed him.

Alex lifted his hand and looked at the crystal key. "Okay," he said quietly.

The three angels drew their swords in case any demons waited on the other side for a chance to enter heaven.

Alex stuck the key into the lock and turned it until it clicked. He grasped the handle and slowly opened the door.

Sariel put his hand on Alex's shoulder. "You are ready for this, Alex. God has protected you thus far. Walk in Him now. Be the light in that place of darkness."

Alex looked affectionately into the eyes of his mentor. "Thank you, Sariel. I will. Be here at the door. I'll be back with the girls." Alex stepped through the threshold.

Dark gray walls of hardened lava sandwiched an endless stone staircase that descended beyond what his eyes could see. As he started down the stairs, he heard the door close behind him and lock fast again.

Darkness surrounded Alex. He willed his sword into his hand, and it lit up the stairs.

At first he danced down the steps, the way he did on his stairs at home. But he didn't seem to be getting any closer to the bottom. He tried to move faster, bounding down three and four steps at a time, but the stairs still seemed endless. He wondered why there wasn't an elevator to hell or some better, more efficient way to get there. At this rate, he'd arrive hours too late. And then he had an idea. Alex willed his shield onto his arm. He slipped his arm out of the strap and held the edges of the curved kite-shaped metal plate.

He took a deep breath and yelled, "Geronimo!" and hurled himself chest-first down the stairs, using his shield like a sled. He bonked forward in something close to a complete free-fall, yelling and laughing as much from terror as from glee.

This was the greatest thrill ride ever.

Bumping and scraping downward at breakneck speed, he looked ahead hoping to see the end of the stairs.

No such luck.

*

"So what is this place?" Hope asked. "It's not . . . what I expected. I mean, an island of light in the middle of the Hell doesn't make any sense."

"Ah, then ye are not fully learned of the Good Book, are ye lass?" the ancient man asked.

Hope shook her head and coughed. "The Bible? No. It wasn't really part of my upbringing." *Boy, is that an understatement!*

"Well then, I think ye will appreciate the telling." Addison beckoned them to walk with him. He brought their attention to some of the carvings. "The story begins with the death of our Savior and Lord, Christ Jesus, on the cross. The Good Book saith that after He gave his life, He descended into this place and preached salvation to all who would lend him their ears. On the third day hence, He resurrected from the dead."

"Jesus preached…in hell?" Katie asked.

"Aye, He did. He gave them *all* a chance to taste the sweetness of salvation—the thieves, the murderers, the reprobates, and the sinners." His face grew somber. "But, alas, they loved the darkness more than the light and clung to it. With the door to heaven wide open and the gift of salvation offered freely, they chose to remain here in Hades."

Hope could relate. She picked up a bright stone that lit up her hand. She asked, "Where does all this light come from?"

Addison continued, "Well now, in the three days our Lord resideth here, in the state betwixt death and resurrection life, preaching His holy kingdom to the fallen souls, the effect was what ye see with thine own eyes. This ground was made holy with His presence—even the likes of hell cannot refuse His holiness. Come, there is more for ye to see."

The man grabbed a black walking stick and led them to more figures chiseled in a nearby lava-rock wall. The girls followed the progression of the carvings and found the story he was telling them about Jesus in Hell was portrayed on the wall in beautiful 3-D, a detailed bas relief that could easily have adorned any church in Rome.

Katie tried to add all this up. Still, one part didn't make sense. She frowned. "So, Mr. Addison, sir, how did *you* get here?"

Addison sat on a hard chair fashioned from a lava boulder. He sighed. "When the scallywags brought me to their vile pentagram and their window to hades, they did a most unholy ritual. At its conclusion, the evil creatures came pouring forth from the mysterious circle. But they had only sixty seconds—one full minute—to complete the deed. When the minute ended, the portal to hell returned to its original estate. It became, once again, a doorway into this place."

Katie reflected on her recent ordeal. "Excuse me, Mr. Addison, sir. They kidnapped me and were going to kill me. Why?"

The ancient man nodded his head as his memories flooded back. "Aye, the last time the portal was used, fair young lassies like ye were there as well," his voice cracked. "He slit their throats, he did. Most unholy."

Hope nodded. "But, I still don't understand how you ended up here."

"The leader, a vile creature we all knew as Jonathan Cain, went to cut me throat with his knife. But, before the demon reached me, I bolted across the room and, like a daft man void of all reason, I foolishly threw myself into the ring." He chuckled again, coughing and losing his breath. "To this day I don't know what I was thinking." His laughing subsided, and he wiped tears from his eyes. "Anyway, I was chased by the nasties until I found this holy place." He caressed the gleaming stones nearby.

Katie turned to Hope. "Cain? That's your father's name. So, your ancestor tried to kill this guy? Mr. Addison's . . . ancestor?"

Hope cleared her throat. "Not exactly. Remember the clock tower? The demonic monster that was in charge of everything? That's my father. He's a demon—a creature that never dies. It wasn't my ancestor who tried to kill Mr. Addison's ancestor. It was my father."

Katie could hardly believe what she was hearing. "So, what does that make...I mean, he's your father? I...I don't get it."

"Look," Hope replied strongly, "I didn't choose him to be my father. I'm not proud of my past. But I've chosen which side I stand with in this war between good and evil. That's all you really have to understand."

Addison put his hand on Katie's shoulder. "Aye. That is all that matters in the end, lass."

Hope's eyes widened. "So, you've been here for over four hundred years."

Addison looked at the sculptures around him and nodded.

Katie jumped in. "Okay, one more thing. So, what was with that, um, Superman routine?

Addison raised his eyebrows. "Superman?"

The girl used her right hand to simulate flying. "You know. When you picked us up and flew us through the air to this place. What *was* that?"

Another twinkle in his eye. "Ah, that. I must say, never have I enjoyed the pleasure of conversation so. It is a delight." His smile fell and he looked into Katie's eyes. "Flying is one of the gifts given exclusively to an athleta Christi, a warrior for the Holy God. I was trained in youth to fight for righteousness. Now, I stand for God in this place."

"But, don't you want to get back to our world?" Katie interjected.

The man nodded heartily. "Aye, if only I could."

"Are you saying there's no way out of here?" Hope choked.

"I can think of but one," Addison replied.

Both girls asked, "What is it?"

He pursed his lips. "This portal shall reverse again, and we shall use it to get back home, God willing. Tis the only way I am aware of."

"But, isn't that where all the monsters are?" Katie whispered.

"Aye, lass. I never said it would be easy."

*

Struggling to cling onto his shield, now red-hot from friction, Alex sledded, scraped, and bounced down the hardened lava stairs. At times the shield would hit the rock beneath him so hard, sparks would fly. His fingers felt like sausages cooking on a backyard grill.

He reached the end of the stairs and skidded forward like a flat stone skimming a pond's surface. His sword illuminated the rock hallway before him and cast eerie shadows onto the jagged rock face.

Alex leaned to the left and right to avoid rocks and stalactites and to navigate the many turns in the narrow tunnel. As he began to slow, he hit a rock he couldn't avoid. Airborne, Alex spun out of control. His shield flew from underneath him. He hit the ground, rolled violently forward, and crashed into a stone wall.

Everything went black.

*

Addison explained the layout of Hell to the girls, pointing out sections of his map with his cane. "Ah, and seeth this large section here?" He leaned his head toward Hope. "It may be of some particular interest to ye, lass."

She scooted closer and listened intently while Addison scraped the cane across an empty circular space, like a stone salad bowl, carved in the floor.

The ancient man continued, "Back in the time of the patriarch, Noah, demons, like your father, took human women to fulfill their vile lusts. 'Twas their plan, orchestrated by their unholy leader, the devil, to destroy the holy intentions of the one and only God, by," his cheeks reddened, "…by polluting the race of men with unholy demonic seed. Their union brought forth progeny, and these offspring contaminated God's humanity. So, the Holy One stepped in and shackled these demons here," he tapped his cane on the round section of the floor, "in this space. It is known here as the Bowels of Hell. The nasties there scream and moan in darkness and will do so throughout eternity."

Hope stared at the carving in the glowing rock face. "My father should be one of them."

"Aye," Addison agreed.

"Note to self," Katie murmured under her breath, "don't piss off God."

"I stay away from that place," Addison added, a chill in his tone. "Now, we are here," he continued, referring to a place on the map with streaks around it. "We shall traverse betwixt these corridors and end up here." He brought his cane to the largest part of the map.

"This is where we will find the window back to our world. It is where I found you."

"What's that?" Katie asked, pointing to what looked like a plateau located some distance from the portal.

"I call that The Infernal Castle. They say it is inhabited by one of the foulest of the demons—some kind of creature feared by the rest of the nasties. They say he is the biggest of creatures and does naught but gorge himself continuously. The other demons, they feed him. The saying goes, *He ne'er eats the ones who doth feed him.* I stay away from that infernal place. Tis probably why I've stayed alive this long."

The girls looked behind the ancient man. An enormous being approached from the shadows. The huge demon clad in black armor closed in with steady thundering strides, displaying absolutely no fear.

Katie and Hope screamed in unison.

*

Alistair Cain glanced at his watch. Seventeen minutes to go. All his planning and organizing had produced excellent results, thus far. The last variable, the greatest threat to the coming demonic infusion, was gone. If Alex dared return, Cain's demonic forces would be ready.

Cain considered Hecate and Katie and an evil grin creased his face. He imagined his starving brothers in Hell feasting on the girls' flesh—a delicious appetizer. He wished he could have seen it.

He studied the portal and pondered the celestial infraction of sending humans into hell. His brow furrowed like a farmer's field. Who did the enemy dictator think he was, anyway, imposing his arbitrary rules in heaven, hell, and earth? Still, Cain was happy he was not the one who actually put the girls into hell. Horrible punishments were imposed on those who broke the enemy's arbitrary rules. He'd heard of demons chained and tortured in the deepest pits of hell for such infractions. He shuddered at the thought.

Why wasn't Cain apprehended and ushered into this same horrible place? After all, most of these demons were imprisoned for extra-species reproduction. Hecate *was* his daughter.

He smirked.

Of course, heaven was run by morons, a bastion of incompetence, slipshod maintenance, and weak application. That's how he had fallen through the cracks. He shook his head. The change in regime couldn't happen quickly enough.

Another thought—perhaps heaven feared him.

That was it! He was too powerful to be messed with.

He stood a little taller and raised his chin.

The witches stationed at each vertex around the pentagram chanted and sprinkled incense on the candles. The flames sputtered and sparked, sending up plumes of yellow smoke that smelled like rotten eggs. A bowl of dark crimson blood, drained from Alex's mom's slit throat, sat on the floor near the pentagram. Every few minutes the fluid was carefully ladled over the evil symbol.

Cain breathed deeply. Soon he and the strengthened demonic army would remove the enemy's intrusive influence from the earth, gathering more and more territory, until Satan ruled this planet.

The hard part was what came afterward. The dark lord, Satan, had loftier goals.

When the next portal came on line, there would be a final massive assault. The forces of evil would storm the gates of heaven itself. It had been written, *The gates of heaven will not stand against us*. Once he and his brothers accomplished this hostile takeover, he would finally be rewarded with his dream job—he would become the Chief Systems Analyst of the universe, in charge of restructuring heaven and earth into an efficient, well-oiled machine under lordship of a new dark master.

Cain patted the radiant circle with affection.

*

Katie screamed next to Hope.

Fifty feet away, the ominous creature approached. The flickering bursts of spurting lava nearby threw red light and black shadows across the armor plates that covered his chest and arms. Katie gasped as his face, which looked like a scary skeletal mask a child might wear on Halloween, entered the harsh light of the outskirts of this holy place. The massive demon stopped, squinted as if the light caused him pain, and took a step back into the darkness.

Cornelius Addison motioned his hands downward, trying to quiet her.

Hope stood tall and took a fighting stance. Her black pajamas turned into a brilliant floor-length white gown. A sparkling sphere of ball lightning the size of a softball formed in her right hand.

Katie shielded her eyes from the brightness.

"Now, now, lassies. Please, settle down. Ye will be a fright to my gentle visitor."

"Visitor?" Hope gulped.

"Aye."

Addison strolled toward the beast.

"Be careful!" Hope yelled. She kept her fighting stance. White energy danced in her right hand like bolts of lightning in a plasma lamp.

Addison waved back.

The pear-shaped man gently swayed as he walked past the statues. In about a minute he'd reached the boundary of the light.

He turned to a roughly hewn cylinder cut into the rock. He lifted the two-inch-thick lid, reached in, and pulled out the most disgusting insect creature the girls had ever seen. It was green and purple and nearly a foot long. Its body writhed like a snake and hundreds of yellow segmented legs wiggled beneath it. Pointed insect wings batted feverishly, and three-inch mandibles snapped open and shut. Addison held it firmly behind the wings so it couldn't bite him, although it kept trying.

He turned to the demon and asked, "Has it come to pass, then?"

The demon nodded his head and opened his mouth wide.

Katie and Hope approached cautiously.

Referring to the insect creature, Addison called back to the girls, "I've given these buggers the name 'Rock-chewers.' They eat at the lava. And my friend here?" He referred to the knight demon. "I named him Lips. Rather an irony, really, for as ye can clearly observe, he has none. He informs me in this infernal place." He moved his hand in a broad circle. "It is he who keeps me apprised of the goings on, ye see. And he tells me now that it is time for us to be on our way. Hurry lassies, the portal back to our world will open anon, and it is vital we be there when it does."

He tossed the squirming creature into the air toward the shadows, where the knight caught it in his open jaws and devoured it with a noisy crunch and a slurp.

Cornelius Addison lifted his right arm. His black hat, doublet, breeches, stockings, and shoes transformed to a full suit of shining armor once again. A brilliant gleaming sword appeared in his raised right hand, illuminating the space above him.

The girls stood. The monster led the way while Addison followed and Hope took the rear, holding her ball of sparkling light energy and glancing from side to side. Katie stayed between them.

Together they passed through a dark winding corridor that the girls remembered from the map carved in the floor.

They stopped in a portion of the hall with deep recesses on both sides.

"Shush," Cornelius said, bringing his gauntlet to his lips. "I heard something."

A midnight demon appeared out of nowhere. It gave a screech and positioned itself in front of the holy knight.

Katie screamed at the top of her lungs.

Hope threw her light energy, but the midnight demon ducked and the sparkling ball stuck to the wall where it blazed and lit up the whole area.

Addison hefted his shield and lifted his glowing sword toward the creature, ready to slice him out of existence. But before he could bring down his blade, Lips tackled him and the two of them crashed in a clanging tangle of armor.

With Cornelius out of the way, the midnight demon's talons reached out to grab Katie. Hope responded quickly, jumping in front of the girl and kicking the creature hard in the chest. She threw a small crackling ball of light energy at it, but the monster rolled and dodged the bolt.

The midnight demon fired a handful of dark energy, which hit Hope's shoulder and wrapped around her right arm, sending out black sparks. Her arm fell limp as a wet noodle. The monster then rose and shoved his talons onto her chest, knocked her down, and pinned her fast to the floor.

The midnight demon let out a banshee cry. His gnarled claws swirled with deadly dark energy. He raised them both above his head, put them together, and the energy inside formed a beach-ball-sized nuclear reaction. The midnight demon heaved the crackling sphere at Hope's head.

There was a sudden flash of light, and the bolt sizzled against a green shield. Lightning spilled over the surface of the cross and dissipated.

Alex pulled the shield to his left side and thrust his sword up into the demon's gut with a mighty shout.

The creature's black eyes widened. It wailed in frustration and pain and dissolved in a tree-sized cloud.

Alex jumped over beside Addison, who was fighting for his life. They were knights from two different eras, united in purpose. Alex swiped his sword in front of him. The demon charged him. The two blades met with a shower of sparks and wisps of smoke.

The creature responded quickly and threw a right cross, trying to take off Alex's head.

The athleta ducked, spun, and kicked the demon hard in the side. He followed through with a thrust of his sword into the monster's back.

The demonic knight's hideous face contorted in pain before he exploded into a shower of shiny ashes.

Addison lifted his face shield with a squeak. "Well done, lad! Well done." The holy knight clumsily pushed himself to his feet.

Alex moved over to Hope. "Are you okay?" He helped her up.

"I will be." She used her left hand to shoot light energy into her right arm. She lifted her arm and wiggled her fingers.

Then her eyes met Alex's. "Thanks, Alex. You really saved us. I can't believe you're really here." Then she looked around and asked frantically, "Where's . . . where's Katie?"

"Was she here? I didn't see her," Alex said, starting to panic.

"I saw it," Addison choked out. "While we were fighting, two of the wee nasties grabbed her and carried her off. I tried to stop them, but—"

"We've got to save her! Which way did they go?" Alex yelled, facing the knight.

Tears welled up in Addison's eyes. "Nay, there's naught we can do. They will take her to their infernal castle. We cannot venture there. Besides, once the portal opens, we must go through it, or we will all be doomed to this place."

"I'm going to save her, no matter what." Alex put his hands on the knight's metal shoulder plating. "Tell me how to get there!"

"I'm going with you!" Hope declared.

"You'll never make it." The knight shook his head.

"That's where you're wrong." Alex took his fighting stance and summoned his sword and shield. Hope stood defiantly with him balls of energy crackling in her hands.

"I meant to say, you'll never make it—that is, without my help," the knight added.

"You'll help us?" Hope choked on the words.

"Aye, that I will. I cannot turn me back on ye. After all, what's another four hundred years in perdition, ay lassie?" The knight's eyes twinkled as he lowered his visor. "Take my hand." He offered his right gauntlet to Hope. "You, athleta, I hope you can fly."

"I can…a little." Alex took a deep breath.

"Good. "Now take her other hand." Alex threw down his shield and sword. They faded out of existence. He took Hope's right hand in his left and squeezed.

When their eyes met, Alex said, "Hope, you're amazing."

She smiled and blinked away tears. "Thanks."

Addison bent his legs. "All right, now, ready?"

Together, Alex and Hope said, "Ready."

Addison looked up. "Lord be with us in this act of foolishness."

The three warriors shot forward as a streak of light. They maneuvered through the labyrinth of shadowy tunnels and lava-spewing caverns.

*

Smok, the North American Demon, looked over the Infernal Castle—little more than the top of a butte covered with stalactites. These spires ranged from small pumice mounds to wide rock spikes towering fifteen feet tall. Formed from lava that had fallen from the swirling, molten ceiling, they made the castle look like the surface of a spiny cactus.

In the center of the castle was a clearing. In the middle of the clearing, stairs led to a rough altar, its sides covered with blood of all colors. Surrounding it, as far as the eye could see, were mounds of debris—the exoskeletons of millions of bugs, shells, bones, and many other unnatural things. The stench was so overpowering, even the demons gagged when they approached to present their offerings.

Smok led a band of ten demons to the top of the altar, pointed to a flat place on the pumice floor, and growled. "Restrain the bait here."

The demons dragged Katie, who screamed the entire way, to the top of the altar where they roughly laid her on her back and held her down. The demons stretched her arms outward, and curved stone stocks were placed over both of her wrists. Two midnight demons placed their claws over the seams and fused the stones to the floor.

Katie retched at the stench, yelled curses at the demons, and violently pulled against her bonds.

Two of the creeper demons looked around in dismay, their brows furrowed and horrified scowls on their faces.

"What is it?" the Demon Lord demanded in a firm hiss.

"Another powerful athlete has been seen in our realm!" one of them squeaked.

"They say he has defeated many of our strongest brothers!" the other one chimed in. "We are afraid he might find us."

The Demon Lord wailed in fury and viciously backhanded both demons across their ugly faces, knocking them off their feet. "I am counting on it, you idiots!" He railed with fiery hatred in his eyes. "This athlete must die!"

He unfurled his large, dragon wings and launched off the plateau toward the lava ceiling. "Keep me posted!" he ordered as he ascended.

Before he made contact with the molten rock above him, he arched magnificently in the air and flew back to the portal that would soon take him back to the front lines in the battle against God.

*

Alex transformed from a blazing streak of energy, still holding hands with Cornelius, and Hope. It was something Cornelius had done, somehow. They soared just above the ground, slowed further, righted themselves, and touched down at the end of the tunnel. Choking on the smell of sulfur, they moved together close to the pumice wall, leaned forward, peered around the corner, and shuddered.

In the middle of a massive fiery cavern, amid flowing rivers of lava, they saw the pillars of the Infernal Castle, a small hill rising toward the swirling molten ceiling. On the side, they saw a zigzagging pathway lined with demons hefting giant squirming bugs. They all stood in line, waiting.

Alex turned toward Cornelius. "You're sure they took Katie up there?"

"Aye, I am certain," the ancient man gulped.

Alex nodded. "Okay. Let's do this."

The three warriors held hands again and rose into the super-heated air near the swirling ceiling. They landed with a crunch at the top of the castle and braced themselves for battle. Trudging cautiously through the ankle-high piles of debris and past the towering stalactites, they reached the open courtyard.

Alex tensed when he heard Katie scream. He saw her chained to the roughly-hewn lava altar with two creepers flanking her. A boulder, the size of a small house, rested fifty yards away.

Warrior demons stepped from behind the altar and attacked.

Addison sliced the first two in half at the waist, and they vaporized. Alex ducked a demonic sword aimed at his head.

Hope fired blazing energy balls from each hand, which immobilized one of the demons. She followed this with a karate kick to the chest that sent him flying into a nearby stalagmite.

307

Alex thrust his sword sideways, cutting the legs off two demons at once. They cried in agony and puffed into a shimmering dust cloud.

Addison sliced another horrified demon in half vertically, and both sides fell away and turned to piles of dust on the ground.

The rest of the evil group screamed and fled.

The three godly warriors marched up the stairs to the top of the altar.

"Alex!" Katie yelled.

The creeper demons' eyes went wide in horror. Their mouths fell open.

"Let her go!" Alex commanded.

The creatures looked to each other in panic. When they unfurled their wings and tried to escape, Alex was on them. In one clean swipe of his sword, they became demon dust.

Alex approached Katie.

"Alex, thank God! Hurry, it's a trap," she shouted.

He hit the shackles with his sword, and they cracked open with a loud crunch. Katie jumped into his arms. He walked her back to their friends, with his arm around her.

"I...I prayed you would come," Katie moaned, choking on her tears and the foul air.

"We must proceed with haste." The older athleta Christi spoke over the gurgling sounds of the swirling lava ceiling. "The window will be opening any time now. We may still be able to make it."

Katie's eyes widened, and she shook violently. She tried to scream but had no breath.

At the bottom of the stairs, the warriors turned and looked behind them. The massive stone they saw earlier was really a gray-skinned, house-sized creature. It bounded right for them, galloping on four powerful legs.

Alex yelled, "Hope, protect Katie! Get her out of here!" He jumped forward, facing the charging beast.

The girls ran for cover among the towering stalagmites.

The ancient knight came alongside him. Both warriors—one ancient, one modern—stood united in battle.

The stone castle shook under the charging beast. Small rocks and chunks of debris danced from the thunderous vibrations. This thing was going to smear them on the ground like a couple of plump grapes.

Alex yelled, "Split up! Whoever gets away takes the girls to safety."

"As good a plan as any," the knight yelled back. He grabbed Alex by the scruff of his neck, yanked him off his feet, and sent him rolling down the stairs toward the girls.

*

Addison then screwed up his courage and faced the monster he'd spent four hundred years hiding from. "Come on, ye fatty nasty. I intend that this meal be thy last."

The creature reached the knight. He came to a sliding stop, scattering a wave of debris. The gigantic demon stood on his back legs, unfurled his massive wings, and roared.

A fountain of chunky, multi-colored spit showered over the knight.

"Now, that's nice, isn't it?" Cornelius glanced at the pasty goo sliding off his shoulders and scowled.

The demon studied his meal, his enormous head slowly moving from side to side.

Addison surmised that this creature had once been a knight giant, changed through centuries of gorging himself, reduced now to a powerful gluttonous being with only one conscious thought—*EAT!*

The nearly-fifty-foot demon reached his massive clawed hand toward the knight to grab him. Addison lunged forward and pierced it with his gleaming sword. The creature pulled back his arm and wailed in pain.

The gargantuan beast reared up again on his back legs, bringing his wings to brush the floor behind him. He reached his hand to the side and snapped off a crusty lava stalagmite about the size of a Christmas tree. He lifted it over his head and brought it crashing down.

Addison jumped aside. The stone struck the floor with such force that the whole area shook. The beast tried this again and again and again, while Addison nimbly avoided the blows.

The demon wailed and angrily tossed the stalagmite into the distance and off the edge of the castle. It rolled down the hill, knocking into the line of demons, sending five of them off their feet and tumbling down the side of the hill.

In half a wink, the monster snatched up the knight, pinning his sword arm in his massive claw. He shook him and slammed him on the ground. Addison's sword fell loose and hit the stone floor with a clang and dissolved.

The knight was shaken, but not spent. He yelled, "Come on, ye nasty! Let me go, and I'll tear out thy throat with me bare hands."

The creature pushed his thick gray tongue—the length of a ship's plank—out of his bony mouth and slid it over the gleaming armor.

The knight turned his head and winced in disgust.

The demon quickly retracted his tongue and spit. "Yick! Metal. Taste bad. Hmm, shell?"

He brought up his other clawed hand and wedged a talon between the armor plates.

The knight yelled in pain as the creature pulled hard, bending the shiny metal.

*

A brick-sized rock hit the demon between the eyes. He turned his attention away from his well-packaged meal and looked around him.

"Hey, beautiful!" the young warrior yelled, hovering in the stale air nearby. "I'm cutting in."

Before Alex could dodge, the monster reached out a lightning-fast hand and snagged him as well. The creature looked back and forth between the knights in each hand.

Alex's green shield was wedged in front of him against the creature's powerful fingers. When the beast brought Alex close to his skeletal face and ran his tongue over the shield, he flinched in pain.

Alex pushed himself down, slid past his shield, and dropped to the ground. When he hit, his legs buckled and he fell on his side into a rancid pile of rubbish. Before the demon could react, Alex was back on his feet. He lifted his sword and raced forward.

The demon pushed off the ground and flapped his enormous wings, launching twenty feet up. He bobbed in the air, barely able to hold up his weight.

"Not that I do not appreciate thine valiant efforts, my young friend," the knight called out from the creature's gnarled hand, "but I hardly see what this will accomplish."

"Just be ready!" Alex yelled up to him. He ran forward, pushed off the ground, and rocketed right in front of the creature's face.

"No, lad! He heard Cornelius shout.

In a split second the perpetual eating machine snapped its jaws over Alex. Alex's glowing sword lit up the cavernous mouth. He stretched out on his back on the soft tongue and thrust his sword upward, shoving it into the creature's soft pallet. The demon howled in pain. Alex scurried out of the mouth and jumped. At the same time, the beast dropped Addison.

311

Ales prayed inwardly as he fell, completely giving himself over to the Spirit. A surge of energy renewed him.

He hit the ground, his armor and the debris cushioning the blow. He scurried up, stood, and took his warrior stance, the sword and shield appearing in his hands once again.

The ancient knight came up beside him.

The creature reared up on his hind legs, roared another shower of spit, turned, and galloped away.

"Must have decided we weren't worth the effort," Alex commented.

"Aye. He'll find a meal that doesn't bite back. Where are the lassies?"

"I flew them back to the only place I was sure would be safe."

"My holy oasis?"

"That's right. Let's go get them and head to the portal. I just hope we have time."

"Aye. Let us make haste."

The two knights shot into the air streaked down the bluff and into the labyrinth that led back to the girls.

*

Cain theatrically pulled a cape over his muscular back and slowly approached the pulsating circle to hell. He looked over the multitude of creatures he was about to bring into this realm.

Thousands of smaller demons would serve the cause as infantry and messengers and do the grunt work. Satan would keep them in line with pain and the threat of evaporation.

A sea of creeper demons jumped up and down in expectation. They would capture the hearts and minds of humans. He imagined heads of state and industry with creepers sinking their needle-like teeth into their skulls, bringing them completely under his master's oppressive control.

Lastly, he gazed on the towering knight demons and midnight demons. Their brute force would be vital to their ultimate goal—storming heaven.

A tall demon trudged through the crowd, the other demons quickly parting to let him through. It was his master, the North American Demon. He strutted to the front of the line like he owned the place.

Cain rubbed his gnarled claws together in front of his face. "Couldn't be any better," he whispered.

Soon Cain, Satan, and his legions of demons would rid the universe of its infernal brightness. Light and love would be forever banished and replaced with hatred and darkness.

Cain ran a curved talon over the portal's metal rim. Once it opened, there would be only a minute to complete the task.

Thankfully, demons were known to move quickly—when properly motivated. According to his calculations, a ring ten feet in diameter could hold approximately a hundred of the smaller demons. If the creatures poured in as planned—taking into account the inefficiency inherent in any endeavor—more than five thousand would pass through before the portal reversed itself. The results would be similar to the last time, in Salem. What a glorious day that had been! Hell poured forth its captives and evil claimed a celebrated victory.

Cain rubbed the thick metal and smirked with malevolent elation.

Then he turned and looked at the teacher, Henry Addison, unconscious on the gurney.

There was also another. Addison's younger cousin, Nicholas, was forty-nine. Soon he would be strapped down and would become the conduit for another portal reversal, and another five thousand demons would return. The forces of Hell would overrun their enemies—on earth and in heaven. Satan would ascend, take his rightful throne, and put all things in their proper order.

The Executive Demon reflected on the clever deal Satan tricked the enemy into that made this all possible. Cain had to admit, he'd never sealed any deal with this level of monumental significance.

No one had.

He exhaled. The portal reversal was imminent. The Executive Demon raised his arms high and chanted an incantation over the radiating circle.

Those watching, including Satan himself, leaned forward expectantly. The surface of the circle churned, distorting the image. Dark energy crackled at the edges of the circle, sending out veins of black lightning.

Behind him, Cain heard Satan hiss with delight.

*

The two holy warriors streaked through hell's snaking tunnels, transformed from light to men, slowed, and landed in Cornelius' holy place.

Katie ran over to Alex and threw her arms around him. "I was so afraid you wouldn't come back," she whimpered.

"Come on, we have to go! You can ride on my back. Hope, you can ride on Addison's back."

"I don't know if I can go out there again, Alex." Katie's voice cracked.

Alex held her close and whispered into her ear, "Katie, I'd die protecting you. But we only have one chance to get out of here. You don't want to stay here forever, do you?"

She shook her head.

"We have to go now. Please, trust me." Alex wrapped his strong arms around her.

Katie nodded. She looked into his soft eyes and breathed out the words, "I'll go anywhere with you, Alex."

"All right, then," the older knight said. "Look lively all."

The girls climbed on their backs and held on tight while the twin knights shot off the ground and became light streaking down the winding tunnels.

When they slowed and landed at the entrance to the portal cavern, Alex's jaw dropped. The portal was a thick metal circle embedded in the wall nearly 200 yards away. It stood nearly forty feet off the ground. A crude, freshly-built lava-rock ramp fanned out in all directions from the hole. Between them and the portal, a massive crowd of demons clawed over each other, pushing toward the swirling circle. A buzzing swarm of smaller imp-like demons darted in the air.

"We'll never make it!" Katie cried.

"Aye, but we *can* slow the tide," said the knight, lifting his metal visor. "Although we will most surely die in the attempt."

"Wait!" Alex called to the others. "There's another way out."

"Young lad, I've been here four hundred years. If there was another way, do ye not think I would have found it by now?"

"It's how I got here. There's a . . . stairway to heaven. Really. It's in a giant cave full of tunnels. I put a mark above the one I came from."

"Do you think you can you find it again?" Hope asked.

An overwhelming surge of the Spirit rose within Alex. "Come on, I'll show you."

Alex turned and flew back into the tunnel with Katie hanging on.

Cornelius and Hope followed.

The group became light and raced through the halls, made a couple of quick turns, and slowed when they arrived in another large, empty cavern with dozens of caves bored into the craggy lava wall. They transformed back to four humans and landed.

"I like this place a lot better," Katie's voice quivered.

315

Alex pointed. "Look! Over there! It's my mark." A few hundred yards ahead of them, one of the holes had a cross etched into the rock above it. "Follow me."

Katie, her arms still around Alex's neck, kissed him on the cheek. Alex smiled and pushed off the ground, carrying Katie with him.

Cornelius and Hope were right behind.

They slowed, turned upright, and landed, walking a few steps to ease the impact. The girls dropped off the Aletha's backs, and they all jogged toward the hole.

Before they reached it, something soared above them and landed between them and the tunnel.

The North American Demon.

The monster growled at them, then grew and transformed, large scales covering his growing body. His neck stretched forth like a 15-foot snake, and its tail extended. His wings grew wide and long. His crocodile face became that of an enormous dragon.

The creature reared back his head, took a deep breath, and spewed a river of fire.

Alex and his companions jumped back.

"What *is* that?" Katie shouted.

"I know him." Hope responded. "He's the North American Demon, lord over all the demonic forces in the North American continent. He's also the strongest demon, next to Lucifer himself."

"Of course he is," Alex said. "But right now, he's standing in my way!" He lunged forward, his sword and shield in hand.

The Demon Lord reared back again and inhaled a deep breath.

The girls and the ancient knight ran off to the side.

When his massive lungs were full, the dragon lurched forward and blasted a stream of fire directly at Alex, who ducked behind his shield, closed his eyes, and held on for dear life. It was like being inside a blast furnace.

When it was over, Alex stood tall again in his warrior stance. Smoke curled around his armor.

The dragon-like creature raised up on his legs and stretched out its enormous wings, ready to pounce on Alex and tear him to shreds with his razor-sharp talons and teeth.

A large drop of lava fell from the molten ceiling and landed in a fizzle at the dragon's feet.

The beast looked up to see Cornelius hovering eighty feet in the air near the swirling ceiling. The godly warrior hacked at the molten rock with his gleaming sword. Lava poured from the ceiling in a column and coated the dragon. It writhed under the glowing red and orange lava, then hardened into a dark gray stalagmite the size of a tall tree.

"Run!" Alex yelled. They started for the opening he had marked.

Thunder resounded throughout the cave as the smoldering lava column cracked and lurched their direction.

Alex grabbed the girls and pushed off the ground.

The massive stalagmite toppled, crashing into the rock face in a pile of jagged rubble. Cracks formed in the wall and tons of boulders and loose stones cascaded down covering the entrance.

Cornelius landed with Alex and the girls.

"That was amazing," Hope exclaimed.

"Aye, lass," the knight agreed, "but look at our escape route. We'll never get those rocks pulled away."

"Whadda we do now?" Katie grabbed Alex's arm, near hysterics.

They all faced the cavern's entrance. A gray mountain galloped toward them.

"It's that thing that tried to eat us!" Katie yelled.

"Aye, one and the same," Addison quipped.

"It just gets better and better," Alex complained.

The girls screamed.

The monster reached them at top speed.

Alex pulled Katie to the right, while Hope and Addison ran to the left.

The creature tried to stop, but the momentum of its incredible mass carried it barreling forward. It slipped and slid over the rocks and sand, unable to gain purchase, like a house sliding down a hillside. It crashed face-first into the pile of rubble and boulders.

The girls jumped onto the athleta's backs, and they shot into the air once more.

"Follow me back to the holy place!" the ancient knight commanded, shoving his visor into place.

"No!" Alex said. "I have a better idea."

He shifted his weight and turned around. He leaned forward and flew straight for the monster that was now back on his feet and facing them. It wailed in fury, showering the entire area with its yellow spit and chunks of debris.

Katie closed her eyes, tightened her grip around Alex's neck, and screamed.

When they came close, the monster lunged at them and snapped his jaws. They were too fast and sailed past his face unharmed.

Addison paused in the air with Hope on his back. He exclaimed, "The poor boy's gone daffy." He lifted a gauntlet and spun his finger in a small circle next to his ear.

"No, I think I get it. Try to stay with him," Hope countered.

"Are ye serious, lass?"

"Dead serious."

24

Friday, 11:59 p.m.

Cain chanted incantations in Latin, his voice the only sound in the musty clock tower attic. Flames danced on the points of the pentagram. Black energy swirled around the portal, sparking wildly. The metal rim became blood red and so hot that curls of yellow smoke rose from it. A metallic hum filled the air.

Satan leaned forward in his chair.

"Four hundred years," the devil hissed, his voice a faint whisper that pounded in all of their skulls. Cain stopped chanting. "Salem was glorious, was it not, Cain?"

Cain faced his master. "It was indeed, my lord. The demon flood gave us the forces we needed to turn the tide away from the harsh brightness of the Christian faith and toward the warm darkness of your kingdom."

Satan's red eyes glowed brighter. "Just when my foolish enemy was gaining momentum, I stopped him dead in his tracks. My legions spread new religions. We infiltrated universities and indoctrinated students with our dark philosophies. And then Cain, we took over the economy."

Cain took a deep breath. "I am thankful to your immanence for allowing me the opportunity to serve you in business and industry. We have been able to turn men to greed and to widen the gap between the sinfully rich and the desperately poor."

Satan nodded. "Best of all has been our influence in the enemy's own earthly stronghold—His church. Hmmm, most satisfying."

"And yet…?"

"And yet the war is not won. The battle rages still. And there is always the possibility of a resurgence of that infernal light. It happens where we least expect it. And our forces continue to dwindle. We must end this cycle—win this war once and for all and displace the usurper." He patted his bony hands on the armrests. "I crave to sit on my proper throne!"

The portal hummed and whined louder.

The time was at hand.

Cain and his master both turned to the opening. Dark lightning streaked across it. The pulsing metal ring blazed bright red, washing the entire room in its radiance.

The Executive Demon took his seat.

The witches stepped aside, next to the thrones, and braced themselves for the impending demonic flood.

The portal's black surface was streaked with jagged purple webs of dark lightning. The portal showered sparks and became a window into hell.

Two brilliant lights blasted out of the portal, extinguished the candles, and passed through the back wall in a flash.

An enormous skeletal head—a Giant Knight Demon—pushed through the circular portal. The raging creature's skull wedged in the opening. It wailed, chomped his frothing jaws, and licked its tongue toward the witches.

They screamed and ran out of the room, slamming the door behind them.

Demons panicked on the Hell side of the portal. Their way back to earth was plugged. Knight Demons grabbed at the massive creature's legs and arms, trying to pull it away, only to be kicked and launched into the air. Creepers covered the creature's massive back. They shot their hooks into the bumpy gray hide and pulled back hard on the oily strands.

Their hooks tickled the beast's leathery skin and it shook violently, causing the creepers to swing wildly and fly off.

The Executive Demon's black eyes turned red. His wings unfurled and he strutted before the snapping jaws of the enormous creature.

"Stop, you fool!" he commanded, pointing his gnarled finger between its bulging eyes. "Back up! Now!"

The beast snapped his powerful jaws in Cain's direction.

The Executive Demon jumped back just in time, almost falling.

The two light streaks returned through the splintered hole they'd made. They landed and became four humans.

The Executive Demon turned and saw his daughter drop from the back of a knight in medieval armor.

"Hecate!" He yelled. "You've ruined everything!"

A sword appeared in the demon's hand, and he lunged at his daughter.

Alex's and Cornelius's glowing blades stopped his sword from striking its fatal blow. For a moment, the three swords held fast.

The two athletas leaned forward and pushed Cain toward the hungry jaws.

Alex cried out, "This is for my mom."

Addison added, "And for me time in hell, ye ugly beasty."

But as Cain drew closer to the wildly snapping jaws, he shifted his weight forward and gained purchase.

The three held still for a moment.

Cain declared, "You are so weak. Did you really think the two of you could defeat me?"

Cain leaned forward and pushed hard, overcoming both knights. They struggled to keep their footing and hold onto their swords. Cain beamed in victory as he reached for Alex's throat with his left claw.

Then Cain heard another voice.

"And this is for seventeen years of hatred and fear," Hope declared.

She raised her arms, threw both hands forward, and hit her father square in the chest with twin bolts of holy light energy. Sparkling white lightning crawled over him from head to foot. He howled and fell backward, landing between the monstrous jaws. The creature closed its mouth, raised its chin toward the ceiling to straighten its throat, and swallowed the Executive Demon whole.

Cain slid down the slippery gullet and dropped into the creature's gigantic stomach, landing on a rotting pile of partially digested bones, flesh, and giant bugs. He willed his sword into his hands and chopped wildly into the sagging fatty flesh. The gigantic monster jumped and shook and tried to stop the excruciating pain. Inside the clock tower, he roared a deafening cry.

The creature's belly ripped open, putrid yellow fluid and debris splashing onto the ramp beneath him. Cain dropped out of the long slit, landed hard on the ramp, and rolled into a group of midnight demons.

The giant monster writhed and howled. It stopped suddenly, opened its eyes in fright, and became an enormous cloud of ash.

Cain recovered and jumped to his feet. He pushed aside the knight demons and scrambled up the pile of debris to the inviting portal. He could see the inside of the clock tower and Alex, Addison, and Hecate staring down on him.

"Stand back!" Cain yelled at the demons before him. They stepped aside.

Racing to the top of the ramp, Cain's sword appeared in his hand. He threw himself into the air and aimed for the glowing circle.

When he reached it, the portal had closed. He hit the surface hard and fell awkwardly to the rocky ramp below.

Wails rose from the demonic horde.

*

The portal's surface sputtered and became the normal back of a clock, with greasy axels, toothy gears, and rusted springs.

Cain was gone.

Demons shrieked, dropped from the ceiling, and scrambled like roaches out the window and through the ragged gaping hole in the back wall. The bloody pentagram faded and disappeared. Flames on the five candles grew smaller and died out. Smoke curled above the cold wicks.

The room was quiet.

Alex, Katie, Hope, and Cornelius looked around them. They'd won.

Overwhelmed with joy, the four victors cheered and fell together in a group hug. They squeezed each other tightly, high-fived, and patted each other's backs.

"That was amazing!" Katie exclaimed.

"Quite satisfactory," Cornelius added, a gleam in his eye.

"Alex, you're a true hero." Hope gave him a hug.

"Me? What about you? I thought we were done for. You . . . with that light energy . . ."

A shadowy figure slowly rose up from the largest of the three thrones behind them. Wings the size of a pterodactyl's spread across the back of the room. Satan's brow furrowed on his black skull-like face, his fiery eyes glowing crimson in their hollow sockets. He hissed with rage, and webs of dark energy crackled off his gnarled claws. The energy waves filled the storeroom, catching all four humans like a tidal wave.

Alex's body went stiff and he dropped to the floor, shaking spasmodically in the foul wake of the relentless evil energy flow. When the discharge ceased, he fought to retain consciousness.

The devil retracted his wings and slowly strutted across the room on heavy cloven hooves. He stood above Alex and cackled, then grabbed him by his neck and lifted him off the floor. He brought Alex's face an inch from his. Satan stared intently into his frightened eyes as if gazing into Alex's very soul.

"Before I kill you," the evil one hissed, "I will hurt you."

Alex tried to move, but his arms and legs hung limp and unresponsive. He called for his sword but wondered if he could even hold it.

The sword didn't come.

Cornelius, Hope, and Katie stared wide-eyed and paralyzed.

The devil tightened his grip on Alex's throat, raised his left claw, and released an explosion of deadly black energy. Jagged arcs of raw maleficent power sparked and crawled over Alex like a lightning bolt. His eyes rolled back in his head. Every nerve ending in his body screamed in pain. It was as if his flesh was being scraped off with a potato peeler. The fluid in his eyes bubbled, and blood ran from his nose and ears.

The devil's hand closed into a fist. The jagged bolts of evil energy suddenly stopped.

Satan pulled Alex close once more. He studied him like a bug under a magnifying glass. "Where is your God, athleta? Where is your guardian angel, Sariel? You are alone and abandoned. They used you for a time, while you were helpful to them. But now you are discarded like a useless piece of garbage. They have given you to me. I alone have power over you. Your life is mine."

"Aiy…lthes. Aiy…lthesss," Alex muttered, his swollen tongue rolling back and forth in his open mouth.

"What is that, athleta? You wish to beg for mercy? Are you pleading for the lives of your pathetic friends? Or, perhaps you wish to worship me?"

"Aiy lthesist ooo," Alex choked out.

"Relax my new disciple. Breathe deeply and speak your worship plainly. Perhaps I shall spare you after all."

The devil's grip loosened enough for Alex to breathe. He struggled to suck stale air into his lungs. He moved his tongue in his mouth and swallowed hard. Nearly blind, he looked Lucifer straight in the eyes, took a last deep breath, and set his jaw.

"I r-resist *you*!" Alex declared.

Under an ancient curse, Satan shrieked and his hand popped opened.

Alex fell to the floor in a heap.

*

The devil recoiled from the athleta, trembling. He turned around in panic and dove through the opening in the back wall, taking wing on the other side and quickly disappearing in the clouds.

His evil influence left with him and all were released from his power. Outside the window, the word spread among the demons. They shrieked, scrambled, took wing, and filled the sky with their dark fleeing forms.

The clouds parted. Brilliant moonlight washed over a clear night sky.

"Alex!" Katie yelled as she crawled over to him. He was out cold. She patted his face and shook his shoulders. "Alex, wake up. C'mon, Alex. Please, wake up." She sobbed.

Cornelius Addison came up behind the boy, knelt down, and placed his hands on Alex's sweaty forehead. "Almighty God, Who causeth the lame to walk and the blind to see, please find favor with thy servant, Alexander. Grant him healing in thy precious name. Amen. Amen. Amen."

The three Christians laid hands on Alex and silently waited on God.

For several minutes, nothing happened.

The boy's eyes fluttered open. He looked up at Katie and grinned, took a deep breath of fresh air and sat up.

Katie smiled and wiped blood from his face with the sleeve of her pajamas. She gazed into his deep blue eyes.

"So, I don't get it. Why'd Satan run away?" Hope asked.

"The lad remembered the Scriptures." Cornelius stood. His armor transformed into his fancy sixteenth-century clothes. "The Book of James, chapter four, verse seven states, 'Submit yourselves therefore to God. Resist the devil and he will flee from you.'"

Hope's brilliant armor changed back into her pajamas.

Alex was suddenly in his street clothes.

For a moment they all sat in silence.

Alex looked to his left and his face dropped. He pushed himself to his feet, rushed to the corner of the room, and fell to his knees next to his mother's lifeless body. He gathered her up in his arms, held her tight, and wept.

Something crashed hard into the back of the reinforced door. It hammered again and again, making large dents in the metal.

Hope and Cornelius jumped to their feet.

Suddenly, the door burst off its hinges and fell into the room.

Alex, Katie, Hope, and Addison all stared into the dust and debris that clouded the doorway.

Beams of light pierced the air.

Three uniformed policemen charged into the room, guns drawn.

"Police!" One of them yelled.

The officers stared at the hole in the back wall, the girls in their pajamas, the unconscious man on the stretcher, the boy holding a lifeless woman covered in blood, and a portly man who looked like he was on his way to a costume party.

"What's going on here?"

25

Wednesday

Billowing cumulus clouds with deep gray highlights covered the sky like a quilted blanket. Sunlight diffused from behind, illuminating the creases. A soft breeze rustled the trees, bringing short-lived relief to the stifling stale air.

A hundred white plastic foldout chairs in five straight rows, mostly empty, faced a freshly dug grave. A shiny pink coffin covered with flowers stood behind the rectangular hole. Soon it would be lowered and covered with dark dirt.

The graveside service dragged on. Alex felt as dead as the inhabitants of the graves around him. He sat in the front row next to his mother's scowling parents. They never spoke a word to him or even made eye-contact.

The prattle of the minister flowed past him like the wind. This man, who spoke like an intimate friend of his mother's—sharing anecdote after anecdote he'd gleaned from others—didn't really know her beyond her first name.

Alex didn't need a stranger to tell him that he had lost the most wonderful mother a young man could ever have. How was he going to live without her? The pain was more than he could handle. In spite of all his efforts to "be a man," he brushed a continuous stream of tears from his red cheeks.

The service finally ended.

Alex's grandparents stood, turned their backs on him, and walked away.

His mom's friends and coworkers, many of whom Alex had only met once or twice, or heard his mom mention, passed his front-row seat, bent down, and hugged him or shook his hand, and told him what his mother had meant to them.

Of course, none of this made him feel any better.

The pastor approached Alex. He took his hand firmly and said, "I'm truly sorry, Alex. Here's my card. I've written my personal cell phone number on the back. You can call me any time, day or night. I *will* be there for you. I mean it."

Alex muscles relaxed a little. With sincerity he muttered, "Thank you, pastor."

The man leaned over and patted Alex's shoulder. "I'll be praying for you, Alex. Stay strong in your faith. God is with you."

Alex nodded.

The man stood, bowed his head to Alex, and walked away.

Hope and Katie stood nearby. When the pastor left, they approached Alex. Their eyes were puffy and red from crying, but they both tried to be strong for their friend.

Alex stood and they fell into a three-way hug. They allowed themselves a few moments to hold each other and sob.

Alex found his voice and asked Hope, "So . . . what's going to happen with you?"

Hope took a deep breath and smiled. "You'll never believe it! I have an aunt, right here in Willowbrook. I found her on Facebook.

She's meeting me tomorrow. I'm going to live with her. I get to stay at Kingman High. I get to stay with you guys!"

"That's great." Alex forced a smile.

They all hugged again.

"We have big news," Katie beamed. "Hope and I are getting baptized Sunday! We want you to come. Will you? Please?" The girls both looked at him expectantly.

Alex hugged Katie. "Of course I'll be there. I'm so happy for both of you." He turned toward Hope. "Have you seen Conor?"

"Still in ICU. They're only letting family in with him. The doctors are still waiting for the swelling in his brain to go down. They've said that his youth is the best thing he has going for him. He could make a full recovery. They just don't know yet. We're all praying for God to heal him and bring him back to us."

"I've been praying for that, too."

"What about you, Alex? Any word yet on what's going to happen to you?" Katie asked.

He looked uncomfortable. "Well, I refused to go and live with my grandparents. We're not exactly . . . Well, that's not an option. My social worker told me today that they're planning to make me a ward of the state. I'm looking into emancipation. My mom had some insurance. That'll keep me going for a while. But, honestly, I don't know what's going to happen to me."

"Well," Katie said, taking his hands in hers. "Wherever you go, Alex, my heart will be with you." She leaned forward and kissed him softly on the lips. Their bodies came close and they held each other as if they could make time stand still with their embrace.

They parted, held hands, and stared longingly into each other's eyes.

After a few moments, Katie looked down. "We gotta go. Look...um...call me whenever you want to...get together and...talk...whenever you're ready. You know, whenever you feel like it." She smiled shyly and let go of his hands.

"I will," he smiled.

"Promise?"

"Promise."

Hope gave Alex a final hug, and whispered, "Thanks again, Alex. You saved me, and I'll never forget it."

Alex lifted the silver cross from her neck and said, "No, *He* saved you, Hope, by an act of love and sacrifice like none other."

"Well, you helped." She winked at him.

Katie and Hope turned away and walked arm in arm through the graveyard, toward the line of cars parked at a nearby curb.

Alex sat for a moment alone. He looked to his right, to the place where Adam had attacked him and tried to throw him into a grave like this one. In his memory he saw Sariel in all his angelic glory, shining like the sun, and commanding the demons out of Adam. Was it really only a few weeks ago? So much had happened since then.

He wondered where Sariel was now.

Alex watched his social worker, Mrs. Frost, approach in her cream-colored business suit that made her look like a big scoop of ice cream. Her bright red hair curved under at the ends. Alex thought of it as the cherry on top.

This woman had authority over his life and would decide his fate.

He stood as she drew near.

Mrs. Frost adjusted her heavy brown glasses and huffed. "Alex...I have news. Please...sit down with me."

They sat on the wooden chairs.

"Alex..." She took another breath. "Alex, I've found your father! He's been looking for you and your mother for years. He passed all the background checks. I talked to him about half an hour ago. He's meeting us here to sign your papers. If you like, you can go home with him, you know, try things out. You can go today."

Alex couldn't breathe. Of all the monsters he had fought over the last few weeks, none approached the horrific image he had in his mind of this man who'd abandoned him and his mother before he was born. What would he say to this loser? Thanks for knocking up my mom and then splitting? Thanks for making my mom have to work so hard all these years and raise me alone? Alex balled his fists tightly and got ready to release sixteen years of fury into this jerk's ugly face.

Mrs. Frost giggled and waddled away.

Alex stood and stepped to the foot of the open grave. As he stared at the metal coffin, the voice behind him startled him.

"I am so sorry for your loss, Alex, and for the pain you are feeling."

Sariel.

Alex sprang at the angel and embraced him. Tears flowed freely down his cheeks.

Sariel nodded toward the grave. "She was a woman of quality. She loved you, Alex, and did a great job raising you." The angel rubbed his back.

He choked through his tears, "I just can't accept . . . she's really gone, Sariel."

Alex wiped his eyes. Sariel put a comforting arm around his shoulders. They stood together in silence facing the grave.

The wind rustled the leaves and cooled Alex's face. He breathed deeply, filling his tired lungs with life. Would he ever feel fully alive again?

He looked over at Sariel. Ever since this being had thrust himself into Alex's life, he'd been on one great adventure. He'd discovered a larger spiritual world he barely knew existed. He'd acquired the full armor of God and had learned how to wield the Sword of the Spirit. Best of all, Sariel knew when to leave so that Alex could begin to stand on his own two feet.

Sariel had been the perfect mentor.

"So," Alex said, "what's going on with you? Anything you can talk about?"

"Actually, I have been reassigned," the angel said soberly. "A most challenging endeavor, fraught with many dangers."

"Aren't they all?"

Mrs. Frost returned—all smiles. "Well, I see you two have met," she said, handing Sariel some papers. "Just sign on the lines highlighted in yellow." The angel scribbled and handed the papers back, sincerely thanking the woman.

"I don't get it," Alex said, confused.

"Oh, you don't know? Alex, *this* is your father, Mr. Sariel. He's just moved into town. He's been looking for you for months. He lives alone but says he has plenty of room for you. He wants to make up for lost time." Tears welled up in the woman's eyes.

Sariel gave him a look that said he would explain everything in due time.

"What do you say, son?" Sariel asked. "Will you come and live with me?"

Head swimming, Alex shouted out, "Yes! Yes! I can't believe . . . Yes!"

"Then it's all settled," Mrs. Frost said. "I'll turn in the papers. Call me if you need anything." She firmly shook Sariel's hand, hugged Alex, then turned and waddled off, leaving them standing alone.

"Son?" Alex asked.

"We had better sit down."

"No doubt," Alex agreed. They sat on the chairs facing the grave. "So, is this like Hope? You're my father? I'm half . . . angel?"

"No, not at all. Cain shall pay dearly for his unholy union. And if I were your father, it would mean becoming a demon myself. No, you are thoroughly human. Your real father has been dead for over two years."

"So what's going on then?"

333

"Taking the role of your father is my new assignment. It was only a matter of modifying paperwork, changing files, and manipulating electronic data. Anyway, on paper, I am your father who recently discovered that your mother had a child about the same time we were supposed to have been . . . together. The authorities believe I have been searching for you. They did a background check, a DNA test, and everything checked out."

"Mrs. Frost took a swab from my cheek last week. She wouldn't tell me what it was for."

"She did not want to get your hopes up. She is a very caring person…like your mother."

Alex nodded and looked back toward the grave. "I miss her so much, Sariel." Tears rolled down his cheeks.

"As you should. Your pain proves how deeply you loved her. It shall always be with you. In time, you will learn how to live with it." He put his hand on Alex's shoulder. "I shall help you."

"She's really gone."

"From this realm? Yes. But she lives now in unspeakable glory. She is counted among the martyrs, those who showed extreme courage and made the ultimate sacrifice for their faith. Her heavenly reward is great. She has never been happier."

Alex nodded again. "So, this is real? You're going to be my father? I'm really going to live with you?"

"Is that what you want?"

Alex managed a smile. "Look, everything happens according to God's plan. It's what's best for Him to reveal Himself, right?"

"Correct."

"Well, if this is God's perfect will, who am I to argue?"

They both smiled and leaned back in their chairs.

The leaves around them danced.

Sariel put his arm around Alex. They stared into the sky together. A lone red-tailed hawk extended its wings and circled above them. Alex looked at the many beautiful flower bouquets set up on stands next to the grave. He hadn't noticed them before. His mom would have loved them.

After a long, satisfying moment, the angel broke the silence, speaking soberly. "Hmm. Just one more thing…"

"What's that?" the young warrior braced himself.

Sariel spoke in a fatherly tone, "About your falling grades, young man…"

Alex groaned.

End of Book One.
The story continues in Godsend 2: A Hero Falls

A children's book with deep meaning for all:

You can follow me on Facebook and Instagram. You can use the QR code below to reach my website:

Godsendbook.com

You can use this QR code to reach my page on Amazon:

Apodaca Amazon

www.ingramcontent.com/pod-product-compliance
Lightning Source LLC
Chambersburg PA
CBHW061323170626
46817CB00001B/279